TICK

A NOVEL

ALLISON ROSE

Printed in the United States of America
First Edition Paperback, 2015
RockRose Books

ISBN 978-0-9864351-0-2

for the man who let me dream …

most of the time

TABLE OF CONTENTS

PART ONE
the city

1 tick or treat

She screams through the tape over her mouth as I tie her hands and feet to the classroom desk. The Los Angeles skyline twinkles behind her as she's perched at the edge of a construction rig in an unfinished floor of a building. I kick the desk with my boot and she topples twenty-five stories to the street below—

"Jo! Are you listening to me? Don't you dare pull this trick again."

The ringing fades and the fog clears and there is Mrs. Garcia. She looks pissed, her brow pinched together to make her appear cross-eyed. A security guy peers over her shoulder, wearing a gray suit with a red ACTA emblem embossed on the sleeve. The guy's name is Jake, and I know that because he's escorted me to class twice this week when he caught me trying to ditch Engineering and Construction. I told him I was lost. I'm pretty sure he didn't buy that. Today, Jake is here to escort me to the principal's office.

"What's wrong with her?" says Jake as he looks me over.

"She has dizzy spells," Mrs. Garcia says with a roll of her eyes, as though I hadn't just had a vision of pushing her off a building to her death, but she doesn't know that. She doesn't know anything about my tick. If she did, she'd send me to some foreboding neurosurgeon who'd splice and dice my brain so I could be a properly functioning human. I should be grateful I'm only being sent to the principal.

"She's pulled this trick three times this week," says Mrs. Garcia. "And now I've caught her drawing during my lecture."

A video about structural engineering plays on a wall screen at the front of the classroom, and next to it is a display of the digital sketch I'd been drawing on my desktop moments before my tick sent me into a vision. It's right there, in front of everyone, inviting their judgmental eyes. A pulse of energy flows through my body, and I jump to my feet—a gut reaction ignited by my compulsion to snatch the drawing from the wall, as though it weren't actually a digital projection. The reality of the technology doesn't even matter, because my thighs slam into the edge of the desk, and I flop back into the seat. Several of the students snicker and sneer at me.

"You can't show that to everyone!" I say, thrusting my finger at the screen.

Mrs. Garcia bellows through her nose. "Miss Bristol, it is against the rules to play on your desktop during class. You were supposed to take notes on the video. You've done nothing but disregard the rules for the two weeks you've been enrolled in this school." She aims her remote at the screen and the projection of my drawing enlarges. "I'm sending this straight to Principal Torres."

That's a terrible idea, lady. Mr. Torres will tell my mom and I can't have her knowing I'm drawing in class, not after what happened the last time she saw one of my paintings. "Don't do that. I'm sorry, but this video is pointless. I'm not going to be a construction worker. I don't even belong at this school."

The students shoot me hostile glares. The girl in the seat behind mine whispers into my ear, "Eeh fancy, don't think you're better than us. You aren't getting outta here any sooner than we are."

I swivel in my chair. "What do you know about it? I'll find a way back into the PEAD program."

She clucks her tongue. "Good luck with that."

The muscles in Mrs. Garcia's neck strain like twisted vines on a tree trunk; the woman is well on her way to having an aneurysm. "Miss Bristol, you are a disruption in my classroom and I will not stand for it anymore."

"Let's go, kid." Jake grabs my arm and pulls me from the seat. The five-year-old in me wants to throw a tantrum and start kicking and screaming, but then the ringing returns.

She's tied to the classroom desk and this time Jake is next to her. I kick him off the building first so she can hear him scream all the way down—

I'm standing in the middle of the classroom as I come out of the vision. Every student is hunkered over their desks, trying to figure out what's wrong with this new kid in their school. I've only been here for two weeks and already I'm the weird kid. How am I the weird kid? I was a PEAD kid before this, dammit. *Programmed Education And Development, Accelerated Curriculum, Eleventh Year*. But here at East Hollywood Trade School? I'm the weirdo with the psychotic tick *slash* dizzy spells, who will be lucky to graduate at all if I don't die of boredom first. The PEAD program is designed to learn the academic strengths of its students and specialize the curriculum for each of them. So what if *Fine Artist* wasn't on the list of selections? I know I'm destined to be a painter, no matter what any computer program tells me. I'm sixteen, nearly seventeen, it's too late for me to learn how to be anything else. I'm sure as hell not cut out to be a laborer, not like these other trade school kids.

Jake rolls his eyes and pulls me toward the door, and just as we reach the threshold, his wristlet flashes and beeps. "What do ya know, he's coming to fetch you himself."

A series of *ooohs* and muffled chuckles flutter behind me, and I glance over my shoulder to see the girl in the seat behind mine flashing her middle finger. Bitch. It has to be her fault Mrs. Garcia even knew I was drawing. I swear the girl has had it out for me since I started here. I stick out my tongue, which draws a wink from the girl, and I'm still making the face as Jake swivels me into the hallway so I'm standing a foot away from Principal Torres's necktie.

"Good afternoon to you too, Miss Bristol," says Mr. Torres. "I take it you're still having trouble making friends at East Hollywood Trade."

I can't summon the guts to look at the principal's face. Instead, I focus on the end of his tie, which is a hypnotizing blend of purples and greens.

Mr. Torres holds out his hand. "Thank you, Jake, I can take it from here."

"I wouldn't recommend that," says Jake as he tightens his grip on my arm. "She tried to ditch twice this week. She needs an escort. Besides, she gets these *dizzy spells*."

There's something about the way Jake says dizzy spells, as though it's some kind of joke, as though my years of suffering with these visions has all been a theatrical display for attention. I look up to babble an excuse for my condition, when I'm caught by the gleaming white smile of Mr. Torres. Yes, the man is smiling, although not in the sense that he agrees with Jake; it's more like he's trying to ease the alarm of a toddler caught on the verge of a crying fit. I feel a familiar swell of heat in my belly. If these two aren't careful, I'll be getting another dizzy spell involving both of them right here in the hallway.

Mr. Torres flicks his hand at Jake. "I'll take care of her. We have a few things to discuss anyway."

Jake moves to protest. "Sir, we need to take her downstairs. Like I told you—"

Mr. Torres waves him off. "Yes, I know about the new protocols. We'll go to the basement in a minute."

Mr. Torres clasps his hands behind his back, nods his head forward, indicating I'm supposed to follow him, and casually walks down the hallway. Jake stands with his mouth open, like he wants to speak but can't get the words out. Then he looks at me, and a creepy grin crosses his face.

Mr. Torres continues down the hallway, completely unaware. "You know, I saw that drawing, the one Mrs. Garcia caught you in the middle of. It's pretty good."

"No it's not." I move too abruptly to catch up to him and nearly trip over my boots. "It's just a doodle. It doesn't mean anything. It's actually really terrible." I glance behind me to see Jake strolling casually behind us with his suspicious smile.

"Would you be more comfortable if we enrolled you in an art class?" says Mr. Torres, drawing my attention to him.

"This is a trade school. You don't have art classes."

"You don't have art courses in the upper-levels of the PEAD program, either," he says.

"No, but I can't get into art school without a PEAD degree."

Jake's voice rings out from behind us. "If she's not being productive in her tech classes, then we need to perform a reevaluation."

Mr. Torres turns around, moving so fast his hypnotizing tie blurs like a hologram. Jake's words cause my own body to seize up, my muscles tense and contract. Jake isn't even looking at me, but at the walls of the hallway which are lit up with TV screens, projecting a news report about a heightened level of cyber alerts from FutureTech. One screen shows a reporter on the steps of the main FutureTech building in West LA, where dozens of drones hover in the air, shooting their blue scanning lasers onto innocent passers-by. It's a drill. It has to be a drill. Alias is not stupid enough to stage an attack on FutureTech. Not now, not with all these new security procedures in place.

Mr. Torres moves in to get a closer look at the TVs. "That's not how we do things here," he says to Jake. "This is a public school, and I have determined we will conduct our student evaluations in a traditional sense."

"With all due respect, sir," says Jake, "when it comes to national security, ACTA makes the rules." He taps the ACTA emblem on his sleeve.

Mr. Torres glances over to me with heavy eyes, his once causal demeanor now distressed. I never thought I'd say this, but I'd prefer to see that ridiculous white smile. I know where this is going, and I don't like it one bit.

"I don't need to be scanned," I say. "It hasn't even been six months since my last PEAD scan."

Jake tilts his head. "This isn't a PEAD scanner. These have new lasers. These are designed to find abnormalities."

My voice trembles because my body is suddenly so stiff it feels like I've been incased in liquid nitrogen. "I don't have an abnormality."

"And the brain scan will tell me that," says Jake. He reaches out for my arm and Mr. Torres puts a hand on him.

"This isn't necessary," says Mr. Torres.

"We're on the highest security alert," Jake says, brushing him off. "Every suspicious person is required to be scanned for thoughts of cyber terrorism. It's government protocol, I don't make the rules. And it's not my fault she picked the worst time to throw a fit in the middle of class." He gives him a once-over, then clasps his hand on my arm.

All at once my body turns into stone, as though Jake is Medusa, snake hair and all. Mr. Torres is stuck in his position in the hallway, watching as Jake drags me down the stairs, straight to my impending doom. I can see the concern in Mr. Torres's eyes, and even though I doubt he has any thought that I am a cyber terrorist, he must know these new scanners are bad news.

And if *he* thinks they're bad news, then they are the worst news for me, because for as long as I can remember, I have feared the day when the brain scanners discover my tick.

I have been through many brain scans in my sixteen years of life. In the PEAD program they're simply part of the curriculum, but those scanners are basic, aimed at the outer regions of the prefrontal cortex to evaluate a student's learning capacity. But an

Anti-Cyber Terrorism Agency scanner is another beast entirely. Those scanners are meant to peer into every neuron, every signal pathway, every cell of tissue to find a glitch in the hardware. To ACTA, if you have an abnormality in your brain, you have the capacity to be a threat to national security.

I don't call it an abnormality. I call it a *tick*. I don't remember when I started using the term, probably back in elementary prep when my teacher's husband left her in the middle of the night, and the next day she sold her house, shaved her head, and became a interpretive dance performer on the Venice Beach Boardwalk. One of the parents said, "Sometimes all it takes is a single moment in time to learn what really makes a person tick," and the term just stuck in my mind.

I *wish* my tick were something harmless like having the need to be a free bird and never stay in one place for too long. I *wish* I were driven by money, or motivated by fear, or that I straddled the edge of insanity right at that place where it meets genius.

But I don't have a normal tick. I have visions of killing people.

I know it's not normal to think about killing people, and I do a pretty damn good job convincing people I'm perfectly fine. After all these years of brain scans, no one has discovered the darkness in my mind. I've had these visions for as long as I can remember and never has anyone been any wiser to it, and I made certain of it because I have always feared what they'd do to me if they were to discover it. They'll scramble my neurons, pick apart my brain to fix me of my abnormality and release me as a splintered version of my former self. I'll never be able to paint anything worthwhile after that. I'll lose all sense of myself. I'll be useless.

I have kept my horrible tick a secret for this long, but times have changed, and my luck is running out.

Jake and I descend the stairs to the basement floor of the school and he leads me into a room filled with yellow light and piss-colored walls. A row of plastic chairs line the perimeter, and a dozen students slouch down in the seats. Most of these kids I'd believe are up to no good—especially the blue-haired guy with black ink all over his hands and arms. He looks like an anarchist; he has to be the one they're really looking for. I'm just an innocent girl trying to break out of trade school.

A frosted glass window at the back of the room slides open and a frumpy woman pokes her head through. "Seriously, Jake? Another one?"

"It's not my fault this school is filled with hoodlums," Jake says.

"We're backed up as it is," the woman says, and waves to the other kids. "She'll have to wait in line."

"No waiting. She's a flight risk." Jake pushes me through a door. "Let's go, kid, before you get another dizzy spell."

The next room is cold and dark, with one chair in the middle illuminated by an overhead light. Beside the chair are three scanner cranes and the most elaborate holographic interface I've ever seen. Everything labeled *by FutureTech.* This is definitely not a typical PEAD-assigned psychological development scan; there wouldn't be such a technological display. This is something else entirely. This is high-grade FutureTech Corporation brain infiltration bullshit.

I have to get out of this.

Jake shoves me into the chair, and a scrawny young lab tech comes into the room and sets up the equipment. A scanner crane moves automatically and positions itself over me, aiming a blue laser at my forehead. I catch a reflection in the glass of a display terminal and it takes me a moment to realize the thin, angular face is mine. In these bright lights my skin is grotesquely pale, even more than usual in contrast with my black hair reflecting the blue scanner light.

Jake shifts in the doorway as the lab tech works in silence.

"I'm not a terrorist," I say. "You can't possibly think I'd know anything about hacking cyber systems."

"I've seen stranger things, believe me," Jake says. "Besides, you should feel lucky you're getting this scan for free. People pay big bucks to be fixed."

My stomach lurches. "People *pay* to get fixed?"

"That surprises you?" he says with a sneer. "We all want to be perfect. My ex-girlfriend sold her car to get her whole face reassembled. Yeah, she was hot after that, but I'd have preferred she spend the money to get her brain adjusted. The girl was a total whack job."

The lab tech grimaces. "That's a depressing story."

"Oh, piss off," Jake says. He settles against the wall and looks me over. "So what's your abnormality?"

A tightness forms in my belly, and I know if I can't keep it together I'll have a vision under these scanning lasers and I can't let anyone be suspicious of the madness in my brain. I take a deep breath and try to keep my voice steady.

"I don't have an abnormality." I say.

"Huh," says Jake. "So what's the deal with the dizzy spells?"

The lab tech jerks to look at Jake, then back at me. A cold chill runs through the air, sending a shiver down my spine. My breath is shallow and loud, echoing off the walls. Jake seems to sense my apprehension because he steps to the side, blocking my path to the door. My eyes land on the stun gun belted to his hip, and he moves his hand to rest on it. My arms contract as I try to pull them in, but they're tied down; the lab tech had strapped me into the chair when I wasn't paying attention. I'm their prisoner now.

"Josephine Bristol," says the lab tech. "Sit still. We're about to begin—"

A deafening high-pitched siren rips through the air, piercing my unprotected eardrums. I strain against the arm straps.

"Let me go!" I holler over the noise. The lab tech uncovers his ears long enough to free me and I squash my palms over my head.

Jake rushes over, seemingly unaware of the siren. "What are you doing? We have to do the scan!"

The lab tech stares wide-eyed. "We can't do the scan. They have the system."

"What are you talking about?" says Jake.

The lab tech swivels around a display. Instead of technical brain scan data, the screen is covered by a giant red *AX*.

"You've gotta be shitting me!" says Jake. He taps open his holo-wristlet and speaks into it. "Alias hacked the system. I repeat, Alias-X has hacked the scanner system!"

My breakfast churns in my stomach, and I do my best to not have it make reappearance. At this moment, I don't know which is worse, ACTA and FutureTech having my brain data, or the cyber terrorists known as Alias-X.

I jump from the chair and get to my feet, knocking over a table of equipment in the process. Jake slides out of the way of the toppling table and I'm able to sneak past him, burst through the door, and pass the kids in the waiting room who eye me suspiciously.

Voices call after me. "Wait!"

I don't wait. I run. The siren rings through the entire school, and red lights flash in every hallway. I race up the stairs with Jake at my heels. I'm paces from the front door of the school when a purple and green tie catches my attention.

"What's going on?" Mr. Torres says as he emerges from a corner.

Jake catches up, heaving and sweating. "She's evading a brain scan, that's what's going on."

Mr. Torres frowns. "I mean the siren."

"Alias hacked the scanner system," Jake says. "Don't worry, we'll have it back on line in a moment. Alias is no match for ACTA."

A handful of ACTA security officers race around the corner and up to us. One woman approaches Mr. Torres. "Sir, the whole security system is down. Order everyone inside the building. ACTA is sending out the drones to find anyone who might be involved."

"So the hackers got more than just the scanners?" Jake says, his eyes clouded with bewilderment. "How is that even possible?"

"It's a temporary glitch," the woman says. "Believe me, it won't last."

"We'll keep the school on lock-down," says Jake, and waves at the other officers. "Secure the perimeter."

"I think not," Mr. Torres says. "Lunch hour is in five minutes. You can't expect me to keep the students locked inside until the end of the school day."

Jake stands tall. "I expect you to follow the ACTA protocols as you've been instructed."

Every part of my body is trembling, tensing, aching with anxiety as the lights flash and the sirens beep and I feel like I'm a half-step from insanity. Jake and Mr. Torres and the security officers are more concerned with their battle for authority and they're not paying the slightest bit of attention to me.

Mr. Torres stands on a stool in the middle of an auditorium, his purple and green tie secured to the rafters above him like a noose. I kick the stool out from under him and his neck snaps—

"Miss Bristol, are you all right?"

Mr. Torres takes his time looking me over. I twitch with the need to run, and when Jake reaches out for me I have the instant thought to ninja-slam the guy into the wall, but that won't do me any favors among all these ACTA officers swarming the hallways. So I do the next thing on my list of escape plans: I run.

I slide past Jake and Mr. Torres before either can move to catch me. I run the length of the hallway, plow into the building door, and smell the sweet scent of freedom. Or … a forest fire. The sky has an eerie brownish tint and the air reeks of smoke. But still. Freedom.

My mobie is parked in the charging stations, which, thankfully, are also linked to the now defunct security system, and I power the bike on and ride away from the school and toward the first person I think of.

"Call Lyle," I say, and my wristlet hologram pops up. Lyle answers the v-call, and his shock of blond hair bobbles out from the interface. I ride along, keeping one eye on the street and one on my wristlet, because Franklin Avenue is not an auto-route and gasser drivers are a mobie rider's worst enemy.

"Lyle! You there?"

"Hey, Jo. What's up?"

"Where are you?"

"Having lunch with my dads," he says. "On Vermont."

"On a Friday? I thought the dads were strict about your PEAD classes? You told me they don't let you leave your bedroom until you're done."

Lyle squints his already squinty eyes. "I got my assignments done early. And anyway, aren't you supposed to be in school?"

"Everah. That place is wrett."

I decide to leave out the story of my near-calamitous brain scan because I can't give Lyle another reason to be wary of my delinquency. A gasser changes into my lane. I swerve and cut off the gasser behind me. His speaker beeps on. "*Get outta the lane, you dumbass kid!*"

Lyle's eyes widen in worry. "Are you on your mobie? You know you can't ride and make v-calls. They won't let you get away with another warning."

"I'll turn it off in a sec. I'm coming to meet you. Stay there."

I end the v-call and turn onto the Vermont auto-route where dozens of auto-electric vehicles zip along in perfect alignment, their drivers poking tablets or eating. Every one of these people—the fancies in their AEVs, the teenagers on mobies—all keep an eye trained on the sky above them, their lips quivering and ready to smile. Perhaps they're aware of the coming drones; perhaps they anticipate the whirring propellers and the camera lenses and the scanning lasers, which are designed to pluck out the abnormals in the city. Any one of these civilians could be damaged or defective, and that flaw alone is enough for the Anti-Cyber Terrorism Agency to peg them as a potential menace to society. It doesn't matter the person's tick—or personal eccentricity, behavioral habit, psychological disturbance, whatever twaddle babble they call it—if they are found to be abnormal, then ACTA and their parent corporation FutureTech will capture and adjust their brains, and release them back into the cement jungle of LA as a normal human being. At least that's what their plan is. So all these dumbasses spend their days smiling at the sky, praying to whomever is listening that there is someone else more abnormal than they are and that they'll capture the other guy first. For most people, it's a good plan. They're not dangerous. They're not threatening.

And then there's me. I am not like most people. I've never been the type of girl who tears the heads off birds in the backyard, but I've heard about those kids. There was this boy on the news that got sent to the brain adjusters because his mom caught him skinning squirrels and selling the furs as mittens to the neighbors. He didn't actually kill the squirrels—they were already dead—but that didn't matter. His mom still sent him away. She was afraid of him.

The worst part about my tick is that anyone can make an appearance in my visions. Even people I know, people I love. At least once a week I have a vision where I hold a gun to Lyle's head and fire. And in my mind I pull the trigger, every time. Every time that gun goes off and the noise is deafening and I watch the bullet penetrate Lyle's skull and his blood spurts onto my face, and every time I hope that I'll feel bad about having shot my best friend in the head, and yet I feel nothing. It's the same with each of these other poor souls whose lives I so vividly imagine ending. I feel nothing.

There is something wrong with me. I know there is. But I can't dare let anyone find out. God knows what they'll do to me, who knows how many neurons they'll have to scramble to rid me of this terrifying curse.

And today, I'm speeding through East Hollywood, through a part of town that dons it's best facade, and I just know I'm the sucker who is going to be found by a drone.

I'm right. By the time I spot the spy-drone it already has its blue scanning laser fixed on my head as I'm speeding along on my mobie. The AEV drivers stare and point, their faces full of worry and distress. These people think the drone sees me as a cyber-terrorist, but I have no Alias ties; I have no criminal record. What I do have is a million thoughts of murder.

I'm having a stare-off with the drone as we're racing down Vermont, and all I can think about is how screwed I'll be once the scanner finds the broken parts of my brain and deems me a menace to society, and therefore I'm not paying the slightest bit of attention to where my mobie is taking me. It's not my fault the sidewalk suddenly jumps into my path and sends me flying over the handlebars of my mobie and straight to my convenient yet untimely death.

2 perfect family

I'm soaring through the air and—oh thank god there's grass here because otherwise I'd be busting my teeth on asphalt.

"Jo! Are you all right?"

It takes a moment for my senses to adjust before I can sit up, and now I'm staring at some guy's crotch. It's Lyle's crotch. I don't know why I know that because I make a point to not look at that part of his anatomy, but I could swear his new pants have some eyeball-magnetism technology built into them. I look up to see his blond hair glowing like a halo in the fire-clouded sun. "What?"

"I said, are you okay?"

Am I? I don't know. A moment ago I was riding my mobie and now I'm crumbled on the grass and everything hurts. "I think I broke my ass."

"You can't break that. There's nothing back there but muscle and fatty-flab."

"That's what you got out of PEAD biology? You've really gotta lay off the holo games, Lyle. You're wasting brain power." I sit up straighter and now my face is even closer to his crotch.

He steps back and chuckles. "Get up. You're getting dirty." He reaches down for my arm and the moment I'm on my feet he cleans his hands with anti-bacterial airspray.

Lyle's dad Dylan rushes over and wipes grass from my elbows. "What happened, Jo? Are you all right?"

"I was being followed by a drone."

Lyle's face contorts with terror as he scans the sky. "You *what*? Drone? Where?"

Dylan frowns at me. "I keep saying those drones are more than a nuisance. They're dangerous. It's only a matter of time before someone really gets hurt."

"I'll be all right," I say. "I actually don't know how I lost the drone. It seemed pretty intent on—"

"Spy-drone!" Lyle calls, the most absurdly creepy grin plastered on his face. The drone laser sweeps over his face, then lights green.

The scanner finds my head, sounding their signature *buzz*, much like that sizzling *zip* of a fly hitting a heat lantern. I freeze and stare back at the blue rays of the laser light. It's that noise, that damn buzzing, that I swear I hear in my sleep. I simply cannot avoid these things today.

Lyle panics because I haven't moved, and it feels like forever that the drone has been scanning me. "*Smile*, Jo!"

"Relax, everybody!" Lyle's other dad Nolan comes out of the restaurant, wraps his arm around me, and waves his wristlet at the scanner. The drone flashes green and continues down the street.

I sigh with relief now that the buzzing has gone, but mostly because I've survived another encounter with my personal sworn enemy. Still, I scan the sky in case there are more drones hiding out of sight, waiting for the next opportunity to pounce on me.

Nolan squeezes my shoulders. "It pays to know someone who works for the city, doesn't it? Now tell me, why were you being tracked by a spy-drone? You know they've been sweeping up a lot of suspected Alias sympathizers today, especially after the hack scare."

"Oh god, they think Jo's a cyber terrorist!" Lyle says and backs away a step.

As much as I'd like to admit my real fear about being followed, I can't tell Lyle or the dads the truth. Maybe that's a mistake, but I've had my tick for as long as I can remember and quite frankly it may be a little late in the game to admit my issues after all this time. So, I do as I've done for most of my life: I lie. "I thought it was after me because … well, I ditched school."

Dylan sighs. "Oh jeez, I'd nearly forgotten you're at East Hollywood now."

I'm expecting the dads to give me a lecture about the importance of my education and how much trouble I'll be in if the truancies end up on my record, but they just gaze at me solemnly, their heads tilted to one side.

Lyle rolls his eyes. "Can we eat now?"

Nolan claps his hands. "Yes! Won't you join us for lunch, Jo?"

I don't care much for this particular restaurant because the food is grown on top of FutureTech buildings and it's genetically engineered to follow the LA health standards, and quite frankly I think it tastes like dirt, but my growling stomach tells me to say yes. "Sure, why not."

We find two small tables in the courtyard along the street—one for the dads and another for Lyle and myself—and Lyle spends a good three minutes spraying it with anti-bacterial airspray before declaring it safe for touching.

Today is a hot day for March, certainly too hot to be outside, even under the cooling towers, yet every patron and passers-by pretend it's all fine and hunky-dory, sweating in their clothes while showing off their best fake smiles, eyes trained on the sky in anticipation of a spy-drone. Or maybe they're all lobotomized botheads … it's hard to tell anymore.

Lyle thumbs the menu display on the table while my attention is drawn to the ad-screen set against the outer wall of a bank across the street. The screen is huge and obnoxious—as are all ad-screens—and having lived in LA all my life, I've grown used to their bright, flashing holograms and incessantly disturbing advertisements for FutureTech security systems and brain realignment centers. But this screen in particular seems to be a bit wonky. It flashes back and forth between a series of ads with no particular consistency, and I could swear I spot an Alias-X symbol flicker with its big red AX.

Nolan notices my distraction. "Are the screens acting up? The system has been glitching all day."

"I told you," Dylan says, "when they've put everything on one system—"

Nolan slaps his husband's arm. "*Shh*! What have I warned about saying stuff like that in public? If you keep acting paranoid, ACTA will schedule you for an adjustment."

"I'm not paranoid, I'm concerned," Dylan says. "It's never a good idea to have everything connected. If it goes down …"

"It won't go down," Lyle says with certainty. "It's FutureTech. You can't breech FutureTech."

"They tried to hack it ten years ago," Dylan says. "And what about the hack today?"

"The hack lasted all of three minutes," says Nolan.

Dylan won't give in. "They'll try again. They're bigger now. They're calling themselves Alias-X. You know, Alias *International.* Like, *worldwide.* I'm not saying I want Alias to hack the systems, because we all rely on FutureTech security, but I'm worried that now—"

"I'll tell my mom about the ad scanners." I interrupt Dylan's rant because even while I agree with him about the devil inside FutureTech, I know all this chatter is bound to attract another spy-drone, and I can't risk that happening again.

Nolan raises an eyebrow. "Lauren doesn't work with ad-screens."

"No, but software programming is a similar department. I'll have her look into it."

Nolan nods but Dylan still looks troubled, especially when he sees me glancing at the ad-screen, waiting for another Alias-X symbol to pop up.

Lyle finally orders his lunch in the table display, taking forever checking off his long list of food allergies and seasoning preferences. I order a sandwich straight from the menu, but thumb through every section for the next ten minutes because the dads are making a hushed ruckus with their cyber-terrorism conspiracy theories, and I want to pretend I don't know them should that damn drone return. Even worse is the man sitting at the table next to us, wearing a dark visor so I can't read his eyes, leaning in our direction. I swear he's eavesdropping.

"So what's it like at East Hollywood Trade?" Lyle says, and it takes me a moment to realize he's talking to me because his face is buried in the holograms of his wristlet. "My cousin Charlie went there when his dad got laid off from FutureTech. He said it's a special kind of hell. Can't even pop a spinner after lunch because there's always someone watching."

"What do you care, you don't do spinners."

"Nu-uh. Those things will fry your nerve cells. But still … it's the principle behind it, ya know?"

"Everah, it's boring," I say with a sigh. "They're two years behind. I spend most of my time drawing graphics in my desktop. Until I get caught."

"Are you still going to get your PEAD degree?" he asks, ignoring my admission of delinquency.

"I've told you, my mom can't afford the program. Not since my dad died."

"You can't get into college without a PEAD degree."

"I realize that."

"I'm just worried about you, Jo. You can't get a good job through a public trade school."

"No shit, Lyle."

"I'll tell you what, though, the PEAD program is getting harder each year. I've heard rumors about how hard Twelfth Year is. Like screw-this-I'd-rather-be-a-sewer-repairman hard."

"You wanna switch places with me, then?"

He looks up and notices the smirk on my face. "Jeez, Jo. When'd you go all sarcasm-master on me?"

He knows why. But this is Lyle, Mr. Perfection and Shiny Things, the boy oblivious to the shortcomings of the outside world until he breathes a bad cloud of air and suddenly his brain cells are dying a slow and torturous death. I'm surprised he's even outside right now, considering the huge plume of smoke rising from the mountains. If anyone needs a brain adjustment, it's him.

This is why I can't talk to Lyle about my dad. It's why I can't talk about my mom and her new shithead boyfriend. This is why I can't tell him about my tick.

And quite frankly, I don't want to talk. No one ever listens anyway. I could paint my feelings onto a canvas, and then maybe they'd see the images in my head, but then I'd get that look from my mom, that terrified stare that turns her into a comatose statue because my paintings remind her of my dad.

Lyle interrupts my thoughts, which is good because I don't like how my wrists tingle when I think about my dad. "I'm going to the Holo Art Show at the old movie studio tomorrow night. It's supposed to be really wicky. Wanna come?"

"Depends who's going."

"Everybody!" Lyle explains with far more excitement than I am in the mood for. "Ashlyn and Sapphire, Matteo … Harley is back in town. She's doing a holo-graphic display. She told me she really wants to see you again."

He's rambling off all the names of people whom I've hardly spoken to in years. I don't know how Lyle managed to keep in contact with this many people. I haven't kept any of my friends from elementary-prep, none other than Lyle. I'm not really looking forward to explaining the current state of my life to a bunch of peppy PEAD kids, but it sure beats hanging out with my mom and her druggie boyfriend all weekend. And honestly, I'm actually eager to see Harley again. She was supposed to help me get into art school, but I haven't even heard from her since she moved away last year. The girl has some explaining to do.

A waiter brings out our food and begins setting it on the tables, and suddenly Lyle starts shouting, "It's back! The drone is back!"

My heart sinks. This is it, I just know it. I am now officially out of passes.

Three others join the spy-drone, and they flash their blue and red lights. "Do not move," they blurt in robotic voices. "The authorities are on their way."

Nolan waves his wristlet, but the drones remain. "What's going on?" he asks. "What do they want?"

Lyle screeches. "This is what you get for saying anything bad about FutureTech, Dad!"

But the drone isn't after Dylan. Or me. There's a clatter as the eavesdropping man drops his plate on the ground. He sits with his eyes wide, shaking violently, as the drones scan his face, the sizzling *buzz* getting louder by the moment. Not thirty seconds later, two shimmering ACTA cars zip up to the sidewalk, and four agents in silvery body suits and dark visors get out and point their stun guns at the man.

"You, sir!"

The eavesdropper jumps to his feet and holds out his hands. "I didn't do anything!"

A drone scans him again, and one of the ACTA Agent's wristlet flashes. "Your brain scan shows you have thoughts of cyber terrorism and you are an Alias-X sympathizer. You are being detained."

Another agent fires his stun gun. The eavesdropper convulses on the sidewalk. They drag him into a car, and the agents and the drones speed away.

It's over in the blink of and eye, and I'm shaking so hard I nearly fall out of my chair. And I could swear it … out of the corner of my eye, the AX symbol flickers in the FutureTech ad-screen on the bank wall across the street.

"Holy crap," Lyle says, "I thought they were after me."

Nolan frowns. "Why would they be after you?"

"I wrote an essay for my PEAD class against the brain adjusters."

"That's no reason to detain you, Lyle," Nolan says. "Now everybody just calm down. They were clearly after that man."

"At least now we can eat," Dylan says, and he shoves a huge forkful of his lunch into his smiling face.

"We don't want the terrorists ruining your lunch, do we?" Nolan smirks. He waves his wristlet over the table menu display, which responds with a cheery *"Ding! Thank you for being a merry patron!"*

Dylan chuckles and chokes on his food sending it flying onto Lyle's pants.

"Eew! Get it off! Get it off!" Lyle dances around like his pants are on fire, and I can't help but laugh because it's a relief to find humor in someone else's misfortunes for once. Nolan squints at me, and now I feel like a jerk.

"I'm sorry, it's just—"

"Don't worry about it, Jo," Nolan says with a smile. "I know how easy it is to pick on kiddo over here. Most of the time he deserves it."

"Yeah, Lyle, lighten up, will ya?" Dylan pokes his son in the stomach and the guy blushes.

Nolan gleams at his husband with his bleached-white smile, and Dylan gleams at their son with a mirroring toothy grin, as Lyle gives this childlike *awe-shucks* shrug, and it is such a flawless postcard image of a perfect family it makes my stomach churn. The ringing starts. I've had this vision before. I hope it passes quickly because it's pretty cruel.

I line up the Wang family on their backs in the grass, the son between the two fathers. I stab hooks into their cheeks and stretch their lips into a smile. Then I remove their heads and stake them in the ground—

"I should go," I say the moment the ringing fades. No one even noticed I was *away*. "My mom will be expecting me home from school."

"Be careful around those drones on your way home," says Nolan.

"Everah," I sigh. "I'll see you tomorrow, Lyle."

"So you're coming to the Holo Show?" he says with a twitching grin.

"Sure, if I can convince my mom to let me." I roll my creaky and now dented mobie down the sidewalk and hear Perfect Family chatter together at the restaurant.

"What does *everah* mean?" Dylan says.

"Hell if I know," Nolan says. "These kids and their slang. They're not even real words."

Lyle groans. "You guys are such botheads sometimes, I swear."

"What's a bothead?" one of the dads asks, but I've turned on my mobie and can't hear the answer.

My crash did damage to my bike, and now the motor screeches like a dying cat. I coast away from the fancy hills of Los Feliz, weave through the jam of AEVs that are eerily silent next to my noisy mobie, get caught behind a foul-smelling gasser that somehow ended up on the auto-route, nearly run over two giggling women popping spinners, dodge three drones, and make my way home.

Hollywood Boulevard. I've heard stories about my street, about the glitz and glamour that used to be LA. Whatever it was, I've never seen it be anything other than a total dump. Lyle won't come near my block because he's afraid someone will sneeze and give him hepatitis. In this part of town there isn't a street corner open enough to walk on because the bums have turned them into campgrounds. There are more people living *on* Hollywood Boulevard than there are living in the buildings along it. The glitz is covered in dirt and trash, and the glamorous people who used to walk these avenues have either moved away or locked themselves within the gated Zero-Toleration Zones.

My apartment building is just off the Hollywood auto-way, behind the FutureTech Hollywood-Highland Center. The complex is massive compared to our building and is covered in giant illuminated signs that flash ACTA propaganda and advertising and all kinds of FutureTech gadgets and gizmos that no one should ever need. It's also a main location of brain adjusters, so, you know, it's super convenient that I live right behind it.

I plug in my mobie in the apartment garage, and the moment I reach my floor I know Rick is here. My legs twitch and I have the urge to flee, but I need something from my mom. And that means I have to see Rick.

Rick is yelling at my mom in Spanish. My mom doesn't know a lick of Spanish. I don't know why he's never figured that out, but he just keeps on insulting her in a foreign language, and all she can do is make excuses for whatever it is she doesn't know she did wrong. She's dressed in her work clothes, a clean-pressed pantsuit, her light-brown hair tied neatly into a bun. I have to wonder why she's home at one in the afternoon.

"I know you're upset, Rick. I'm trying to understand why you're upset with *me*," my mom says in a voice far too sweet for such a conversation. "I can only do so much on my own." She spots me standing in the doorway and flashes a smile. "Hi, honey, you're home early."

Rick squints at me. "Yeah, aren't you supposed to be in school?" He squeezes a clear plastic spinner capsule onto his tongue and shudders.

"It's not your problem," I say.

My mom tilts her head. "Jo, don't be rude."

"What are you arguing about?"

"We're not arguing," Rick says, his eyes crossing as the spinner takes effect. He's dressed in business attire with his hair slicked back. I've only seen him once in the company of other FutureTech employees and he spoke quite eloquently, but most of the time, when he's around my mom, the slur comes out, that lazy drawl that makes him sound like his lips are about to slide off his face.

My mom eyes Rick carefully. "That's right, sweetheart. We're having an adult conversation."

"Mom, I'm not a kid anymore. I know the difference."

Rick sways over to me. "I'm trying to explain to Lauren why we can't stay in this apartment. We have to move."

"*We*? You don't even live here."

"Honey, Rick lost his job today and now I'll be supporting all three of us—"

"How did you get fired from FutureTech?"

Rick grunts. "What makes you think I got *fired*?"

"I made an educated guess."

He moves toward me like an asteroid drawn into the earth, his huge belly bursting through his button-down shirt. "What do you know? Who told you? Tell me what you know!"

"What are you talking about? I don't know anything."

My mom moves in, but stops short of getting within arm distance. "Rick, dear, please calm down."

But Rick doesn't listen. Instead, he points a gigantic finger at my forehead, pressing his fingernail into my skin. "I'll figure you out, fancy. I know there's something in that brain of yours, and I'll find out. Just because it's in your head doesn't mean it's safe from the scanners."

I've never heard Rick talk like this before. He usually ignores me. In fact, most of the time he pretends I don't even exist; he spends his time in our apartment yelling at my mom about everything under the sun. I hardly remember them acting like a couple, and I still can't imagine why my mom would have gotten involved with a guy like Rick in the first place.

And that's when I see the equipment in the corner of the living room, all marked with FutureTech labels. There are laser lenses, optrodes and diodes and wires and light tubes, and a whole mess of stuff I recognize but have no idea what it does.

Rick is lying in a medical exam chair, his arms and legs strapped down. I take a saw and slice off the top of his skull—

Rick's stinking hot breath on my face pulls me from the vision. "You stole that equipment, didn't you? They fired you because you stole FutureTech property!"

My mom looks to the corner where I'm waving, and she squints like it's the first time she's seeing any of the equipment. "Rick, where did you get all of this?"

Rick turns to glare at her, never moving his giant finger from my forehead. "Leave it alone, Lauren."

"I don't think you're authorized to remove the equipment from the labs—"

Rick bellows at her. "Lauren! Cállate!"

My mom abruptly stops talking as a thin sliver of blood trickles from her right nostril. She touches her nose with the back of her hand, and her eyes widen at the sight of the blood. She frantically searches the living room for something to wipe it up with, and when she looks back at me it's as though she's surprised I'm in the room. "Jo, honey, I didn't hear you come home."

I shove Rick's arm away and glare at him. "What are you doing to my mom?"

Rick's eyebrows knit into a scowl, and he sways because the drugs have subdued his physical control. "I'm not doing anything to her. She was like this when I found her."

My mom pulls a bloodstained tissue from her purse and dabs at her nose. "I told you, Rick, I asked for more hours at FutureTech, but they can't justify giving me more money. And if I ask for more, they'll probably let me go."

"You cannot lose your job at FutureTech."

My mom waves him aside. "I can get a programming job anywhere, maybe someone else pays more money."

"No! You have to stay at FutureTech!"

I point to the pile of equipment in the corner. "I'll tell FutureTech that you're stealing from them."

"Jo, don't be absurd. Rick isn't a thief." She tucks a strand of hair behind her ear with such a casual movement I'd think we were talking about the weather.

Rick's belly jiggles as he chuckles. "Stay out of my business, fancy girl. You go anywhere near FutureTech and they'll discover how screwed up you are and you'll become their next lab rat. Lauren has a job to do at FutureTech and don't you dare get in the middle of it. I'm warning you!"

"She's my mom!"

"Any more of this and we're moving to South LA with my brother."

My mom straightens her posture and runs her palms down the front of her skirt. "Jo, we need to do what's necessary."

"But, Mom, this isn't necessary. None of this has to be this way."

Rick glares at me. "It is all the way it is supposed to be."

I don't have a clue what he means. Rick is sweating through his dress shirt and heaving in my face, and it is completely grossing me out. My mom has been dating Rick for months now, and I cannot for the life of me figure out why. I've never seen them pretend to be happy together. Rick is nothing like my dad. In fact, he's the complete opposite of my dad. Nothing has been the same since he died. Nothing will ever be the same. If I were braver, I'd go straight to the brain adjusters and insist they turn me into a bothead, because at least then I wouldn't give a shit about how wrett my life has become.

But I am just not that kind of girl.

3 the westside

I don't care who says otherwise, but I'll argue any day that my mom's tick is worse than mine. Sure, almost anyone would diagnose me as a psychotic freak of nature, but at least my tick hasn't hurt anyone. My mom's tick hurt everyone. Even my dad. *Especially* my dad.

I didn't figure out my mom's tick until recently. It never really occurred to me before then. At first I thought it was her obsessive need to always do laundry on Thursdays—which I suppose *could* be a tick, but I remember Grandma was the same way, so maybe that's just a habitual thing. Then I suspected her tick was her fear of driving on the auto-ways, but that's because she'd gotten into an accident with a gasser before the 101 highway was converted for AEVs.

I didn't know what my mom's tick was for all those years because I only saw the end effect of it, and it really didn't seem so bad. In fact, Mom was fine, always fine, chipper and cheery and *oh no, Grandma just passed away, let's go to the beach!* My mom's ability to brush past the stressful events of life was admirable to everyone. She was strong. She was resilient.

Then one day I asked her a question about Grandma and she told me to ask her myself. "She's just down the street, probably watching those TV shows she likes."

"No, she's not. Grandma's been dead for five years."

And my mom gave me that blank stare that I never understood and now makes complete sense because my mom has the amazingly horrible ability to forget any painful event that happens in her life. Just like that. At the snap of her fingers. *Oh, it's not something I want to think about? Just fuggedaboutit.*

Lyle jokes that I have it easy because she'll forget if I get busted for doing something illegal, but it warps to have a parent like that. It's especially bad if one parent is gone and the other doesn't remember what happened to him.

My mom's tick is the biggest reason why I can't stick around the apartment. Rick is reason enough, but he spends most of his time in South LA with his brother. Usually I spend my free time with Lyle and Perfect Family, or I wander the bum-covered streets by myself, but today I actually have somewhere to go. Today I'm going to see Madri. And to do that I need my Pass signed.

My mom is on the couch watching TV—actually, not *watching* TV, more like blankly staring at the colors as the holograms pop out from the screen.

"Mom, I need you to co-sign my Pass." She doesn't blink. I move in front of the TV and the projection of the action movie floats around my body as though it's trying to attack me. "Mom."

She looks up. "You need a what?"

"I need you to co-sign my Pass. To get past the Zones gates."

"Where are you going?"

"The Westside."

She tilts her head. "*Where* in the Westside?"

She always does this, tries to be all *parental*, as though it ever made any difference. But I don't dare tell her where I'm actually going. I have to dig into my box of lies. "West Hollywood. With Lyle's dads. Nolan signed his half, but you're my parent, so you need to sigh the other half."

My mom's eyes drop, and she seems to force herself to look at me. "You're always with Lyle's dads."

"What do you have against the Wang Family?"

"Nothing. It's just ..." She sinks further into the couch. "Maybe you could spend more time here. At home. With me."

That sounds like a terrible idea. "Mom, you spend all your time with Rick. Most days I don't even think you want me here."

"No. Sweetheart, I need you here. To keep me company."

She's totally out of it, trapped in one of her *forgetful moments*, so she'd not likely remember this conversation. Still, her demeanor is depressing, and I need to get this conversation moving so I can get out of here.

"Yeah. Sure. Maybe next weekend. But not today. They're expecting me."

My mom sighs and it seems like forever before she speaks again. "All right. Be home for dinner."

She voices commands into her own wristlet and waves it against mine, and I'm grateful she's not paying enough attention to notice that the Pass has actually come from Madri. My mom has no idea she has just granted me permission into Beverly Hills.

I stand out like a sore thumb on the Westside. There the people are tidy and trimmed, hardly a person who's the least bit overweight or underdressed. In the Zero-Toleration Zones the rules are not based on race or background or sexuality or even occupation. But there are strict policies, and to stay longer than your pass allows will result in—at the very least—a solid kick in the ass on your way back through the gate.

Madri's neighborhood in Beverly Hills is one of the worst places for a Free-Zoner like me to wander through. Madri insists on giving me outfits to wear when I visit her so I at least look like I fit in, but I hate the way her clothes hang on my body. I prefer to wear what's comfortable, which Nolan refers to as "retro." I know my mom hoped I'd grow out of my tomboyish phase and start dressing like a girl, but really, I don't know how any of these girls can stand wearing the clothes they do.

Even if my fashion isn't really fashionable, there is one part of my outfit I stand by: my boots. Stiff, glossy white, black laces and rubber soles. I was neurotic about keeping them clean, until I dropped paint on one and I suddenly had the urge to color them completely. The paint chips off in the heat and washes away in the rain, but I don't mind because I can change the design based on whatever I'm feeling that day. They are my walking canvas.

My other canvas is at Madri's house in Beverly Hills. The journey is an undertaking in itself because it is an hour-long ride on my mobie from Hollywood to the Mehra's house, and by the time I finally drive through their gate I'm sweating and huffing from weaving around gassers and AEVs under the scorching sun. I park my mobie in the driveway and stand on the black pad on the Mehra's porch while the camera scans me.

Madri's smiling face appears on a screen by the door. "You're late," she says.

"My mom—" I start, but Madri's face disappears and the front door swings open.

Madri's house is huge. Like, really huge. I have spent many days here, and it never fails that I still get lost going to the bathroom. And even though the house is plainly decorated with some very old antique Indian accents—certainly more modest than I'd expect from such a wealthy family—there is one admirable quality to their home: the artwork. Dr. Mehra is a self-professed art collector. The whole house is covered in it, and not the stupid vintage blobs of paint worth five million dollars kind of artwork, but *real* art. Beautiful, provocative, awe-inspiring pieces from famous and unknown artists alike.

And that's why I come here, because down the halls of the Mehra home hang the last remaining pieces of art created by my dad. Dr. Mehra has offered to let me take a few home and keep for myself, but I can't. I just can't.

Madri leads me through the house, and I pause in the hallway in front of one of my dad's pieces, a mish-mash of paint and textures. In the middle of the imagery of a burning city, there is a young girl clutching a paintbrush in her hand. He never said so, but I think the girl is supposed to be me.

"They delivered the canvases today," Madri says from the doorway of her art room. "You won't believe how hard they're getting to find."

"Did New York stop selling them?"

"Either they've run out or they're hoarding them for themselves. I had to order these from Japan."

"You got imports from Japan? How did you manage that?"

Madri gives a sly smile. "It helps when your mom works for the city. She pretended they're for some commission thing."

She steps aside as I burst into her art room. Madri has an unprecedented collection of materials to work with because she's got the money to buy any kind she wants, including the four giant canvases from Japan. Each is taller than I am, and they smell of freshly bleached fabric and feel thick and organic under my fingers.

"Oh! Madri, they're beautiful!"

Now she's really gleaming. "Aren't they? I knew you'd like them."

"I almost don't want to paint on them."

"Well, if you won't, I will," she says with a smirk.

Dr. Mehra appears in the doorway as we're sorting through her collection of paint, and his dark face wrinkles when he sees me. "Hello, Jo. I didn't know you'd be here today." He gives his daughter a disapproving head tilt as he says this.

Madri dips her chin with a sigh. "Yeah, I know, Dad. I'll get to it tomorrow. The canvases came today and I knew Jo wouldn't want to wait to see them."

"Madri, your brother nearly did not get accepted into college, and you know what that did to your mother. You can't expect to just walk in."

Madri's skin is pretty dark—though not as dark as her father's—but I still see her blush. "Dad, I know. I'm going to get into college, okay? I'll be a doctor or a scientist or whatever you want me to be, but right now I really want to paint."

Dr. Mehra fumes. "Madri! This is not for me, this is for *you*! This is your *future*! What will you do if you have no future?"

Madri sinks back behind the canvas and Dr. Mehra seems embarrassed to be having this conversation with me in the room. He sighs dramatically and leaves without saying another word.

I hand Madri a paintbrush as she stares at the blank canvas. "Hey," I say. "I'm here, we might as well paint."

"It's no use," she says, shaking her head. "I can paint all I want, but it'll never mean anything for me."

"Sure, it could. You've got a better chance than anybody to make it a career. It would be easy to get your mom to commission you."

Madri rattles her head. "Gimme a break, Jo. You know better than anyone how risky that is."

"Yeah, but your mom would have a harder time turning you down for a commission since you're her daughter."

She squints at me. See, Madri's smart—like, freakish baby genius smart, and she's always had that going for her—but she's also intuitive and clever, and that's why I like her. She sees right through my bullshit.

"You know my mom wanted to give him the commission—"

I don't want to hear this. "Everah, it's fine. And anyway, that's not why he killed himself."

Madri sighs and folds her hands in her lap and off she goes, mirroring her father's psychologist mannerisms. "So tell me, Jo, why *did* your dad commit suicide?"

I flash her a pout, but she's pulling it out of me, not because she's mean or because she's really wanting to be a psychologist, but because we're sitting in front of four blank canvases and I haven't painted anything substantial in weeks.

"Look, Jo, I can buy all the paint and canvases I want, but I don't have the right kind of talent. Not like you do."

"It's not like I'm going to change the world with the crap I paint."

"It's not crap, it's good. Don't get me wrong, you're no genius, but you're good. Better than me. Better than most."

"Well, I'm not gonna paint anything for the city or FutureTech, no offense to your mom."

"Don't paint for my mom. Paint for yourself. Paint something for your dad."

And I do. Out of nowhere the paint flies from my brush and splatters all over my pants and I don't care because I've been bottling up so many images and I finally want something to show for it. Madri is resilient in her efforts to break into my soul, and maybe that's why I never have any visions about her. She's safe from my horrible tick because she provides the canvases, both literally and figuratively. It's in this room with all this paint that my visions leave me alone while I put my mind on paper.

Once I'm done with my painting, I snap a picture of it on my tab because it'll be another week before I see it in person. I can't take it home; I never take any of my own paintings home.

As much as I'd love to take Dr. Mehra up on his offer and acquire my dad's artwork, I can't bring it anywhere near my mom. The last time she saw a piece she had such a violent panic attack she had to be hospitalized for three days. Until that moment she'd forgotten about my dad. She'd forgotten he was dead. She'd forgotten all about the night she found him with his wrists cut wide open and bleeding to death in the bathtub.

4 trade secrets

Saturday morning my mom is in the living room, as usual, staring into the TV. It's eight o'clock and soon she'll be leaving for her weekend shift at FutureTech, but she's not even dressed in her work clothes. It's unusual to see her in tight jeans and a flowy top instead of her usual pencil skirt and blazer, but she's still wearing those ridiculously high-heeled sandals to let me know she's not fallen off the rails completely.

"Good morning," I say pleasantly, trying to judge her current state of mind because I'm really hoping she'll let me go to the Holo Art Show tonight.

She frowns and I know I'm in for something terrible. "Jo, sit down, please."

"What's wrong?"

"I got a message from Principal Torres."

This can't be good. "On Saturday?"

"He says you ditched school yesterday."

Ah shit. Redirect! Redirect! "Mom, that place is wrett. I can't learn anything there. I'll be stabbed in the throat by one of the other kids. That's why the PEAD program is designed to be done at home, because parents were worried about their kids getting killed. Aren't you worried about me getting killed?"

"Jo! Sit down!" Her face flushes and I plop down on the couch. "I know you're smart, so stop using dumb words like that. If you mean to say *wretched*, then say—"

I groan. "Blame it on the school. It's making me dumber by the day. They're so far behind I can't stay awake through a whole class. And even if I ace through it, I'll still never qualify for college."

"So you *do* want to go to college?"

"Yeah. Maybe. I donno. If I can get into art school, then yeah, definitely."

My mom cringes. "No! I can't have you running off to art school!"

"I won't be *running off*, I'll—" I have to take a breath because I'm about to start yelling and that will send my mom straight to shutdown. "I haven't figured it all out. I mean, things have changed. But I can't deal with the trade school. I can't go back."

"Then you'll have to get a job."

I can't believe she said that. "*What?*"

"Jo, I can't support all three of us on my salary, and the way things are going, we won't be able to live here much longer. So if you're not going to school, you'll have to work."

"I can't get a job, I'm only sixteen. I have to be eighteen to work."

"Tell them you're eighteen."

My mom just suggested I lie to get a job. What. Is. Happening. "They'll check my records. And if I'm caught lying against the data system, I'll never have a proper career after that."

"Goddammit, Jo! Stop making excuses!"

And here we go. I hate having visions about my mom. I don't enjoy having visions about anyone—well, that's not entirely true; some people deserve it, like Rick—but the visions about my mom are just creepy.

My mom is soaking in a bubble bath, shaving her legs with a straight razor, from ankle to knee and over again. I sit behind her, outside of the tub, and I take hold of her arm and retrace her motions, only I turn her hand so the edge of the blade pierces into her skin and a long sliver of blood drips down and stains the bubbles red—

"Jo, stop that. I'm taking you to the school. Now."

It takes a moment for my mom's words to sink in as the fog clears from my sight. "Wait, what?"

She gets to her feet and adjusts the collar of her blouse so it tucks inside her bra. "That's why Principal Torres called me. He wants to have a parent-student conference this morning."

"This is a joke. There's no reason for him to care so much about me."

"We're going, and if you choose to ignore him, then you're on your own." She grabs my arm and off we go, straight to the guillotine.

If my mom could afford a modern AEV, it wouldn't be such a nerve-racking experience to be in the car with her behind the wheel. Instead of being led safely along the major auto-routes by computer automation where there is no need—or excuse—for road rage, we're stuck on the side streets with the gassers and the other outdated electric cars. Which gives my mom all the room and opportunity to rage up a storm of insults for other drivers.

"C'mon, you moron, there are two lanes here, can't you see that? I can walk faster than this! Don't flash your lights at me! Keep moving or I'll run you over!"

"Mom, your speaker is on."

"Oh crap!" She flips the switch and glances around. Every other driver glares at her.

I distract her by pointing to the road ahead. "Take the next right, it'll be just past—"

But she doesn't go right. She makes a hard left through incoming traffic, and suddenly we're in the hills where the houses are smashed on top of each other and the roads are so narrow our car barely squeezes through.

"Where are you going? You missed the turn."

"I know a shortcut," she says, and she yanks on the wheel so hard two tires leave the ground.

"How do you know a shortcut to the school?"

"I graduated from East Hollywood High," she says, and she glances at me just as we're about to crash into a tree, and then swerves a few more times until we're in right in front of the school.

How did I not know that my mom went here? I assumed she'd gone to school with my dad, but now I remember he's from Burbank. My mom grew up here, in the heart of LA, just like me.

We stand on the front walk for a few moments, and I tilt my head back to gaze at the main tower as it soars over us like a cathedral fortress. My first day here I expected to see a hunchback greeting students at the door.

"Wow," my mom says, "this place hasn't changed."

"It's wrett."

"I don't know, it's kind of historical."

My mom knows the way to the principal's office, and I have to wonder if she spent a lot of time there. My mom's heels clack and my boots squeak on peeling linoleum floors as we make our way through the dark hallway, which is especially creepy on the weekend. Heavy, foul air fills my nose, making me queasy—beach and tobacco smoke are not comforting scents.

The office door swings open before we even reach it, and Principal Torres pokes his head out and flashes me a bright white smile. "Miss Bristol!" He spots my mom and smiles wider. "And you must be… *Missus* Bristol. It's a pleasure." That smile makes him look human, and almost attractive. Almost.

My mom is so fixed in place and gazing dreamily at Mr. Torres that it's clear she thinks he's the most handsome man she's ever seen. I stand there awkwardly as my mom holds out her hand like she expects Mr. Torres to kiss it, but he shakes it instead.

"Please, come in."

Mr. Torres's office is very hi-tech. The whole back wall is covered in security screens, and tabs and terminals clutter the rest. He speaks to his desk computer, "Josephine Bristol, Junior," and a hologram pops up with my name and some other backwards text I can't read.

Mr. Torres weaves his fingers together and peers at me. "Miss Bristol, I was rather disappointed that you decided to leave school yesterday. Care to explain why you did that?"

Okay, this is where I'm supposed to get all apologetic and say how sorry I am for disrupting his school, and how much I appreciate his authority because he's the wise old adult and I'm just a kid. "I won't go in for another brain scan."

My mom gasps but Mr. Torres isn't the least bit startled by my statement. In fact, I think he expected it.

"I didn't ask you here to finish the brain scan. I don't agree with those protocols anyway."

"Then why am I here?"

Mr. Torres leans back. "Miss Bristol, I know this is difficult for you. I've seen many students who had to drop out of their PEAD Programs. I know this must seem like a step in the wrong direction, but I assure you, we at East Hollywood Trade want to do everything we can to make this as productive and successful an experience as possible."

I know my face is contorted in some perplexing expression, but I don't dare say anything. I just stare at my hands.

"It's a shitty job, you know." I look up and Mr. Torres tilts his head and smirks. "Mine. I've been here going on fifteen years, before the PEAD programs started. And suddenly my school was turned into this place for kids who've been told they have no chance at a real future. Can you imagine what that's like, telling kids the state can't afford to give them a chance? These students know they'll end up being machinists, or construction workers, or office clerks because that's what they're taught here. How can any student even try to get into college to become a doctor or a nurse when we don't even teach biology?"

"You don't teach biology?" my mom says with great concern. See, now she's getting it.

"What's worse is when I get a student like you, Miss Bristol. Not only do you already have some PEAD education—which puts you leagues ahead of other students—but you probably have some affinity for your future, for what you're going to study in college. And suddenly you're thrown into the mud pit without a chance of ever getting to go to college."

"Jo doesn't want to go to college," my mom butts in. "She wants to go to *art school*." I know my mom's not on my side here, but does she have to make it sound like I'm joining a band of mountain hippies?

"I'm not surprised," Mr. Torres says, and he waves his hand over his desk again and the hologram expands to display the incriminating drawing from Mrs. Garcia's class.

I hide my face in my hands. "Oh god, not that thing again."

"You have been told the rules many times, Miss Bristol. Desktops and tablets are meant for school assignments only."

"I was just doodling. Besides, that video was wrett, what am I going to do with notes about building structures?" Great, now I'm getting defensive and my voice is cracking like a pre-teen boy.

Mr. Torres grins again. I wish he'd stop doing that, because as handsome as he is when he smiles it makes my skin crawl. "Miss Bristol—"

"Oh god, stop calling me that. My name is *Jo*!"

"Jo! Don't talk back to the principal!" I can't figure out why my mom looks like she's about to cry. This is *my* warped-up future on the line, not hers.

"All right, *Jo*, if that's what you'd prefer ..." I give a pouty nod and he goes on. "I didn't ask you here for a scolding, so you can get over that."

Mr. Torres waves away the image of my drawing, and I'm grateful because I'm tired of looking at it. It's not even that good, just a rough sketch, the perspective is a little janky and I don't like how I shaded the background so dark.

"Jo, I don't want you at my school any longer."

"Are you kicking me out?"

"I want to help you get back into the PEAD program."

My mom stops crying, and I'm so happy I bounce in my seat.

"But I can't afford it," my mom says. "She can get back in, sure, but not without a way to pay for it."

"Yes, that's how I aim to help."

"How?" I say. "Can I get a grant?"

Mr. Torres sighs. "No. Unfortunately, grants are out of the question. The state hardly has any money to pay the electricity bill for this school, let alone give grants."

"Federal grants?" my mom says.

"Mrs. Bristol, I realize it's been many years since you and I were in school, but times have changed. The federal government no longer has any say in the public school system. It's all in the hands of the state. There are, however, private scholarships."

"Private?" I say. "You mean …"

Mr. Torres lets out a long sigh. "If there is one thing FutureTech good for, it's their abundance of money, and they give scholarships to students who need help paying for the PEAD program."

A lump forms in my throat and I swallow it down. "Okay, sign me up."

"Well, it's not quite that simple."

Of *course* it's not that simple.

"FutureTech doesn't give the scholarships to just anyone. You have to show them how you stand out from the crowd, how you in particular can benefit from the PEAD program, and in return be of benefit to the state once you've achieved your degree. The committee reviews the applicants, and if you're in the top rankings they'll award you a scholarship."

"How do I stand out?"

Mr. Torres waves his hand and my sketch hologram reappears. "You should submit your artwork."

I think my mom stopped breathing. All this talk about *committee*, and *submission*, and *artwork* ... Yes, my mom tries her best to forget what's happened to our family, but there's no hiding from the triggers. And there's no denying this situation is a little too familiar.

My mom is crying again—no, *sobbing*—and her nose is bleeding all over the place and I'm sitting here trying to keep myself from punching Mr. Torres in the mouth. I don't mean to hurt the man, I just want to shove those words right back through his handsome white teeth.

"Is everything all right?" he asks. He's worried about my mom's nosebleed and confused about her crying and hasn't the slightest freaking clue as to what's just happened.

My mom snorts all the grossness into her bloody handkerchief and grabs my arm. "Jo, we're going."

I brush her off. Something about this doesn't add up. "Hang on a minute. This drawing is crap—"

Mr. Torres interrupts. "I don't think it's crap."

"Everah, that's not the point. You're assuming, based on this doodle, that I'm going to be able to get a scholarship from FutureTech?"

Mr. Torres rests his elbows on the desk. "I've seen some of your other work."

"No, that's impossible. I don't have any of my artwork online. I took it down years ago. There were some stalkers …" I shudder at the memory of the days when people dissected my artwork down to the most miniature brush stroke and claimed they knew everything about me. "I took it all down and shut off my port. And then when my dad died …"

My mom howls and blows her nose again.

"I didn't say I saw your work online," says Mr. Torres, and he drums on the desktop. Anther image pops up in the hologram next to the doodle, and even though I haven't seen this drawing in a long time I recognize it instantly.

It's a painting of a phoenix, in the brilliant colors of a fire, flying toward the sky, balancing scales in her beak. I painted it years ago—I was maybe thirteen—and it was one of the last I'd done with my dad before he started locking himself away in his study.

"How did you get that?" My voice crackles with a whisper. I'm too stunned to be angry.

Mr. Torres grins. "That's not important right now. What is important is that you get yourself that scholarship."

Yes, that *is* what's important. Why it's so important to *him* is perplexing, but regardless of his motivation, he's throwing me a bone. As much as I despise FutureTech with every fiber of my being, I need to get back into the PEAD program so I can get into art school. Only there will I truly be understood. Only there will I not be considered the weird kid. Only there will I have a chance of not ending up in the hands of brain adjusters, or alone in a bathtub. I can't screw this up.

My mom sobs in my ear and Mr. Torres is stares hard at me and my phoenix painting floats above his desk and I'm so nauseas I taste bile.

"How much time do I have to submit?"

"You can submit any time, but the longer you wait, the longer you'll be expected to attend class at East Hollywood Trade."

A clock beeps 9:00 a.m. and we're all startled back to reality. My mom even stops crying.

"Crap, I'm late for work. C'mon, Jo, we need to leave."

I can't move, I can't tear my eyes away from Mr. Torres and my painting, but my mom is suddenly Superwoman and she drags me from the office.

5 fool on the hill

My mobie screeches as I walk up the street to Lyle's house. Lyle lives in Los Feliz, up on a hill near Griffith Park. The street is so steep that my mobie has a difficult time getting up here on a normal day, but today the damn thing won't cooperate. I have to walk the three blocks uphill, pushing my bike all the way.

I pass by my old house, the house we lived in before my dad died. I loved living there. I could see the Griffith Observatory from my bedroom window, with its twinkling lights and eyes on the infinite sky. Even still, the Wang home had always been nicer than mine. I begged my parents to put red clay shingles on our roof and lay Spanish-style tile on the floor. Instead, my mom covered the roof in solar panels and installed some recycled temperature-controlled flooring that made the house smell like a wine cork.

I reach Lyle's house and stand on the black mat on the porch as the security scanner sweeps over me. The door swings open. I find the dads in the kitchen in front of the TV screen as a news reporter interviews the hologram projection of some ruffled civilian. The dads are so enthralled with the program that they barely notice I'm standing behind them.

"What's going on?" I ask.

Dylan squints at me, his slanted eyes so narrowed they appear closed. "This man's wife was abducted by brain hackers."

My throat tightens. "Brain *what?*"

Nolan shoots his husband a disapproving look. "Don't call them that."

"I'm not calling them brain hackers, *they're* calling them that." Dylan points at the TV. "And what else would you call them?"

I'm terrified to know the answer, but I have to ask. "What's a brain hacker?"

"These poor people are having their brains turned to mush by these criminals," Dylan shudders. "It's all an Alias scheme, I'm telling you."

Nolan shakes his head. "This is what happens when people want their brains adjusted for cheap, and they don't do their research and find a real doctor."

"These people are scared, Nolan. They're trying to beat the ACTA drones and they're willing to risk their livelihoods by having their brains torn apart and be turned into robot heads."

"*Bothead!*" Lyle calls out from the living room. "The word is *bothead!*"

Dylan shudders again. "The point is, it's bad enough that we have to deal with the threat of the actual neurosurgeons going around fixing everyone with their optic implants and lobotomies, but now there are brain *hackers* on the loose. When are you gonna convince the city to regulate this?"

Nolan heaves. "Brain adjusting *is* regulated. And you've got nothing to worry about because your brain is fine. Just don't go spouting any more of your paranoid ranting and you'll never have to deal with these hackers."

Holy crap. I thought being caught by real brain doctors was bad enough, but now there are hackers on the streets turning people into botheads? What if they were to discover my tick?

"But what if they find *me*?" Dylan says, mirroring my own internal thoughts.

The holograms of the TV screen begin to blur, the graphics crossing and bleeding into one another, but it's not the TV. I know this because I hear the ringing—

Nolan grabs my arm, holding me steady on wobbly knees.

"Stop shouting, Dylan," Nolan says. "You're upsetting Jo."

I wave him away. "No, I'm fine. I want to sit down."

Nolan leads me into the living room where Lyle is in front of the TV, crouched in a firing position as he shoots at grotesque alien creatures that jump around him from the holo display.

"Jo is here," Nolan says, but Lyle doesn't respond.

I lie down on the rug and fiddle with my tab and wait for Lyle to finish saving Earth from the alien invasion. I go straight to the news app on my tab, and sure enough the story of the brain hackers is everywhere. This is the real deal. There are people who will literally scramble your brains for a few dollars.

"*Gaah*!" Lyle groans as he throws his visor across the room. I look up to see him cornered by holo-aliens. He collapses on the floor next to me and the graphics disappear. "Whatcha watching?"

I hold out my tab. "The news."

Lyle gags. "I don't know why you torture yourself, Jo."

"I like to know what's going on in the world."

He rolls over to get a better look at the video while the newscaster babbles on about Alias-X plots and our threatened cyber-security. "Because it's so uplifting, right?"

Lyle, practically on top of me, has his leg flung over mine, his bony hip smashing against my ribs. Normally, I'd be arguing with him over his ignorance to the issues of the world, but I'm too distracted by the feel of his body.

I've never been able to understand my relationship with Lyle. We've known each other forever and we've always been friends, yet things have gotten … *complicated.* To Lyle I'm just Jo, but every once in awhile he seems to remember I'm a girl. I'll catch him looking at me, like the summer when my boobs finally came in and Lyle's eyes twitched over my not-quite-bikini-body and hardly said a word. And then there are times like these when Lyle and I are touching, but in a *friendly* way because no one has made a move. I'm enjoying it, but at the same time I'm confused and I don't know what to do, and Lyle doesn't do anything either. Finally the awkwardness is stifling and I don't even realize Lyle is breaching my privacy as he's browsing through my tab.

"What's that?" Lyle says, his breath blowing my hair into my ear. He's pulled up the photo of my latest painting.

"I did it yesterday at Madri's." I'm out of breath, partly because I'm gasping for air after remembering to breathe, and partly because Lyle has his elbow on my back as he reaches over.

"Send it to the holo."

"Oh. Yeah, okay." I send him the image and he flicks on the TV holograph and my painting lights up so vibrantly it looks real.

"Jeez, Jo, that's freakish. In a wicky way. What's with the eyeballs?"

I don't really know where the imagery came from—flat shapes and bold colors of a vase holding a bouquet of eyeballs, and one hand is reaching down to pick a stem out. I really have no idea what it means. I pretend I didn't hear the question, but Lyle has moved on already.

"So what's up?" Lyle says. "You seem a little off today."

Probably because he's touching me and I'm confused as to why it's making me excited. "The principal at the trade school offered me a scholarship to finish the PEAD program."

"Seriously? That's wicky!"

"No, it's not. I have to prove I'm worthy of the money. He wants me to submit my artwork."

"That's easy. Just do it. Done. You're in."

"You don't understand, Lyle. You don't know what that means. Hell, *I* don't know what that means."

"It means you can get into the U of Denver with me and we can finally leave this wrett place."

I take a really deep breath, and Lyle's body moves on top of mine. "I'm not going to Colorado."

"You're not?"

"I want to go to art school."

He rolls over and looks at me like I've just told him I have a terminal disease. Honestly, what is it about art school that freaks people out so much?

"Jo, I don't know if that's such a good idea."

"It's a great idea if I can get back into the Program."

"Get back in the Program, sure. But aren't you a little *worried* about what might happen if you become an artist?"

"Dammit, Lyle! I'm not going to turn into my dad!" I jump to my feet and tower over Lyle as his face turns pale.

"I'm not saying you're going to *kill yourself*," he says, "but you know what could happen if you get a job through FutureTech. And you won't make any money if you don't."

"You *are* saying I'll kill myself!"

Lyle doesn't understand. He never did understand. I've told him time and again that there's no place for me at a traditional college, that I'll never be able to fit in with the bubbling, chipper, pretty girls at a university. My place is not where Lyle wants me to be. My place is at art school.

Everything goes blurry and I can barely make out the sound of his voice over the ringing.

Lyle stands in front of me. The pistol is heavy in my hand as I raise it up and aim it at his forehead, the muzzle but an inch away. My finger finds the trigger and the bullet penetrates into his skull and his blood splatters on my face—

The doorbell rings. Lyle jumps to his feet, adjusts his shirt, and runs his fingers through his hair just as Ashlyn and Sapphire walk in.

"*Hey*, Lyle." Ashlyn struts across the room in the shortest skirt I've ever seen, and I have to move out of the way of her swaying hips.

"You're here early," he says, blushing. "Where's Zander?"

Ashlyn tosses her head back as though the mention of her boyfriend has ruined her afternoon. "Oh, I donno. He'll be here soon."

I catch Sapphire's eyes—which sparkle the deep blue of her namesake—as she stands in the doorway, balanced on one leg like a flamingo, dressed like an over-done fashion model with pink-streaked hair stiffened high above her head and her eyeliner shaped like a star. I could never pull off a look like that, even if I was actually convinced I was as pretty as her.

"Hey, Jo," Sapphire says. "So you probably heard about our brother, huh?"

I'm a little stunned she's actually talking to me. Then again, she's been oddly empathetic since my dad died. "Is he back from Vegas?" I ask, trying to sound interested.

"Yeah." She weaves her necklaces between her fingers. "ACTA got a hold of him. Put him in a hospital in the Valley, got him all…" she shudders "…*fixed up*."

Ashlyn rolls her eyes. "Jesus, Saph, you make it sound like it wasn't his own fault he had to be adjusted. He was an addict."

"He tried to get better," Sapphire says with a shrug.

"And the doctors finished the job," Ashlyn said. "Stop acting like it was a bad thing. He's no less conscious now than he was when he was drugged out."

Sapphire seems a half-step from crying. "We're just happy to have him back."

"I know I am," Ashlyn says with a flick of her hair. "I was getting tired of explaining him to people."

"No one should even be allowed to get to that point," Lyle says matter-of-factly. "Everyone should get fixed at the first sign of an abnormality."

I don't know how to respond to that in a way that doesn't include smacking him upside the head, but no one even heard him.

Ashlyn has moved on to checking her reflection in the window, and Sapphire stands there clinking her overabundance of necklaces.

Without warning, Matteo struts into the room and twirls in front of Sapphire as she bats her pretty blue eyes.

"Hi, ladies," Matteo says as he brushes his silky black hair from his forehead. He's not talking to me. Technically, I'm not considered one of the "ladies." He moves to peck Ashlyn on the cheek, and she grabs his face for a full-on mouth kiss, then the room fills with sloppy smushing sounds. She's lucky her boyfriend isn't here to see this, but I doubt she'd care either way.

Lyle fusses with his shirt as his eyes flicker over me. "Hey, Matteo, you got the tickets, right? You promised you'd get us in to see Harley."

"*Oooh*!" Ashlyn breaks her mouth from Matteo. "You're still hung-up on Harley, are ya?"

Sapphire rolls her eyes. "Ugh. I hear she's covered herself in those night-glow tattoos."

Lyle turns red. So that's why he was so eager to go to this art show. He despises crowds, especially the sweaty-dancing, drunken-moshing ones, but Harley will be there. His old next-door neighbor, the rebel girl, the artist, the realist, the one who was supposed to help me get into art school but ran off to tour with a pop-art crew.

"Let me check," Matteo says, and he whips out his wristlet like he's some important businessman.

"What the hell is *that*?" Ashlyn frowns at the TV like it hurts her, and I realize my eyeball painting is still in the holo.

"Oh, sorry," Lyle says as he waves his hand in front of the TV sensor and my painting disappears.

"Zander is meeting us there," Matteo says as he taps his wristlet closed. "Let's go before Harley gets on."

"Right," Lyle says. And then he turns to me. "Are you wearing that?"

I look around the room and realize I'm the only one not dressed for the occasion. Even Lyle is wearing one of his nice shirts, and he never dresses up unless it's for a family event or if he thinks he has a chance to impress a girl. I'm still in my old standard tank and jeans.

"I thought it was an art show," I say, and hold out a boot. "I cleaned up the paint job."

Ashlyn rolls her eyes. "It's an *event*, Jo. Everyone's gonna be there. You don't wanna embarrass Harley, do you?"

"Harley's an artist. She of all people will appreciate my boots." I look to Lyle for support because I'm starting to feel ganged up on, but he's staring off into the corner of the room.

"C'mon," Sapphire says, "our mom is waiting in the car."

We pile into Mrs. Baez's massive AEV. I get in first and Lyle scoots in next and smashes me against the window like there isn't enough room in our row. Ashlyn squeals with Matteo in the back while Sapphire chats with her mom up front.

It's not a long ride over the hill to the abandoned studio lot, but it feels like it takes ages. Lyle is as stiff as a board, his fingers scratching the knees of his jeans. I lean forward to get a look at his face when I notice his gaze is stuck on the dashboard.

I've known Lyle forever, and I know that look. That is his guilty look, not because of something he's done, but something he hasn't done. There is something Lyle isn't telling me.

"What is it?" I ask.

Lyle's eyes shift, but he stays still. "Nothing."

"I know something's wrong. Why won't you tell me?"

Sapphire turns to shout at Ashlyn to quiet her flirting, and Lyle looks down at his hands.

He leans over to whisper, "I don't want to be the one to tell you. You'll find out when we get there."

My heart lurches, and I'm suddenly regretting coming along to this art show in the first place.

6 the fourth wall

The asphalt vibrates with a *thump thump thump thump.* Soundwaves bounce off the row of studio buildings, and everyone jumps around in a massive mosh pit in the middle of the alley. Lights flash in beat with the music, and I know someone is bound to suffer a seizure. A few people sit on a water tank with gold and blue lettering as it rests on its side, concave where it smashed into the ground. In the rare instances that I come to these events I like to pretend that the studio is still functioning, like back when they actually made movies here. No one makes movies in LA anymore; they haven't in years. Now the lots are swarmed by holo shows and dance parties.

Ashlyn and Sapphire lead us through the crowd with ease, catching glances from men who know perfectly well they're too old to be ogling at teenage girls. The Baez sisters are pros at this game; they know how to smile and flick their hair and strut their way into the biggest sound stage. The crowd acts as an organic organism and seems to know I don't belong with these people, pinching off the path before I can squeeze in behind. One guy smashes my foot through my boot, a girl spills neon liquid on my pants, and I swear someone just grabbed my ass. Once through the wide door into the sound stage I reach out in a last-ditch effort to grab Lyle, and someone holds on.

"Oh hey, Picasso!"

Only one person I know thinks he's clever by calling me that. Zander. He flashes a smile as he reels me in like a fish on a line. The douche will kiss anything with boobs—even me—so when he throws his face into mine, I move away, only to get bumped from behind, and our skulls crash together.

"Hey, bothead!" Zander calls after someone. "Watch where you're going!"

Lyle appears from the sea of sweaty bodies and turns me away from Zander, who has already moved on to the next girl.

"Harley's up front," Lyle says. "You can see her on the stage."

"Can we go up there?"

Lyle's eyes shift around the crowd. "I'm not sure that's a good idea."

"Why not? It's just Harley." I look at him carefully and notice the tension in his cheeks. "What, you don't want me talking to her because you *like* her?"

His eyes narrow and he leans down to me. "That's what you think this is about?"

"I don't know, Lyle. I don't know why you're being so weird. I haven't seen the girl in a year, and now you're trying to keep me from her."

"Jo, that's not—"

He doesn't have the chance to protest further. I've forced myself to deal with the Los Feliz groupies to get here, I've pushed aside my anxiety and trudged through the thicket of people, all so I can finally see Harley again. So help me, Lyle will not stop me now.

Harley isn't hard to spot. She's high on a platform in the middle of the stage above a DJ who creates music by weaving his fingers into beams of lasers. Harley's hair is bright blue and she has, in fact, covered her skin in night-glow tattoos. She's smiling and laughing and dancing and waves her hands in the air. 3D hologram projections float above the crowd and on the walls of the sound stage. This is pop art. Harley used to be a painter, like me. And now she's making graphics of mutant animals and naked people.

Harley smiles wider when she spots me, her teeth shine purple under the lights. "Jo! How are you, sweetie?"

"Hey, Harley. This is … um … *fancy*!"

"Yeah, well, gotta pay the bills somehow, right?" She dances to the music and the crowd hoots and cheers. The sight of her is intoxicating.

My voice cracks when I shout, "I thought you were going to art school?"

"I've been on the road with this crew for the last year. We went to Toronto last month. Can you believe it? We actually got into Canada!" She's completely avoiding my question.

"What about your artwork?"

She flicks her hand. "I tried art, but it's hard, ya know?"

"So you dropped out?"

"Never went. Couldn't pay the tuition. Also, I never did get my PEAD degree."

"What? Why not?" Now I'm worried. Harley is three years older than me. She was my study partner for a while, and if she didn't pass the PEAD program, then does that mean …?

"I love being on tour! It's so liberating!" She smiles and waves her arms in the air and her tattoos shimmer as her blue hair catches the illumination of the holos. Everything is just so *shiny*. "I'd never go back, you know," she says as though continuing a conversation I wasn't aware of. "There's no way. It was all so dark. I was tired of not being happy. Now I get to be happy all the time!"

"Harley, what are you talking about? You are an artist, a good one!"

"I still *am* an artist!" she says and waves a holo of a naked woman into the crowd. "Just a happier one!"

Harley closes her eyes and tosses her head back, lost in the movement and the music. I'd maybe think she was high or drunk, but I've seen Harley in both those states and she was irate and miserable, itching to get out of her own head. She wasn't loose and giddy like this. This is something else entirely.

"At least she seems happy, right?" Lyle is at my side. His hands are stuffed deep in his pants pockets, his bony shoulders brought up to his ears. The realization strikes me like a blow to the head, and I understand what it was that he didn't want to tell me.

Harley has been fixed.

The crowd seems to have compressed around us, touching every inch of my body and all of its pressure points as though I have been submerged in mud. The force rises up to my chest, around my neck, strangling me, suffocating me. I can't move or breathe, but I can still see Harley up on the stage, dancing and laughing, eyes rolled back in her head, body limp and flopping around like a puppet. A puppet on strings.

My head spins and it's not because the music is too loud or because the crowd is swaying and making me seasick.

I go to the DJ station and crank the volume up and up until the sound pressure pops everyone's eardrums and blood seeps from their ears—

I can't figure out if I've moved or if the crowd has pushed me closer to the DJ platform.

"You should join me, Jo," Harley says with a childlike smile. "This is the kind of art that people want to see. You should do it with me!"

Some guy reaches out for Harley's leg and she has to kick him away, and for a brief moment I see a flicker of anguish in her eyes. The sensation is over in a flash as Harley breaks out into laugh and throws her hands in the air. It's my cue to get the hell out of there.

It takes a tremendous amount of energy to shove my way back though the forbidden forest of people. Even once freed from the mosh pit in the building, there are more people walking the alley: giggling girls and groping guys, drinking beers or popping spinner capsules.

"Jo, wait!" Lyle races after me, his shirt ruffled and bunched on his shoulder.

"This is what you didn't want to tell me?" I'm shouting at Lyle even though the music is quieter in the alley. "If you didn't want me to know about Harley's adjustment, then why did you bring me here?"

Lyle waves his hands like he's trying to quiet me. "I did want you to know. I wanted you to see her."

"Harley was my friend! She was my inspiration! She understood my pain, and my need to paint!"

Lyle's lips pull around his teeth in a grimace, like he's about to reach into something gross. When his hand lands on my arm, I shiver at the sensation of his cold fingers.

"I wanted you to see that she's okay," he says. "She's been fixed and she seems to be happy."

"She *seems* to be," I say, my voice shaking as much as the rest of me. "You don't know what's going on inside her head."

"But that's the point, Jo. There's nothing bad going on in her head. They removed the bad parts from her brain. She's okay now."

The world shifts into slow motion. Dancing people hover above the ground, suspended in action, paused in time. A breeze blows through Lyle's shirt, poofing it out slightly, ruffling every fiber of the cloth.

All at once I realize what Lyle is trying to tell me. He wants me to be like Harley. He wants me to remove the dark spots in my brain, the broken parts of my soul. He wants to send me to the brain adjusters. He wants to fix me.

Lyle stands in front of me. The pistol is heavy in my hand—

Wait. This isn't supposed to happen. I've had repeating visions, sure, but never the same one twice in a day.

I raise it up and aim it right at his forehead, the muzzle but an inch away—

I don't like this. It's the exact same vision, yet it feels real. I have always had a disconnect from my visions, as though I were watching myself from afar. But this is different. I'm here, I'm right here, I'm as close as I can possibly be …

My finger finds the trigger and—

"Jo, what are you doing?"

The vision fades and my eyes adjust to the lights. And then I see it. I'm standing in front of Lyle with my arm raised. I'm pointing at the middle of his forehead, but I'm not just pointing.

I've shaped my hand to look like a gun.

"Oh god!" I yank my hand away. It's shaking. My whole body is shaking. Lyle's eyes are wide and he's looking at me like I'd been holding a real gun. I might as well have been.

The people around us have stopped moving. They're staring at us, frozen in awe, as I'm clutching my fist in my other hand. I've had these visions for as long as I can remember and I have never acted them out. Ever. Until now.

"Why did you do that?" Lyle asks barely loud enough for me to hear him.

"I'm sorry. I didn't mean to. I just got upset—"

Lyle holds up his hand, and for a second I expect him to point a finger-gun in my face. "I'm calling my dads. We should leave." Lyle pays no mind to the Los Feliz friends as he pulls me though the crowd of dancing people.

Nolan picks us up without any questions. Lyle sits in the passenger side and I curl my legs in the backseat, trying to hold my shaking body together. I'm overwhelmed and over-stimulated, and my ears are ringing but I can't tell if it's from a vision or residual effects of my music-damaged eardrums. I can't focus on anything, let alone try to figure out what I've just done, and I'm startled when I see Lyle has turned completely around to stare at me.

And there he goes, repeating the same mantra he's said for years because there have been so many moments that have inspired him to wonder: "Are you okay?"

I used to be able to answer that question with a lie. I'd come up with so many excuses to pretend that I'm just fine, and usually I am because I've more-or-less gotten used to the wrett reality of my mind. But now? I don't know.

Something has changed.

7 creeps and spies

I swear I don't imagine things, but there's no other way to explain the breathing noises I heard in my sleep last night.

I'd spent all of Sunday hiding in my bedroom, too terrified to come across someone and act out another vision, unwilling to talk to Lyle or the Los Feliz groupies. Then Rick came over and yelled at my mom all evening, and I fell asleep before I heard him leave.

Before dawn on Monday morning, my room is illuminated by the FutureTech ads flashing outside my window, and I lie in bed, wiping sleep from my eyes, when I realize the breathing isn't in my imagination. I fumble around for my room terminal and switch on the lights.

Rick sits in a chair next to my bed, leaning on his elbows with his mouth gaping open.

I scoot away pull the covers tighter around me. "What the hell are you doing in my room!"

Rick is dressed in his business clothes, wrinkled like he's slept in them, and his eyes are red and glazed over. I don't know how long he's been watching me sleep, but it must have been awhile because there's a wet spot of drool on his pants … at least I hope that's drool.

I leap from the bed and throw my pillow at him. "Get out, you creep!"

He snaps to and he bobbles his head as he gathers his bearings. When he sees me standing before him in my tank and undies, he wags a finger at me. "No one likes a sleazy girl, fancy. You'll upset your mother."

"Why are you sneaking into my bedroom?"

"Someone's gotta keep an eye on you. You're up to no good."

"I was sleeping!"

He heaves a flemmy chuckle and leans back, revealing something in his hand, something familiar but oddly out of place in my bedroom.

A scanning laser lens.

A flickering thought sweeps through my brain at that very moment, the memory of Lyle's face as he told me about Harley's adjustment. And for a moment I panic at the thought of Lyle and Rick joining together to trick me into being fixed. The thought passes quickly, but the ghost of Lyle's voice echoes in my head.

I fumble backwards, away from Rick, pulling my bed sheets with me. "What are you doing with that scanner?"

Rick blinks. "Nothing."

"That's one of the stolen parts, isn't it?"

"I'm a scanner repairman," Rick says, unmoved.

"Not anymore. FutureTech fired you."

Rick tilts his head, squints, and gets to his feet. He holds the brain scanner at me, and the blue light sweeps over my body and sends data to a tab in his other hand. "You're just as messed up as Lauren, you know that?"

"Leave my mom alone!"

"She's abnormal. You're both abnormal. You're primed to be fixed."

I watch the blue laser hover on my chest as Rick's words ring through my bedroom. His belly heaves through the open slot of his button-down, his dark eyes peer out below a jutting brow. He's up to something; I've always sensed this. There's no reason for a man like him to be interested in a woman like my mom. Sure, she's still very attractive for her age, but she's tidy and elegant with a lingering attachment to the upper side of Los Feliz and a yearning for the security of the Zones. And here's Rick, barely a step above the South LA neighborhoods, brimming with hostility to anyone of the Zone mindset. And now he has that brain scanner.

Rick's wristlet flashes with a call, giving me an opportunity to take the upper hand.

"I'll tell my mom about this."

"You go right ahead. She won't remember anyway." He answers his wristlet while the scanner still lights me with blue lasers. "Hey, Lauren. Did you get the data I sent you?" Finally the laser disappears, and he winks as he backs out of my room while continuing his conversation with my mom. I listen as Rick grabs something in the kitchen, fumbles around in the living room, and leaves the apartment.

I didn't expect my mom to already be at work, but of course she has to work overtime to support all three of us. It would be easy enough for me to stay home from school since there's no one here to force me to go, but there is still that chance Rick will come back. I don't believe he's smart enough to do anything with the data spat out by the scanner; there's no way he could be dangerous. But then, what did he mean about by mom being abnormal? Sure, her brain is all kinds of screwed-up, and, quite frankly, I'm surprised she hasn't taken herself to the adjusters.

I'm being paranoid. Rick is not a brain hacker. He's an asshat. He wouldn't know what to do with a brain if he was holding one in his hands.

The apartment is weirdly quiet and gives me too much space to think. I force myself to go to school because if I ever have any chance to get away from Rick for good, I still need that damn FutureTech scholarship to get into art school.

By the time I get to school I already want to leave. I suffer through my first few classes and try desperately to not fall asleep. When our first break finally rolls around, I call Madri. Her face pops up in the screen of my wristlet. Her hair is a mess and she rubs her eyes like my call woke her up.

"Jo?"

"Hey, Madri," I say.

Someone screeches behind me, and I see a beefy teenage boy chase after a girl in a really tight skirt.

Madri squints. "Where are you?"

"School," I say with no attempt to hide my distain.

"Are you allowed to make v-calls at school? I thought they had rules about that."

"Yeah, probably." What are they gonna do, confiscate my wristlet? They can't do that because then the school's security couldn't track my attendance and they wouldn't know if I was on campus or not. Wait, that's brilliant. I should talk louder.

"Hey, listen," I say, "are you busy tonight? I need to work on my portfolio."

Madri sighs. "You know I'm not allowed to have company on week nights."

"Then I'll go over now, before your parents get home."

"And how will you get out of school and through the gate without a Pass?"

She's gonna hate this suggestion. "Your brother?"

"Jo!"

I hurry on before she can argue. "Satesh is the only one who can hack the system."

"He was put under house arrest for two months after the last time. He's on the Alias sympathizer watch-list!"

"Yeah, I know. I'll make it up to him, I promise."

A deafening siren goes off in a nearby building. A handful of security officers race across the courtyard toward the building as the beefy kid stumbles through the door with a bloody nose, the girl in the tight skirt shaking out her hand behind him. When I look back at my wristlet, Madri has her head in her arms.

"Ah, dammit," she says. "All right. If you can get out of school, you can come over. I'll talk to Satesh."

"Thank you! Madri, I owe you."

Now all I have to do is get off campus. With one siren wailing, security won't notice another one. It's exactly the diversion I need. Well, Principal Torres will probably see me skipping through the door—hell, he's probably watching me *right now* …

A shiver runs down my spine. No time to waste. It's now or never.

I race to the nearest building and bound down the hallway, slam my hip into the door, and next thing I know I'm flat on my back. I didn't think they locked *all* the outside doors. What is this, a prison? Something blocks the ceiling lights from above. Security has found me.

"Going somewhere, Jo?"

It's not security, it's Principal Torres.

"Apparently not." I struggle to my feet despite the sharp pain in my hip, and Mr. Torres holds my elbow to help me up.

"You do know you're not supposed to make v-calls on campus," he says.

So he *was* watching me. Really? I've had enough with men spying on me today.

The siren stops and both our wristlets flash with a message: *EHTS Classes Resume.* The hallway fills with students as they return to their classrooms, and many snicker at me as I stand there with the principal's hand on my elbow. I pounce on the distraction.

"I guess I'd better get to class."

"Why don't you walk me to my office first?"

He's not asking, and he hasn't yet let go of my elbow. We head out across the campus at such a slow pace I have to pause on one foot before I take the next step. He finally stops touching me, and I can't help but plan yet another escape route.

"So how's the scholarship portfolio coming along?" he asks.

I don't know how to answer, so all that comes out of my mouth is a heavy sigh.

His voice takes a deeper, more serious tone. "Listen, Jo, I heard about what happened to your dad."

What? How could he possibly know anything about my dad? Who in their right mind would do something that backstabbing?

"Your mom called me last night."

"She *what*?"

"Jo, it's all right." He tries to wave me through the building so I'm not standing in the hallway hollering, but I can't move any muscles other than the ones that control my mouth.

"You can't listen to her. My mom doesn't know what's going on, and she never has. She didn't understand my dad and she doesn't understand *me*!"

Faces appear in the classroom windows and Mr. Torres tries again to get me moving, but I won't budge.

"Jo, I want to help you. I'm not your enemy. Your mom wants to help too. She's just caught up in a lot of other things and it's hard for her to see the big picture."

"No, she *forgets* the big picture."

Mr. Torres tilts his head but continues. "Jo, your artistic reputation precedes you." He jerks like he didn't mean to say that. "Clearly, I mean, because that phoenix painting is not new, is it?"

"No, it's not, I drew it years ago and I took it off the ports, and I still don't know how you got it in the first place."

"Jo, I want to do everything I can to help you get you into art school. I made you a promise. But first, you need to get that scholarship."

"That's why I was leaving school. I can't be here if I'm going to get my portfolio done."

"That's not part of the arrangement. You still need to attend East Hollywood."

"But I won't have the time to do my artwork. Everything is at my friend Madri's house, and I've gotta ride my mobie all the way across town just to get to her, and even then her dad doesn't like me being over there—"

"You can't ditch school!"

"Why not?"

"If you get too many truancies on your record you won't even be *considered* for art school."

Okay, I get it. He's an old-fashioned guy with a school to run, I understand that, but he's trapped me in limbo. I know I can't do both. I've only been at this school for a few weeks and I already feel it sucking the life out of me. And if my soul is drained dry, then where will I find the inspiration to make art? This is madness. This is mad—

I creep into the principal's office which is dark except for the tabs and panels flickering images of nearly every drawing and painting I've ever done in my life. A large office chair swivels around and I see it's Mr. Torres. His bright white teeth light up with a smile and I take hold of his necktie and tighten it around his neck—

"Jo, are you all right?"

Mr. Torres's eyes are wide, and I see the confusion in his face. Did I say something? Did I act out part of my vision as I'd done with Lyle? He looks okay, his tie is still securely in place.

"I don't feel well." I'm impressed my voice is that sturdy, considering how much I'm trembling. "My dizzy spells have been bad this week. I'd like to go home, please."

Finally Mr. Torres is sympathetic. "All right. See the nurse and get a medical pass."

"Thank you so much," I say and as innocently as possible because I have no intention of going home. I'm heading to Beverly Hills.

8 pull back the wool

The ten mile journey from East Hollywood to Beverly Hills is like a tourist's expedition, a history lesson of the old Los Angeles and the new. Gated ZT Zones stand clean and sparkling, a preserved rendition of what LA was like before the entertainment industry left, before the *haves* crossed the border and beat the Canadian Immigration Laws. The rest of the LA basin is left rotting and crumbling, streets reduced to broken asphalt and graffitied TV studios, where the *have-nots* are left behind, secluded and segregated by the Zone gates.

Life outside the gates is a gamble, at the best of times. To afford a house in the ZT Zones you need a well-paying job. And to get a well-paying job you need a college degree. And to get a college degree you need a PEAD degree. And to get a PEAD degree you need to finish the PEAD program. So as it stands, I'll end up as a plumber or on the streets in the Free Zones with the other ten thousand bums. Or, I risk breaking the law and get into Madri's art studio and finish that damn portfolio.

There is a long line of gassers and outdated electrics outside the Beverly Hills visitor's gate, professions noted by animated window decals: a pool man, a construction company, a maid service. This gate has beefed up security due to the recent Alias hacks, and handful of ACTA agents are being meticulous about their vehicle inspections. At the moment, a TV repairman is in a heated discussion with an agent about the restrictions of his Zone Pass, giving me all kinds of reasons to question my decision to break the Zone laws today, of all days. All they'd have to do is take a close look at my fake Pass and realize I don't belong here, and I'll be banned for life.

But the urge to talk to Madri outweighs those concerns. I can sneak past. I just have to pretend I belong. *No, sir, I'm doing nothing wrong. I know my outfit is odd. It's laundry day.*

I turn off my mobie so the screeching motor doesn't attract attention, and wheel it up to the separate gate for mobies and pedestrians. An ACTA agent spots me as I'm holding my wristlet up to the scanner, and he takes a few steps in my direction. I smile politely and wave my free hand and do my best Westsider impersonation. The scanner rings a dull *bonk*, telling me there's something wrong with the Pass. I try again. The agent comes closer, I keep on smiling and waving, and finally, just as he reaches the fence, the scanner beeps a cheerful *ding* and the gate slides open.

I force a laugh for the agent. "Ha. Must be acting up again, huh? They really hire idiots to be scanner repairmen." I laugh for real at the accuracy of my statement.

The agent isn't amused, but I'm inside the gate and out of his reach. I ratchet on my screeching mobie and ride down the Santa Monica auto-route toward Madri's house.

When I arrive at the Mehra mansion, Satesh is at the front door with his tall and lanky body and this amazing chiseled chin that I'd like to slice cheese on. He doesn't smile much—at least that's what Madri says—but as he watches me ascend the steps to the porch his lips curl on one side, and his chiseled cheekbones pop out even more.

"Hi!" I say in a freakishly loud voice.

The other corner of his mouth curls. "Hey."

"Thanks for getting me the Pass. I know I owe you for last time."

He raises his long-fingered hand. "Just don't get me caught by ACTA again."

I give a subtle flip of my hair and Satesh chuckles.

"Madri's upstairs. Come on in." He slinks aside and waves his arm into the house. Such a gentleman.

"Thanks!" I make a point to brush up against him as I pass by. I'm not sure what effect that has, but as I reach the top of the stairs I see he's still standing there with the door open.

Madri sits on her bed, messing with an intricate 3D hologram tab. At a closer look I realize she's manipulating a simulation of a brain hologram.

I plop down on the bed next to her. "Jeez, did that come with your PEAD packet?"

She sighs and moves her hands and the brain simulation explodes.

I stare amazed at the image. "You blew up your brain!"

This sets Madri off in a fit of hysterical laughter, rolling around on her back and almost kicking me off the bed. I laugh a little, but I didn't really think my joke was that funny so I spend the next minute watching her squirm and clutch her stomach in amused agony. Once she's out of laughs for the day—or the month—she collapses on the mattress, heaving for breath.

I look her over. "If I'd have known psychiatry was so entertaining, I'd have studied that instead of this fickle art crap."

She wipes the tears from her face. "I'm sorry. I'm so stressed out with this exam coming up it's only a matter of time before I blow my brains out in real life."

Now I'm thinking about Lyle. "At least I was here to help you choose the holo instead."

Madri pats my leg with a grin. "Yes, you're a good friend for that."

Satesh appears in the doorway like a guard looking in on his princess. "Everything all right in here?"

Madri waves her hand. "Oh, we're fine, Satie." He leans against the doorframe, and Madri ignores him. "So what was so urgent that you needed to break the law to get here?"

I feel the blood rush to my cheeks. "I'm not *trying* to break the law."

"ACTA has been cracking down. Every day there's a new firewall," Satesh says as he cracks his knuckles.

Madri frowns at him. "Then don't you think it's a good idea to be a little more careful? You've seen the news, they're swooping up Alias sympathizers all over the place."

"Yeah, but Satesh isn't a sympathizer. They'll learn that the moment they hook him up to the brain scanner." I look at him. "Right?"

Satesh lifts a shoulder and give his sideways grin.

Madri jumps from the bed. "Satesh! They'll arrest you! They'll send you to prison!"

"They'll have to catch me first." He winks at me and slinks from the room.

Madri throws her hands in the air. "I swear, he feeds off this illegal crap."

"But he's not a terrorist … is he?"

Madri rolls her eyes. "Hell if I know. He's just weird. Anyway, what's going on with you?"

I peek through the doorway, wondering if Satesh is listening. "It might be best if we go for a walk."

Her eyes scan over me. "Well, okay, but you can't go out like that."

"No!" I wave her off as she grabs for me. "No, no, no!"

"Jo, you know I like you just as you are," she says with a smirk, "but you can't walk around here dressed like that. They'll kick you out."

I groan but I know she's right. It takes a half-hour for me to find something in her gigantic walk-in closet. Madri is shorter than me so all her clothes are a bit small, but she manages to find something my size: a shirt with puffy sleeves and tight shoulders, fitted around the waist. It's so sheer I'm really glad I decided to wear a bra today. Sometimes I'm envious of how easy it is for Madri to be girly. My mom would probably have preferred to have her as a daughter.

The streets of Rodeo Drive are blinding in the spring sun. The sidewalks are spotless and bright white as though made of marble. We walk down block after block and never pass a single person; the only movement comes from gigantic ad-screens and 3D hologram models.

Madri pokes me. "Will you stop squirming? You look like you're trying to escape from a straitjacket."

"I hate things on my shoulders."

"Well, you look good in it."

I stare at my pink-shoed feet. "Listen, Madri—"

She rolls her eyes playfully. "Here we go."

I don't like asking this much of Madri, but she's the only person I think understands what happened to my dad and how it affected me. At this point, she's the only person in the world that I trust.

"You know I really appreciate what you've done, letting me use your art studio and all ..."

"Are you breaking up with me?" She's joking, but not really.

"That's not what I mean." I sigh. "I have an opportunity to get a scholarship to finish the PEAD Program and maybe even get into art school."

"Oh, that's great!"

"Yeah. Well, the scholarship comes from FutureTech."

Her smile drops. "Oh ..."

"I just have to impress them enough to get the scholarship, and then I can carry on and never deal with FutureTech after that." I bite my lip to keep from retracting my statement.

Madri doesn't even blink. "Are you sure about that?"

My spine turns to rubber because I don't have the endurance to keep pretending. "No, I'm not. I have no idea what else is involved with the scholarship. The principal at the trade school insists I make a portfolio, but I don't know if I can surrender a part of myself to FutureTech, not after what they did to my dad."

Madri keeps her eyes on me while I'm shivering on the sidewalk. She leads me to a bench and I slide down on the hot metal framing while she waits patiently for me to continue talking. Thankfully, Madri breaks the silence.

"I remember the day my dad brought home the first painting," Madri says. "He was so excited, said a patient gave him this piece in exchange for treatment, and my dad couldn't turn it down because he liked the painting so much."

"My dad paid for the therapy with his artwork? I didn't know that."

Madri nods. "Dad insisted my mom commission your dad for city artwork because he clearly needed the money. It wasn't until he brought home one particular piece that my mom finally agreed."

I know exactly the piece. "The one with the girl in the burning city."

"Yeah. My mom fell in love with your dad that night we had your family over for dinner. In the weeks after, I remember my parents fought a lot. More then usual. Mom argued about FutureTech and Dad argued about your dad and then—"

"And then my dad lost the commission."

"No." Madri speaks so abruptly I'm startled. "No, Jo, he turned it down."

My heart lurches in my chest. "He didn't turn it down. There's no way he would have done that, not for that kind of money."

"He did, Jo."

"If it was *his* fault he didn't get the commission, then it didn't make sense for him to kill himself."

Madri takes my hand. "FutureTech knew about his schizophrenia, and they required that he go to the brain adjusters before he could work for them. He knew if he did, he'd lose his artistic sense. So he refused the commission."

"But that was his chance! He told me—*he told me*—if he could get this one commission then we'd have more money and he could go on and make all the art that he wanted to make."

"But he wouldn't have been able to make art if his brain had been adjusted."

"So he *killed* himself?"

Madri doesn't have an answer for me. No one does. The only person who could possibly have some meaningful explanation for this slit his wrists a year ago. This can't be true. It can't. My body tries so hard to reject this information that I feel like I'm splitting at the seams. Slowly and painfully. Like lava seeping from cracks in the earth, incinerating everything in its path.

"Was it worse?" I say quietly, my lungs quivering. "Did my dad consider it worse to take the offer from FutureTech than to kill himself and leave his family behind? Is that what the world is trying to tell me, that if I too become an artist, I'm destined to bleed out in a bathtub?"

Madri swallows hard and squeezes my hand. "Jeez, Jo, I hope not."

I gaze off into the shimmering stores, searching for the right words—at least, the *best* words. "My dad wasn't always depressed. He was okay when I was a kid. Maybe not *happy*, but content, you know? I was ten when I first found him on the floor of his studio. He had a bottle of drugs in one hand and a bottle of liquor in the other."

Madri's eyes are wide now but she stays quiet.

"That's when I first realized my dad wasn't happy the same way everybody else was. The schizophrenia drove him mad. He couldn't get through the day without drugs. And when he took the meds, he couldn't paint the same."

"I didn't realize—"

But I don't let her finish—that's not the point of my story. And now, more than ever, I know I have to come clean. I have to tell someone my secret because there's no telling where I'm headed.

"Madri, do you know what a tick is?"

"Like, a personality flaw? I heard my dad talking about that. It's exactly what ACTA is trying so hard to fix in people."

"Yeah, *what makes a person tick.*" I pause and she waits for me to go on, and now I'm not really sure if I should because at any moment my tick could attack and I don't want Madri, of all people, to be a victim of it. But my mind is the calmest it's been all afternoon, and I'm convinced she is momentarily safe.

"I have a tick," I say with a strange bark of authority.

Madri raises her eyebrows. "Okay. What's yours?"

"What do you mean? Do you have one?"

She shrugs. "Sure. Doesn't everyone? I steal things." She looks a little too pleased to have shocked me with this news. "Just small things … mostly."

"You're a *thief*?"

"Well, hell, when you say it that way!" She chuckles and gazes at her lap. "It started in prep school. I was definitely *not* the wickiest kid, and there was this other girl who kinda became my friend. She saw me messing with a stylus … Do you remember those red ones?"

"The one that followed the movement of your eyes?"

"Yeah! I really wanted one. My parents wouldn't buy it; I wasn't supposed to be messing around with art toys. Anyway, this girl spotted me playing with it and she told me her plan to break into the class during lunch and steal stuff. Sure enough, we snuck in and, for no reason at all, took off with an armful of art supplies."

I have to smile; it's an entertaining story.

"It went downhill after that," she says. "It's like an addiction. Everywhere I go I have the urge to steal something."

"But you're so rich. You can buy whatever you want."

"That's not what it's about, though. It's more of a possession thing. Like, once I see something I become obsessed with the need to claim it. It doesn't matter if I can buy the item, the point is taking it from *them*."

Of all the ticks I'd expected Madri to admit, this is certainly not it.

She's studying me. "You think I'm a horrible person, don't you?"

"No, actually. I'm relieved."

"Really?"

"Yeah. It might not be such a crazy idea to trust you to not send me to the brain adjusters."

Her eyes go wide again. "Why would anyone do that? You're not schizophrenic."

"No, but my tick is kind of scary. And I'm going to need someone on my side if things get worse."

Madri jerks upright. "What are you talking about? Did something happen? What happened?"

"Nothing's happened! At least, not yet. But things are changing."

"Tell me," she says, and she grabs my hand again. "What is your tick?"

I tell her. I tell Madri every last gruesome detail. I tell her about the visions of my mom, of Lyle's family, of Mr. Torres from the trade school. I tell her how I get them over and over again, and no matter who I have the visions of, or how terrible the deaths are, I've had so many for so long that I've become numb to the gore.

"Whoa …" Madri's brown skin has turned into a light tan, and she lets go of my hand a little. "Have you ever had one about me?"

"No. Actually, you're one of the few I've never had a single vision about. You and my dad."

She narrows her eyes and for a moment I don't think she believes me, but then she sighs and leans back against the bench. "Well, okay, so you have visions about killing people. But it's not like you're actually killing people." I hesitate to answer, and Madri jumps to her feet. "Oh god! Jo!"

"I haven't killed anyone! Why would you think that?"

"Then why are you worried about your brain being adjusted?"

This is where I have to decide if it's a good idea or the worst idea to tell Madri about Lyle and the finger-gun I held to his head. Once I cross this line, there will be another person who not only knows my tick, but also knows of the possibility of the visions coming true.

I never get the chance to tell Madri the whole story.

9 eighty-six

The spy-drone is on us, hovering above, blasting that awful sweeping siren, flashing lights brighter than the sun. Madri and I are frozen on the sidewalk with our hands smashed against our ears.

"What's going on?" I shout.

"I don't know!" Madri shouts back.

Three ACTA cars swarm the street, their lights flashing. A speaker beeps on. "*Stay right where you are!*" The agents get out of their cars and surround us, and finally the sirens stop.

"Jo Bristol?" says one of the agents. His body suit is the fanciest I've ever seen, a dazzling display of shiny armor and flashing colored lights, and I'm so transfixed by his stimulating uniform I forget to answer. "Are you Jo Bristol?"

"Yes!" I say and throw my hands up.

"She's too stupid to be a hacker," a lady agent says.

"Just get them in the cars," the first agent says.

A younger agent snaps tracker cuffs on Madri's wrists and he's nice about it. The lady agent attaches a pair on me and she's definitely not. It's a short ride to where we're going but Madri is quickly turning pale.

I've never been in a police station, but a ZT Zone station is the wickiest place to get arrested. The building is brand-new and shiny, and the floors are smooth and don't have a scratch in them. There are cameras and monitors and spy-drones everywhere, and it's all so mesmerizing I forget why we're even there until Madri starts crying.

"Don't touch me!"

"We need to scan you for weapons," the first agent says as he leads her to a body chamber.

I'm in a police station, and I have tracker cuffs around my wrists so I shouldn't even be opening my mouth, but Madri's cries are terrifying. "She doesn't have any weapons! She didn't do anything wrong!"

"Get her out," the agent says.

Mean Lady Agent drags me into a room and leaves me there alone. A table and two chairs are the only furnishings, and I sit facing two walls with floor-to-ceiling windows that look into the hallway. Behind me is a giant screen that displays all sorts of FutureTech advertisements and anti-Alias propaganda.

Madri's borrowed shirt tugs at my shoulders when I slouch, and I have the thought that these ACTA Agents are on to me. They can see right through me, and they know I don't belong here. This is it. This is the end of the line for me. At least I finally told someone about my tick, maybe now I'll be awarded a lesser sentence from the brain adjusters.

I'm getting paranoid again. The pink shoes pinch my feet so I kick them off, and the shirt is so wrett I'm about ready to tear that off too and sit in my bra when I look up and see the young agent smiling at me from across the hall. I can't figure out why he's got that expression until I realize I've pulled my shirt down so far I'm exposing my cleavage.

There are other agents walking past, but this guy stands there with a stupid grin, unaware of anything else around him. Ashlyn and Sapphire, with their practiced ability of manipulating the male sex, suddenly pop into my head and I have to wonder if there's a real usefulness in the skill. Sure, I'm no Baez girl, but I already have this guy's attention and maybe it's not so crazy to think I've got something worth flaunting. After all, I got Satesh to get me an illegal Zone Pass. Perhaps I can convince this guy to bust me the hell out of here.

I leave my shirt open and rest my elbows on the table so I'm leaning over in the young agent's direction. He tilts his head and smiles wider. Surely they must have rules about the ACTA agents not flirting with the detainees, but this guy clearly didn't get the memo. I'm grateful for his incompetence because he's twitching now, and I think my plan is working. Then our gaze is broken when Satesh walks down the hallway.

Satesh! What is he doing here?

I sit up so fast my shirt catches on my elbow and rips the collar wide open and now I'm completely exposing my bra to the world. And of course, Satesh notices the movement. At first I think he's stunned to see me, but then his chiseled chin shifts and his lips curl into that heart-stopping grin. He's not smiling because he's got a clear view of the top of my boobs—not *just*, anyway—it's something else. Two huge ACTA agents lead him down the hallway and they look pissed, but Satesh seems pleased with himself.

He winks at me and all of a sudden I realize Satesh's tick: He's a hacker. It was his techie skills that got me into Beverly Hills, but he didn't do it because he can. He did it because he *likes* it. Maybe he's not an Alias terrorist, but he's certainly a rebel. That mysterious boy, he gets off on breaking down the system. What a strange family they are, Madri with her thieving and Satesh with his hacking.

Mean Lady Agent comes into the room and sits across the table from me. She's still dressed in her silvery body suit and visor, and everything flickers and flashes like a holiday window display.

"Hands flat on the table," she says. She's even less friendly now, so I comply without hesitation. My tracker cuffs magnetically link to the steel table and scanner screens light up beneath my hands. The heat tingles against my palms.

She reads information as it is displayed on the desk in front of her. "Name."

"Jo Bristol. What's going on?"

She doesn't look up. "Occupation."

"I'm sixteen. I don't have an occupation."

"You are about to undergo a lie test. Do you comply?" I notice the palm scanner flicker red as I hesitate. "Answer the question."

"Do I have a choice?"

"No."

"Oh. Then, yes. Can you call my mom? She should know I'm here. She's a software programmer at FutureTech."

Mean Lady Agent peers at me through her visor. "Are you working for Alias-X?"

"What? No, of course not." The palm reader flickers orange and yellow.

"Are you an Alias sympathizer?"

"No!"

"Are you aware of Satesh Mehra's involvement as an Alias sympathizer?"

Well, before today, absolutely not. But now? The palm scanner glows red, the information flashes on the desktop at increasing speeds. "He's not a sympathizer. I wanted to see Madri and I asked him to help get me in because he's done it before. I didn't want anyone to get in trouble. Please call my mom!"

The palm scanner is a sunset of colors and the skin of the lady's face is so taught it looks like leather. "Tell me what Lauren Bristol is doing for Alias."

"My mom isn't working for Alias. She's a programmer."

"What do you know about Ricardo Salazar?"

"Rick? He got fired."

"What do you know about The Plan?"

"What *plan*?"

For once the palm scanner is solid green. Good timing too, because my mom appears in the doorway with an older ACTA officer.

My mom looks mortified. "Josephine! What is going on?"

The officer peers at Mean Lady Agent. "We can't possibly be interrupting an interrogation, can we? Certainly not of a minor without a guardian present."

Mean Lady Agent taps her tab and all the display information disappears from the desktop, and my tracker cuffs detach from the table.

"Of course not, sir," she says without a hint of subtlety. "We were just chatting."

My mom rushes over to me. "Are you all right?"

"I'm fine, Mom."

"You're supposed to be in school. I got a v-call from Mr. Torres asking if you got home all right, and now I find out you've been arrested!"

"I haven't been arrested."

"You're in jail! They think you're working with Alias!"

Mean Lady Agent jerks and the officer shakes his head. "All right," she says, "this way."

We're led to another room crammed with desktop displays and hologram maps and simulators and even more agents in silvery body armor. Madri sits in a chair at the other end of the room. Her eyes are red and puffy and she'll barely look at me.

"Are you okay?" I ask.

Madri twitches as a woman behind her turns around. It's Mrs. Mehra, and the moment she sees us she frowns.

"Hello, Lauren," Mrs. Mehra says with a not-so-polite nod.

My mom doesn't say anything. Her body goes rigid, her posture as perfectly straight as a catwalk supermodel.

I speak for her. "Mrs. Mehra, I am so sorry about all of this—"

She holds up her hand. "You know what you've done, Jo. I've had quite enough of this. First it was Satesh and now you've brought Madri into it. ACTA thinks we're Alias sympathizers and it's ruining my position with the city. Please, leave my family alone before you cause any more damage. I forbid you from coming near my children ever again."

Ever again? Madri is my friend, all my artwork is in her bedroom, she's my only hope of not getting sent to the brain adjusters when they find out about my visions.

Madri sits there, staring at the floor. She won't look up at me, and she won't look at her mother. We're crammed in this stifling tension and I can't take it anymore.

Mrs. Mehra stands in the middle of a large empty room. I tie her feet to ropes that lead to opposite corners. Then I tie her wrists to the ceiling. The ropes lead to a crank, and I turn the wheel and cinch the ropes tighter and tighter and her limbs spread apart and tear off—

My heart is pounding when I snap back from the vision, and I don't know why because I don't usually have physical responses to my visions. But this time I think I actually wanted to do it. This time I wanted the vision to be real.

Madri is looking at me now. Her eyes are wide and she knows. She knows I've had a vision about her mom and that's bad enough, but I hear my mom wailing and Mean Lady Agent yelling. Someone pulls me back and that's when I realize I've been holding onto Mrs. Mehra's arm.

I've done it again.

I let go and Mrs. Mehra winces and grabs her shoulder. My arms are pulled around my back and I feel a *zap* as my tracker cuffs clasp together. I turn to see the young smiling agent, only he's not smiling anymore.

"Young woman, you are in a serious amount of trouble!" Mean Lady Agent waves her finger in my face, and I don't have the words to defend myself.

My mom cries in my ear. "Jo! What did you do? I can't believe this. What's wrong with you?"

Mrs. Mehra wants in. "First you get my children in trouble, and then you go and attack me!"

Mean Lady Agent yells louder to be heard over the barking moms. "Now you have *two* points on your record, one for breaking Zone laws, and another for assault!"

All this yelling floods my senses, tripping the wire that leads to the darkness. I hear the ringing and I see the fog, and shit it's gonna happen again.

"Everybody *stop*!"

Everybody does stop. No one makes a peep because the one who blurted those words is dainty little Madri, and she's standing between us with her arms outstretched like a karate ninja.

"Madri—" Mrs. Mehra makes a bold move, but Madri's palm is in her face and she shuts up.

"Jo?" Madri leans in to get a close look at my eyes. "Are you all right?"

She saw it. She saw the signs I was about to fall into another vision and she stopped it. Jeez, she's quick. And thanks to her, yes, I'm all right, so I nod.

Madri nods back. "Mom, you're not pressing charges against Jo." Mrs. Mehra and Mean Lady Agent protest, but Madri won't have it. "No! We've both had a stressful day. Hell, Jo's had a stressful *year*. But aside from that, both Satesh and I knew perfectly well that we were breaking the law and we did it anyway. We're sorry for everything. Aren't we, Jo?"

Honestly, I don't know that I am. I don't actually want to injure Madri's mom, but I can't help feeling like she's responsible in some way for my dad's suicide. Even if it *wasn't* her fault, she works for the city and they're in bed with FutureTech, and by extension that makes me loathe all of them. Right now I've no leverage with which to argue, so I look Mrs. Mehra in the face and apologize for trying to kill her.

"I'm sorry, Mrs. Mehra," I say in my most mature voice. "I did not mean to hurt you and I apologize if I did. I don't know what came over me."

"We've had a lot of stress, haven't we, honey?" My mom is back from the depths of Mordor and I'm a little afraid of her sudden sweetness, but all things considered I decide it's best to play along.

"Yeah, it's been a rough week."

Mrs. Mehra nods and grabs her arm again exaggeratedly. "I accept your apology, Jo."

Mean Lady Agent frowns. "Really? You're not going to press charges?"

Right on cue, the older ACTA officer bursts through the doors to the room and rushes over to us, with two agent lackeys shuffling behind him. "Mrs. Mehra, I'm sorry to say that your son Satesh will be held here overnight. We have the evidence to charge him with Zone Regulation violations, and possibly enough to charge him with a felony in accordance with ACTA laws."

Mrs. Mehra gasps.

"Unfortunately, ma'am," the officer goes on, "that means Satesh may be sentenced with a neural adjustment and you and your family will be forced to leave the Beverly Hills Zone permanently."

Mean Lady Agent looks pleased, and Mrs. Mehra goes off to argue with the officer. Madri is quiet, staring blankly at a spot across the room.

"Madri," I say. "I am so sorry—"

She holds up her hand and I flinch. When her eyes meet mine I see they're brimming with tears. "Satesh was gonna get busted eventually, even I knew that. It's not your fault. But I think it's best that you go, before you hurt…" she winces "…someone else."

Her words choke me. And while I thought that was sadness in her eyes, I now realize it's fear. She's afraid of me. Madri is afraid I am going to kill her.

I want to stay and talk to her, explain what is happening, that I don't mean any of it and by god I'll do whatever I can to make sure she's safe. But I'm not even allowed the chance to try. The tracker cuffs come off my wrists and before I can reach for her, my mom grabs a hold of me and drags me to the door.

"Madri, I'm sorry …" is all I can mutter before she's out of sight.

10 southern charm

I can't tell if my mom is angry or if she's gone to the empty place in her head, but she's driving us home with both hands gripping the wheel so tightly her knuckles are white, staring straight ahead with barely a blink.

My head rattles against the window. I want to close my eyes and shut out the world, but I've got to keep a look out on the road. And it's a good thing too, because we're barreling toward a red light and my mom hasn't slowed the car even a little.

"Mom! Stop!"

She jerks back to life but it's too late for her to react and we drive straight into the intersection. Signaling my impending doom, the car's console screen beeps with an impact warning, and I look out the passenger window to see a big car coming straight for me. I'm certain at that moment that this is karma kicking me straight in the ass, but our car's auto-brakes apply and we skid to a halt. The AEV flashes orange and red lights and it too stops automatically. If it had been a gasser coming at us, I'd surely be dead.

The big car's speaker comes on. "*What the hell are you doing?*"

My mom has gone stiff so I flip on the speaker and wave. "Sorry. Our mistake. We'll get out of the way."

"*Hurry it up, then,*" the big car driver says. "*I'm already late!*"

The other cars wait for us to move. "Mom. C'mon." She nods and we're off again.

We sit in awkward silence until finally I have the need to say something. "Mom, I'm really sorry about what happened—"

"I lost my job." She speaks so abruptly it takes a moment for her words to sink in.

"Uh—*what?*"

"FutureTech fired me today. After fifteen years, they fired me."

"Ah, crap, Mom. I'm sorry. It's because I made you late on Saturday, isn't it? Because we went to see Mr. Torres?"

"No, this has been coming for a long time."

I wait for her to explain, but she just sits there. "I don't understand. You were moving up, you got promoted a couple years ago."

"And then your dad died and I didn't have the conviction for it anymore. I'm surprised they didn't fire me a long time ago." She flinches at the memory of my dad, then shakes it off.

"Sweetheart," she goes on, "I don't want you growing up thinking you can't do something because your parents screwed it up their time around." She looks at me and I'm drawn in to her intensity. "I'm sorry that it's been so difficult. I'm doing the best I can. Things are gonna get a little worse before they get better. But I promise you, it will get better."

"Worse? How can things get worse than this?"

She sighs and I know what's coming before she even says it. "We have to move."

"No! We can't move down there. I won't survive in South LA. I'll get jumped. Or murdered!"

"You're not going to get murdered."

"Rick's brother is a criminal, and I'm sure Rick is too."

"Rick helped me."

"Dad was barely cremated before you got in bed with Rick."

"Josephine Abigail Bristol, you take that back!"

Yep, she's used my full name. Shit just got real. "I will *not* take that back! Rick is a creep. He uses you. He takes all your money to buy drugs and god knows what he's up to with all that equipment he's stealing."

"Stop accusing people of things you know nothing about."

I have to take a huge breath because I'm starting to hyperventilate. "I don't trust him, Mom. His brother is even more suspicious. They're both using you."

"Using me for *what*?" My mom turns to me, completely removing her attention from the road. I'm about to take control of the car myself when I see her helplessly mystified expression. Blood trickles from her nose. She stares at me, her eyes empty and afraid. Either she doesn't want to know the truth or she really doesn't know anything.

I know that Rick is a manipulative shithead even if no one believes me, but for the moment there's nothing I can do about him or the fact that we can no longer afford to live in our apartment in Hollywood.

I'm allowed to skip school for the next couple of days so my mom and I can pack our things. Mr. Torres calls a few times but my mom doesn't answer. Lyle bugs incessantly with his postings on my Connex port about his band's gig this weekend. I wish he'd call me, but I know he's still confused about the night at the art show when I pretended to hold a gun to his head.

Before I know it, we've loaded our things into a moving truck and we make our way to South LA. It's a wrett place, a terrible place to even drive through that smells of piss and gasoline. Broken-down gassers line the streets, the houses are the same as they have been for forty years, and it shows. The electrical lines haven't been updated below the Santa Monica auto-way, and the streetlights and signs are standing ruins. It's nearly medieval.

Rick and his brother Santino are on the crusty, brown lawn when we drive up. Usually I'd not be able to see the resemblance between these two when Rick is dressed in business clothes, and Santino looks nothing like him with his tattooed and broken face, but when they stand next to each other in their white undershirts, the resemblance is uncanny.

Santino grins when he sees me. "Hola," he says with a slur. "Welcome to the 'hood."

Rick stands on the lawn with a beer in his hand as we haul our stuff inside the duplex that Rick shares with Santino and his slutty girlfriend. There are no keypads or terminals or cameras anywhere in the house. There's not a sign of real security, only ill-fitting bars over the windows.

Everything is open for any burglar, rapist or murderer to bust in, except for the last bedroom down the hall. There are three deadbolts on this door alone. I haven't seen anyone carry an actual key in years, and yet here are three keyholes, all of them locked. There are so many possibilities of what Rick could be hiding behind this door, and while my curiosity is piqued, something tells me I'm better off not knowing what's in there.

The duplex doesn't feel like home. I'm not the least bit compelled to try and make it comfortable. I put a few of my things in the drawers but leave the rest taped up in boxes because I'm not sure how safe it is out in the open. My room is tiny and the one window looks right into the neighbors', where a little kid peers through his window and waves. It's a friendly gesture, but I can't help thinking he's signaling for rescue.

We haven't been here twenty minutes, and Rick is already arguing with my mom. I'd much rather stay away from him, but the place is too small to find a hiding spot. Besides, I'm determined to prove to my mom what an asshole Rick is.

My mom's voice rattles. "But Rick, they fired me."

"I don't give a shit that you got fired, Lauren, you have to get another position." Rick sways under his intoxication.

"I can get a position at AppleSoft. I hear they have some openings."

"There's a position in Human Resources at FutureTech."

"I'm a software programmer. I'm not qualified to work in human resources.

"Eeh, si," Santino grumbles. "Ricardo, she won't have access to the system from H.R."

My mom looks confused, but she agrees. "Right. I need to find a job that I'm qualified for. That's why I'll apply to AppleSoft—"

"Screw AppleSoft." Rick says. "You need to get your job back at FutureTech."

"But I got *fired*!"

"Eeh, Ricardo, I said you were wasting your time with the señora. Should'a left her in Hollyweird." Santino pulls a spinner capsule from his pocket and dabs it on his tongue.

The Salazar brothers are even worse as a pair, and now they're ganging up on my mom. I'm so furious I blurt my words before I can stop myself. "We'd all be better off if you'd just leave us alone!"

Santino chuckles and winks at me. "Hey, maybe she can get a job at FutureTech."

"She's not old enough," my mom says, suddenly against the suggestion of me working.

"What is so important about FutureTech?" I say.

Rick and Santino exchange a glance, and my mom's presence drifts away as she stands there staring off into the distance. She's getting another nosebleed, and I swear she's never had them this often. Maybe it's the stress—like with me and my tick—but still, the timing is strange.

Santino burrows his gaze into my head. He's half smiling, half scowling, his lips twisted and folding into his teeth.

Santino is tied down in a medical chair. I come at him with a tattoo gun with a needle the size of a ballpoint pen. I dig the needle into his face and draw nonsensical shapes in his skin and it makes a bloody mess—

"She's got it too, eeh?" Santino's voice leaks through the ringing in my ears. My eyes focus and I see Rick and Santino staring at me.

"Nah," Rick says to Santino. "I don't know what her deal is. I can't work her the same as Lauren."

I look to my mom for a sign of life but she's still gazing at the wall. "Leave my mom alone."

"Oh?" Santino gives me a sarcastic grin. "She's gettin' feisty. Ricardo, you better act fast or señorita is gonna blow the plan."

"I'd rather just be rid of her," Rick says as though I'm not even there.

"Eeh, just send her out to the streets," Santino smirks. "They'll eat her up like a greasy taco."

He and Rick laugh and then grab some beers and head back out to the lawn, and I lead my mom to the couch.

"Mom, are you all right?"

She's looking right at me, but I know she can't see me. She seems okay, and I can't bear to stay another second in this house. I grab my mobie and head out into the streets.

Down south, it doesn't matter anymore which color your skin is. People in these neighborhoods have united against everyone else, particularly the *fancies* in the Zones. And now here's me, the whitest girl for miles, riding atop my screeching mobie, which is still loads better than what most of these kids have ever owned.

I gather quite a bit of attention riding through the ghetto. Today I swear my mobie motor is even louder than normal, and every single person turns to gawk at me. I have no clue where I'm going, and I have probably made an even bigger mistake by going *anywhere* by myself. Not two blocks down, my mobie sings a horrible tune of a dying cat, and I'm forced to walk.

And then I realize I have a tail.

"Hey, fancy white girl!" someone whistles. "Look atcha. You're so pretty, aren't ya?"

It's like ninety degrees out here, and I really wish I were wearing a jacket. The guys are on me, steps behind. I don't dare turn around, but I can hear them huffing.

"You don't wanna play? Eeh? Think you're too good for us? You fancy girlie with your fancy mobie and your fancy boots."

I pick up my pace. They shuffle after me. People watch from their lawns but no one moves in to help.

"You're all the same, ya fancies," he goes on, and I notice real anger in his voice. "You don't know what's coming, do you? It's all gonna be over soon. You Americans have no pride, you're weak at the seams. Alias is gonna break it apart and Mexico is gonna take *all* this back. Viva la Mexico!"

Out of nowhere the whole block shouts back and whistles and raises their fists in the air. I don't know how I suddenly became the figure of American hatred, but I don't want to stick around and find out. I take off in a sprint and ratchet the ON switch of my mobie. Finally it sparks to life and I leave the chanting Alias sympathizers behind.

11 spinning lights

The vibration of my wristlet startles me awake, another notification about Lyle's band gig tonight. I don't know why he's so into playing music again; they haven't played a show in months and all of a sudden it's the most important thing ever.

I check out his Connex port. The header has a photo of the band in which Lyle and Matteo battle for the center of attention. The show is apparently a big deal because *everybody* is going. Zander, the Baez sisters, all the Los Feliz friends. Even Harley posted an open invite to her hotel for an afterparty art extravaganza.

Being at school today actually brings me some relief. I was kept awake all night by the moaning and rhythmic banging of the bed against the wall from Santino's room, and the incessant arguing from Rick and my mom. I hardly slept at all, and I'm really feeling it now. Thanks to my vibrating wristlet, I pick my head up just as Mrs. Garcia's eyes land right on me, and I nod like I've been listening the whole time. I can't bear to suffer another escort to the principal's office for a lecture about my portfolio that I'm likely to never finish, at least now that I can no longer paint at Madri's house.

Maybe it's my dreary appearance, but no one bothers me at lunch. I sit on the concrete and let the sun soak into my skin; the heat helps calm my trembling. My wristlet vibrates again. It's Lyle—he's finally calling me.

"Lyle!"

He seems surprised by my enthusiasm. "Hey, Jo. Happy Birthday."

"What?"

He frowns. "You forgot, didn't you?"

Ah crap, he's right. It's March 11. I read that on my wristlet this morning and it didn't register. How could I forget my own birthday? Oh, right, my life has become such a ridiculous melodrama I haven't had a chance to remember. Hell, my mom hasn't even mentioned it.

"Thank you for remembering, Lyle." Despite my inner angst, my voice sounds sweet and it makes him blush.

"I could never forget your birthday," he says. "So how's it feel to be seventeen?"

"Just as shitty as sixteen."

His laugh fades faster than I'd like. "Look, Jo, I'm sorry about what I said at the Holo Show. I didn't mean to upset you. I'd heard about Harley's adjustment and she seemed … and you … Well, I just want to be sure you're okay."

My insides seize at the thought of the brain adjusters, that my fate may be decided without me, regardless of how hard I try to hide from them. Lyle, at least, only wants me to fit in. Still, what he knows of the darkness in my mind doesn't even scratch the surface.

Lyle clears his throat to speak again, because I haven't said anything. "Hey, you're coming to my show tonight, right?"

"I don't know, Lyle."

"My Dad Nolan wants to take you out. We can hop around downtown and grab some dinner and celebrate your birthday before the show. And then we'll go to Harley's hotel party and you can sleep at my house. How does that sound?"

Actually, it sounds like the best thing ever, even if Harley has changed. It sure beats staying in Rick's house for another night.

"That would be great, Lyle."

"Wicky. We'll pick you up at six."

"You'll want to leave a little earlier than usual."

"Why?"

I have to tell him what's happened. I have tell him about my mom and Rick, but I leave out the details about what happened at the ZT Zone police station with Satesh and Madri. Maybe that's a mistake, but he's already staring at me through the wristlet with eyes so wide they might pop out of the holo display.

"Holy crap, Jo …"

"Yeah. I'm looking forward to getting out of there for a night."

He smiles. "Good. Send me your new address."

As six o'clock rolls around, my mom is on the couch, watching the flat images of Rick's old-school TV, her face drooping like she's fallen asleep with her eyes open.

"Hey, Mom, I'm going out with Lyle and the dads. I won't be home until morning."

She struggles to lift her eyelids. "Why are you going out tonight?"

Well, Mom, it's my seventeenth birthday. Clearly you've forgotten that today marks the anniversary of me being pulled from your uterus. Thanks for remembering.

I'm about to storm from the room when I see a glass of liquor in one of her hands, and a blood-soaked hand towel in her other. She's having a worse day than me.

"Lyle's band is playing downtown," I say. "And my old friend Harley is in town."

My mom nods. "Oh yeah, Harley. I remember Harley. She was pretty."

"She was also an artist."

"Oh. Right," she says, and looks back at the TV.

I shift my duffel bag to my other hand as Lyle's face pops up on my wristlet. "They're here. I'll see you tomorrow."

"Have a good time, honey," my mom says without looking away from the TV.

Rick and Santino are sitting in folding chairs on the lawn, beers in hand. "Where you goin', fancy?" Santino says. "Gonna make some cash on the streets?"

Rick pipes up. "You better come back here with a job."

I brush past them and slide into Dylan's car as fast as possible. "Go. Now. Before they say anything else."

Dylan speeds away and Lyle stares out the window at the pathetic neighborhood I'm now a resident of, his nose wrinkled like he smells something foul.

Nolan turns in the front seat. "So that's him, huh? That's the guy Lauren's with?"

"Yeah, he's horrible. I don't know why my mom is dating him. He's nothing like my dad."

Dylan and Nolan share a look of understanding.

"They worked together at FutureTech, right?" Dylan says into the rearview. "Maybe she appreciates someone from her side of the world."

"You mean, because she never understood my dad," I say, but it's more of a rhetorical smirk than an agreement.

Nolan tilts his head. "The opposite was also true, you know. Your dad didn't really understand your mom."

"Then why did they get married in the first place?"

"They did love each other," Dylan says, "in the beginning."

Dylan's comment rings true in some part of my brain—perhaps my mom finds relief in Rick's understanding of her career. Still, they hardly have anything else in common, and they're always arguing about something. And there's no getting past the sinking feeling that Rick is using my mom for something other than drug money.

"His brother called me a taco," I say, trying to break the tension.

Nolan bursts out laughing. "Oh no! Please don't tell me you're moving into a roach coach."

Lyle grimaces. "What's a *roach coach*?"

"A taco truck," Dylan says. "On the street. Where you buy tacos."

"And salmonella!" Nolan says.

"Oh god!" Lyle gags, and we all laugh at his squeamishness.

Dylan drives us to Downtown North. Downtown South is where all the dealers and pimps hang out, and everyone knows to never go below 3rd Street unless they're keen on being mugged by a hooker. Downtown North, however, has been well-maintained by the artists and musicians and actors that remained in the city, and they do everything in their power to keep it a viable place, despite the incessant towering of FutureTech buildings. It is *the* place to be on a Friday night.

"Okay, Jo," Nolan says as we stand on a street corner. "Our birthday present to you is a brand-new outfit."

I chuckle. "You don't think I'm dressed for the occasion?"

He looks me over but there's nothing new to study. "New year, new you."

We wander down the block and the dads suggest store after store, yet none of them are quite my taste. Of course, I don't really *have* a taste so I'm not even sure what I'm looking for, but I tell myself I'll know it when I see it.

"Hey, retro girl!" Nolan calls out. "How about this one?"

He pushes me into a store that looks like a cross between a music shop and a design studio. Screens display intricate graphics, and the speakers blast old rock music. As Nolan suggests, this place is *retro.*

The orange-haired storeowner beams when we walk in, her night-glow tattoos and flashing piercings contrasting against her mahogany skin. "Well hello! What can I get for you tonight?"

"This is Jo," Nolan says. "It's her seventeenth birthday and we're here to make her look like a *star.*"

The girl eyes me as I'm gawking at the display of boots. "Birthday girl, huh? What do you say, shall we fancy you up?"

She puts me in a dressing room and tosses in all sorts of clothes and shoes and accessories. I spend a good hour going through all of it until I find the perfect outfit I didn't even know I was looking for.

Knee-high boots, glossy black with sparkling jewels all over. Faded black pants with white stitching. A shimmering blue halter-top that looks like the surface of rippling water in the sun, with an open back that exposes my skin to my waist. And to top it all off, a pair of jangling metallic earrings that twinkle against my black hair.

I barely recognize the girl looking back through the mirror wearing these fancy clothes, but I know it's me. I can feel it's me. And I feel … *sexy*. And totally badass. I've never felt so strong and feminine at the same time. More exposed than I've ever been in public, I'm on the edge of a vulnerability I've never felt, yet at the same time there's a part of me begging to expose more. A breeze blows under the top and the fabric brushes against my skin, heightening the sensation. The tension inside me is exhilarating.

I wish I could capture the look on the dads' faces when I step out of the dressing room. Their younger, more flamboyant selves come out, and they flock to me and scrutinize every bit of my outfit.

"My girl!" Nolan squeals. "Hot damn, you look amazing."

Dylan flips my hair. "You are definitely wearing this tonight."

Lyle is slumped against a display table. As soon as I catch his gaze, he stands straight and looks away. But then he looks at me again, and turns away. And back at me. I smile and he blushes.

Nolan pays the store girl for my outfit, and she offers to hold onto my painted boots but I don't want them anymore. That was an emblem of my past, and tonight I want to be someone new.

The boys let me lead them down the sidewalk. There's this swagger in my step, and I have the sudden desire to be in South LA, me and my invincible outfit. I would walk straight up to those assholes on the street and punch them in the throat. *Eeh fancy—BAAM!*

Nolan takes us to an expensive restaurant where the food is lowered from the ceiling. The dads chug their drinks and chat wildly as we wait to be served, and Lyle messes with his wristlet. I make light conversation because people are watching and it's making me antsy.

"Are you nervous about the show?"

Lyle jerks as though I've startled him. "No. Why?"

"Oh. Well, you've been pretty quiet since back at the store."

He blushes and looks away. Two ACTA agents walk past and Lyle stiffens. "Oh crap!" He reaches into his pants pocket and holds out his fisted hand. "Here, take it!"

"What is that?"

"Just take it." He opens his hand and reveals a spinner capsule.

"Lyle! What are you doing with that?"

"*Shh,*" he says, and drops his hand under the table. "It's not for me, it's for Zander. They'll arrest me if they find it. You have to take it."

"I'm not legal to have it either. You'd rather *I* get arrested?"

"They won't search you. You're a girl. And you look..." he pauses and scans my body "...*older.*"

We both realize his hand is resting high on my thigh and he jerks back, dropping the spinner capsule between my legs just as the agents walk past us. Lyle hunches down in his chair, and I'm left there with a spinner caught between my thighs.

The cops don't even look our way, and the dads are too drunk to notice the ruckus. Our food lowers down and creates enough of a diversion for me to make the awkward search of my seat for the loose spinner, which I stuff in my pocket. Lyle spends the entire length of dinner staring at his plate.

"Hey, Lyle," Dylan says, thumbing his wristlet, "from the look of it you'll have all of Los Feliz at the show tonight."

Lyle grumbles something incomprehensible and the dads laugh.

Sure enough, the nightclub is packed. I recognize nearly everyone. And yet, hardly anyone recognizes me, at least not at first glance. My body tenses when we walk past a crowd of boys hovering around the Baez sisters. I catch Sapphire's gaze, and she looks me over and smiles, and then Ashlyn's eyes go wide and all the boys turn to gawk at me in my shimmering outfit.

"Hey, Jo!" A flicker of bright colors slithers up to me; it's Harley and her night-glow tattoos. She gathers attention as she moves through the room, but does a much better job pretending everyone isn't looking at her. She grabs my arm and spins me around. "Look at you, all sparkly and fancied up. And here I thought you'd never turn into a real woman."

Hopefully the lights are dim enough to hide my blush. "Harley, I heard about your …"

I heard about your adjustment is what nearly came out of my mouth, as though it's casual conversation to ask about someone's boob job or recent stint in rehab. But then, Harley probably wouldn't have been upset had I said anything. After all, she's been fixed to not feel any negative emotions. I remember the days when she and I would crack mean jokes about the Los Feliz groupies and their conformist ideals. Now, Harley looks like she fits right in.

Is this who Lyle wants me to be?

Harley hasn't noticed my pause in conversation because she has closed her eyes and stands swaying to the music.

I start again. "I heard about the afterparty. Lyle says other artists will be there."

She grins and keeps her eyes closed. "Oh yeah. There's this one guy … *oof,* I've had such a jazz for him ever since I saw his 3D graphic work. Such carnal stuff too, gets me all keyed up. I want to introduce you. I think you'll vibe with him."

I'm so confused as to what she's talking about, and then some dude grabs her around the waist from behind. She laughs, slaps him on the arm, and the dude disappears into the crowd. She didn't used to be so distracted by guys. She used to be distracted by *art.*

"So you're coming, right?" Harley says. "To the party? You'll be a smash in that outfit, I promise." She winks and goose bumps run down my arms.

"I told my mom I'll be spending the night at Lyle's."

She tosses her head back and laughs. "Oh shit, Jo! I forgot you're still a kid." She pets my arm. "Dontcha worry, we'll fix you up."

My skin tingles at the word *fix.* The house lights flash and that's Harley's cue to move on. I'm glad to watch her leave. I lived next to her for eight years, and now I feel like I hardly know her. I don't know her, truthfully, not as Harley the Adjusted.

Lyle gathers his band, and the dads and I make our way to our reserved table on a platform high enough to see over the kids standing at the stage. I have a clear sight of the Los Feliz friends, with their fake attitudes and cozy lives. I suddenly realize that I don't care. I don't need to be like Harley. She gave in, she surrendered to the brain adjusters, but I'm stronger than that. I can hide behind this new version of myself—this bolder, sexier, more confident exterior—and no one will be any wiser to my tick. As I glance around the nightclub from my perch I realize everyone is looking at me, and for the first time I don't fear what they think. What these people see is exactly what I want them to see.

"Are you having a fun night?" Nolan asks and wraps his arm around me.

His smile is contagious and I feel the tug on my lips. As much as I scoff at Perfect Family and their positive image next to my negative and very un-perfect life, they sure are a great bunch of people to have on my side. After all, it was they who bought me this invincible outfit.

"The best," I say. And I mean it. I haven't felt this good in a long time.

The house lights go out, and Lyle and his troupe take the stage. The band is terrible. Sure, they look good, but the music is just repulsive. Lyle plays the keyboard and he's not too bad when he's playing more than a four-note melody, which is rare. The bass player is too old to be in a band of teenagers, but he's the best musician so no one can really argue. There is a new guitar player every time I see them, and this guy doesn't want to be here. The drummer has twenty pads and uses only three, and I can never tell what Matteo is singing because he has this weird yodeling voice with a flutter that sounds like he's vibrating.

Nolan and Dylan are supportive parents, and they bob their heads and clap politely, but I can tell from their constant wincing that they hate the music even more than I do. The songs go from bad to worse, and I'm about ready to bash my head on the table when I remember Lyle's spinner in my pocket.

I've only popped a spinner once, last winter during the earthquake blackouts. Lyle and I hiked up the hill to look at the stars, and he'd brought two spinners and suggested we give it a try. We lay on our backs and watched the stars twinkle and swirl around us. Then my body felt like it was falling into the earth, so I reached over and grabbed Lyle for help, and before I knew it we were kissing. I'm not sure how long it lasted, but my lips were sore the next day.

We never kissed again after that. Neither of us even mentioned it. In fact, I'd completely forgotten about it until right now, but it's too late for any concerns because I've already popped the capsule and let the liquid flow onto my tongue.

The music is far more bearable now. Or maybe I can't hear it anymore, I don't know. I don't care, because for a night I'd like to not be in my own head. So I sit and bounce in my chair until Lyle says my name over the speakers.

"Yay! Go on, Jo!" Dylan pats me on the back. He's so blurry.

"What?"

Lyle's voice booms through the speakers. "We learned to play this song because it's her favorite and today is her birthday, and we want her to sing it with us."

The room bursts into applause. Lyle appears in front of me and pins the mic to my shirt. "C'mon," he says, "sing for us."

I'm too inebriated to protest, so I let him drag me to the stage. The lights are blinding and I've hardly any sense to know if I'm even standing upright.

And then the music starts. I'm surprised the band knows how to play any song this well. I'm grateful they're not butchering it. Lyle is right, it is my favorite song, back from when my mom was in college, and the sound of it brings to mind the imagery of muscular cowboys with their shirts off riding through the desert—a fantasy I prefer to appreciate in private. The drums are slow and sensual like the walk of a horse, the bass rattles with a slinking harmony, and the keyboards are sparse and bluesy. All I can think about are shirtless men on horseback, and for a moment I forget I'm not alone in my bedroom. The spinner pulses through my veins, blurring my senses yet heightening them at the same time. I've lost complete control over my body, my hips tug me back and forth, and I hear someone singing the lyrics in a sexy growling voice, and it must be me because my lips are moving.

I can't see anything beyond the blinding lights, so I pretend to focus on someone in the audience. I picture the young agent from the ZT Zone station, standing there with that goofy smile. And then I picture Satesh and his chiseled face, and I wink. Someone whistles and I see I'm actually staring at Zander, who is lost in the deep blue ocean of my shirt. My outfit shimmers under the bright lights and reflects around the room. Everyone is watching me. *Everyone.* The girls—and most especially the Baez sisters—have their faces contorted in awe. The boys give drunken smiles, and for no reason at all I pretend their eyes are peeling away my clothes, leaving me dancing naked on the stage.

I turn to Lyle and I swear his face is melting. I didn't think his jaw could hang so low, and I'm afraid it might actually hit the floor. He locks his eyes with mine, and I'm amazed he's still playing the keyboard. I keep on singing. I'm singing the song to Lyle like it's meant for him, howling the lyrics with the ache of a thousand lust-drenched hearts, and Lyle can't take his eyes off me.

I give one long, final wail, and the song is over. It feels like forever that the room is dead silent, so quiet I can hear the thump of blood in my ears.

And then the roar comes. The cheers startle me, rumbling the floor beneath my boots, making my entire body tingle with a glorious sensation of pleasure and relief.

Matteo takes my arm to steady me, his touch sends a shiver up my spine. "Nice job, beautiful."

Zander grabs for my other hand and pulls me toward the edge of the stage, to a dozen grinning guys in the audience. Lyle is there in two seconds flat and leads me back to the table. The dads are cheering. Everybody is cheering.

"You're beaming!" Nolan shouts over the crowd.

I know I am. My heart pounds and the room spins and I can't tell up from down, but I have never felt so alive.

12 beyond the pale

The show is over. The nightclub's house lights come up, and everyone moves about, drunken and high and mumbling and pointing at me. My body tingles and buzzes with every touch, and my cheeks ache from the smile I cannot tear from my face.

Matteo comes by to compliment me again, even though he has three girls clutching his arms. "Wicky song, Jo."

The Baez sisters swoop in. "I like your shirt," Sapphire says. "I'll have to get one. It matches my eyes."

Ashlyn groans, and twitches like she's being poked in the ribs. "I didn't know you could sing. You should do this instead of that art stuff."

"Jo, my girl. You were amazing." Harley wanders over to the table, her eyes wild and flickering like her night-glow tattoos. She tosses her head around and laughs, and even through my own drug haze I can tell she's drunk. "You did it, didn't you? You got fixed!"

Everyone jerks, shifting their heads between Harley and me. It takes me a moment to focus on her words, to understand her implication, to realize Harley suggested that I am broken. She's suggested I'm like her. But I am not like her.

Then Lyle says something I don't expect. "She doesn't need to be fixed. Do you, Jo?" He stands right in front of me, the toes of his shoes scraping against my boots, gazing down as I sit slumped in the chair I've been molded into. His eyes are so intense I feel them pushing against me, through me, into me.

Our silent conversation is interrupted as Zander shoves Lyle out of the way and smashes his body on top of mine and bites down on my neck like a bloodthirsty vampire. Ashlyn hollers, and Nolan gives Zander a hip-check sending him toppling onto the floor.

"C'mon, birthday girl," Nolan says, laughing. "We should go before your groupies get any more hands-on."

Harley laughs, like she's forgotten all about her suggestion of my brain adjustment. "You're all coming to my party still, aren't you? There are so many guys who will want to meet the birthday girl."

Lyle takes my hand and lifts me to my feet. "I should take her home."

"Aw!" Harley says with an exaggerated pout. "Are you sure about that, Jo?"

I sway under the influence of the spinner, and Lyle wraps his arm around my waist to steady me. I've never known him to feel so sturdy.

"Yeah," I say, "I'm sure."

It's a long and quiet ride back to South LA. Dylan snores in the passenger seat, and I press my face against the window, watching the lights of the city blur past.

Music plays through the speakers, and Nolan peers into the back seat through the rear-view mirror. He's looking at Lyle, who is staring at me.

"You were great tonight," Lyle says. He jerks like he's embarrassed. Nolan chuckles and turns up the music a little more.

"Thanks," I mumble.

Lyle lowers his voice even though the music is loud enough to drown him out. "I just … I … well, you …"

He won't spit it out. Whatever he wants to say is stuck on his tongue as it hangs out of his open mouth. I can't tell if the spinner is distorting things or if Lyle really is leaning toward me, but the car stops and he looks away.

We're on Rick's street. The whole block is pitch-black except for Nolan's car lights and a few TVs glowing in windows. Lyle leads me under a building awning next to the Salazar duplex, and I will myself to stand upright.

"Lyle," I say. "I had a really great time tonight. Thank you."

He comes in close and a chill runs through me. "Me too," he says. "I'm glad you were there. I hope you're not upset we didn't go to Harley's party."

Any other time and I'd be upset that Lyle was bringing up Harley while we're sharing such an intimate moment, but for once I don't care. "Harley has changed. You can tell the adjustment did something to her."

"Yeah, I know. She was a really good artist."

Okay, now he's taking it too far.

Lyle closes the gap between us. "Jo, your stuff is better. I could never admit that to Harley. But I've always thought you were the better artist. Your paintings have more … soul."

My heart swells. He means it too. Even on this dark street, I can see the gentleness in his eyes. I want to see deeper in those blue wonders. I want to know exactly what he's thinking about me, I want to—

His arms wrap around me, and I fall into his chest. An instant later his lips are on mine. I don't remember them being so soft. I hiccup and Lyle starts to push away, so I put my arms around his neck and pull him in closer. His fingers graze down my bare back and my entire body shivers, and I fall into him even more. He knows I like his touch because he does it again, and again, and it feels so good I never want his fingers to ever leave my skin.

Our bodies are mashed together, and our lips and tongues are a sloshing mess, but I don't care because I want him and I know he wants me. His hands go up and down my spine, and I wriggle against this body. My blood pulses through every vein, and my nerves feel like they are on fire. The lasting effects of the spinner make my head swirl. My knees go weak and my lips slide away from his, and he clutches me tight to keep me from collapsing onto the sidewalk.

His breath tickles my ear. "Are you all right?"

I smile into his chest. "Never better."

"I guess it's a good thing we didn't go to the party, huh?"

I chuckle. "Too bad you had to take me home."

Lyle shudders and leans back a little. I grab a handful of his shirt to keep him close because I can't let this moment be over yet, but I know there's no place for our encounter to continue on this night. I'll have to wait until next time.

"I'll call you tomorrow," Lyle says. "Happy Birthday, Jo. I know this will be a better year than the last one." He looks at me, his eyes glinting in the dim light. Then he turns and walks back to the car.

The street is dark and creepy, but I'm so high from the events of the night that I feel invincible to any terrors in the neighborhood. Come at me, world, I'm ready for you. Lyle is right; this is going to be my year.

There is a light in Santino's window, but Rick's side of the house is dark. Even the TV is off. Rick is usually up all hours of the night watching some horrible movie. I'm surprised he would have already gone to bed. Or maybe he and my mom went out. Who knows. Who cares? All I care about is the lasting sensation of Lyle on my lips. And how thirsty I am.

The fridge is full of beers. There's not even a single canteen of water. The filtration system doesn't work either; I had the unfortunate experience of discovering that yesterday.

I barely have the fridge closed when I hear it, but I can't be certain. Maybe it's the spinner. That's it, I'm hearing—nope, there it is again.

The sizzling *buzz* of a scanning laser.

The sound is faint. My head is still swimming in spinner soup and I can't tell for sure but I think it's coming from inside the house. Rick must be home messing with his stolen scanners. And this time, I aim to catch the bastard in action and get him arrested.

I creep through the living room, fumbling with the camera of my wristlet. My breath bellows through my nose, and I fear I'm going to get caught because I'm breathing too loud. I reach the hallway, aim my camera lens, and hold my breath.

The mysterious locked door at the end of the hall is open. Not by much, a few inches at the most. Blue and orange lights flicker against the walls. I hear another laser *buzz*. I try desperately to stay quiet, and put one eye to the door opening.

I see Rick. The two inches of space between the wall and the door allows only the visual of him sitting on a stool with his back to me, and a small table next to him which holds a bowl of spinner capsules and push-pin syringes. Colored lights bounce off the sweat on his neck, his face aglow from a bright source in front of him. I move closer, my eyes crossing from the spinner. Misjudging my proximity to the doorframe, I lose my balance, over-compensate my step, and hurdle through the door and into the room, and what I see causes the whole world to come to a halt.

This isn't just bits and pieces of scanners stolen from FutureTech, this is a mad scientist's lab. A brain hacker's sanctuary. Mismatched pieces of electrical equipment, tools that belong in a mechanic's garage. Saws, drills, tubes, sensors. Tape and clamps hold things together. Above a tab hovers a 3D hologram projection of a brain, neurons flashing in real time. Below the graphic are three words: *Patient: Lauren Bristol.* My eyes follow the length of a fiber optic cable connected to a transmitter box on the floor, streaming bits of blue light into my mom.

My mom.

She's lying in a recliner, not moving. The optic cable is stuck up her nostril, the one that always gets nosebleeds. Rick doesn't know I'm here; he's still going at it, sweating like Santa Claus on Christmas Eve, and I'm surprised he's still upright given the quantity of empty spinner capsules next to him.

The tab flashes and beeps a warning, and my mom convulses in the recliner, shaking so violently the floor vibrates. Rick fumbles with the tab and my mom's brain hologram flashes red, and then orange light travels the length of the optic cable and the brain hologram flashes some more. My mom is in a sedated stupor, her eyes rolled back, frothing saliva oozing from her mouth, thrashing around in the chair with her head tossed in a neck-breaking position, and Rick just keeps on screwing with her brain.

He'll kill her. He'll kill my mom, and even if he doesn't, her brain will be mush and she'd be better off dead.

The spinner effects are now completely gone from my body, and I'm so aware of everything but I can't do anything more than stand here like a petrified bothead. Rick reaches over to the table, and that's when he sees me standing in the doorway. His face drains of color, his eyes go wide, and sweat pours down his face.

I hear another *buzz*. That sound, that terrifying noise that I swear I heard in my sleep came from Rick. He's been hacking my mom, he's been torturing her for god knows how long, and it's only a matter of time before he comes after me.

I snatch a syringe and jab it into Rick's arm. He slides off his stool and onto the floor, knocking over a tower of equipment. He lands with his back against the wall. His body goes limp. He's still breathing. Rick is still alive, paralyzed by sedatives. I grab a small circular saw and turn it on. Rick's eyes flicker as I press the whirring blade into his forehead, cutting through the bone. Blood spurts across the room. I saw all around, chopping off the top of his head. I reach in and rip Rick's brain from his skull, taking with it all the veins and nerves, and place the brain in his own lap—

"What have you *done*!"

My mom's voice. My mom's voice snapped me from my vision but my mom is brain dead. I saw her in the recliner, getting light signals sent through her nose, but now she's fine, legs curled underneath her, wiping saliva from her mouth, gaping at me in horror.

"Josephine! What have you done?" She points across the room and I turn to look.

It's Rick. On the floor. Missing the top of his head. His own brain resting in his lap.

Dead.

"You killed him! Jo, you *murdered* him!"

"Mom! I didn't—"

Oh, but I did, because as I'm waving my arms to argue, I see the saw in my hand. And the blood. My beautiful birthday outfit is covered in Rick's brain blood.

My mom wails. "Why would you do such a thing?"

"I thought you were dead! He was hacking your brain!"

"Don't lie to me. He wasn't doing anything to me."

It hits me all at once: the equipment is gone. The room is nearly empty, except for my mom and Rick and his brain and the saw and the buckets of blood splattered on the walls, but the equipment is gone. All of it. The transmitter box. The tower of electronics and sensors. The fiber optic tubes. Even the hologram-projecting tablet. Gone. Not a trace, no clean spots on the floor where the blood would have missed.

"This can't be happening ..." Blood trickles from my mom's nose and her gaze drifts as she disappears into her empty space.

And then Santino bursts in, his cheeks bright red. "Ricardo! Ricardo!" He comes at me and yells in Spanish, and I think he's going to hit me but I still have the saw in my hand and he backs away. He looks across the room at my mom curled in the recliner, and I can swear I see the hint of a smile curl at his lips.

"It's your turn, senorita." Then he runs from the house, yelling in Spanish at the top of his lungs.

A crowd gathers in the yard, and Santino stands guard at the door to ensure I don't escape. I can't move. My body is so stiff I can't even let go of the saw. That's how the cops find me: holding a bloody power tool while hovering over Rick's dead body and his own brain perched in his lap.

Investigators scan the room, take 3D images of the crime. A cop talks to my mom as she cowers in the recliner. The saw is taken from my hand and tracking cuffs are bound to my wrists, and before I know it I'm led through the crowd on the lawn in my shimmering outfit with my hands behind my back and shoved into the back of a police car.

This cannot be happening. This. Cannot. Be. Happening. It was a vision, dammit—but it was all so real. Too real. It *was* real.

I murdered someone.

But it was Rick. It was that shithead Rick, and I swore my mom was dead, and even if she wasn't he was still hacking her brain. The bastard deserved to die.

What happened to all that equipment? I couldn't have imagined it … could I have? No, I'm not my mom, I don't forget things, and I don't hallucinate like my dad. I'm not crazy. It could have been the spinner screwing with my eyes, but the effects were gone the moment I saw my mom on that recliner. He was doing it. Rick was hacking my mom's brain. Goddammit, someone find out what happened and get me out of this mess!

I'm pissed off and furious, and I'm about to start kicking the door open when I see faces peering in the windows. It's the neighbors, Santino, his slutty girlfriend, media reporters and cameramen, and then the windows black out. It's really quiet all of a sudden. I can hear my own heartbeat. My tracker cuffs break apart. A screen folds down from the ceiling of the car and a woman in a suit appears in the display.

"Hello. My name is Alexia Malkovich. I have been assigned to your case by the Superior Court of the City of Los Angeles. What is your name?" Her dull brown hair falls in her eyes and she blinks constantly. It's distracting.

"Uh, what?"

"Your name. What is your name?"

"Jo Bristol."

"Good. Now, see the palm scanner there?"

A box on the seat next to me pops open and reveals a scanner screen. It hurts to unclench my hand and place it on the glass, and I'm so covered in blood it takes a while for my prints to register.

Mrs. Malkovich looks off-screen. "Ah, okay, here you are. Josephine Abigail Bristol, born March 11. Correct?"

I nod.

"Good. You have one minor infraction on your record, and wait—my god, you're only seventeen?"

"Since today."

Mrs. Malkovich frowns. "Hum. I don't typically represent juveniles." She looks away. "Are you sure I have the right case? Murder? … Really? *Her*? … Oh, all right."

"What's going on?"

"My apologies, Miss Bristol. I was unaware you were so … young, but never mind that. I understand this is a very difficult and confusing time for you, but I will make certain you will get the most fair and just trial possible. They will read your Miranda rights once you arrive at the station. I won't be able to speak to you again until tomorrow morning, so is there anything you'd like to ask me now?"

"Um, yes, actually, there is."

"And what's that?"

"Are they going to send me to the brain adjusters?"

She glances away and back again, and shakes her head. "No."

"Why not?"

"Because there's nothing wrong with you."

PART TWO
the slammer

13 the schoolgirl slicer

There is nothing wrong with me.

Since I was a kid I've imagined killing people in gruesome and gory detail, but there's nothing wrong with me. I've been possessed by this nasty tick and unknowingly acted it out, but there's nothing wrong with me. *I've chopped someone's head off and ripped their brain from their skull,* but hey, I'm perfectly normal.

That's good to know. I was getting worried.

I am driven away from the scene of my crime without a word from the police, and I can focus on nothing but Mrs. Malkovich's words. They reverberate in my ears: *There's nothing wrong with you.* It doesn't make sense. None of this makes the slightest bit of sense.

And then it occurs to me: I have never had a vision during a brain scan. In fact, I've never been through a full neuron scan, only those learning development ones issued by the PEAD program, and the results showed that I have an affinity for problem solving and am prone to hyper-activity, but certainly nothing to suggest I am a pathological killer. The only other chance anyone had to find my tick was that day at school when Alias hacked the system and granted me a free pass. There is no reason for anyone to believe that my tick and the event that just occurred are remotely related. So if I'm not going to the brain adjusters, where am I going?

Murder, Mrs. Malkovich said. I'm going to jail.

The cops pull me from the car and into the police station, which lacks any resemblance to the stations in the ZT Zones. This place is horribly outdated with computer systems from a decade ago, and the whole place is cracking and crumbling and saturated with body odor.

I'm not just escorted through the station, I'm paraded through it like a poodle at a dog show. Everyone turns to witness my passage—cops and criminals alike—and there's a lot of hooting and whistling and racial slurs. Instead of being ushered past the spying eyes of drunks and druggies, I'm made to pause and wait for the cops to take their sweet ass time with my ID entry, and even when a diamond-toothed pimp reaches out to grab my shirt, the cops ignore the whole interaction. I'm examined and prodded and tossed about, and I really have no bearings anymore. The whole place spins around me and it makes me so dizzy I feel I'm about to puke. With a persistent shove, I'm stuffed into a small square room with concrete walls, no windows, and one bright light in the center of the ceiling.

"Sit," one cop says and waves me toward a chair at a large metal desk. He takes a seat across from me and reads from a tab while never breaking the scowl from his pock-marked face. "I am Officer Ibanez. That is Officer Bell." He nods at the cop by the door. "You are under arrest for the murder of Ricardo Salazar. You have the right to remain silent. Anything you say can and will be used against you in a court of law. You have been provided an attorney by the City of Los Angeles. If you wish to be represented by your own attorney you have the right to do so at no harm to your case. Do you understand the rights I have just read to you?"

I concentrate on focusing my eyesight under the bright light. "Huh?"

Officer Ibanez leans in and I get a whiff of his liquor-heavy breath. "Do you understand your rights?"

My rights are the least of my concern right now, jerk. "What's going to happen to me?"

Officer Bell comes over from his post by the door. "Miss, you have to say yes or no." His perfectly round, bald head reflects the light, and his voice is smooth and sultry. I like him. He can stay. Take the mean one away.

"Uh … yes, I understand."

"Jesus, finally," Ibanez says. He pauses and looks down at his tab, but he's not reading it anymore. "Why'd you do it? Huh? You think because you're some privileged white girl you can kill a decent Mexican man?"

The air is sucked from my lungs, and I can barely breathe out, "No!"

"Ibanez! Back down!" says Bell.

Ibanez leans over the table. "You sure about that? *Fancy*?"

"He hacked my mom!"

"You crazy white girl. Whose side are you on? Who do you work for?"

I've never felt more exhausted and full of adrenaline at the same time, and I imagine the tension in my muscles fracturing my bones like brittle clay. "Rick was killing my mom!"

Officer Bell grabs Ibanez by the collar and lifts him from the seat. "Ibanez! Out!"

Ibanez straightens his uniform calmly as though this interaction were a common occurrence. He points a long jagged finger at me. "We will finish this, I promise you." Then he mumbles something in Spanish and leaves the room.

Bell sighs, then takes the seat across from me. "I apologize for my partner's behavior. That was uncalled for."

Officer Bell is good cop. Officer Ibanez is bad cop.

"What do I have to do to get out of this?"

Bell sighs again. "You're up shit creek, doll. There's no getting out of it."

Okay, maybe not *good* cop.

"Mrs. Malkovich said there's no reason for why I killed Rick, and I don't know if you'll understand it either, but the only one who can speak for me is my friend Madri, so if we can give her a call, she can explain, but if you want me to confess it's going to sound a little weird …" I'm rambling frantically as Officer Bell thumbs through his tab, and he looks up at the last moment.

"You won't be confessing," he says, with a wave. "I don't get to interrogate suspects anymore. The brain scan will do that for me."

"I'm not going to give a statement?"

"You're not going to tell me any more than the brain scan will."

"I *can* tell you more, trust me. You have to listen to my side of the story!"

Officer Bell stands and blocks the overhead light. "Like I said, that's not my job anymore. C'mon, time to hook you up."

He doesn't offer me the chance to retort before he grabs my arm and leads me into an adjacent scanning room. It's not the scary gerry-rigged setup like Rick's, but still my heart skips a beat as we enter. A tech straps me in the bed and aligns the laser, and I'm left alone in the room.

I don't want to be here. Maybe it would be easier if I had a friend beside me, someone to say this is all going to be okay, someone to speak on my behalf to convince these people that I didn't mean to kill Rick, and even if I did, he damn well deserved it anyway. I wish I knew who was standing on the other end of these wires, peeking into my brain, trying to find a scientific explanation as to why a girl like me would do a thing like that.

Maybe this time they'll see my tick in the brain scan. Maybe this time a decent scientist will be able to determine the source of my visions, and prove that I have been a hostage of my own mind for my whole life. *Are* there any decent brain scientists? Is there anyone in the world who would be more willing to help me than drive a light tube up my nose and flip the off switch? Is there anyone out there who can help me?

The test is over. I receive no summary of the brain scan, and there are no scientists to greet me with an apologetic plea. Officers Bell and Ibanez take me down the hall to another set of doors and into a room, and I am instantly bombarded by the smell of stale piss. A half-dozen other women sit on the benches, and the second they see me their eyes go wide like they've spotted a glossy piece of cheesecake. Ibanez gives me a shove and I stumble into a dirty woman's lap.

"Ah look, fresh meat," she says through the gaps in her teeth. "She's still bleeding."

I reach out to steady myself on the bench and see the dried blood caked on my hands and arms. I have not even been given the chance to clean off the evidence. I turn to ask for a restroom break, but Ibanez closes the door with a spiteful grin.

"See you in the morning."

And that's it. I'm left in this filthy room with women who are drooling like they want to devour me. I sit in the corner furthest from the others and three of them shift toward me.

One young woman leans in. I can see the glaze in her eyes, and she's wearing so much makeup I can't tell if those are her real eyebrows. "So what are you in for? You a hooka too?"

A burly tattooed woman chuckles. "Ah, she's no hooker. Look at her, she's barely been popped."

"I donno," says the clown-faced girl. "She don't look so innocent to me." She reaches for my arm and I think she's going to hurt me so I flatten myself against the wall.

Another woman shouts to no one in particular as her eyes dart around the room. "You're all government spies! Get out of my brain!"

The women gabber on, the crazy lady shouts to herself, and the clown-faced girl breathes in my face. I cover my ears and shut my eyes and hope with all my might that I'll wake up and this will have been some horrible dream.

But this is no dream. This has been the worst birthday in the history of bad birthdays.

"Josephine Bristol!"

The voice cuts through my covered ears. I force my eyes open and find the women looking at me, except for the clown-faced girl, who is fast asleep on my shoulder.

Mrs. Malkovich appears in the doorway, all pale and clammy and blinking like something is stuck in her eye. "What's this? You kept her in the public holding cell? She's a minor!"

The guard shrugs. "She's here for murder, ma'am. The sheriff didn't want her in with the juveniles."

The clown-faced girl wakes and gasps at the mention of my crime.

The tattooed woman laughs. "Ha! I knew it. There's a devil in her."

"Quiet, you!" the guard says, but the woman laughs more.

"All right, Miss Bristol, let's go," Mrs. Malkovich says. I stand and she grimaces. "Look at you. You're a bloody mess. Couldn't they have at least cleaned you up first? Guard, get us some towels."

The dried blood is so stuck to my skin it hurts to wipe it off, but I'm grateful to be rid of it. Though there's nothing I can do for my destroyed shirt.

Mrs. Malkovich and the guard lead me to another floor, and we pause at a heavy wooden door. "Okay, the judge will read your charges. Don't say anything unless the judge asks you a question, and don't argue your innocence. This is just the first appearance, not the trial. Then we'll come back and discuss the details of your case. Understand?"

There's nothing at all about this that I understand.

The hearing room is madness. People cry and argue, the judge slams his gavel into the desk, and no one pays him the slightest bit of attention. I sit as still as possible and wait my turn to stand before the man in the black cloak.

"Josephine Bristol. You have been charged with first-degree murder. How do you plead?"

First-degree? I killed him, yeah, but they're suggesting I premeditated the whole thing.

Mrs. Malkovich speaks for me. "We plead not guilty, Your Honor."

At least she didn't say *guilty*.

"Very well," the judge says. "Bail is set at one million dollars, preliminary hearing is scheduled for March 20." *Slam!*

"Come along." We settle into another room, and Mrs. Malkovich plops her bags on the table and fumbles around for her tablet, yet she seems to be having difficulty seeing anything because she's blinking so much. "How are you, Miss Bristol?"

Oh, I donno. I spent the night in a holding cell with a handful of flesh-hungry women and I've just been charged with first-degree murder and I'm cold and starving and exhausted, but other than that I'm freaking fantastic!

"I'm a little … lost."

Mrs. Malkovich doesn't bother to look up from her rummaging. "Yes, that's understandable. This is a confusing and arduous process, but we'll get through it together, won't we?"

"When can I see my mom?"

"From what I understand your mother is in the hospital. I'll make certain she'll come and testify on your behalf, don't you worry."

Was there a concern that she wouldn't? "Did Rick hurt her? I knew he was a brain hacker, that's the only explanation for any of this. His brother is in on it, he has to be. That's why all the equipment was gone."

Finally, she squints at me. "What equipment?"

"The brain hacking equipment. The optrodes and lasers and tools and everything else."

"There was no equipment found at the crime scene."

"It was there. I swear it. I don't know what happened to it."

"Miss Bristol, I need you to say focused on the trial. The man you murdered—*supposedly* murdered—was under surveillance by ACTA, on suspicion of his ties to Alias."

"So he *was* a brain hacker?"

"There's no evidence of that, and even if there is I can't discuss it with you. But there will be a lot of questions as to what you knew about him. Accusations will come falling out of the sky, and the details of this case are going to be misconstrued now that you're a media sensation."

"Media sensation?"

She raises her eyebrows and blinks a few times. "Oh dear, you've been on the news since last night. You're a huge story, the fancy PEAD girl who murdered a man. And not to mention the *way* you murdered him. I mean … holy Moses. They nicknamed you The Schoolgirl Slicer."

I feel like I'm choking. "The *what*?"

"Take a look at this."

She plays a video on her tab of me being escorted from Rick's house through the shouting crowd on the lawn. Flashing cameras bounce light off my shimmering outfit, at least the parts not covered in blood. With my gaping eyes and the curl of my lips I look like an animal fresh from a kill. *The Schoolgirl Slicer.* Yup, sounds about right.

"That's already on the news?"

"Oh yes. The city is eating up your story. It's unfortunate that the murder may be tied to Alias and the ACTA investigation, but we'll do our best to keep the two stories separate. For the sake of the trial."

"I didn't know he was under surveillance. I killed him because he was hurting my mom."

She blinks furiously. "Don't say that! Never admit to the crime, especially before the trial. Your position is sensitive since the details about your mother's state at the time of the crime are debatable."

"How are they debatable? She's in the hospital. He had an optic tube up her nose. They can tell she's been hurt."

"There's no evidence Mr. Salazar did any harm to Lauren Bristol's brain, especially with the absence of this *equipment* you're going on about. Optrode light stimulation requires proprietary materials. It's highly unlikely any civilian would have access to such technology. And remember, there was no evidence of it at the scene of the crime."

"It was there. Somebody must have cleaned it up."

"Miss Bristol, I suggest you take care with what you say. I'd hate to see you implicate yourself any further. In a case with so much media attention, the jury is likely to have made up their minds previous to the trial. I'll do what I can during the jury selection to weed out the predecided from the pool, but it's a challenging task. And then there's the crime. Self-defense is one thing. Manslaughter, the accidental result of death, would have worked in your favor. But you sawed a man's head in half and ripped his brain out. In the eyes of a jury, that's clear intent to kill. To the world you are a cold-blooded murderer."

Cold-blooded murderer? Does she even know what happened last night? What evidence *does* she have to go on? And what about the brain scan? Is there any argument on my behalf, anything at all for my defense? She's assuming I'm guilty!

My hands shake uncontrollably and there's nothing I can do to keep them from reaching out …

I leap across the table and wrap my fingers around Mrs. Malkovich's damp neck. I clamp down, right over the pulsing veins in her throat. Her blinking eyes go berserk and her face turns blue—

There's a sharp zap of electricity in my side and I'm thrown back onto the floor. I look up to see Mrs. Malkovich gasping for air and rubbing her throat just as I feel a pinch in my arm and the world goes dark.

14 until proven deadly

The last few days have been a blur. I have been confined to my own cell with clear plexiglass walls, pumped full of sedatives to keep me calm, driven in an armored car to another building, and dragged from room to room to meet an assortment of people who make no secret the distance they're keeping from me.

This is my life now. Tracker cuffs. Full-body jumpers. Plexiglass walls. Armed escorts. Drugs.

I miss my mom. I wonder if she's okay, if she's safe in the hospital. I miss the dads and their goofy humor. I miss Madri and her sturdy friendship. I miss Lyle so much that whenever I think of him my heart feels like it's breaking out through my ribs.

I don't know what day it is, or how long I've been here, but today I'm being moved again. Ibanez and Bell drag me through a garage to an awaiting armored vehicle, and I'm stuffed inside. My cuffs magnetically link to the seat, securing me in place. Once my eyes adjust to the dimness of the cab, I see Mrs. Malkovich blinking and sweating. There's a panel of plexiglass between us, yet she still flinches when I spot her. Remnants of bruises discolor her neck.

"All right, you just stay calm."

I am calm. They've got me so pumped full of sedatives I can't be anything *but* calm.

"You're probably surprised to see me," she says. "I wanted to drop your case. Other than the fact that you tried to *kill* me, you're a losing gamble. But you're a media sensation. They can't get enough of your story. You're the biggest criminal drama since The Nightclub Clubber."

Don't tell me that. The Nightclub Clubber was a serial killer. He was the modern-day equivalent of Jack the Ripper. I'm no Jack the Ripper. Or Nightclub Clubber. I'm Jo Bristol, The Schoolgirl Slicer. Ah, shit.

"Regardless," Mrs. Malkovich says, "my boss insists that I remain your attorney because it's great publicity for the firm. And I'll give you the best trial possible because this is my goddamn neck on the line." She winces and puts a hand on her throat. "So if I remain your lawyer, can you promise you won't try to kill me again?"

Actually, no, I can't promise that. "Yeah, of course."

She nearly smiles. "Good. We're on our way to your preliminary hearing. I realize this is bad timing since we haven't had the opportunity to go over your case, but is there anything you'd like to tell me beforehand?"

Yes: my tick made me do it. "I didn't intend to kill him."

The look of shock on her face is incredible. "Really? You didn't think ripping out his brain was going to end his life?"

"No, I mean … I was in a kind of dream state. I wasn't aware I was doing it."

"Huh." She thumbs her tab. "Your brain scan didn't show any abnormalities."

"I'd also taken a spinner earlier that night."

"Nope, no signs of intoxication either." She peers at me. "Listen, Miss Bristol, you're not gonna fool anyone by making up stories like this. I'm your lawyer. If you're not clean with me—"

"I'm telling the truth." If I weren't drugged out, I'd be yelling at her. Instead, my voice is calm and spooky.

"The more lies you pile up, the more difficult this defense will be."

"It's the truth. I didn't mean to kill him."

She lets out a long sigh. "Look, I'll be honest. I don't trust you. You strangled me. I don't understand why the doctors say your brain is normal because you're clearly not. But this isn't about what I think. This is about a trial. I am to do my job and prove I'm a good lawyer, and I will not let you interfere with that. Do you understand?"

This woman is lucky there is plexiglass between us because I hear the ringing in my ears. My own damn lawyer wants to send me to prison. I don't have a fighting chance of making it through this.

The car stops and the door swings open and Ibanez is there with a push-pin syringe that he plunges into my arm. More drugs. The ringing fades.

There are hundreds of people outside the courthouse, and I'm led right through all of them. They shout my name, shout my media-created nickname, shout obscenities, shout sympathies, shout marriage proposals. Cameras flash, lights blind, people swarm. Please welcome the Schoolgirl Slicer. Stay for the aftershow, bloody brains all around.

I'm locked inside a plexiglass cube on one side of the courtroom. The judge's voice booms through speakers next to my ears. Mrs. Malkovich argues over misleading evidence. The prosecutor looks like a rippling ape and points at me a lot. A projector comes down from the ceiling and displays a holographic recreation of the crime scene, of me with the saw and Rick with his brain in his lap. The prosecutor waves his arms wildly. The judge is horrified. Mrs. Malkovich peers at me from the corner of her eye.

It is decided there is enough evidence for a trial. Due to the nature of my crime, I'll be tried as an adult—no juvenile detention for the Schoolgirl Slicer. I'm released from the cage, escorted through the flashing cameras and shouting crowd, and driven back to the jail.

I'm exhausted and saturated with drugs, but my day is not yet over. I'm taken to another room with a table in the middle and a plexiglass divider through it. I'm told to sit down. A door on the other side of the glass opens. And I see Lyle.

I jump to my feet and let out some animalistic whimper, and Lyle stands frozen in the doorway, holding some kind of large paper rolled up in his hand. Nolan and Dylan push their way in and their solemn expressions do nothing to raise my spirits.

"Oh my sweet, Jo!" Nolan says. "I'm so sorry this ever had to happen to you."

I don't want them to see me like this, so I bow my head in shame.

"How are you?" says Dylan. "Have you been hurt? Are they treating you well?"

"She's in jail," Lyle says from the doorway.

"I know, I know," Dylan says. "It's just ... jeez, Jo. I can't believe this is happening."

"It's all over the news," Nolan says. "They're calling you—"

"The Schoolgirl Slicer," I mumble into my chest. "Yeah, I know."

Nolan leans in. "I'm sure you're worried about your mom. They tell me she's been moved into a hospital in the San Fernando Valley. Have you heard from her?"

"No. I haven't seen her. She didn't even show up for my hearing."

"Well, I'm sure she'll be fine. Jo, just know ... we know who you are, okay? We still love you. All of us."

"Thank you." I choke on my words, but I must do my best to keep from crying. I will not cry. Not in jail.

A voice comes over the intercom. *"Bristol, three minutes."*

"Jeez, we barely got here," Dylan says. Nolan nods him away and they make room on their side of the desk.

Lyle finally looks at me. He's devastated. Angry. And something else that I can't read in that face I have so longed to see again. He comes over and stands near the glass and I lean against the divider to be as close to him as possible. When our eyes meet, the waterworks start. I can't stop bawling. Lyle looks at me with a most woeful expression, and it makes me sob even harder. So much for not crying in jail.

"Bristol, one minute."

Lyle clears his throat. "They threw it out, Jo."

"What are you talking about?" I heave through sobs. "Who threw what out?"

"The paintings. The ones from your dad. They're all gone. Your friend Madri found me on Connex and told me. She kept one. She said she knew you'd be heartbroken, but even more if you knew they threw out this one."

He opens what he's had rolled in his hand and holds it flat against the glass. It's my favorite of my dad's art pieces, the one with the girl holding a paintbrush in the middle of a burning city.

I collapse onto the floor as the guards come in to retrieve me. Lyle wipes his eyes, and I know he's crying too. He keeps the painting there against the plexiglass as the guards grab my arms and drag me across the room.

I should have done it. I should have done the one thing I never wanted to: I should have told someone about my tick. The whole truth, not just the nicer details like I told Madri. I should have come clean and let them send me to the labs to adjust my brain neurons, as they did with Harley, as Lyle suggested. I should have fixed myself for the safety of everyone else.

But no. I did none of that. And here I am.

Innocent until proven guilty. Isn't that a law? Bill of Rights? I should know this, I was a PEAD kid before they kicked me out, before my dad slit his wrists and my mom went nuts and started dating a brain-hacking druggie, before I became the monster I knew I always was but never wanted to admit to.

I am not innocent. According to my lawyer, I shouldn't even be getting this trial.

Today is the day. Spectators pack the courtroom and watch as I'm led to my plexiglass cube, like I'm some circus freak on display. The whole Los Feliz neighborhood is here. Lyle and the dads, Madri and her mom, Harley, Zander and Matteo, and the Baez Sisters. Even Principal Torres. They're watching me, shooting disgraceful stares through the glass of my cube. I want them all to go away. *Please stop looking at me … Please.*

Officer Bell is called to the witness stand to present the evidence from the crime scene. There's the bloody saw, my own DNA samples and fingerprints, the holo images of Rick and his brain. The jury is horrified, they sneer at me from across the courtroom. One juror gets sick and has to be excused. The prosecutor smiles and Mrs. Malkovich flutters her eyelashes and rubs her neck.

A witness for the prosecution is brought forward, some stuffy neurosurgeon in a thick suit. Holo-projectors show a twirling 3D image of my brain. The ape man asks a question and laughs, acting like he's some kind of court-ordered jester.

The neurosurgeon laughs right along, somehow in on the joke. "Well, as you can see from the scans—and, might I add, these were taken with the latest and most accurate FutureTech technology—the defendant's brain shows no signs of abnormal behavior. In the brain of a violent psychopath, I would expect to see a decreased or damaged prefrontal cortex, but that is not the case with the defendant."

The prosecutor folds his arms. "These scans were taken after her arrest. Her brain could have been acting abnormally prior to the scan, could it not?"

The neurosurgeon smirks. "Yes, well as I said, we have the *latest* in FutureTech technology. If the defendant had been acting under some kind of anomalous influence, the scans would have recognized the left-over effects of the activity—a kind of residue, if you will. Her brain is, by all accounts, perfectly normal."

Perfectly normal, sure. That's why I'm locked in a plexiglass cube with enough sedatives to knock out a horse.

The prosecutor smiles at the line of jurors. "So, doctor, in your professional opinion, the defendant did in fact commit this crime with a conscious intent?"

The neurosurgeon scrunches his nose at me. "In my professional opinion, the defendant is no psychopath. She knew exactly what she was doing. There isn't anything wrong with her brain to justify any light therapy or neurological adjustment. It's a shame, really, I'd have enjoyed the challenge."

A few observers in the room chuckle. Go ahead, laugh. I'm so far up this creek I might as well become a salmon.

Mrs. Malkovich calls her own scientist, because apparently one brain-scrambler isn't enough. This guy isn't quite as confident as the prosecutor's; his eyes hide under floppy graying hair, and he constantly scratches the shadow of scruff on his cheek.

"Dr. Frey," says Mrs. Malkovich, "I understand you study unconventional and experimental neurology in San Diego, is that correct?"

The neurologist squirms in his seat, his voice barely audible to the room. "Um, yes."

"Speak up, Dr. Frey," the judge orders.

The twitchy man clears his throat. "Sorry, yes. I study abnormal brains. Mostly, those with mental disorders."

"Clearly, this is not a crime committed by a normal teenage girl," says Mrs. Malkovich. "You stated in your assessment of the defendant's brain scan that she does in fact have some abnormal cognitive capabilities. Can you elaborate on that?"

Dr. Frey glances at me, then quickly looks back at my twirling 3D brain. "Well…" he clears his throat again "…her medial temporal lobe has a highly engaged pathway with her visual cortex. This is typically associated with a photographic memory. But when I took a closer look, I realized something else; she has both an enlarged hippocampus and large amygdalae, and both are highly active in her visual encoding. Yet further, despite her enlarged amygdalae, there is a considerable amount of memory engrams stored in her hippocampus which lack emotional encoding."

Mrs. Malkovich twists to glance at the panel of jurors, most of whom are not even watching the interview. "Dr. Frey, if you will, please, in laymen's terms?"

"Right." He shifts in his seat. "Typically, someone with enlarged amygdale will suffer from anxiety disorders because every memory passed through has a higher concentration of negative emotions encoded onto it, meaning most memories relate to strong emotional connections. This girl stores visual memories at a high capacity, but her enlarged amygdalae does not encode *any* emotional tags onto those memory engrams. It's as though there are certain visual memories stored in her brain that are completely disassociated from everything else, including emotion."

Mrs. Malkovich flips her hair over her shoulder. "So, your assessment is that her memories lack emotional connections. Could this mean the defendant lacks the normal empathy regarded with violence?"

"Not necessarily," Dr. Frey says as he digs his fingernails into his cheek. "If that were the case, her memory engrams would be encoded with tags of reward, causing violence to give her pleasure, but these stored engrams are completely devoid of emotion altogether. It's unusual. I've never seen anything like it. But I can't determine how those engrams were stored without emotional encoding in the first place. If I could further examine—"

The prosecutor waves his hand. "Objection, Your Honor. The witness had his chance to evaluate the data."

"But there's more to study," Dr. Frey says before the Judge can butt in. "The emotionless engrams are taking up a huge chunk of her brain. It's like the information is just sitting there, waiting to be used."

Mrs. Malkovich pulls her shoulders up to her ears, as though to hide the bruises on her neck. "What you're suggesting, doctor, is that she suffers from a form of emotional instability, which would prove my defense of an abnormality."

"No, that's not my interpretation." Dr. Frey waves his arm, then pulls it back. "According to my data, her brain is quite remarkable."

Mrs. Malkovich wrings her hands. "Dr. Frey, I called you to testify on the mental abnormality of my client, not to present evidence for the prosecution."

"Well … I … There's not …" Whatever Dr. Frey wants to say just won't come out, and Mrs. Malkovich has gone red in the face. The prosecutor twirls in his chair, letting the whole room see his smug smile.

"Have you nothing more to offer my defense argument?" says Mrs. Malkovich.

"The investigation requires further examination," Dr. Frey says hurriedly. "If I could be allowed to scan her brain myself, with my own equipment—"

The prosecutor laughs. The jury laughs. The spectators laugh. The judge tries his best to conceal his smile. Everyone finds this ordeal hilarious—everyone except me and my pathetic excuse for a lawyer.

"Dr. Frey," the judge says, "unless you are requesting scientific review of the admitted evidence in regards to the charges against the defendant, I cannot allow any delays in this trial. Is this your intent?"

The neurologist sinks in his chair. "No. I suppose not."

And with that, Dr. Frey is dismissed.

The next witness for my defense is called. Someone else to tear me down, someone else to stuff me in a package, wrap it with a bow, and ship me off to hell. Who's it gonna be now?

"I'd like to call to the stand, Lauren Bristol."

Mom! Where have you been? I've been locked behind plexiglass walls for weeks and you've not once come to thank me for saving your life from that pathetic asshole you called your boyfriend. Am I so disgraceful that you have abandoned your own daughter?

My mom walks to the witness stand, dressed in brand-new business clothes. She won't even look at me, but everyone else does. I'm so furious I could scream. I hear the noise echoing in the cube and I realize I *am* screaming. Mrs. Malkovich waves at me to shut up, but I just keep screaming. I hear the ringing in my ears. A guard comes up to the glass and pokes a syringe through. It hits my arm and I'm looking forward to subduing the fury, but it's barely enough to make me dizzy. It won't be enough to calm the pull of my tick, I know it won't.

My mom's voice comes through the speaker. Her voice is dull, her body stiff, shoulders pulled back and ears flat against her head as if in a perpetual state of hypnosis. "I met Rick three years ago. I was a Security Software Programmer at FutureTech and he was a laser repairman, so we worked together frequently. We began dating shortly after my husband died a year ago."

She's gone. My mom was my one chance at redemption, but her tick has overtaken her. Mrs. Malkovich doesn't know the difference, so she continues her questioning.

"I understand he was let go because of drug abuse?"

"That's what they claimed, yes."

"Were you the victim of any emotional or mental abuse from Mr. Salazar?"

"It was mostly verbal, a lot of yelling. He was frustrated about having lost his job."

Don't you do that, Mom. Don't you dare make Rick look good.

"And what about the night of March 11?" says Mrs. Malkovich. "Can you tell me about that?"

"Rick went out with his brother. They came back intoxicated. He yelled at me about having lost my own job and then I fell asleep."

"What did you see when you awoke?"

Come on, Mom. You have to remember something about that night. You have to remember the stolen equipment. The nosebleeds. Look at me, Mom. Look at me and tell the truth. I'm begging you.

"I woke up and I saw my daughter holding a saw. She was all bloody. And Rick was dead."

"Your daughter? You're referring to the defendant?"

"Yes. That's right."

Snap out of this, Mom! You have to remember something!

Mrs. Malkovich's eyes twitch around the room. "I understand there were some allegations of illegal optrode technology in the victim's apartment, yet the investigators did not find any. Can you tell me about that?"

My mom flinches, but keeps on going. "I don't know anything about that. I don't believe Rick stole any equipment. I don't know what he would have done with it if he had."

He used it to *hack your brain*!

What is happening? This is supposed to be my defense? This is batshit crazy madness! My mom was the one person who might have been able to keep me from spending the rest of my life in prison, and she won't even try. I don't know if she's even looked at me. I hate her. I hate her tick. I knew it—I *knew* my mom's tick is worse than mine. Yeah, my tick made me kill someone and strangle my own lawyer, but at least my tick doesn't do *this*.

The prosecutor is next. He drills my mom about me breaking the Zone violations, about my supposed drug problem, about my violent history, about my complete lack of respect for the law.

"Mrs. Bristol, I understand the deceased Ricardo Salazar was under surveillance by ACTA, is that correct?"

My mom doesn't even blink. "I was unaware of that until they mentioned it on the news."

The prosecutor tilts his head. "Are you aware that he *was* in fact stealing scanning lasers from FutureTech as part of an operation for the cyber-terrorism organization Alias-X?"

"Your Honor!" Mrs. Malkovich hollers. "If there is evidence of this stolen material, then it should have been presented to the defense. This is evidence *for* the defense. What use does the prosecution have for undermining their own arguments?"

The judge leans over the bench. "Sir, are you switching sides?"

The prosecutor grins. "Your Honor, the state has acquired new information to explain the motivations of the defendant to murder the victim. To complete my argument of this conspiracy, I must continue questioning the witness."

Mrs. Malkovich starts to protest, but the judge waves her off. "Continue," he says.

The prosecutor nods and turns back to my mom. "I have recently learned that you, too, were under investigation for assisting Ricardo Salazar with his connection to Alias. Mrs. Bristol, what do you know about The Plan?"

The Plan? That's what the Mean Lady Agent asked about in ZT Zone police station. What is *The Plan* and what does it have to do with *me*?

My mom sways in her chair. "I was just doing my job."

"Are you denying the accusations by ACTA that you were not only tampering with security programming at FutureTech, but that you were doing so under the guidance of Ricardo Salazar?"

Wait, *what*? I don't have a clue what he's talking about. And my mom just sits there, taking the bullshit the ape-man throws at her. Mom! Wake up! We're both drowning here! Wake! Up!

Mrs. Malkovich jumps to her feet. "Objection, Your Honor! The witness is not the one on trial!"

The prosecutor waves his arms in the air. "Your Honor, I am presenting evidence that the Salazar Brothers were using Lauren

Bristol to illegally penetrate the security systems of FutureTech for the use of Alias-X, and that she and the defendant Josephine Bristol *conspired to murder* Mr. Salazar to hide their own involvement in The Plan!"

What.

The.

Hell.

Everything sounds muffled, like hands are covering my ears. My body tenses and suddenly I am moving forward.

I run at the prosecutor at full speed, my fists stuffed in iron gloves. I take one jab, then another, and another, his face is bloodied, sunken in, beaten to a pulp—

The guard pokes me with another syringe and this time the drugs are strong enough to tear me from the vision, and I collapse onto the floor. My hands are throbbing. There are red smears of blood on the glass. Everyone is looking at me, their eyes wide, their mouths hanging open, their faces ashen. Mrs. Malkovich has her hands at her neck. The prosecutor is disgusted. And my mom has finally turned to me.

Mom, keep looking at me, please. I see you in there somewhere, trapped behind those blank eyes. What did they do to you? Did they hack you? Did the tick overtake you? I know you're in there, Mom. Please, more than ever, *I need you.*

Slam! Slam! Slam! goes the gavel. "Order!"

People find their seats, their eyes glued on me.

"Your Honor," the prosecutor says, "the witness is still on the stand and is required to answer my questions."

My mom turns away and gazes off into the blank part of her mind once more. "I don't know anything about it."

The prosecutor's jaw drops. "Mrs. Bristol, you are under oath. If you're found guilty of perjury—"

"I don't know anything."

"Mrs. Bristol! Did you conspire against the Salazar Brothers?"

"*Objection*!" Mrs. Malkovich jumps to her feet. "Your Honor, all ACTA investigations are sensitive material, and unless the prosecutor has acquired this material, then he has no basis upon which to back these claims!"

"Yes, all right," says the judge. "*Do* you have any evidence for these accusations?"

The prosecutor huffs. "No, Your Honor."

"Very well. Objection sustained!"

"But it is an active investigation and I can prove it!"

The judge won't have it. "Do you have any more relevant questions for this witness?"

The prosecutor sulks back to his chair. "I have no further questions."

I'm curled on the floor of my cube, but I feel all eyes in the courtroom on me—Lyle, the jury, the press, the Los Feliz groupies—but there's one pair in particular that draws my attention. It's my mom. There is life in her eyes. Finally. Only now it's too late.

Mrs. Malkovich notices the exchange and quietly steps up to the podium. "Your Honor, I request a redirect."

"Continue, Mrs. Malkovich."

"Mrs. Bristol, is there anything you would like to say on behalf of the defendant, your daughter?"

There's a really long pause. No, she doesn't have anything to say. Good. Get her out of here before she does any more damage.

"Jo's a good kid. She's smart … maybe too smart." Her voice cracks. "It hasn't been easy for her, all these changes in her life. I think she did the best she could. And whatever happened that night, she did it for the same reason that she does anything in her life … because she had to."

She's back. My mom came back just in time.

And then I see him. Santino Salazar. He stands up, he's got something in his hand. A gun. Aimed at my mom. He fires.

15 contingency plan

Two shots. One at my mom. One at me. The bullet ricochets off my reinforced plexiglass cube and hits a bystander. The courtroom erupts in total pandemonium. Officer Bell tackles Santino Salazar. Officer Ibanez backs away, his gun holster empty. Armed guards burst into the room. The windows black out and bright lights flood every corner. Someone runs for the stand toward my mom, who is hunched over the rail. All of this happens in a matter of seconds and I'm watching it in slow motion.

"Have you been hit?" Mrs. Malkovich shouts over the noise. "Are you hurt?"

I feel the pinch of a syringe in my side. I don't want anymore drugs. My brain is mush already and my mom has been shot. I try my best to stand but my legs give out and a darkness fills my eyes like thick oil running down the side of a glass bottle.

* * *

My eyelids weigh a ton as I open them. The darkness hovers in the corners of my sight. My brain swirls in my skull. My hands ache with every throb of blood through my veins.

The room comes into focus, an infirmary. I'm tucked into a bed. Someone is here, a man, with a dark goatee and colorful tattoos all over his neck and arms. It's an Alias terrorist—a Mexican sympathizer come to avenge the death of his fallen brother Ricardo Salazar and finish off what Santino started.

"Whoa, calm down! You'll pull out the tubes, and from the looks of it you need what they're feeding you."

The man is talking. He looks Mexican but I don't hear an accent. He's just sitting here, right next to me, not trying to suffocate me with a pillow. I don't know what he's waiting for.

"Here, hang on a minute," the man says. He taps the terminal beside me and a warm, soothing substance flows through the tubes and into my veins.

"There. Better? Hospital drugs are the best, I swear, there's nothing like it on the street. Once I broke my hand on purpose just so I could pump myself full of this shit. Best day ever." He opens and closes his left fist a few times. "Still hurts sometimes, though."

He's playing nice. He's going to butter me up before he kills me. I try to scream for the guard but my mouth is glued shut.

"You coming around now?"

He stands and leans over me and studies my face, then breaks into a smile. He's younger than I first thought, and his hazel eyes glimmer under the lights and match his wide, sparkling grin. He's sexy when he smiles. Why am I thinking about him being sexy? The guy is about to murder me and now I can't stop staring at his neck tattoos. There's a white wolf in there and it's really quite beautiful. What the hell is wrong with me? It's the drugs. It must be the drugs.

"Oh, yeah, sorry," he says. "Probably should have covered up more. That was my fault. I didn't really think about it, but after what you've been through—"

"Who are you?" Oh thank god my mouth still works. I just hope he heard me because I don't have the strength to repeat it.

He chuckles and pulls his grin even wider, showing off a perfectly straight row of teeth. "I'm your friend."

I shake my head and it makes me dizzy. "Don't kill me."

"You think I'm here to kill you? Oh, okay, yeah I don't blame you for thinking that … but I'm not. And anyway, if I was here to kill you, you'd be dead already, wouldn't you?"

Is that supposed to make me feel better? "Where is my mom?"

"Ah! Yes, your mom is fine. She wasn't hurt too bad, just her shoulder. Salazar is a terrible shot, lucky for her."

"Who are you?"

"You're repeating yourself." There's that grin again. Dammit, stop doing that. "All right," he says. "My name is Diego Felix. The higher-ups call me Oscar Romeo, but you can call me Felix."

"Get away from me."

"Hey now, you might wanna be nice to me. I'm your last line of defense if you wanna get out of this in one piece. I know your trial seems like a shitstorm right now, but Santino did you a favor by shooting up the courtroom. Officer Ibanez is under investigation for his involvement, and half of the evidence of your case might get tossed."

My eyes finally focus and I can sit up a little. "What are you talking about?"

Felix paces back and forth at the foot of my bed. "This isn't just about you. You heard what the prosecutor said back there, right? About your mom hacking into the FutureTech security systems? It's all true. For the last year, ACTA had her and Ricardo Salazar under surveillance. ACTA was close to busting the whole operation open when you went and killed the bastard. And—may I say—*dude*, that was some hardcore shit. I don't think I'd have the balls to cut some guy's head off."

"My mom does not work for Alias!"

"Rick did. He was being used as a pawn by Alias to hack the system. But he wasn't smart enough to do it all himself, so he used your mom."

"She would never agree to working for cyber terrorists."

"She didn't. At least not *knowingly*. Rick may have been a drugged-out tool, but he figured her out. He found her weakness. He realized she's a little—" He whistles and circles his finger around his ear.

"My mom is not crazy!"

"Okay, fine. Maybe not crazy, but she's definitely not all there. She's got major selective amnesia and some other scientific shit I don't understand. In any event, he used her amnesia to trick her into hacking FutureTech."

"So it's true, Rick is a brain hacker?"

"Not technically, no. It's more likely he was using optrodes to trigger preexisting opsin genes."

"I knew it! I saw the equipment. Someone cleaned it up, you have to believe me."

"I *do* believe you. Alias has their own sweepers. That's the whole point—in and out without a trace. There's no way to trace the hacking, especially since your mom already had the opsin genes implanted in her neurons years ago to treat her depression."

"My mom isn't depressed. My dad was the one with the mental problems."

"She had postpartum depression after you were born. It's all in her records. She went through that light therapy bullshit, and from then on she had the open socket, if you will. All Rick had to do was plug a fiber optic cable up her nose, set the programming, flip the light switch, and *ta-da*, your mom's a bothead!"

"She's not a bothead. She was still functioning."

"Was she?" He puts his hands on his hips and tilts his head. "Really, *was she*?"

This guy is pissing me off. "She just forgets things. She always has."

"There's more to it than that. You know there is."

"If you know all this, then why can't the neurologists and detectives prove it?"

"Because the scientists work for ACTA, and ACTA is run by FutureTech. It's all a gross love-fest."

"All right, fine. But what about me?"

"What about you, Jo?"

"What's wrong with my brain?"

He bows his head and sighs, then sits by me on the bed. He smells like leather and gunpowder, like a cowboy. Not that I've ever met a cowboy, but I've spent plenty of time fanaticizing about them and—dammit, there I go again.

"Jo, no one can agree on an explanation for why—or how—you were capable of doing any of this. A one-time event in a fit of rage and fear because you found your mom being hacked? That's a believable story. I believe that story. But strangling your lawyer? Punching the glass at the courtroom? Assaulting your friend's mom in Beverly Hills?"

"Mrs. Mehra?"

"Yeah, you bet she filed those charges against you. They put her on TV, had this whole panel discussion about teen violence."

"How do you know all this?"

"I've been studying your file. I've been getting to know you vicariously, and I like you, Jo. I don't think you are who they say you are. I know you're not a monster."

"How can you be so sure?"

"You're too pretty to be a monster." He smiles again and goose bumps rise on my arms. "And I've seen your paintings. Monsters don't make art like that."

"That's a stupid thing to say."

He chuckles. "Of course it is. The reality is you could be a goddamn supermodel and have the mind of a pedophile serial killer, but that's not my point. Whatever it is that's got your head wrapped up in this violent spiral will be your undoing if you don't find a way to control it."

I've been having this conversation with this guy for several minutes now, and I still have no clue who he is or why he's here or how he cares to know all this about me, but there's something familiar about him. I feel like I know him. I have the vague sensation that I've met him before.

Regardless, if this is all true—if he really is here to help me—then I have to come out with it. I have to tell him. I can't get myself caught in yet another net because I was too afraid or too ashamed or too proud to admit that I need help. I have to tell the truth because if I don't, there's no saying what will happen to me. He may be my last hope.

"Um … I have a tick."

"The bug?"

"No."

"Personality tick."

"Yeah."

His brow flutters in a wave. "Yeah, well, don't we all …"

"I have visions."

He narrows his eyes and leans in. "Visions of what?"

I can barely whisper the words. "I have visions of killing people."

Felix's face is a flurry of emotions. First his eyes go wide, and then he tilts his head in thought, squinting at me. "How bad are they? Violent? Bloody? Gory?"

I nod.

"How often?"

"Nearly every day since I was a kid."

He shifts his jaw. "They were all in your head?"

"No one even knew about them."

"So what happened?"

"I don't know. They're not just visions anymore. A week before my seventeenth birthday I acted one out on my friend. Not full-out, just … pretended. Then Mrs. Mehra—"

"The assault."

It sounds bad when he puts it that way. But really, how can *assault* be worse than *murder*? "I wasn't aware I was doing it. Same with Rick. I had the vision, and when I came out of it Rick was dead and the equipment was gone. I tried to explain that to my lawyer, but she doesn't believe me. She doesn't trust me. I thought it was a vision, I swear."

"They didn't find anything in your brain scan—"

"But I'm telling you, it was a vision!"

"Jo, I know." Felix takes my hand even though the cuffs are still attached to the bed. My knuckles are bruised and bloody from hitting the cube wall, and all I can think about is how warm and comforting his fingers are. "I believe you, okay? I know that doesn't mean much because right now your lawyer is making a plea deal with the prosecutor and you *will* go to prison, that I can guarantee. It's gonna be a really shitty time for you. I'm sorry."

I feel like someone's just run me over with a truck.

"There's no way to prove anything about your visions and they've yet to find any evidence of the optic equipment."

"Santino—" I start, and Felix squeezes my hand.

"Santino Salazar will go to jail for shooting up the courtroom, but for now there's still no evidence to tie him to Alias. That's not going to help you."

"Then why are you here?"

Felix pauses and lets out a huge gust of air. "I work for ACTA. A subgroup, code name: Lone Wolf. We're part of the ground force."

"You're an agent?"

He winces and looks away quickly. "Not exactly. I was in the army before all this, before Washington got stuck with their dicks in their hands and forgot to press the *military funding* button. My army division was dismantled, and in came ACTA with the offer of a hefty compensation for being an active investigator. It's my job to sort out inconsistencies in all things related to security and cyber hackings. So here I am."

"What does that have to do with me?"

"I've been watching your case since the beginning," he says, and his eyes come back to mine. "You've got one homicide and an attempted murder on your file. It's a clear line to the pen, but there's a blip in the radar, Jo. You killed a very active Alias member, and in the process revealed a very active Alias infiltration and the possible involvement of the LA Police Department. You somehow ended up in the middle of it, holding the sharp end of the stick. Your trial has Alias-screwery written all over it, so I'm going to try and break your case out of state court and move it into the ACTA Criminal Division. With all these cracks in the case to start with, it might get thrown out completely."

I shake my head again and the whole room blurs. Felix taps the terminal and more drugs rush through my arm. "You're saying my killing Rick was a *good* thing."

I don't expect him to laugh. "Are you kidding? You snagged a loose thread in the whole Alias operation. ACTA now knows where the hacks originated in the FutureTech system. I just hope it's not too late."

"Too late for what?"

Felix rolls back his shoulders. "To stop The Plan."

There it is again. "What the hell is this *Plan*?"

"I think you know, Jo. The Plan is the invasion from Alias."

"Alias already tried their cyber attack. They failed."

"Alias is bigger now. Alias-*X*, remember? They've gone international. We've gotten weaker, and they've gotten stronger. We're in big trouble this time. The invasion is coming and there's no telling who—or what—they'll bring with them. Once it happens, the whole country is gonna go to hell."

"But I'll be in prison."

"Where do you think they send all those captured Alias members? Listen, Jo, the whole reason why I'm here is to tell you that I'm gonna try and get you out. I'm gonna do whatever it takes to get you out of that prison, but I can't if you screw up while you're in there. You've gotta keep your head straight, keep those visions under control."

I know I can't. I lost complete control over it a long time ago. But perhaps, maybe if they keep me in a drugged-out stupor, I might be able to keep on pretending my tick doesn't exist.

"What's going to happen next?"

"Well, we first have to hope your sentence isn't bad. Anything over twenty-five years and I'll never even get a hold of your case. But if your plea bargain goes well—if your lawyer cares about her career, she'll make sure it does—you'll spend a few years serving out your term while I'm busy getting the ACTA case organized."

The reality is starting to sink in. "I'm going to prison ..."

"You did murder someone, and since there is nothing in your brain scan to suggest a medical or psychological reason for it, *you* are to be held responsible for it. You'll do your time like they tell you to. But you can't screw this up, do you understand? This is important. One false move and it's all over. Any more visions or outbursts or any of that and you will be spending the rest of your life in prison and there will be nothing more I can do for you."

My head won't stop pounding. My mind hops from thought to thought, unable to focus on anything. I have a million questions to ask yet there is no forming the words.

"I don't know if I can do it."

"You have to. You so much as threaten someone with a toothbrush, you'll be screwed." I squint at him and he laughs to himself. "Sorry, I just can't get over … never mind. Just figure it out, okay?"

"I'll try …"

"You *have* to."

"I don't understand why you're helping me."

He takes my hand again. "Everyone is connected somehow, but that's not important right now."

"Tell me."

"I can't tell you yet. You need to focus on this first." His hazel eyes are fierce, focused, beautiful. "You will survive this, Jo Bristol."

I need to believe him.

16 four-piece suit

Twenty-five years.

"That's the best I could get. I tried for fifteen since you're a minor and your case ran off the rails when the victim's brother tried to kill your mother ... but you *did* strangle me, and there's no denying you're dangerous. If the judge had any hope for your rehabilitation, your sentence would have included light therapy with the brain adjusters, but the state cannot justify spending any funding on someone who shows no signs of remorse for her actions, or any general hope for the future.

"I must warn you, Miss Bristol, you're on thin ice. The warden knows you're prone to violent outbursts, and you'll be under strict surveillance. I advise you, keep your wits about you or you'll be in even more trouble than you are."

Yes, thank you, Mrs. Malkovich, for your kind and encouraging words. I'll remember how hard you tried to prove my innocence to keep me from entering into this hell. I'll remember your adorably blinking eyes every day when I'm locked in the darkness of prison for the next twenty-five years of my godforsaken life.

Piss off, Mrs. Malkovich. You're lucky I'm drugged.

"When can I see my mom?"

She's surprised I'm asking. "Your mom is back in the psychiatric hospital. Has no one informed you of this?"

Of course not. The only thing I've been told for the last few weeks is when it's time for my next drugging. "Will I be able to talk to her?"

She shrugs. Are you kidding me? Is there *anyone* here to see me off to prison?

No, there isn't.

You will survive this, Jo Bristol. That guy, Diego Felix. Who the hell is he? Why is he so intent on helping me? Me, the Schoolgirl Slicer, the nutjob brain extractor? He's convinced I can get through this, that I can survive to see the light of day again. I have to believe him. How, I don't know. But I can't go out like this. I can't live out the rest of my life engraved with an identity that does not define me. I am not a monster.

I must survive this.

These are my last moments on the outside. They stuff me in an orange jumper that is thick and stretchy and very tight. No place to conceal a weapon, even if I needed to. Then the tracker cuffs: one ring on each wrist, one on each ankle. The wrist cuffs snap together like magnets at a push of a button on the guard's tab. *Stand still. Sit down. Move here. Move there. Have more drugs.*

A guard comes to fetch me. "Time to go to the bridge."

The bridge is a room in the basement of the jail, a holding cell. The door opens and more women come in, wearing all different colors of jumpers. Some haven't bathed in weeks. One woman in red sits next to me and I nearly puke from her stench.

Another woman is as tall as a basketball player, her green jumper stretching to full-capacity. "Hey, they got you in a four-piece suit," she says, amused at my expense. She nods to my cuffs. "What 'cha do to get a top and bottom?"

All the other women are in wrist cuffs; I'm the only one with my ankles bound as well. I stare down at my hands, but the tall woman doesn't like that.

"Hey, girl, I asked you a question!"

Zap! go her electric cuffs. She hollers.

"Pipe down!" the guard says.

We're instructed to go outside. My ankle cuffs are magnetically linked as though tied together with a foot-long invisible rope. We shuffle through the door and there's a lot of pushing and shoving, hooting and insults. Someone bumps into me and I can't take a wide enough step to catch my balance and I topple into another woman—the tall one.

"*Oooh*, pretty white girl wanna get in on this?"

She grabs me by the collar of my jumper with both hands, and her cuffs are right against my chin when they *zap*. I've never been electrified before and it hurts like hell. My jaw clamps shut and I bite my tongue and taste blood. The big woman lets go and I fall to the floor.

"Hold it right there, you!" hollers a guard.

Everyone freezes in place and I'm still slumped on the ground. My mind is cleared, the zap must have shocked me out of the drugs. The ringing starts.

I take my cuffed arms and wrap them around the tall woman in a headlock—

"Bristol! Don't you dare move another muscle!"

My eyes focus. I'm not strangling the tall woman, yet based on my stance I was likely on my way to do so. She squints suspiciously, sizing me up even though she's a head taller.

"All right," says the guard. "We're getting on the bus. Any more nonsense from any of you and you're headed straight to the bin the moment we get to the facility. Got it?"

No one makes a peep. We're shuffled onto an armored electric bus with walls like vault doors and a label on the side that reads *FutureTech High-Security Transportation*, as though to make certain everyone on the outside knows the nature of the cargo. We're lined up, shoulder to shoulder, our cuffs magnetized to the seats. It's a miserably hot and tense two-hour drive east to the SoCal Institution for Women.

And it only gets worse from there.

I try my best to block it all out. I don't want to be witness to any of this madness, but the drugs have faded and I'm aware of everything. Most of these women know the drill. They line up where they're supposed to but make a fuss while doing it. They yell obscenities at the guards, and the guards yell back. Our photographs are taken, and the tall woman flips off the camera. My turn comes and everyone hoots at me to make a show like I'm a stripper. Then we're stuffed in body scanning chambers that peek into our insides, and when one woman is discovered to have contraband in her, there's more wrestling and cuff-zapping. The guards tackle the smuggler and she squirms on the floor. And then I'm zapped.

"*Aaouh*!" My body tenses and my wrists throb. It's worse than the zap at the bridge. I see a young guard holding a tab, and he's looking at me with a guilty expression. He glances at the tab and finds the right button and the smuggler hollers.

"Bristol!"

A giant female guard comes right for me. She's more than six feet tall with short reddish hair and a most unfriendly face, which could be due to the long, red scratch marks that stretch from her eye sockets down to her mouth like she'd been attacked by an angry monkey. But something about the hardness of her eyes gives me sense she always wears this soured expression.

She looks over the top of my head. "Are you Bristol?"

The crowd of women hushes, and then the whispering starts.

"*Bristol*?" one says.

"*Jo* Bristol?" another says. "*The* Jo Bristol?"

I've been made.

"*Oooh*! We got ourselves a celebrity in our house! The Schoolgirl Slicer, oh yeah!"

The women dance around and cheer, and then I feel another *zap* and every woman screeches.

"Quiet down!" says the giant female guard. "Bristol. Level Three. Come with me. Now."

She heads down a corridor away from the hooting women, and I scramble along taking the tiny steps that my magnetic anklets allow.

"My name is Hathaway. You have been assigned to me in high-security Level Three cell block. You will be wearing the full set of tracker cuffs at all times. If you so much as tamper with them, I'll put you straight in the bin."

Hathaway leads me down corridor after corridor, keeping her back to me. At the end of one is a set of escalators that are smooth until she waves her wristlet and two steps pop up. I cram in behind her and hug the rail on our way up to the next floor. She shuffles a bit, and I am nearly sent sliding back down.

She goes on, spurting a mantra that she's likely repeated a hundred times. "Level Three is for the most dangerous offenders, that's why you're orange. In Level Three you eat, sleep, and shower on my watch. I don't care if you're on the rag, have diarrhea, or want to call your mommy. You will do everything I tell you and don't do anything I tell you not to or what little privileges you have will be revoked indefinitely."

Down another corridor, through some more doors. Every inch of this place is made of steel and concrete. The air is cold and damp and every breath echoes. I have to shuffle my magnetically-linked feet just to keep up with the giant guard through the maze of hallways. It's exhausting. And she still hasn't looked at me.

"Dinner is served at seven on the dot. If you're not in the mess hall, you will go to bed without food. Lights out at ten, breakfast at seven a.m. You will be quiet, you will not engage the other prisoners, you will behave yourself, or you will not see the sun again for a very long time."

We reach a door marked *Level Three.* Hathaway waves her wristlet in front of the terminal, and a light flashes green and the door swings open, and we enter the next section. Dozens of individual cells line one side of the corridor, all sealed with a clear plexiglass walls. Cameras everywhere. Motion sensors. Siren horns. Everything labeled *by FutureTech.* It's like the corporation is taunting me, letting me know just how much of my life they've controlled: my dad's art, my mom's mind, and my freedom. I should get a tattoo, *Property of FutureTech*, right on my ass. Maybe I could get paid for advertising.

Near the end of the corridor, Hathaway stops at the cell marked 317, holds her wristlet against the terminal and the door slides open. She waves me inside and I stand in the middle of the strangely empty room, heaving because I'm out of breath. She hovers in the doorway and her eyes flicker around the cell, as she touches her scratched face with her fingertips. "Do I make myself clear, Bristol?"

I nod because I'm too afraid to speak and she hasn't approved it.

"Good," Hathaway says. "Do you have any questions before I leave?"

Which hundred should I start with? "When am I scheduled to get my drugs?"

She frowns and I'm afraid I've asked the wrong question. "What drugs?"

"The doctors and guards gave me sedatives. They help keep me calm."

Hathaway glances behind her through the door and then back over my head. "I'm not in charge of regulating any drugs. If you have a medical need for some, that will be in your report and the doctors on staff will administer them to you, but if you're just looking for flake, you're in big trouble. Once caught using you'll be headed straight to the bin. However, if they've been pumping you with jail sedatives, then I'm sorry to say you're in for a tough ride coming down off those. Dinner is at seven."

She doesn't so much as pause after her statement before leaving my cell. The glass door closes so fast I wonder how many people have lost arms in this place.

No drugs. She thinks I'm an addict. She thinks I just want to get high. I'm in this high-security prison with a twenty-five-year sentence because everyone in the city of Los Angeles thinks I'm a violent monster, and the only time I'm *not* is when I'm sedated. The drugs were going to be my only hope of getting through these first few years before Diego Felix comes to rescue me. I made a promise to him. I swore I was going to find a way to make it through this without causing any trouble.

But I'm in prison. With violent and angry women. Women who want to bully and harass me. Put me in a confined space with agitators like that and no drugs to subdue the tick, who knows what the hell I'll do.

17 all the girls

I know very little about life in prison, but I imagine if it's anything like public school, you become a target if you show any sign of weakness. It's a big flashing sign if they catch you crying. And I can't stop sobbing.

I want to lie down. I at least need to sit. It's been a long and bizarre day, and my cell doesn't have a bed. Why doesn't my cell have a bed? Do they expect me to sleep standing like a horse? The floor is disgusting, covered in some slimy gray material that I can't place as a natural substance. There's no way I'm sleeping down there. And what about a toilet? Or a bucket, at least? Do they think I am nothing more than a barn animal and expect me to shovel my own crap every morning?

I'm having a panic attack. My heart is pounding out of my chest and the tears are so thick in my eyes that I barely notice the terminal set into the wall behind thick glass with a display for the time and date and touch screen. I hover my finger over the icon of a bed and the camera dome above me lights green. Then there's a beep, and the opposite wall opens and a bed folds down.

Oh thank god. I don't have to sleep on the floor. I've stopped crying because of the distraction. I sit on the bed and the hard surface pokes my tailbone. This is not going to be the most comfortable place to spend the next quarter century of my life.

My eyes fly open and I jolt upright as the plexiglass door slides open. I don't remember falling asleep. The clock display reads 6:55. *Dinner is at seven.* My stomach is in knots, and I'm really not looking forward to community time, but I'm so afraid to disobey Hathaway's orders I'd eat a rotting fish in front of the entire hooting prison just to keep her happy.

There's a woman in an orange jumper at my door. She has very dark eyes set inside a very dark face. Her hair is cut short and she looks like she was pretty once, before time thinned out her skin and she got that scar across her cheek. Her eyes go up and down, up and down, scanning me.

"The last woman in this cell cut her own throat with a spoon." Her voice is as jagged as her expression. "*Candy*, we called her. She was my yard-wife. She died two days ago. You're in her bed." I don't know how to respond to that. The woman doesn't give me a chance anyway, for she disappears down the hallway without another word.

Locks beep, lights flash, and cameras scan me in every passageway, every door, and every stairway as I make my way through Level Three. As I pass through the threshold of the mess hall, my tracker cuffs yank me to the wall, slamming my face into the cold, steel plate, forming spots in my eyes.

"You'll learn to brace yourself, ya know," says a strangely chipper voice, and I turn to see a blond woman in the same position against the wall. "I broke my nose the first week. It seriously hurt like hell."

I can't say anything because my lips are throbbing. Scanners come down from the ceiling and the guards take roll call, and as soon as the magnets release us from the wall the whole group shuffles to the other side of the room. I stumble to the serving windows where robotic arms shove out plates of food that smell like eggs but look like soggy beans. I'm grateful I'm not hungry.

By the time I have my food, the rest of the women have found their seats. They're grouped together, like cliques in a school, huddled in tight bunches, matching appearances and dispositions. For a moment I hope there's a table for girls like me, but I'm the only skinny teenager from the PEAD program.

I've stood here too long. They're like wild animals, they can sense they're being watched. As if on cue, they all turn and look at me, catching me frozen in place, my lip swelling, my meal tray balanced on shaking arms.

I dump the contents of my meal tray onto the head of the first woman I see, then break my tray in half and jab the sharp end into her throat—

I can't even yelp before the woman has me by the neck. She's got at least two hundred pounds on me, wearing a jumper just like mine, and because of her size she looks like a busted orange, pulp and juice spilling out between rolls of fat.

The mess hall erupts. The women jump from their seats and start hollering like they're at a boxing match. The guards keep their distance, fingers hovering over their tablets, bouncing on the balls of their feet. I feel a *zap* on my chin from the woman's cuffs and my teeth clatter together, but she hasn't let go; the shock is no match for this beast.

Hathaway barrels through the crowd. "Baby Cub! Put her down!"

This just got worse. I'm going to be murdered by a beast named *Baby Cub.*

A mustached guard with a gold-colored collar appears next to Hathaway. He stands with a smug look, his arms folded across his chest. "Looks like she's made a new friend."

"Klein! Do something!" Hathaway says. Klein shrugs. Hathaway presses a button on her tab. My chin gets *zapped* again and my eyes cross, creating two versions of the orange behemoth before me. "Klein, you have to sedate Baby Cub! I can't stun her without killing the girl!"

"Then get in there and break it up," Klein says.

Are the guards really going to let this woman kill me? I thought they were supposed to keep the peace, keep the inmates from hurting each other, but the guards aren't doing a damn thing. Except Hathaway, who leans forward like she's contemplating jumping in but is held back by invisible wires.

"*Bristol.*" Baby Cub doesn't even sound like a woman; her voice is so deep it rattles the windows. "You're the Schoolgirl Slicer."

Goddamn you stupid heartless media people. You just had to give me a nickname like that, didn't you? Now I'm in prison and about to be mauled by a grizzly bear because you were *so entertained* by my story.

Baby Cub's fingers cut off the circulation in my neck and my consciousness starts to fade. I know my tick would be sending me into another vision if it weren't for the zapping of the woman's tracker cuffs against my jaw, and I'm grateful I'm not fighting back because this woman could crush my bones by sitting on me.

The brute heaves suffocating sour breath in my face. "You killed Ricardo Salazar. He was on our side. Now you're in *my* house and *you* are the enemy."

This woman thinks I'm an agent, but I'm not with ACTA. I'm not with anyone. I'm just a girl with a shitty tick. With an Alias murder on my rap-sheet. And an ally on the outside who claims to be an ACTA Soldier.

I'm doomed to die in prison, aren't I?

Hathaway's scratched face appears in my peripheral. My sight blurs and I know I'm about to pass out, and that's when the electrical shock rips through my body. The giant's fingers let go of my neck, and I fly backwards onto the floor, my muscles seizing and contracting, every inch of my skin tingling with electricity. I look up to see Baby Cub standing in a bewildered haze, her shoulders slumped over and her eyes closed like she'd fallen asleep. Hathaway holds a stun gun in a firing position, her brow scrunched in fury. The room is silent.

Klein struts over, tapping something into his wristlet. "Put the girl in confinement."

Hathaway growls under her breath. "You heard what the warden said. No more inmates in the bin until they investigate the cause of Candy's death."

"The warden hasn't left her office in two years," Klein says. "She doesn't have the say to make such a call. The girl started the fight, and she must be punished for her behavior." He picks up the two halves of my food tray from the floor. So it's true, I did start the fight, and I nearly got myself strangled to death because of it.

Hathaway stands tall. "I'm not putting the girl in the bin!"

Klein gets in Hathaway's face. "How diplomatic of you to now be so concerned with the safety of these whores. I don't give a shit why you suddenly changed your mind, but get a handle on your cell block or I'll send you to gate duty."

Hathaway stands her ground. "You don't have the authority."

"The hell I don't," says Klein. He swivels around and shoves his way through the crowd of guards who stand like a row of statues on a lawn.

Hathaway watches Klein leave, eyes Baby Cub carefully, then looks down at me. "Are you all right?"

I manage to mumble something that mostly resembles English. "I … well … kind of."

Hathaway nods once, and races after Klein. Baby Cub snaps from her daze like nothing happened, gives me a glare, and returns to her dinner. Everything is still for awhile. Then one by one, the women and guards go back to their business.

The chipper blonde is at my side, and she pulls me to my feet. "You'd best be careful, ya know. You can't just go around busting people's heads with food trays."

"I didn't mean to."

She flicks her hair out of her eyes. "You're fresh meat. These girls can smell chow like you from a mile away. And believe me, you'll wanna get rid of that target on your back, right quick."

She scurries off to the other side of the room, and I'm left standing there like I've been magnetized to the floor. I haven't been in prison for twenty-four hours, and already I've made both friends and enemies.

Dinner is over. Hathaway's voice booms through the speakers. "Line 'er up!"

Back to the wall, pinned to the steel. I remember the blonde's advice in time to keep my face out of the way. We're scanned and tagged and sent back to our cells.

The dark woman pauses in my doorway. "Don't let me hear you crying again, Princess."

Lights out at ten. Women argue down the hall, and their voices echo through the cell block. Hathaway threatens to turn on the floodlights. I lie on my hard bed, pull the one blanket up to my chin, and try my damnedest not to cry.

"Only you are responsible for your fate. Only you can determine your mark on the world. Only you can choose how you will be remembered." My dad used to say that. I don't know the last time I thought about my dad other than in the context of him being dead; I couldn't handle it. But I can't help it now. I wonder what he'd think if he knew I was in prison, trapped inside these plexiglass doors and magnetic steel walls. Of course, if he were alive, my mom wouldn't have been with Rick and I'd have no reason to kill him and I wouldn't be in prison in the first place.

I have to keep myself together. I don't have a choice. Any more visions and I'll be spending the rest of my life in this hellhole. I can't let that happen. I just can't.

Lights are on. It's already morning. I don't think I slept. I certainly don't feel like I did. My head is pounding like gnomes are chiseling for gold inside my skull. Breakfast at seven. Face against the wall. Scanners. Roll Call. Oatmeal slop and toast.

There aren't many empty benches. There's one that looks broken and another at a table full of women who are laughing at a fumbling chubby girl. I can't go through the same ordeal as last night, so I stand near the windows and pretend to eat my bowl of bland oatmeal.

"Bristol!" Hathaway waves at me. "Get away from the windows. There's no loitering allowed in the mess hall. Sit down."

The women laugh at me. Even Baby Cub laughs at me. And I swear all the remaining empty seats are suddenly taken.

A voice whispers from behind. "What did I tell you about getting that target off your back?" It's the blonde. "Just come sit with me and get outta the way, will ya?"

I follow her to the other side of the room, and she sits down at a table with the snarling woman. I didn't expect these two to know each other. The girl's bleached hair is a stark contrast to the woman's dark skin, as if their demeanors weren't opposing enough. The woman scowls at me, and then scowls at the blonde, who is conveniently ignoring her.

My stomach gurgles and I feel a sharp pain above my hip, and I'm forced to plop down on the bench.

The blonde mirrors my wincing face. "I know, right? The breakfast takes some getting used to. I don't know where they get the stuff. It's like they're thinking if they starve us they can weed us out. I hurled for like a week when I first got here."

"You were high, that's why you hurled," the dark woman says, darting her eyes around the room.

"Yeah, well, they're a bad mix," the blonde says. Her words fly out of her mouth so quickly I barely have a chance to absorb her statement before she moves on to the next one. "This here's LaRae. I'm Goldie. Real name's Goldberg. Goes with the hair. It's not my real color, you can see my roots coming in. Dye's expensive in here.

And it's crappy stuff too, 'cause they won't let us have all those chemicals. They're afraid we're gonna poison someone."

LaRae groans. "You gonna keep up this chatter all goddamn morning?"

Goldie goes on. "I know who you are, though. Everyone does. We don't get many celebrities in here. *Schoolgirl Slicer.* We watched your story on the news before the fights started, and they had to turn off the TVs. There was some talk you'd done it because you and your mom were undercover. But, uh..." she looks me over "...you look a little young to be an ACTA agent."

Finally, I have a chance to say something. "I'm not an ACTA agent."

"Well, that's good to hear. Lemme tell ya, I ain't wanting to make friends with an ACTA agent. Not in here. Not with Klein in charge."

"We're not making friends, ya bimbo," LaRae snarls.

"I'm just saying," Goldie says. "If she *were*, then we'd be targets for the Alias bitches in here."

"You mean there are *more* Alias women in here?" I glance around the room to try and figure out who else in this lot of violent criminals knows I offed an Alias member.

"Of course! Where do you think ACTA sends those terrorists they snatch off the street? It's an Alias breeding ground in here. That explains why Baby Cub is all over you; she's thinking you're with ACTA and you killed that guy to get yourself in here to take 'em all down."

My throat closes up. "I didn't kill him on purpose. I killed him because he was hacking my mom's brain."

Goldie shrugs. "Yeah, well, it doesn't matter what you try and tell them. Once you're on their list, that's it."

"What did I say about attracting attention?" LaRae growls at Goldie. "You want Baby Cub to come after you next?"

Goldie brushes her off. "Hey, I don't intend to die in here. I'm getting out once The Plan goes through and they breach the place. I've been here for nine years already. Can you believe it? *Nine years.* My good days are over, I'll tell ya that. My boobs are already starting to sag. Even so, I'd rather let Baby Cub suffocate me than have Klein send me to the bin."

"It was Hathaway," LaRae says. "How do you think she got her face all torn up?"

"You keep saying that, but Candy wasn't like that."

LaRae slams her fist on the table so hard the bowls jump from the surface. "What the hell do you know about Candy?"

Goldie finally looks concerned with LaRae's state. "She's only been gone three days, LaRae. I know you still love her, but there's no sense in being so angry—"

LaRae is shaking. "I stopped loving her the moment she let Klein put his filthy hands on her."

I have the stupid idea to ask my most burning question. "What happened to Candy?" Goldie stiffens, her eyes fixed on her oatmeal bowl, but I go on. "It's just … I'm in her cell. It might be helpful to know what happened so the same doesn't happen to me."

LaRae leans across the table, and I get a good look at the yellow of her eyes. "The less you know, the less you're my problem, Princess."

My head spins. It could be a vision, but it doesn't feel like a vision.

"Hey, what's wrong with you?" Goldie asks me. "You're turning green. Is it the oatmeal?"

LaRae looks me over. "You're comin' down, aren't 'cha?"

"What?"

"You an addict?" says LaRae.

I flinch. "*Drug* addict?"

"What you think I mean?"

Goldie catches on. "Oh no! You're strung out!"

"They gave me something at the jail. To keep me calm."

"Flake," LaRae growls.

"*Flake*," Goldie agrees.

"What's flake? What does it mean, I'm *strung out*?"

LaRae nods at Goldie. "See what I mean? I told you to stop trying to make friends. First she's with ACTA and now she's gonna be the next flaker to die in the bin."

Goldie's eyes go wide. "Ah, c'mon, LaRae! Don't say that. It's nothing but a tragedy that Candy died in there, but you know she was bound to get caught soon enough, considering how she was with Klein."

Beads of sweat form on LaRae's greasy forehead. "You know nothin' of it, you fool!"

My insides are in knots. "I don't know what you're getting so upset about. Hathaway knows about the sedatives in the jail."

"Yeah, what's with you and Hathaway?" Goldie asks.

"What about her?"

"You two are awful cozy," LaRae says. "I ain't never seen a guard be so concerned with fresh meat. What's it mean?" She's staring at me so intensely that I can't blink, and my eyeballs start to dry out.

Goldie pats the table top as though it were a stand-in for LaRae's arm. "All right, LaRae. I'm sorry about Candy and all, but you gotta get off the whole Klein thing before he puts *you* in the bin."

LaRae's eyes go bloodshot, and if I could see past that dark layer of skin, I'd bet her face is beet red. "Don't talk about Candy like you knew her, ya hear? She's dead. That's all there is to it." She throws her spoon onto the table with a clatter, then slides off the bench and disappears to the other side of the room.

"Is she all right?" I ask.

Goldie sighs. "She's got some conspiracy theory. I don't know if I believe it or not, but she swears that Klein is sneaking flake in here and pushing others to sell it for him."

"They sell it in here?"

"It seems a little fishy, 'cause I don't know who Klein works for. Definitely not the warden. Klein thinks he owns this whole goddamn place. But listen to me. You're a flaker. I know you didn't *want* to be, but you are. You could get a dime added to your sentence and a week in the bin if you're caught using. Then you'll be coming down in the bin—and that's a bad place to do that, trust me. It's best you just dry out now before anyone notices."

Goldie turns back to her breakfast, and I sit trembling so hard I can no longer hold my spoon.

I'm not an addict. I don't want to be an addict. I remember a time when Lyle and I promised each other that we'd never touch any drug. Of course, that pact went out the window when I took that spinner and then gave the stage performance of a lifetime.

Oh, Lyle ... Dammit, I miss your face, that goofy, round and freckled face. What would you say if you knew I was a flaker? You'd probably tell me I've already lost enough brain cells and dropped at least twenty IQ points and I'll be nothing more than a pile of drooling mush in a few years so pull myself together and get off the stuff. That's what you'd tell me.

But what if I told you that I'm in prison for murdering someone when I thought I was having a vision and it's only a matter of time before I have another vision and stab some burly inmate with a pencil and get sent straight to death row? What if I told you that I think those drugs are the only thing to keep me from having the visions?

Maybe the bigger question is, do I have the guts to find out?

18 dirty money

I imagine there are a lot of ways to die in prison. I could be shanked in the shower. I could die of food poisoning or starvation. I could catch some incurable disease. I could be bludgeoned to death by someone named Tinker Elf. I could kill myself with—what did LaRae say? A *spoon*? That sounds excruciating and quite regrettable.

But for now, I'm dying of drug withdrawals. Or, at least, I feel like I am.

My body became addicted to those sedatives the jailers pumped into me, and now that I've been cut off my insides are rebelling against me. I've spent the last four days curled in the fetal position, moaning and crying. My skin feels like it's on fire, and I swear there's an alien digging its way out of my stomach.

Hathaway comes by several times a day for roll call, but she won't send me to the infirmary. Baby Cub bounces her busted-orange body across the hall, laughing. Goldie brings me crackers that I promptly throw up, and a towel to drape on my head that I think is dampened by toilet water. LaRae sticks her head in my cell, but only to *shush* at me to stop the moaning that is keeping her up at night.

I want to go home. Not back to the bastard brain hacker's dump in South LA. *Home.* Not to that wrett apartment in Hollywood. *Home.* Not to the Los Feliz house where my dad won't be there. *Home.* That home doesn't exist, I realize that—my dad is dead and my mom is crazy and I know there's no such thing as *Home Sweet Home*—but dammit I wanna go home!

I'm still having visions. Now there's a new one:

I'm in the middle of the mess hall and all the women are pointing and laughing at me. I reach for Hathaway's pistol, and it's not a real gun but a fire torch. I pull the trigger and a stream of molten liquid squirts out and covers the entire room. The women scream in tortured pain as their jumpers catch fire and they burn to death—

I suppose I should be grateful I'm stuck in bed because I have no idea how that vision might play out in real life.

When the vomiting finally subsides, and I'm able to keep down Goldie's crackers, I drag myself out of my cell. I zombie-step it down the corridor of Level Three on my way to the mess hall when Klein steps in my path, pauses, and gives me a once-over.

"Bristol," he says with a squint of his eyes. "Time for you to get a job."

Is he kidding? My stomach is so queasy I could barf at any moment, and he's expecting me to work?

He's not kidding. He thumbs through his tab and smiles. "There's an opening in Laundry. Let's go."

Klein leads me down a few sets of escalators to an underground floor and through huge steel doors where I'm bombarded by the loud rumble of giant machines and the sickening smell of detergent. It's chaos in here. Robotic arms come down from the ceiling and dunk bedsheets into large steaming vats of water, then another set of arms pulls the sheets out and onto a conveyor belt to a dryer the size of a large car. These are not modern machines; this is ancient technology left over from the turn of the century.

Two steps inside and I'm nearly whacked on the head by a robot arm that had been hiding in the steam, waiting for me to pass by. As I'm skipping and ducking around the threatening machinery, I see small clusters of women in orange jumpers huddled in various spots around the room. Klein leads me to an empty washing vat where four women hold long poles that are attached to the ceiling by cables and use them to scrape down the inside of the vat. I don't recognize two of the women, but the third woman is LaRae and the fourth is Baby Cub. Of course it is.

"All right, here's your spot," Klein says. "Not much to it. If you see grime, scrape it off. And don't be getting skimpy with it, or the super will make you work overtime." He swivels on his boot heels and walks off across the room.

Baby Cub is positioned on the opposite side of the vat, and she pauses cleaning long enough to send a cloud of foul-breath air in my direction. Her face is so chubby that her eyes and mouth pucker and sink into her head, making her look like an infant doing business in his diaper. I spot three guards nearby and plan my emergency escape, and Baby notices my glance. I think she laughs, but the skin of her face pulls taught over her chubby cheeks and her jaw jerks to one side, so she could be having a seizure.

The woman next to me swings over a pole and it hits me in the head. "Well, get to it."

I take the pole and follow her lead, pushing my scraper down the length of the vat to collect the grease and grime in a pile at the bottom. I've only been here five minutes, and I can tell I'm going to fail miserably at this back-breaking work. I'm still hungover from the detox, and I haven't eaten enough to have the energy for such physical labor. The room is stifling in heat and humidity. I'm sweating through my skin-tight jumper, and every time a droplet of sweat rolls down between my boobs, I have to stop and wipe it away. Just when I think I've gained some momentum, the women yell *"overhead!"* and I look up to see a robot arm coming right for me. I duck out of the way at the last possible moment, and my pole crashes with LaRae's. She whacks mine so hard it sends vibrations up my arms.

"Get it together, Princess!"

I'm trying my best to stay focused on what I'm doing so I don't puke in the nearly-cleaned vat. I especially don't want to upset the two animals across from me, but I don't seem to be their concern at the moment. Baby Cub and LaRae are having the most intense stare-off I've ever witnessed, glaring and grunting at each other like bucks about to duel for a fertile doe.

Once our vat is clean we move to the next machine, which is a casket-sized box with exposed gears. I'm handed a scraping pad to shove into the crevasses to wipe away the black grime.

"You're doing it wrong," shouts the middle-aged woman next to me. "You've gotta get your hands all the way in there, else the super will make us clean the whole thing again."

I shout back over the noise. "What if the machine accidentally turns on?"

She shrugs. "If you lose a finger, they'll have to find you another job."

That's almost encouraging. "Isn't it kinda weird, though, that they don't have robots to clean the washing robots?"

The woman rolls her eyes. "If they'd have robots do this, what would *we* do?"

"I didn't expect to work in prison."

"We gotta earn wages somehow, otherwise we'd have no money to spend in the canteen."

"Or in the laundry room," laughs the fourth woman as she elbows Baby Cub in the gut. "Am I right?"

Baby Cub hardly notices. She and LaRae bump into each other for positions at the gearbox, all the while glancing over their shoulders to Klein, who is searching through a few metal crates behind a rumbling dryer. The guard looks up, having sensed the attention. LaRae throws her arm out in front of Baby Cub, and I think these two are about to have at it when a stooped, wiry lady—who could be somebody's grandmother, were it not for the tattoos and shaved head—interrupts the confrontation as she comes to inspect the gears. She looks around carefully, and nods to another vat for the five of us to scrape down.

We're even closer to Klein now, and the tension between Baby Cub and LaRae is building. Through a cloud of steam I can just make out the crates that Klein is fussing with, and from here the contents look like unmarked cigarette boxes. The other two cleaning women aren't paying attention—or they're pretending they don't see anything. Then there's a loud clatter as LaRae slams her pole into the side of the vat.

"Guard!" Baby Cub shouts over the machines. "Guard, she's threatening me!"

LaRae glares at Baby Cub. Klein emerges from behind the dryer and points to LaRae as two other guards run over.

"Get her out of here," Klein orders.

The guards grab LaRae by either arm and she snaps at Klein like a dog. "I'll stop you, bastard!"

She's hauled away and everyone stands frozen for a moment, even Baby Cub. Then Klein shouts, "Back to work, all ah ya!" and everyone returns to cleaning. Except Baby Cub, who joins Klein behind the dryer.

We're on to another gear box, this one right next to the meeting-place dryer. My cleaning crew is now down to three, and we've still got a ways to go when the dryer ends its cycle and the loud rumbling stops. I can hear the voices of Baby Cub and Klein coming from behind it. They talk animatedly about something, and I can't help but eavesdrop.

"It's not the same stuff, I know that." Klein sounds agitated.

"What do you care what it is?" says Baby Cub. "Your cut is the same either way."

"I need to know your supplier is solid."

"They ain't gonna rat you out."

Klein's voice cracks. "How can I be certain if I have no reason to trust them? You can't expect me to pass the new stuff through security and not know where it's coming from. It's my ass on the line here, even if the warden is blind to the whole thing."

"You'll still get your cut," she says.

"Listen, ya beast, this is *my* operation. You work for *me*—"

"I don't work for you."

"The hell you don't!"

"You get the supplies in, I sell it, and you get your cut."

"Goddammit, I'm the head guard of Level Three, this prison is under *my* control, not anyone else's, not any of those assholes on the outside, you hear? If you even think about undermining my position, I'll put you in the bin and let you wither away and die a skinny little bitch."

Baby Cub chuckles—really, it sounds like a pig snorting—and she comes around the dryer into view while stuffing something down the squishy abyss between her boobs. She stops short when she sees me and, of course, I'm caught staring right at her like a dumbass. Klein pops out and glares at me with such force I nearly jump into the next vat of boiling water.

"Klein!"

Hathaway appears out of the steam. I never thought I'd be so relieved to see the woman. Baby Cub sinks into a curtain of fog, and everyone else goes back to pretending to clean.

Hathaway glances at me from the side of her eyes. "What is the girl doing in here?"

Klein straightens his jacket and grins. "She's doing just fine. See, she already looks like a greaser." He points to my jumper and I look down to see I've colored my chest in black grime from wiping away the sweat.

Hathaway shifts. "She's too small to work in Laundry."

As much as I'm grateful for Hathaway's defense on my behalf, she's doing a bit too good of a job pointing out my weaknesses. She's right, of course, because I've only been here two hours and the muscles in my arms and shoulders are on fire.

"She needed a job, so I assigned her one," says Klein.

"There's an opening in the canteen."

"Not anymore. I gave it to the Hawaiian girl."

"The warden didn't sign off on this."

"The warden hasn't signed off on anything for months. What makes you so concerned for the red tape now?" Klein tilts his head and gives her a sinister grin. "Oh wait … Candy."

Hathaway sighs through gritted teeth then flicks her fingers at me. "Bristol, let's go." I hurry over despite the many nasty looks from the women.

Klein frowns. "Where are you taking her?"

"To find her a better-suited job," Hathaway says, then heads to the door with me at her heels like a shivering Chihuahua.

Hathaway takes me to the shower room, which is thankfully empty of inmates because I still haven't gotten used to the idea of showering with other people. She stands just outside the wetroom as I toss my jumper in the steam-clean machine and let the sprayers blast the grease and grime from my body. I'd stand here forever if I could and let the pressure of water massage my aching muscles, but Hathaway has already thrown me one bone today and I don't want to compromise that.

As I'm zipping up my freshly-cleaned jumper, my attention is caught by a pair of feet poking out from another shower stall. The feet aren't moving. I tiptoe my way to the stall and find a naked brunette girl lying on the cement floor, on her side, hands beneath her head like she'd lain down and gone to sleep. I tap her foot with my toe. She doesn't move.

"Um … Hathaway?"

"What is it, Bristol?"

"You may want to call a doctor."

Hathaway bursts into the wetroom, grabs my shoulders, and scans my body. “What is it? What’s wrong?”

“Not me. In there.” I point to the unconscious girl’s feet, and I could swear Hathaway breathes a sigh of relief.

She goes to the woman and takes her pulse. “Ah Jesus, not another one …” She speaks into her wristlet, “Main Security, we have a Code Blue in Level Three East showers. Call the doctor.”

“Copy that, Hathaway,” says a voice through the wristlet. *“Dr. Baydar is on her way.”*

A triple-beeping siren sweeps through the room, and the lights flash orange, which is supposed to mean that all inmates are required to return to their cells immediately.

Hathaway peers out from the stall. “Sit down. Don’t move a muscle until I tell you to.”

I slide onto a bench and listen as the clamoring of footsteps approach from the hallway.

Klein is the first to arrive, and he spots me on the bench. “What are you doing here?”

“She’s under my supervision,” Hathaway says from the shower.

“While you’re screwing around on your hands and knees? What the hell is going on? Who’s that on the floor?”

He moves in to get a better look, and Hathaway stands and pushes him back. “Don’t contaminate the scene.”

“Scene? There’s no scene. She’s not even hurt. It looks like she’s sleeping. She probably drowned herself like the other girl.”

“Two girls in two days?” says Hathaway. “You expect me to assume that’s a coincidence?”

“These girls are in prison. They should do us all a favor and get rid of themselves.” Klein nods over to me.

Hathaway closes the gap. "I swear to god, Klein, if you're in on this—"

"What happened?" A woman in a doctor's cloak bursts in and goes straight for the girl on the floor. "She doesn't have a pulse. How long has she been here? Who found her?"

Hathaway glances over at me, which receives an eyebrow raise from Klein. "I found her just now," Hathaway says. "The showers were locked. She could have been here since the last shift."

"All right," Dr. Baydar says and waves in a few guards. "Let's get her to the infirmary." The guards pick up the naked girl and carry her from the room. She surveys the stall then comes up to Hathaway. "Lock this area down. I want to come back and take a closer look."

Hathaway nods. "You'll do a tox-screen, won't you?"

Klein moves in. "It's hardly necessary to waste our funding on an autopsy."

Dr. Baydar squints at Klein then speaks to Hathaway. "I'll do a tox-screen. Anything in particular I should be looking out for?"

"I honestly have no idea." Hathaway glances back at Klein, then swivels to hover over me as I sit on the bench. "Let's go, Bristol, unless you too want to end up dead on the shower floor."

She leads me through the corridors back to my cell, walking so fast I have to skip to keep up. We walk the entire length of my block, past cells 301 through 316. The inmates are secured behind their plexiglass doors—except for 309, the dead girl's cell—and every one of these women watch as I walk past. Most of them are right up against the glass, all with their arms crossed, all with a smug smile pulling at their lips.

19 the librarian

The next morning the mess hall is buzzing with talk about the dead girl in the showers. She was twenty-six, through eight years of a life sentence. I didn't know her name. I barely recognized her, but Goldie did. I can tell she's upset when I plop down next to her and LaRae at their table.

"Shit, LaRae, do you always gotta be so insensitive?" Goldie says, her face scrunched in disgust.

LaRae taps her spoon on the rim of her oatmeal bowl. "She shoulda stayed away from the flake, is all I'm saying. I told all you, don't feed the monster."

"But what *I'm* saying is she wasn't a flaker. She'd been clean as long as I've been here, and now all of a sudden you say she got the itch? It doesn't make sense."

"She looked peaceful," I say. "Do you think she just went to sleep and never woke up?"

Both Goldie and LaRae look like I've asked where babies come from.

"You're joking, right?" Goldie says. "People don't just lie down and wait to die. If you wanna kill yourself, you gotta make it quick so no one stops you in the middle of it." She glances at LaRae who is holding her spoon suspiciously close to her own neck.

"So what killed her?" I ask.

"It was the flake," LaRae says, and a few women turn to give her the evil eye.

Goldie hunkers down and whispers, "It can't be the flake! Girls have been flaking for years and no one's died from it."

"Something's off," LaRae says. "Klein's got his hands in a different hole."

Goldie shudders. "I can't deal with this. Too many girls dying. It's not good to think about that. Besides, if it is the flake, then we gotta be extra careful to stay away from it. And *you*, kid, especially need to get rid of that green in your skin. C'mon, we'll take you out to the yard."

I can't help but feel as though her statement sounds like they're going to take me behind the barn to put me down with a shotgun, but maybe the yard is a good idea. No one has died out there … yet.

The yard is large and dusty, a flat expanse of dirt and squares of asphalt boxed in by a monstrous concrete structure that puts the Great Wall of China to shame. Despite having nothing in it, the place bustles with women. Some busy themselves by exercising. A few chat in a huddle, others stand arguing, and one group sits in a circle saying prayers. Everyone else wanders in circles, bored out of their minds.

We find a table next to Hathaway's day post by the door. I can't see through her dark visor, but I get the sense she's got an eye on me.

"So I hear you're no longer in Laundry," says Goldie. "Have they found you a new job?"

Hathaway shifts but stares straight ahead.

"I haven't been reassigned yet," I say. "I hear they gave the spot in the canteen to some other girl."

"Ugh!" Goldie says. "That girl's a pain in my ass. Always chatting my ear off. The girl *never* shuts up. What's worse is I think she's with Alias, and I know she's gonna spit out something I shouldn't hear—"

LaRae reaches over and whacks Goldie on the leg with a paperback book. "Don't be spurting out shit like that!"

"Give it a rest, will ya? What you think Alias wants with me?"

"They'll come after you if they think you're against them."

"I'm not the one they want, LaRae, you know that."

The two girls are yammering on about conspiracy theories, but all I can focus on is the book in LaRae's hand. A real, solid paperback book. There's a picture on the front of a half-naked man kissing a woman, but still—a *real book.*

"Where'd you get that?" I ask.

LaRae won't answer, but Goldie is eager to change the subject. "The library!"

"I didn't know there was a library," I say.

"Yeah, well, I hate reading so it's no use to me. And anyway, it's been closed for awhile. There's a bunch of art crap in there. That's the only reason I ever went. I had this friend on the outside who did 3D graffiti art—you've seen those shows in LA, right? He's really good. He'd let me use his stuff sometimes."

There's an art room! My hand twitches with the excitement of holding a paintbrush, the eagerness pulses through my arm. The thought of painting sends a wave of calm through my body, like it's washing away a poison.

"Can we go there now?" I say.

"Where?"

"The art room."

"The library is closed until further notice," Hathaway says, finally breaking her silence. "No one's allowed inside."

Goldie squints at me. "You an artist?"

"I was a painter. It's the only … it helps calm me down."

Hathaway jerks in my direction, then quickly corrects her posture.

"Oh wicky!" Goldie says. "Maybe you can teach me."

"I'm not a *teacher* …"

"Neither was my friend, but he really inspired me. I had so much of his stuff saved in my Connex port, but I lost it all when I got sent here …"

Goldie rambles on, but I'm lost in my own head, overwhelmed with the memory of Lyle coming to visit me in the jail. *They threw it all out, Jo.* Everything. My art, my dad's art. Except that one, the one with the girl and the paintbrush in the burning city.

I hear the ringing. I'm simply sitting here on the bench with Goldie's chatter muffled beside me, and I hear the ringing. That's all it takes now, I guess. I only need to be thinking of something painful to start a vision. This is worse than I thought. The cloud drifts over my sight and—*BAAM!*

"Jesus! Whatcha do that for?"

My eyes clear and I see Goldie gaping at my hand. My knuckles throb and are bleeding where I've slammed them against the bench.

"You all right?" Goldie says.

"Yeah, I think so."

Hathaway is also looking at my hand. I can't tell what she's thinking behind that dark visor, but suddenly there's a fight across the yard and Hathaway runs off. One of Baby Cub's girls has another woman in a headlock, and even from here I can see the victim turning blue.

The orange lights flash and the sirens signal everyone back inside. I follow the crowd through the door, but I'm so distracted by my throbbing knuckles that I look up and find myself alone in a dark corridor. I must have taken a wrong turn somewhere. I start to head back into the light when the shadows move and there is Baby Cub, her huge orange monolith coming at me, one thunderous step after another.

"Where do you think you're going, Slicer?"

"I think I went the wrong way."

"I think you went the wrong way in *life*, fancy."

Well, that's obvious. I'm in prison. And now—*again*—I'm about to be murdered. I'm actually quite certain she'll finish the job this time.

"I know you're a flaker," she says. "I can see it in your eyes. All glazed over and needing a fix."

"No, I came down. I don't wanna end up in the bin like that other girl. Just beat me up and get it over with."

She laughs and her whole body jumbles. "As fun as that sounds, I'm gonna make a deal with you, fancy. You need flake. I got flake. You buy flake from me and I promise I won't bust your fancy little teeth in."

"Please, no. I don't want flake."

Baby Cub blows her hot, stinking breath and cracks her knuckles. "Hmm, but I think you *need* it."

My heart races from the thought of this giant's fists making permanent dents in my face.

I jump onto Baby Cub's huge body, my knees in her belly, one arm wrapped around her neck. I jab my bare fingers into her eyes and scratch my nails all over her face—

I'm thrown backwards and my tailbone slams into the floor. Baby Cub stomps toward me and I scramble to my feet, bracing myself to be bowled over. There's wind in my ear, and I jerk around to see a pair of yellow eyes shining in the darkness.

"When you gonna get your stank ass outta my face, LaRae?" Baby Cub says, and cracks her knuckles again.

LaRae growls, confirming her identity as I have heard that sound so many times.

"Oh what, you gonna go tell on me?" says Baby Cub. "Gonna get me sent to the bin? No one will take your word, not after that girlfriend of yours slit her throat. I wonder what made her do that." She pauses and looks LaRae over, then flashes her scrunched shit-taking grin.

There's movement further back in the corridor, and Baby Cub sucks in her belly and stands rigid, staring behind me into the darkness. Then she grins again, turns away, and walks to the main corridor.

LaRae growls into my ear. "Stay away from the flake, Princess. Don't feed the animals." She pushes into my shoulder, shoving me into the wall on her way to follow Baby Cub.

"But I wasn't—" I call after her, but she's already snaked her way out of the darkness.

There's no chance I'm going to follow the same path as both of those women; Baby Cub is probably waiting for me around the corner. I take a deep breath and prepare to brave my way into this oddly dark space when I see there's someone *else* standing here, the real reason Baby Cub stormed away.

It's Hathaway. She waves her arm and the lights turn on and I get a full view of her disappointed face. "This is the second Orange Alert where you've not returned to your cell. That's a sign of defiance and you'll get points on your record."

Hey, the first time there was a dead girl and Hathaway told me to stay put. And this time I was cornered by a man-eating orange. I'd much *prefer* to be in my cell right now, thank you very much.

"I was on my way there—"

"Let's go." Hathaway doesn't want my explanation. Instead, she links my tracker cuffs to her and pulls me back to my cell.

It's impossible to make myself invisible in here. Three nights in a row I find Baby Cub standing at my door, her breath fogging the glass. I'd hear the ringing in my ears and *BAAM!* into the wall my knuckles go. Every meal the Alias women glare at me from across the room and *BAAM!* into the table my fist goes. It's the only thing I can do to stop the visions, but now both my hands are so beat up they ache constantly and I can barely use them.

This morning my hands are covered in blue bruises and red lacerations. I barely have my spoonful of oatmeal steady and it's nearly in my mouth when LaRae's voice startles me.

"Why do you do that?"

My breakfast falls back into my bowl and I whimper. "What are you talking about?"

"Your hands. Are you fixing to use them on someone?"

My ragged state has left me with no patience for the woman's mulishness. "It's just the wall. What's it to you, anyway?"

"You don't look like the violent type."

"She *is* the Schoolgirl Slicer, remember?" Goldie interjects rather casually.

LaRae jerks to scold Goldie, but stops. "So what's your deal?"

"I don't have a deal."

"You've busted both your hands. Either you're building them up to do some damage, or you've got something nasty rattling in your head."

Her piercing glare shoots fireballs into my eyes. She knows something's up with me, that much is obvious. Hell, she knew I was coming off the sedatives. Even though she was rude to me from the get-go, I'd like to think she's more my friend than Baby Cub or Klein. Maybe revealing the truth is a risk worth taking.

"I have this tick … of needing to hit something."

"So you hit the wall?"

I shrug. "It distracts me. I don't have drugs to subdue me. It's all I have. Otherwise, I might …"

LaRae squints. "Otherwise you might hit *someone*?"

"I'm not gonna hurt anybody."

"Like the guy whose brain you ripped out?"

I am an idiot. This was a bad idea. I should have kept my mouth shut. They really need to instate a prison orientation for newbies like myself that includes helpful hints such as "Don't mess with the head guard," or "Don't ask too many questions," and "Whatever you do, don't assume it's safe to make friends with anyone, especially the widowed wife of a recently self-mutilated inmate."

LaRae shoves her spoon in my face. "Don't you get back on that flake, ya hear? I don't care what you say about this *tick* or whatever. If you use, Klein will put you in the bin, and you're no good to me there."

"What are you talking about?"

Goldie is equally confused by LaRae's comment, but we get no answer for LaRae makes yet another dramatic exit from our table, leaving us in a wind of unanswered questions.

"What was that?" I ask.

Goldie shrugs. "Her conspiracy theories, remember? I donno, kid, take my advice and stay out of it."

I'm trying to stay out of it. I don't want anything to do with any of it. But no matter what, I keep getting dragged into this circle of mayhem. I didn't ask to be on the Alias Most Wanted List. I'm just trying to get through this alive.

Goldie is busy finishing her breakfast, and I'm envious of how easily she moves on from one thought to the next. I'd like to ask her to elaborate on her advice of *how* to stay out of the chaos, but Hathaway's voice rattles through the room and interrupts even my own thoughts.

"Bristol! Here! Now!"

"What did you do?" Goldie asks.

"I didn't do anything!"

"Well whatever it is, don't let her see your hands."

"Bristol!"

I scramble to my feet, leave my nearly untouched bowl of oatmeal, and race across the mess hall.

Hathaway seems hurried. "Follow me." She leads me down some corridors to a door at the end of the hall, waves her wristlet at the terminal, and invites me into a dim room with long tables and bookcases against the back wall. I know exactly what this is.

It's the library. And it's an absolute mess, all dusty and littered, books scattered everywhere, and wooden easels and crates of paint stuffed in the corner.

Hathaway stands in the middle of the room and looks around, avoiding making eye contact with me. "The warden has a strict rule that every capable inmate have a job," she says. "You're not suited for hard labor, but you need something to occupy yourself. I have the understanding your case may get moved to the ACTA courts, in which case you may be transferred soon. However, if you keep up these actions you won't last until then."

She's looking at my battered hands. I haven't done a very good job of hiding them. "I didn't know it was against the rules to hurt myself," I say quietly.

She straightens and adds even more height to her six-foot frame. "It's self-endangerment, and *that,* Bristol, is most certainly against the rules. If you keep this up, they'll tie you down in a bed. Do you want that?"

Oh god no. That sounds worse than the bin.

"I'm giving you an opportunity here, Bristol. Screw this up and you'll be washing shower drains. The warden has agreed to let us re-open the library under the condition that it is taken care of. That will be your responsibility. Keep this place clean. If the women make a mess, do something about it. Don't come whining to me. If you can't handle it, I'll lock it back up. Can you do this?"

I take a big breath. She's asking me to convince convicted felons to keep a library and art room clean? That's more than a tall order—that's near impossible.

But I see the easels in the corner. I see the box of paint sitting next to them. My hands start twitching—partly because my knuckles ache, but mostly because the thought of holding a paint-laden brush in my hand makes me the most calm I have been in a long time.

"Yeah. I can do that."

Hathaway puffs out her chest. "Good. Clean it up first. Quickly." She calls another guard to stand at the door. "Be in the mess hall at noon for roll call." And she's gone.

It's just me and the other guard. He doesn't say anything, just watches as I get to work. I dust off the bookcases and line the books on the shelves, sweep the floors, scrub the tables, throw out the trash, and all the while I've got one eye on the pile of paint in the corner. Maybe it's the excitement and anticipation that motivates me, but I get the whole place cleaned up in few days.

Hathaway is meticulous with her inspection but pleased with the results. "Congratulations, Bristol."

The library is open for business.

"Oh, it looks great!" Goldie says as she twirls around the room.

LaRae heads straight for the bookcases. "They're not in order." It's a surprise to see LaRae at all after our last altercation, and now she's being nice … well, as nice as LaRae can be.

"Oh c'mon, LaRae!" Goldie says. "Just be happy you can read something other than that sex book."

"It's not a sex book," LaRae says in her usual grumpy tone, but she's looking through the shelves with her eyes wide.

"Okay then." Goldie plops herself into a chair. "Teacher, teach me to paint!"

"Oh. Um, let's see what we have." I lay out the paint, brushes, and paper on the table. "It's mostly dried out."

"Eeh, we'll make it work. Oh look, tangerine orange! It's the same color as our jumpers. Let's paint self-portraits."

Goldie's enthusiasm is so contagious I actually feel myself smile. I have no memory of last time I smiled. Oh, yes I do—just before I kissed Lyle on my birthday night. Before *all of this.*

I have to take a moment to breathe. My hands still hurt, but the feel of the brush is familiar and comforting: the weight of the metal ferrule, the smooth and tapered handle, the long prickly bristles. Tangerine orange paint scrapes across white paper and everything in the world is okay. My mind is so at ease that when a handful of other women come in and start making a ruckus I don't even care. I focus on my paper canvas and nothing else.

The library is a hit with the women. They're certainly not the most cooperative art students, and I have a hell of a time wrangling back the books they borrow, but it's a nice break from the monotony. Color is added to the drab cells as the women proudly display their artwork. Jumpers are stained with paint, but no one seems to care much. The mess hall is quieter since many of the women have their noses buried in books.

Every Monday Hathaway comes by to give me my salary. In paper money, even. I've never held paper money, let alone earn any. It smells funny and most of it is held together by tape, and my payment isn't much but there's some relief in knowing I can buy something at the canteen if I care to.

Baby Cub brings her girls in to ruffle my feathers—maybe she's hoping I'll break and she can have a reason to beat me to a pulp—but there's no way anything can agitate me in the library.

I haven't had a vision in months. Nothing that the jackass guard or the snarling woman or the man-eating orange can do to set off my tick while I have a paintbrush in my hand. This has been my greatest moment in prison.

And then a fight breaks out.

20 doctor's orders

I'd have expected that, as adults, people grow out of their adolescent impulses and melodramatic reflexes. But this is prison. Even the supposedly accidental splash of water on another's painting sparks that juvenile animalistic frenzy, and in an instant becomes an all-out brawl. A hair-pulling, nail-scratching, saliva-spitting, fist-throwing clash of the orange-suited titans. In *my library.*

Sitting at the end of a table showing an older woman how to color a horse she drew, I have a sinking feeling when I notice our guard step out of the library. Then the yelling starts.

"I know what you're up to, señorita!"

The instigator is a burly woman—appropriately named Buzz Kill—and she's red and huffing and screaming at Baby Cub, who sits slumped in a chair.

"You ain't got no way to prove it."

"I've got friends on the outside too!"

"None of you can stop it." Baby Cub tries to stand up, but the chair has folded into her rolls of fat, and she scrapes across the floor with a spine-tingling screech. This is the third time this week Baby and her cubs have taken up residency in the library, and not with the purpose of staring me down. Lately—like today—they're actually painting. Or, they were, until we heard the news about another mysteriously dead inmate.

"That girl was one of mine." Buzz Kill wags a finger in Baby Cub's face. "You and all your Alias bitches had better back off or you're in for some trouble."

Three other women have the right idea and head for the door, but Baby's girls have created a blockade between the me and exit.

"Don't worry about her, Baby," says one of the cubs. "Our brothers are coming."

Buzz Kill turns red. "Oh gimme a break. That bullshit invasion ain't gonna do nothin' for you in *this* place!"

"Don't you dare call it *bullshit*, bitch!"

Out of nowhere, the table flips over. There are people sitting at that table, and as the furniture comes crashing down on them, everybody starts hollering. Buzz Kill reaches over and grabs a woman by the hair. Two of the cubs jump Buzz Kill, and then Buzz Kill's friends start throwing punches. Before I know it the whole room is in the brawl, except for Baby Cub, who finally manages to wiggle out of her chair.

The sirens go off and the orange lights flash, then the guard reappears in the doorway just as one of the cubs comes at me. The girl takes a swing, and I dodge her punch just in time. She loses her balance and falls over a chair.

I jump on top of her and wrap my fingers around the girl's throat, and I feel the zap of her tracker cuffs just as Baby Cub picks me up and tosses me across the room—

The electrical *zap* pulls me from my vision as I slide across the floor. The next thing I see is a fist flying at my face. The pain in my cheekbone is incredible, made worse by my skull bouncing off the concrete floor. My cuffs snap together and so do the cuffs of my assailant and it only makes things worse because now she's using both of her fists against my face. She might as well be using a crowbar. The pain gets worse with each blow, and I have the real fear she's going to crack my head open. Guards rush in and start zapping everyone with stun guns.

I still have my paintbrush in my hand, and as the girl leans back to prepare her next blow to my face, I jab the sharp end of the paintbrush into her eyeball, bursting it like a grape tomato—

The stun gun hits her first and she convulses on top of me, the paintbrush sticking out of her eye socket. Hathaway appears above and I can barely see her through the tears welling in my eyes. She aims her stun gun, and I black out.

The first thing I notice when I wake up is how much everything hurts. My face feels like it has swelled twice it's normal size, and my nose throbs with the beat of my heart. One eye is swollen shut. I go to wipe away a tear from my good eye, but my tracker cuffs are linked to the bed frame. There are cameras, siren horns, guards at the door, and lots of medical equipment. I'm in the infirmary.

"About time you woke up." Dr. Baydar pushes buttons on the terminal beside my bed and I wait for the soothing sensation of drugs to take my pain away. It doesn't come.

"Drugs?" is all I can mutter through my swollen lips.

"No drugs, I'm afraid. You'll have to heal through the pain. You're pretty busted up. Your nose was shattered. I've set it best I can. The swelling around your eye will go down in a few days and the rest will heal pretty quickly. I'll keep you here for a couple nights so I can administer antibiotics. But no sedatives. I'm sorry."

"They help my … visions."

Her eyebrows raise. "Visions? How long have you had visions?"

"Always."

She thumbs her tab and shakes her head. "Your brain scan is clear. Nothing to suggest any abnormalities."

She doesn't believe me. Of course she doesn't. After all this, who would?

My cuffs detach and I leap from the bed. I go to the desk on the side of the room—

I blink. I'm still in the bed. I didn't even hear the ringing. Oh wait, there it is …

I pull out a large scalpel—

Back again. My wrists hurt as I'm pulling against the cuffs.

I swing open the door and jam the scalpel into the guard's neck, right beneath his ear—

I can't tell whether I'm in the bed or at the door. I feel the scalpel in my hand and then it's gone. Flashes. Back and forth. The panel by the bed beeps wildly. I'm hyperventilating. I can't breathe. I can't speak.

I take the scalpel to the doctor's throat and slice her ear to ear—

No ringing this time. Not even a fog cloud. Just a flash. From reality into vision and back again in at the blink of an eye. My body convulses so violently I feel like I'm going to pop a blood vessel in my brain.

"Bristol? Bristol!" Dr. Baydar's voice swirls around my head, her face twists like wet blobs of paint. "You're going into shock. I need you to focus. C'mon, girl, stay with me …"

The room is much darker now. I don't know how much time has passed. The doctor's voice is nearby, but I can't see her. My good eye is too heavy to open all the way. I try to move my swollen tongue to ask for water, and then I hear another woman's voice. Hathaway's voice.

"No, that can't be it," Hathaway says. "I've been keeping an eye on her since she got here. I'd know if she was flaking, trust me."

"You can't know everything these women are doing all the time," says Dr. Baydar. "You didn't know what was going on between Klein and that girl Candy until it was too late. And by then—"

Hathaway cuts her off. "It wasn't my fault Candy died in the bin. She wasn't herself. She was violent. You saw what she did to my face."

"I know it's not your fault, but you knew she was acting strangely and you put her in solitary anyway. And then she killed herself."

So it's true then. Hathaway was the one to send Candy to her death. My one ally in this prison got another girl killed. Great. I'm really not sure anymore if Hathaway is my best option of survival. And more over, why *is* she helping me?

"What are you suggesting?" says Hathaway.

"I'm wondering if this girl would have stabbed that woman with a paintbrush if she was clean. She may have been hallucinating. She told me she has visions."

"Visions? You did a tox screen on her, didn't you?"

Dr. Baydar sighs. "I found no signs of drugs."

Actually, flake would have stopped the vision and prevented me from popping that woman's eye out in the first place. Got it, Doc? I need drugs. Give me drugs!

"I'm telling you, Bristol is clean," says Hathaway, "I've made certain of it."

"But I didn't find flake in Candy either. Or in the girls who drowned themselves in the shower. And the other four women who Klein claims starved themselves. I'm running out of beds in here. There are too many women who won't eat."

More women have died? What did I miss while I was hiding in my sanctuary of a library? I know I'd be gasping in disbelief right now if I weren't so paralyzed by pain.

Hathaway is also flabbergasted. "It's not flake?"

"No. I did find some other strange chemical signatures in all those women. I have no idea what they are. I had to sneak out the labs because Klein told the warden the autopsies weren't warranted. He's got her convinced he's in control of the prison, and she doesn't seem to care to know the truth."

"I've told her Klein is double-crossing her."

"And yet Klein is still here."

"The warden doesn't work for Alias."

Dr. Baydar sighs. "I know that. But Klein thinks I'm siding with her, and he'll throw me under the bus first chance he gets. I'm risking my job with the hopes of finding something in these lab tests that might not even be there."

"But what about Bristol?" Hathaway says. "Did you find any of those other chemicals in her?"

"No. She was completely clean."

"See, I told you. She's not flaking."

"Hathaway, you're focusing all your attention on this one girl, all the while women are lying down and *dying*, like they've just given up on living. It's not a side effect of flake. You know that. There's something else going on here, and you need to put an end to it."

"I can't stop a conspiracy that I can't see."

"You can't see it because you're hovering over Bristol like you're her mother. More women are going to die if you don't stop it!"

"I can't stop it. You know as well as I do that Klein is in on this, and if I so much as point a finger at him, he'll send my ass packing. And if I'm gone, this girl will be the next to die in the bin."

What the hell is going on here? Why is Hathaway so worried about me? I'm in prison for murder. I strangled my own lawyer. I've just stabbed a woman's eye out with a paintbrush. And still she's insisting I'm her sole purpose in life? Why is this woman so obsessed with me?

My heart starts pounding and I must be going into shock again but ...

I take the scalpel from the doctor's desk and slice it across Baydar's neck, and then Hathaway's—

"Hey, calm down or else—" Dr. Baydar tries to warn me as the sirens go off. A guard rushes through the door and pushes past Hathaway and Dr. Baydar.

"Bristol!" shouts the guard as he aims his stun gun at me. "Calm yourself immediately or I will shoot!"

Hathaway throws out her arm in the guard's path. "You will stand down. That is an order!"

"She needs to be subdued."

"You need to back off!"

"Get your hands off my guard." I focus just enough to see Klein walking across the room. It's suddenly very crowded in here.

"You've been reassigned, Hathaway," Klein says. "Level One."

"*What?*" Dr. Baydar and Hathaway shout in unison.

The response garners a smug grin from Klein, and his mustache twists into his cheek. "You heard me. The warden has had enough with this nonsense with the fancy girl. It's drawing the attention of the other inmates and is likely the cause of the fight in the library. Bristol is my responsibility now."

Hathaway and Dr. Baydar yell and argue with Klein, and all I can focus on is the self-satisfied curl of Klein's mustache.

I'm in a room similar to the infirmary, but it's large with a dozen beds. Klein, Hathaway, and Dr. Baydar are strapped down in three of them—

I blink and I'm back in my own bed.

Klein and Dr. Baydar are in each other's faces, and Hathaway stands staring down at me.

Klein, Hathaway, and the doc are under scanning lasers, their brains sending rapid spurts of data to the bedside panels—

There's no stopping the visions now. They appear like a flash.

I go to Klein first. I press the whirring blade of a circular saw into his forehead—

What's happening? I'm having a vision almost exactly like the one where I killed Rick. Only, Rick didn't survive that vision.

I move next to the doc and saw off her head as well—

"Aaargh!"

All three of them look at me. I've yelled out loud. My wrists throb because I've been yanking so hard on the tracker cuffs.

At last there's Hathaway. I cut off the top of her skull, exposing her brain, which I rip from her head and place on a table next to a dozen other freshly-removed brains—

Sweat rolls into my eyes. The salt burns and makes me tear up. My heart is fluttering so rapidly I can hardly catch my breath. Everything hurts and I really want more than anything to hit something. I no longer fade into the visions with warning. Now they're flashes spliced into my consciousness, blending seamlessly into my reality. And I'm aware of it the whole time.

"Get her out of here," Klein orders.

"You don't have the authority!" says Hathaway.

"I'd like to see you argue with the warden," he says, "as though she's even paying attention. This prison is mine now."

Three more guards come in and wrestle their way through the women. I'm detached from the bed, the tubes torn out of my arm so quickly I feel my veins going with them. There's no slight of hand the way these guards drag me from the infirmary. They plop me face-first on my own bed. Klein and Hathaway stand in the doorway of my cell; one guard amused at my decrepit state, the other visibly disappointed by it.

"You're under probation," says Klein. "No community time for you until further notice."

"The library—" I mutter.

"The library is closed. Permanently."

Klein smirks, then shuts my door and walks away, nose held in the air.

Hathaway hovers in the corridor. Her face has softened, her mouth droops down her chin, and she looks shorter than usual. For whatever reason this woman had for keeping me safe, she's now lost her ability to do so. My protector is my protector no more. Two guards nudge her to move, takes a big sigh and lets herself be escorted from Level Three.

21 givers and takers

Hathaway stands on the other side of my plexiglass door, stiff and comatose. She's missing the top of her skull, her brain exposed, glistening in goo. She lurches forward and her forehead hits the glass, BONG! And again, BONG! Her brain leaves smears on the glass. Klein appears from behind her, a black box in his hand with an optic cable leading into her head. He presses a button and she jolts into the glass. BONG! BONG! BONG!—

"What are you doing!" I hear Goldie, but her voice is distant.

The door opens. Hathaway falls to my feet. Klein doesn't have the chance to move before I take a swing at him—

"This is bad! This is really bad!" Now I see Goldie; she's waving her arms. Why is she waving like that?

Klein is stunned by my attack. He bounces back like a balloon on a string and I hit him again—

"They're coming! You're gonna get caught!" Goldie's voice is clearer now. I can see her standing in the corridor. There's blood all over her face. She looks horrified.

I keep wailing on Klein, punch after punch, breaking his teeth, his nose, his face—

"Stop!"

My eyes focus and it's not Goldie who has blood on her, it's the plexiglass of my closed cell door, smeared with blood from my hands.

"Clean up this mess or you'll never get out of here!" Goldie scurries down the corridor.

This is the third time I've had this vision and slammed my hands into the glass. This time I've broken skin, and it has left a mess. Boots clamor down the corridor and I grab the only thing I can think of—my pillow—and wipe the blood from the door.

"Bristol." Klein is at my cell. "Everything all right in here?"

I toss my pillow on my bed as casually as I can without showing the dirtied side. "Um, yeah. Everything's fine."

Klein scans the room and I can swear he's spotted the faint remnants of blood smears on the plexiglass. He pulls his lips tight, bunching his mustache under his nose. At last the door slides open and hides the evidence.

"It's your lucky day, Bristol. Your probation is over. Two months done. The time has been good for your face too. You don't look like such a mess."

Klein looks me over and chuckles, then waves his guards away from the corridor. Once their footsteps disappear, I take my first step through the threshold and breathe in the scents of the prison. It's musty and metallic, but better than the stale air of my cell.

I feel eyes on me. Lots of eyes. Down to the far end of the corridor a dozen women huddle together, arms crossed, glaring at me.

"*You!*" A woman squeals as she pushes her way through to the front of the pack and huffs at me. Her left eye socket is fitted with a plastic cap. "Look what you did. You popped my goddamn eye out! Do you have any idea how much that hurt?"

Goldie hovers behind me and shouts over my shoulder. "You attacked her first!"

"I did not!"

"You did! I saw you!"

"She looks all innocent and shit, but what they say about her is true. She's a psycho! Psycho Slicer! Psycho Slicer!"

The women follow the one-eyed girl's chant. "*Psycho Slicer!*" The mob moves in, closing the gap.

I lunge at the woman and jab my fist into her mouth—

I blink back to the present. The flickering visions are furious, tossing me in and out of them.

I grab the woman's eye cap and rip it from her socket. Blood spurts all over—

"C'mon, don't do this." Goldie has me by the left arm, my right one is in the air, hand folded in a tight fist. The tension breaks the lesions and blood trickles down my wrist.

The one-eyed girl thrashes around in the arms of two women. "Let me at her! I'll kill her! I'll kill the Slicer!"

I have a paintbrush in either hand, the ends sharpened to a splintered point. I thrust the spears through any soft flesh I can reach, stabbing woman after woman—

Goldie is on the floor, staring up at me like I've pushed her there. The women keep chanting. "*Psycho Slicer!*" I'm outnumbered twelve to one. I don't have a chance of surviving this if I can't stop the visions.

BAAM! BAAM! BAAM! BAAM! Both hands into the wall. Pain shoots up my forearms to my elbows. Tears form in my eyes. My entire body tenses with shock, but the visions are gone. The women have stopped shouting. My attacker gapes at me through her remaining eye.

"What the hell is wrong with you?" she says.

LaRae's voice enters my ears like a ghostly howl. "I warned you to keep away from her. You don't wanna set her off."

"You're lucky Baby ain't here," another woman says. "She'd put you both in a shallow grave in the yard."

"Baby would have to survive *these* first," LaRae says as she grabs my bloody fist and holds it out. I wince in pain, but LaRae doesn't seem to notice. "You don't wanna end up completely blind, do ya?"

The one-eyed girl grits her teeth and stiffens her body as a pair of guards walk into the corridor, followed by Klein.

"You ladies having a party?" Klein says. "And you didn't invite me. I'm insulted."

One of the cubs bravely steps forward. "What do you want, Klein?"

The woman's cuffs *zap* and she hollers in pain. Klein shoves his way past Goldie and me and grabs the woman by the hair.

"You dare speak to me like that again, I'll let the rats pick you apart in the bin."

The woman grits her teeth. "Not if Baby can help it."

"Baby is not in control." Klein lets the girl go and looks to the rest of the pack. "You hear me, ladies? I run this joint."

Klein barrels through the group of women and the other guards follow, careful not to touch anyone. The women glare after

Klein, then at me and LaRae. I avert my eyes to avoid agitating them further.

"Let's get Baby," a woman says to the cubs.

The stare-off dissipates as each woman leaves the hallway. LaRae still has hold of my hand and I pull on her.

"It's not your time yet, Princess," LaRae whispers. She narrows her eyes at me, then releases my hand and walks away.

Goldie scrambles to her feet and stands against the opposite wall. I reach out to her with my bloody hand and she winces.

"I'm sorry," I say. "Did I hurt you?"

She looks at my hand, then at my face. "No, I'm fine, but you have to stop doing that."

I know this is getting worse. My visions are no longer separated from reality—they're melding together. I have no way to stop my tick. I can bash my hands into walls until they're completely numb, and then what, my toes? My face? I'm going to beat *myself* to a pulp before anyone else has the chance to.

"Goldie, I need to ask you something."

"Yeah? What?"

"Not here. Away from the cameras. Let's go to the yard."

"But the girls will be there."

"It's breakfast time. We'll only be there for as long as everyone else is in the mess hall." I pull her arm and we scramble through the maze of corridors to the yard. Down the halls and in the common rooms every inmate and guard stops to stare at my face. When we reach the yard, the few women lounging in the dirt can't take their eyes off me. It takes me a moment to realize why.

"I haven't looked in a mirror," I tell Goldie. "Is my face really that bad?"

She peers at me and I'm worried now that she's taking so long to answer. "Eeh, there's something different. I don't know what."

"Different? How? My nose? It feels a little crooked."

"Yeah, kinda. Now you actually look like you belong in prison."

That's not the answer I was hoping for. "Goldie, I need to ask you a favor."

She makes a grimace. "This doesn't sound like a good thing."

"I can't keep doing this," I say and hold up my broken fists.

"Yeah, no shit," she says with a grunt.

"You know how I said before that I get this urge to hit things?"

"You hit walls. It makes you look like a psycho."

I wish she'd stop interrupting me because she's making this ordeal that much more uncomfortable. "It's getting worse. I can't control it. I need to calm myself down before I actually hurt somebody."

"You killed a man to get in here, then you went and stabbed a girl's eye out, and now you're worried about hurting someone? Shouldn't you have thought of that sooner?"

"The only times I didn't want to hit someone was when I worked in the library—"

"Which is closed now."

I sigh. "*Or* ... when they gave me those sedatives in the jail."

Goldie pauses. "Oh no. No. Don't go there."

"Goldie, I need drugs."

"You'll end up in the bin if you're caught using!"

"I'll end up in the bin if I hurt someone else!"

She shakes her head and her blond hair covers her face. "Oh shit, girl, LaRae's gonna be so mad if she finds out you're buying from Baby ..."

"Why does LaRae care so much about that?"

She squints at me. "Really? You know how Baby Cub gets the flake in here."

"I don't—"

"Klein!" Goldie says a bit too loudly. "Klein sneaks it in and Baby sells and he takes a cut of the sales. It's their deal. You buy from Baby and your money's going straight to Klein's wallet. That's why LaRae hates him. Well, other than the fact that he traded flake for sex with Candy …"

I don't have time for this. I need the drugs before I hit someone, and right now that person might be Goldie. "Look, I know LaRae doesn't want me buying from Baby, but I'm running out of options. If I don't find a way to calm down my tick, I'm going to ruin everything!"

She throws out her hands defensively. "Hey, girl. I'm sorry, but I'm staying out of this. LaRae's the only friend I have in this place, and if she were to find out I got you using, she'll disown me and get me sent to the bin like she did with Candy."

"Wait, what—?"

"LaRae doesn't like to be betrayed. She'll hurt you. Bad. Don't do it. She will end you."

She turns on her heels and leaves me in a cloud of yard dust. I've just lost my one remaining ally in prison. Well, I haven't *yet*, but I most certainly will if I buy flake, which means my solitude is inevitable. I know I've made up my mind. If I don't find a way to subdue my tick, I'll either be killed or end up in the bin. Or both.

This is it. I need flake.

Baby Cub will be in the laundry room. Klein may be there too. And LaRae. But so will the drugs. It's worth the risk.

The anticipation of relief from the visions and the fear of getting caught are doing a frolicking tango inside my stomach, and I feel like I might puke on my way to the laundry room. I must have the deer-in-headlights look of a creeper because all heads turn when I enter. I stand there frozen in place, and a guard looks me over.

"What are you doing here?" he asks.

"I'm … um … here for work?"

"You're late for your shift," he says and hands me a scrubber.

Baby Cub is busy scraping down a vat. She's got so much sweat pouring into her sunken eyes that she doesn't even see me until I'm ten feet from her, on the opposite side of a conveyor belt which forms a convenient barrier between us. The beast smiles and looks me over like prey to be devoured. I need to get this over with. I pull open the collar of my jumper and reveal the small stack of bills in the interior breast pocket. Baby Cub laughs, and so do the women nearby. My cheeks burn with humiliation. I've just reached the lowest low I possibly could in prison.

Baby Cub nods her head to the rumbling meeting-place dryer. I follow the length of the conveyor belt, keeping a close watch on Baby Cub. She does the same, her belly jiggling with every step. I lose sight of her once I reach the dryer, and as I come around I see her standing there, chubby arms resting on her stomach. She's no longer smiling. In fact, she seems disappointed.

"We could have used you," she says just loud enough to be heard over the machines. "You could have belonged to us. You're just too difficult to control."

"I don't belong to anyone." I can't tell if it's the movement of the dryer that makes my voice tremble. "I just want to survive my time in here."

"That won't happen either, fancy. But I'll take your money either way. Do you have enough?"

"I don't know how much I need."

She squints then rolls her eyes. "Lemme see." She holds out her hand and twitches her stubby fingers.

"Oh, you want … okay, here." I hand her my stack of bills, and she thumbs through it.

"This is good for one month."

"One month? That's it?"

"That's all you'll need, fancy."

That hardly makes sense, but I suppose I'll have to find another way to make more money so I can buy more flake. "Fine. I'll take what I can get."

Baby Cub rummages through a crate and pulls out a small bag of capsules. I reach for them and she pulls back. "Prove to me that you're not with LaRae."

"She's not my friend."

"She's chummy with you."

That seems unlikely. "I don't know what LaRae is up to. I don't care. I just want to get through this."

Baby Cub looks me over. "There's no getting through this," she says and hands over the capsules.

I can't stand to hear another word out of her flapping mouth, so I stuff the bag of drugs down my jumper and leave the meeting-place dryer. Behind me, I hear Klein's voice calling across the room. I glance over my shoulder just as he stabs his stun gun right into Baby's gut. She barely winces, but the fury in her face is unmistakable. Eyes spot me passing through the laundry room, shooting grisly stares. I put my head down and race back to my cell.

Goldie isn't on the cell block. I'm relieved that I don't have to explain this to her. I pull the bag from my jumper, take out one capsule, and stuff the rest in my pillowcase. My heart races as I hold the capsule in my palm; I'm trembling with the eagerness and relief of finally subduing the visions.

I squeeze the capsule on my tongue, sit on the bed, close my eyes, and wait for the drugs to take effect. A familiar warm sensation flows through me, but something's different. There's a twinge in my jaw, and when I open my eyes the walls are closing in around me. I jump to my feet I feel like I'm falling through the floor.

This is not the same as the sedatives, nor the spinners. These are laced with something else. I don't know what, but I don't like it. Splashing water on my face helps to stop me from sinking into the floor of quicksand, but I look up and swear I see three times as many cameras in my cell. They're probably watching me right now, dressing themselves in riot gear to drag me to the bin. Footsteps clamor down the hall, and I flop back onto the bed, wrapping myself in the blanket. This is it. They're coming to get me.

LaRae bursts into my cell. She rushes over, takes my head in her hands and studies my face. She growls and tosses my head into the mattress.

"What the hell do you think you're doing, Princess?"

"Me?"

"Yeah, ya fool. *You*!" She paces around my cell and my wonky eyes create three separate versions of her, each more furious than the other. "What did I tell you about gettin' on flake, huh? You're feeding the animals!"

My tongue weighs a ton, and I have to focus to speak. "I'm not doing it to spite anyone. I'm doing it to stop *this*." I hold up a bloody fist.

She pushes my arm aside. "You didn't listen to me. No one listens to me. Candy didn't care. She turned against me. She went with Klein."

"And you got her caught, didn't you?"

LaRae doesn't catch my insult; she's too busy ranting. "You're on their side, aren't 'cha? I knew it. I knew you'd be like the rest of them. If you're with them, then you're against me."

"I'm not with anyone. I'm all alone." I didn't mean to say it that way, but as the words leave my mouth they leave a hollow emptiness in my chest.

LaRae stops pacing and glares at me. "What are you trying to do, Princess?"

"I just want to go away." *It.* I just want *it* to go away. Right? Isn't that what I meant to say?

LaRae pauses, then leans her body over mine. "Listen, Princess. You're so far down the rabbit hole you can't even see light anymore. But this ain't over. You're gonna do this for me whether you want to or not."

She lunges over me toward my flake stash. I have just enough sense to use my body's rolling momentum to pin her arm to the wall, and she yelps and jumps back.

"What seems to be going on in here?" Klein appears in the doorway. LaRae tenses at the sound of his voice. "I didn't think Bristol was your type, LaRae."

LaRae slinks off my bed, never looking at Klein. She flashes me an insufferable glare, then dashes from my cell.

"Whoa! Why the hurry?" Klein chuckles, but she's already gone. He clears his throat and lowers his voice. "You sure know how to draw attention to yourself, Bristol."

I squeeze my eyes shut and I hear Klein's footsteps come closer. There's a beep and the glass door slides shut. Klein has locked himself in my cell. My body is rubber and even though the drugs suppress my tick, I also don't have the sense to defend myself.

"Pay attention, Bristol, I need you to understand something. This is *my* institution. I take my job very seriously. I am the eyes and ears of this prison. No one does anything here without me knowing about it."

I peek through my eyelids and see him leaning against the opposite wall, his arms folded across his chest. Klein has been watching me. He knows I was in the laundry room.

"The warden is an ACTA puppet, and I can assure you they've forgotten she's even here. This place isn't ACTA's concern anymore. So I've taken it upon myself to handle things. Every eye and every camera leads back to me, and I know what everyone is up to. This includes Dr. Baydar." There's a slight rattle in his voice. "I know about those labs she snuck past me. I don't know how she did it, but she's no longer an employee here, I can assure you that. But I read the report. That flake isn't what you think it is. Sucks for you, but good for me."

The room spins with Klein at the center. My body feels like it's stretching around him, being pulled apart at the edge of a black hole, about to disappear into nothingness.

"Now, here's the interesting part," Klein says as he shifts his weight. "The drugs make you girls easier to control, and that makes my job easier. I like easy. I like to keep things running smoothly, with everyone in line, safe and secure. You're lucky Hathaway is no longer on Level Three because she'd send you straight to the bin for using. I won't do that."

The room stops moving, and Klein's uniform hardens and shimmers like a knight's armor. *Klein*? My knight in shining armor? I should be gagging at the thought, yet for some reason I feel safer with him in my cell.

"We're going to make a deal, Bristol." Klein's armor grows spikes, and his stun gun transforms into a gigantic sword. "I'm going to keep you out of the bin because—well, let's face it, you won't last three days in there. So keep your drugs, make yourself easy for me to control and wait patiently for the next step. But here are my terms: Stay away from LaRae. She is the bane of my existence here. I want that woman as isolated as possible. You so much as look at her and I'll lock you up. Do you hear me?"

I have no idea what he's talking about because I'm so transfixed on his sword as it turns into a fiery spire, but I don't *care* what he's talking about because he's not here to drag me to the bin. He's going to let me keep my drugs.

"Yes," I mumble.

"Good," he says. "I'm glad we understand each other. Just know, Bristol … you will survive in here, but not on the outside."

Just like that, the door slides open and Klein is gone.

22 uninvited guests

Klein's words are terrifying. I know they should be terrifying, but I don't actually *feel* terrified because these drugs have turned me into an emotionless blob. I like feeling like an emotionless blob. I don't care that I can't get myself to leave my cell more than once a day to eat. I don't care that when I do wander down the corridors, I can sense LaRae and Baby Cub shooting lightning bolts from their eyes into the back of my skull. I don't care about any of it.

The drugs have stopped the visions, but I still see things. I think they're mostly in my head, but sometimes it's hard to tell. The walls flex like they're made of soft rubber. Eyeballs blink in the camera dome in the corner of my cell. My feet slide on black ice that covers the floor. I feel I'm being watched *all the time.* And then I see Klein in his shining medieval armor, and somehow I think he's here to keep me safe. I don't know why that is, because I despise the man, but he's letting me keep my drugs and I want nothing more than to be a numb blob of a girl. So today I pop an extra capsule on my tongue, and shove three more in my jumper breast pocket should I need another.

"Bristol!" A guard comes stomping down the hallway. "Visiting rooms. Now."

I have a visitor? I haven't been allowed visitors this whole time due to probation. And now, even after all this, I don't want to see anyone, not even my mom. I want everyone to leave me alone.

But I'm in prison and I'm not given a choice.

The visiting room is similar to the one in the LA jail. One desk, two chairs, and a divider of plexiglass. I stand in the doorway and do my best to focus my blurry eyesight so I can see who it is they've forced me to interact with. I hear his voice before I see him.

"Ah! There she is!"

Diego Felix. I don't know whether to feel relived or upset, but it's difficult to feel anything with the extra drugs in my system. I sure picked a bad day to double-up.

"Sit down and let me have a look atcha." He gives me that sexy grin, and I tremble a little. Apparently I can still feel *that.* I saunter over to the chair as carefully as possible because I don't know how stable my legs are.

His chuckles. "Ah damn, Jo! Look what they did to that perfect face of yours. Although…" he tilts his head "…I kinda like you better like this. You look more badass."

"When are you getting me out?"

"You just got here. You wanna leave already?"

He's joking, right?

Felix sits in his chair and folds one leg on top of the other. He's wearing shorts. His legs are hairless and covered in more tattoos. I feel a thump in my chest, and I realize I haven't seen this much of a man in almost a year.

"All right, look. I heard about the fight. You're lucky that girl didn't die, otherwise your punishment would have been a lot worse. And anyway, didn't I warn you about threatening people with toothbrushes?"

He laughs at his own joke, and I wish he'd stop talking so much. My head is too fuzzy for this, and I swear his tattoos are swirling around his arms.

"It was a paintbrush."

"Everah. I'm here to see how you're doing. How is it with that … uh … whatcha call it? Jinx?"

"Tick."

He snaps his fingers. "Yes! That's it. A *tick.* Shit, I've been trying to remember that for the last eight months."

Get to the point, buddy. Your tattoos are coming alive and it's really freaking me out. "Why are you here?"

"Because you're such a beautiful sight! Well, you *were* …"

"I don't want you here if you're just going to tease me."

He folds his arms. "All right, fine. I'm here to tell you I have good news. The ACTA courts agreed to take your case."

The glass divider has turned into a waterfall, and it takes a moment for his statement to travel through the mist. "I'm getting out?"

He grins. "Yep! Well, you still have to prove to ACTA that you're not an Alias sympathizer."

I don't like where this is going. I don't like what he's saying. I don't like the way he looks at me when he says it. "I'm not a sympathizer."

"*And*, you have to prove that you were absolutely certain that Rick was hacking your mom's brain."

My mind floods with something, a feeling I can't put my finger on. It's there, just out of reach, but close enough to make me uneasy. A lump forms in my throat and I try to swallow it down. "I was sent here because they proved that's not what happened."

He flicks his hand. "Your trial is irrelevant now. Ibanez was your arresting officer and there's reason to question whether the evidence was tampered with, whether the equipment actually *was there*. They're suspecting a cleanup, that Santino Salazar was involved. ACTA needs more information about the Salazar brothers, and since your mom's head is all screwy, they'll be needing *your* help. You now have bargaining power." He leans back and grins. "What did I tell ya, huh? You happy now?"

Happy? No. I don't know what I feel, but it's most certainly not happiness. My pulse thumps in my ears and a pressure builds in my belly. Even though I don't want to believe it, something in the back of my mind tells me this is all wrong. I don't trust Felix. I don't believe anything he's saying. I don't know why, but I'm waiting for him to say some magic word to make me feel better.

"Listen, Jo. This isn't an easy ticket out. You still gotta keep your end of the deal. You need to stay out of trouble or ACTA won't help you."

Shadows and shapes fly between us, as though I were standing along a highway with Felix on the opposite side. He wants to get me out of prison, but I don't belong out there, not in the real world. I won't survive.

I need to know why he's here. "Why are you helping me?"

His smile drops and his eyes get serious. "I have my reasons."

"Back at the jail, you said we were connected."

"Well, that's part of it," he says. "We both know Manuel Torres."

"Torres?"

"The principal of East Hollywood Trade School. He's my dad."

A bright light flashes in my brain, because somehow I think I knew that. "But your name is—"

"Felix. Yeah, I do know my own name, thanks. It's my mom's name. My mom told me my dad left us. Turns out, he never knew I existed."

"Why did Mr. Torres want to help me?"

"Oh hell, I donno. I think he's trying to find a good wife for me to settle down with." I snarl at him and he laughs. "I know, right? He doesn't pick the most *available* women."

"Why did your dad try to help me at the trade school?"

Felix's lips quiver. "Because I asked him to."

There has been a conspiracy against me, brewed between Felix and Mr. Torres. I have been their pawn all along. Felix's eyes light up with flashing red beams, a warning signal to *get out.* This man is not my knight. He's here to keep me from my mission. What mission …? There was a mission? There is. I feel it. Someone told me. Klein? I'm not sure. There's something nagging, something telling me that I can't let Felix take me anywhere. I have to stay here. Right here. I can't let him save me. I won't survive out there.

Felix leans closer to the glass and the wolf tattoo jumps off his neck and flies straight for me, and I shield my face with my arms.

"Jo? What the hell?"

I look through my arms to see Felix studying me. I straighten and do my best to act natural, but he's already on to me.

"Goddammit, Jo." His voice is low and rumbling. "You're flaking, aren't you?"

I shake my head and the room spins. "You can't get me out."

His face turns white, all the muscles and skin go slack. "No …" He pushes the chair back and stands. His hands dance in front of him like he's poking his fingers into fire. "No, Jo, please don't tell me you got flake."

"I had to stop the visions." I'm trying to yell back, but my voice is barely a whisper.

"Jo. This is bad." His voice is hard, rough in my ears. "It's not what you think it is, trust me. They're not sedatives, they're—" He stops himself, straightens, and runs his hand over his hair. He glances at the camera on the ceiling, then back at me. "Jo, you have to get off that stuff. Now."

I knew it. He's not here to protect me. He wants me to loose control. "I need the flake to stop the visions. Without the drugs I'm gonna kill somebody and I'll ruin everything."

Water splashes on my hands and I realize I'm crying, but I don't care anymore. I don't care if I get out of here or not. My chance of survival ended a long time ago. I don't care if I die in my cell pumped full of drugs or in the bin with a spoon slashed through my throat. I don't care. I just don't care. Don't. Care.

Felix takes a long breath and leans his hands on the table. "I'm going to get you out of here. I'm going to save you. But I won't be able to if you're …" he swallows "…*gone* before I get to you."

"I don't—"

"Listen to me, Jo. Flush those drugs down the toilet and forget about them. You will survive this. I promise."

The tears stop. The red beams in his eyes vanish. The tension in my throat eases.

Felix said the magic words.

A loud beep rings through the room and Felix jerks.

"I have to go," he says. "You're gonna be okay, Jo. Just stick it out for a little longer."

He backs toward the door, keeping his eyes on me, his brow perched out so far it casts a shadow on his face. I swear I see a glimpse of a knight's sword on his hip as he slides from the room.

I'm left alone. The pulse of adrenaline forces through the drugs as I wait for the guard to come fetch me. I am so confused. I don't know who to believe. My instincts tell me one thing, yet my head tells me another. It's too much. I can't handle this. I want nothing more than to crawl into a cave and wait for the chaos to pass.

I don't get to.

The visitor door opens again. And there in the threshold stands Lyle.

"Lyle!" The sight of him breaks a crack in my drug bubble, and for a moment there is light. "I'm so happy to see you."

"Hey, Jo." Lyle is startled, not nearly as eager as I am. He's skinnier than I remember, his skin more pale, his blond hair down to his shoulders. He sits in the chair and studies me with a frown. "What happened to your nose?"

I feel the rush of blood to my cheeks. "I got in a fight."

He pauses with his mouth open. "The dads say *hi*."

I nod. "Oh. Thanks. Tell them *hi* back."

He nods. Now I don't know what to say. I've known Lyle my entire life and it's like I'm meeting him for the first time.

"How's my mom?"

"She's doing okay. She's at some hospital in the Valley. They're giving her light therapy. Nolan has been to see her a few times. She seems to be making progress."

"Good … good." This is a nightmare. And I suddenly feel really tired. "Lyle, I'm so sorry …"

"Don't apologize. It doesn't matter anymore."

"What do you mean by that?"

He shakes his head. "It's a disaster, Jo. They've turned your life into a freak show. At least once a day we get a call from some TV program wanting to do an exposé on you."

"Oh my god …"

"We won't talk to them, but other people have. Some of our old school friends, the Baez sisters, Harley. They're trying to convince people they saw it coming, like they knew all along you'd turn out to be a killer. They say it's the quiet ones, the artists who internalize their emotions."

I feel like I'm melting into the chair.

"And the family of Rick Salazar is claiming you're all Alias Agents. You, your mom, even your dad. They want to prove it was a setup."

The tension in my throat returns, and this time I can't swallow down the lump.

But Lyle goes on. "They couldn't prove that your mom was hacked, and she can't remember anything. No one can figure out why you did it. I don't know why you did it. You're not the same girl I knew. I mean, look at you. You don't even *look* the same."

My eyesight blurs and darkens. This could be the drugs, but I know better than that. It's coming, and the only thing left for me to do is send my fist into the table.

BAAM!

Pain stabs into my hand. Lyle jumps back in his chair. Two capsules of drugs and I still teeter on the razor's edge between reality and the visions.

"I don't know what to do," Lyle says, his eyes on my hand. "You're my best friend but things are … *different* now. I mean, I wish it weren't. I don't know when you're getting out of here, and … well, things are getting tricky."

Tricky for *him*?

"We're moving. To Denver. Nolan got a job up there. We can't stay in LA. It's madness, not to mention Dylan is worried about Alias and all that. So we're leaving."

I sigh. That's all I can do. I don't even want to plead with him to stay.

"I kept the painting for you, the one with the girl in the burning city. I put it in a safety deposit box in a bank near your mom's hospital. Nolan gave her the key. She'll have it when … well, when you get out."

He's an idiot to think the painting will be safe with my mom. He must know this. He couldn't have already forgotten what happens to her at the *mention* of my dad, let alone the visual sight of one of his paintings. How can he possibly think this is what I would have wanted?

Lyle doesn't care about how I feel. I'm not sure he ever did. He's not here to bring positive vibes or encouragements for the future. He's here to tell me goodbye, *so long and thanks for all the bullshit.* And now my drugs have worn off and my knuckles are throbbing, and I want nothing more than for him to leave.

Lyle gets the point. He sighs and stands up. "I know who you were, Jo. You were an amazing girl. I hope you return to that. Take care of yourself."

I don't look up to see him leave. It doesn't matter. He's going off to live his life away from me and my infectious destruction. I can't say that I blame him. *Take care of yourself* ... Honestly, I don't want to.

The guards come to take me back to my cell. They can tell I've been crying, but I don't care. I don't want to care about anything. I want to flood my brain with drugs and drift into the ether of nothingness.

But on my way back I sense something is wrong. LaRae passes me in the hallway, and she's got a suspicious glint in her dark eyes. She's been in my cell, I know it. I stumble into my cell and to my horror I cannot find my bag of flake capsules, my tiny containers of relief. I frantically search the bed, the floor, the corners of the room, under the sink, under the toilet, inside my pillow case.

But it's no use. The drugs are gone. All that is left are the three capsules in my jumper.

23 the yardbirds

My panic attack is swift and merciless. Fear floods my body like a tidal wave. Prickling pain crawls up my body like hungry spiders, from my toes up to my neck, sparking my jawbone on fire. My muscles are so tense that a slight tap on my shoulder would shatter me into a million pieces.

Warm liquid from one of the final three flake capsules drips onto my tongue and eases the anger and hatred pulsing through me. For now.

Two remaining.

Who took my drugs? It had to be LaRae. It had to. I would demand she give them back, but knowing her she's already destroyed the evidence. She's got an axe to grind with Klein, and I've become her whetstone. Now, thanks to her, my future is in turmoil, and soon I will have no drugs to escape into.

One remaining.

Three days pass as I hide in my cell, desperate to hold together my splitting seams. I'm completely losing sense of reality, and it's not because of the drugs. I feel disconnected from myself, as though I were some fossilized version of who I used to be, nothing more than an empty shell. It's over for me. Felix says he'll get me out, but there's no chance I'll survive until then.

None remaining.

I must find Baby Cub. Maybe she'll be willing to deal to me on a loan of sorts, at least until I can get another job. If I can get the drugs, then I'll be calm and vision-free. I can get another job and pay back Baby Cub and then get more drugs. LaRae won't be able to keep up and Klein will watch over me and everything will be fine.

Everything will be okay if I can get more drugs. I just have to get more drugs.

I stumble down the corridors on the hunt for Baby Cub, but I'm so rigid I can't move my mouth to ask if anyone's seen her. No one is even paying attention to me; they hardly notice I'm there. Nearly every woman trudges through the corridors like zombies, others prop their shoulders on walls and doorframes, their eyes vacant, chins covered in drool. Some women sit on the floor, and I can't tell if they're resting or unconscious.

I pass a common room on the way to the mess hall and notice the TV is on. This seems to be the only room inhabited by women who are not drugged out. A handful of Baby's cubs are crammed in front of the wall, eagerly watching the screen. All I see are blurred shapes and bleeding colors, and I'm not in the mood to watch TV so I start to head on, but then someone says my name. Not *my* name, but rather my media-created nickname.

"Oh hey, you're on the news. The Schoolgirl Slicer!"

An invisible force pulls me toward the TV, as though my battered soul is ripe for yet another beating. In the program, a gussied-up reporter yammers into the camera, making sure everyone remembers all the horrible details of what I did last year. They show the video of me being escorted from Rick's house in my blood-covered, glimmering outfit, and the women in the room burst out hooting and whistling. The sight of myself makes my stomach churn, and I search for a corner to puke into, but the next scene on the TV pulls me in like a hypnotic swirl.

It's the Mehra family, all four of them, sitting on a couch in the news studio. Mrs. Mehra looks furious and wild-eyed. Satesh is there, his chiseled cheeks sunken and hollow. And Madri. My dear friend Madri is crying.

Dr. Mehra avoids the camera. The reporter smiles and asks a question, and Dr. Mehra answers the floor. "Yes, well, the Bristol family had a history of mental illness. Her father, Jethro Bristol, was my patient. I diagnosed him with schizophrenia."

The reporter leans in to get another shot of herself on TV. "He committed suicide two years ago, isn't that right?"

"Yes," Dr. Mehra says. "We were making progress with his illness until he could no longer afford the treatments."

It's Mrs. Mehra's turn for the camera. "I got him a commission with FutureTech and he turned it down because he didn't like the terms of the arrangement."

"Is that right?" the reporter says.

Dr. Mehra winces. "Jethro insisted medication inhibited his artistic sensibilities. Without it, the schizophrenia symptoms got worse and he had visions."

My dad had *visions*?

Madri suddenly stops crying, and she jerks to look at her father. No one else notices.

"Visions?" says the reporter.

"Yes," says Dr. Mehra. "He had visions of his daughter, of Jo. He told me he was scared that if he took the commission through FutureTech they'd send him to the brain adjusters for light therapy and as a result he'd lose his visions of artistry. He couldn't bear to let Jo see that happen to him."

"So he killed himself!" says Mrs. Mehra and thrusts her finger at the camera.

"The Bristols are certainly a family with many issues, aren't they?" says the reporter with a puzzling smile. "It's no wonder this story has turned out the way it has."

Dr. Mehra grips the couch arm like he's getting ready to stand. "Jethro told me one day he had a vision of what would happen once he became an employee of FutureTech. In his vision he saw Jo become angry and violent."

The reporter gasps dramatically. Mrs. Mehra turns red. Satesh is stiff as a statue.

Madri jumps to her feet and screams at her father. "Don't say that! Jo is a good person! This isn't her fault!"

And the program cuts off—just like that—and I'm standing there with the cubs gaping at me. I can't believe Dr. Mehra would say something like that on national TV. But Madri … at least someone still believes I'm a decent human being. It doesn't matter; everyone else believes I was destined to be a monster.

The TV graphics flash something about "*Breaking News from the Border*" and the attention of the room is diverted. A reporter shouts over the sounds of gunfire. "Things are getting very precarious at the Mexican-American border as an army of international Alias foot soldiers makes its way to the wall. The border patrol is doing all it can to keep the advancing army back, but there isn't the manpower to hold it."

"Hah!" one woman shouts. "See? I knew they'd be comin' to tear down the system!"

I step closer to hear the TV. "There are reports that Alias has already hacked into the border security," says the reporter, "but ACTA assures that all FutureTech security systems are secure and cannot be breached. It's a cyber-battle behind the scenes, but as we can see, there's quite a lot of armed people ready to—"

A huge fiery explosion rips through the wall behind the reporter, spouting out metal and concrete in every direction. Hundreds of guerilla soldiers race through the hole and into US territory.

The cubs in the common room burst out cheering and hollering, and the zombied women collapse to their knees. Alarm sirens wail, and then stop and start again.

A guard races down the corridor, yelling into his wristlet. "Come in, Level Three Command. Can you hear me? Anyone? Hello!"

More guards race in the other direction, shouting nonsensical instructions at each other. Baby's cubs push me through the common room door and into the madness, and all I can think about is Dr. Mehra and Madri and my dad. Then the flickering visions return. Visions of yanking off Mrs. Mehra's arms. Visions of stabbing a scalpel in Dr. Mehra's head. Visions of bashing my fists into LaRae, Klein, Ibanez, Santino …

I won't survive this bedlam of inmates and guards, invasion or not. I have to hide. As fast as I can I stumble to my cell block, slamming my fists into the walls, leaving bloodied handprints in my wake.

A group of women swarm me I don't realize what's happening until someone grabs my arm and drags me through a door and into the yard. I'm shoved into the dirt as the building doors slam shut and the sirens stop. We're not supposed to be outside during a lockdown, everyone knows this, but a crowd of orange-suited women stand as a barricade holding the building doors shut. The rest circle around me like vultures above fresh road kill.

"Ah ha! We got you now, fancy little Schoolgirl!" One of the women spits on me. I recognize her from the laundry room. "You ready for your next meal?"

The one-eyed girl moves through the crowd, dragging someone on the ground behind her. It's Klein, his hands bound behind his back and his mouth taped shut. Klein rolls over in the dirt, and when he sees me he starts laughing. He's the one bound and gagged, and he's *laughing*. He thinks I'm still drugged, but my drugs have worn off and he no longer looks like my knight in shining armor. He looks like the asshole he always was.

Even Buzz Kill is here, somehow now roped in with these cubs. "Are you flakin', fancy?"

"No, I'm—"

"LaRae told us you're only psycho when you're clean."

"I told you, I flushed her stash." I know that growl. It's LaRae.

I jump to my feet. "What is going on?"

"I wanted to beat the shit outta you," says the one-eyed girl, "but then LaRae comes to make a deal, says you've got something nasty in your head. Says you get off on killing people."

"Yeah!" says another. "Go on, Psycho Slicer, do your thing!"

The women cheer and one shoves me over to Klein. He stops laughing. He looks up at me, studies my face, and this time he looks scared.

There is shouting at the building door as the inmates collide with a group of guards. My tracker cuffs *zap* with electricity and so do everyone else's, but hardly anyone bats an eye. Something blocks the sun from me. Something huge, something orange: Baby Cub.

"This better be worth the trouble, LaRae," says Baby Cub. "I wasted good drugs on her, she was supposed to die like the rest of them. That was the plan."

"I promised you a deal," LaRae says. "You want Klein outta the way, here's your chance."

Buzz Kill spits on me. "It's a brilliant idea. I sure as shit ain't gonna get myself thrown in the bin for killing him. Let the fancy girl do the dirty work. She'll go down for all of it."

"We all want him gone!" says another woman.

Klein flops around on the ground, moaning and grunting. The women kick and spit and throw dirt on him.

"Stop this!" Hathaway calls from behind the wall of orange jumpers by the door. She's made it back to Level Three, minutes too late. A handful of women jerk from the electrocution of stun guns and collapse into the dirt, but there are still too many inmates and not enough guards.

"Once Klein is dead, your plan will go through just fine," says LaRae. "She'll be the one locked away in the bin."

"She's the Psycho Slicer," says the one-eyed girl. "Let her do her thing! Get this asshole out of our way!"

One moment I'm standing near the boulder that is Baby Cub and the next …

A woman approaches from the side and I punch her in the throat—

Baby Cub heaves. "They might lock us all up."

Another woman shouts out. "They can't put us all in the bin! And besides, who else is gonna mess with us once the asshole is dead?"

A flash, a flicker. One moment I'm here, the next …

I come at the woman and kick her in the gut—

And I'm back again.

One jab, two jabs, and both her eyes are gone—

"Look at her, she wants to do it! You can see it in her face!"

I'm flailing about, rushing in full-speed—

Baby Cub has moved. No, *I've* moved. I jump back behind her. I can't let this happen. I can't let them use me. I'll spend the rest of my life in this hellhole if I can't pull myself together.

"C'mon, fancy! Kill the bastard!"

"Get the riot gear! Now!" Hathaway screams from the building door, but it's no use.

There's LaRae, standing off to the side. I go right at her—

And I've moved again. My arm falls back down because I've thrown a punch in the air. Every woman moves back a step, except LaRae. She's the only one with the guts to approach me.

"You just fell into my lap, Princess," says LaRae. "They were gonna drug you up and let you die like the rest of them, but you're worth so much more than that."

I want to scream at her, but no sound moves though my throat. Another flash and I've jumped forward, my bloody fists thrown out in front of me. I have to stop this. Somehow. But there are no metal tables or glass walls to pull me from the visions.

"I can see it in your eyes, Princess." LaRae moves closer. "You can't stop it. You sure tried to hide it, didn't you, gettin' all flaked out. But straight? You're a monster. Banging your fists day and night, they're like clubs, all the best to bash this bastard's head in. That's all you're good for now."

I scramble back to Baby Cub, but she's moved away. I have nowhere to hide and there is no one to come to my rescue. The guards and inmates are in a full-out battle at the door. It's just me and LaRae.

She comes in closer and I step back …

And push into a run, heading straight at her. I don't stop, I tackle her to the ground—

LaRae is beneath me and she's stunned it's her I'm after. I can't get caught in another fight, they'll lock me away, and that's exactly what she wants, yet it was supposed to be Klein …

With every ounce of strength in my body, I pound into her face—

LaRae hollers in pain.

I take another swing. I crack her cheekbone—

I'm in the middle of the dusty yard on top of LaRae with the vultures all around us, yet no one moves to stop me. I hit her, over and over and over. My knuckles are so calloused and numb from months of banging them into plexiglass doors and steel walls that I can't feel the pain, but LaRae can. She convulses underneath me with every blow to her face.

The sights and sounds of everything else fades away. I can only focus on this. I know I'm doing it—it's not a vision. I'm here, this is me. And it's all so familiar. I've spent so many years imagining beating people to death that it's almost natural. I've felt the breaking bones and warm blood on my hands, heard the screams and cries for help. So many people and so many deaths. LaRae is just the next casualty.

I have killed every single person in my visions. I have never felt the sympathy of that of a moral human to end the rage and have mercy on a victim, and this is no different. This is not a vision but it doesn't matter because now *my life is the vision.*

And I do not intend to leave this woman alive.

24 ain't no sunshine

If this is what Hell is like, the Devil is a fool to endure in such a place.

This is the place of nightmares. Every nightmare ever penetrated into my psyche came from here, traveled through space and wedged into the cracks of my mind, birthing a million fantasies of horror. Nightmares of darkness. Nightmares of torture. Nightmares of death, of purgatory, of Hell. Nightmares of this very place.

The bin.

It's dark, nearly pitch-black. A tiny window at the back of the room lets in a thin sliver of sunlight. Four walls, barely eight feet square. Concrete floor covered in damp filth. One drain hole in the ground. No toilet. No water. No place to sit except in the piss and shit and blood of every person who suffered time here before.

I feel like an animal. Even savage beasts don't deserve such torment. I'm just a girl. A girl who has now murdered two people. And this is where they've sent me.

The bin.

I try to breathe and the effect of the stench is immediate. I vomit all over the floor, heaving and choking. It only makes the nausea worse, and I feel like I'm going to pass out. Maybe it would be better if I did so I wouldn't have to be conscious through this.

No human interaction. I don't even hear voices. A small window opens and a plate of food slides in. Rotten mush. One small paper cup of water, most of it splashed out by the time it reaches me. I'm so thirsty my lips are cracked and bleeding. There's no way I can eat anything. The stench makes me vomit even when I have nothing left in my stomach to surrender.

This is where Candy came to die. She'd sliced her own neck with a spoon. She was here, in this place, until she could no longer take the torture, and her best option was to make her own slow and horrific end. And I don't blame her.

They'll forget about me. They will. Why would they let me out? I'm a monster, a despicable excuse for a human being. They know what I am. They always knew. There's no way those visions could have remained in my mind. I should have seen it coming. *Why didn't I see this coming?*

Because I didn't want to. I wanted to believe I was a decent person, that I could grow out of it, that I was stronger than these violent impulses, that I didn't need to be healed or tricked or re-programmed by the brain adjusters. Oh how wrong I was. I was always a killer. I was *born* a killer. I came out the womb with visions of torture and murder so that I may one day be the heartless assassin I am now.

I had demolished my victim in the yard to a bloody wreckage before the guards finally burst through the blockade. Hathaway was the first to reach me. I couldn't even look her in the face. All I needed to feel was the clench of her hands and her nails digging deep into my skin to know she had changed her mind about me. She dragged me here, pulled me through the building by the hair. It was she who locked me away. I can't help wishing she'd left me with a utensil of death, but this place is meant to break me down. And here I am, longing for a weapon of self-destruction.

This is where monsters deserve to be.

In the bin.

It gets worse. It can't be possible, but it is. I'm detoxing. My body aches for flake, and it's furious with me. I shake constantly. My muscles are so tense I crack a rib. There are no more tears in my eyes; they're dried out and aching. My skin is on fire, burning with fever. I vomit even more. The only thing that helps distract me from the pain in my body is hitting my fists on the wall. *Over and over and over and over …*

Days pass. The sliver of light comes and goes four times. My mind cracks like frozen glass. The sensation of dread spreads through me like a virus. I have no idea how long they'll keep me in here. They want to punish me. They want to break me. They'll keep me locked away until I'm nothing more than the pile of shit I'm sitting in.

On the fifth day my senses start to fade and blend together. Demons dance in the shadows. Ghostly whispers breeze into my ears. The Devil himself pounds on the earth beneath me, likely digging a hole to make a quicker access for me to fall into Hell. But where are the gunshots coming from? Those rumblings, they sound man-made.

Something is happening outside these walls. It's not a normal sort of fight between guards and inmates. It sounds like war. I hear shots from dozens of guns. Explosions rumble through the earth and reverberate against the concrete. Footsteps thump outside my door. Voices holler with anger, others cry in agony.

The bombings and gunshots go on for a day. I lean my head against the door for some indication as to what has happened, but then there's nothing. It's quiet. Silent. Not a footstep nor even a whisper. I wait and wait and nothing comes through my food slot. Not even water. Two more appearances of the sliver of light from the window. Still nothing.

I should get someone's attention, beg for the end of this torture, yet I don't want to. There's nothing in me that cares to try. I have no strength to muster the will to get through this. I've reached the depths of Hell already, and there is no longer any desire for survival left in my soul. The darkness had lived in me all my life, and if I'm to end the rein of my own destruction, then the darkness is where I will take my last breath.

I curl up against the wall, in the cleanest place I find. My lungs heave. My stomach cramps and convulses. I pass out several times and awaken with my face in my own puke. I'm fading.

I am dying and no one cares.

Not even me.

PART THREE

the desert

25 blinders on

The sun is excruciating. There's no other way to describe it. *Everything* is excruciating, but the sun brings something more. Exposure. Judgment. Shame.

"Oh my god ..."

Someone has opened the door. A man.

I don't dare answer. I don't look up or even move. I sit curled in the corner, hiding from the sun like a tormented vampire.

The man coughs. And grunts. And gags. He's revolted by my disgraceful state. Why is he here if he's so repulsed by me? I don't want anyone to see me like this. I'm a half-step from dead, so why bother?

"C'mon, Jo. Let's go."

He takes a deep breath and pulls me to my feet and away from the bin of everlasting nightmares. I have no strength left at all in my body. My legs barely work. My aching hands are useless. There's not an ounce of energy to summon any will to walk.

The man is strong. He holds onto me. He's not dragging me by the hair—me, the monster, the girl who reeks of death and despair. I pull my head up just enough to see his face.

Diego Felix. I can barely make out his features, but I know it's him. He's dressed in heavy soldier gear, covered in the charcoal gray body armor of an ACTA soldier, armed and ready for battle.

"Let's get you cleaned up."

Felix helps me into the building, even though I know I can't go back in there. I don't want anyone to see me like this, caked in nearly every bodily fluid imaginable. My eyes are too blurry to see any malicious inmates, but for now no one says a word, stunned to silence by my vile appearance.

Felix leads me to the showers. He lets me go and my legs give out. I fall to the concrete floor, slumped on the ground as water muddies the filth on my face, drowning me in raining water. Then soap sprays down on me.

"Jo, you've gotta clean yourself up. Get out of that jumper."

Felix grabs me under the arms, lifts me to my feet, and leads my bloodied and throbbing hand to a rail. I can barely hold on enough to keep from swaying. My jumper is unzipped and pulled down, and suddenly I'm standing naked in the shower as Felix tugs the clothing over my feet.

"Scrub," he says. "I'll find you some clean clothes."

I'm too weak to securely hold onto the rail, let alone scrub my body, but I manage to stand long enough to clean my hair. More soap rains down. The warmth feels good on my skin. Blow-dryers blast away the water as Felix returns.

"I found some guard's clothes. They'll have to do." And he's gone again.

I wobble out of the shower and find the clothes on the bench. It takes forever to pull on the pants; my fingers don't have the strength to hold on to the thick fabric. Felix returns just as I get the tank over my head.

"Drink this."

I down the canteen of water in a few gulps.

"Eat this."

The rectangular bar smells of sweet dried fruit. It hurts to chew, my jaw sore from grinding my teeth for days.

"And take this."

There's a pinch in my forearm. He's punctured a push-pin syringe into my vein. A tingling vibration flows through my body, and little sparks ignite in every inch of my insides. My hands stop shaking. My heart stops fluttering. My head stops pounding. My eyes focus and I look up to see him studying me.

"Better?" he asks.

"What was that?"

"Adrenaline."

"You gave me adrenaline? That was a bad—" My arm moves before I can stop it, grabbing the syringe from Felix and jabbing it at his neck.

"Hey! Calm down!"

Lucky for him, by body is still too frail for the attack. Felix has me by the wrists and he unclasps the tracker cuffs, exposing my raw and tender skin, and I feel more naked than I did in the shower. Bending down, he to removes my ankle cuffs and fastens boots to my feet. He shouldn't be tampering with the cuffs; he doesn't have the authority. They'll throw me back in the bin, I'm certain of it.

But he tosses the cuffs onto the bench and nothing happens. No sirens wail. No guards come to drag me away by the hair.

How did Felix even get in here? Doesn't he know why I was in the bin in the first place? He made me promise to not screw up, and I did the worst thing I could possibly do, and now he's *rescuing me*?

He balls his left fist. Then he walks away, calling over his shoulder. "We need to leave. And you need to eat that. Force it down. You're a goddamn skeleton."

The adrenaline, water, and few bites of food have allowed me enough strength to get to my feet. I wobble after him and pass a shiny window. I wish I'd never looked at my reflection, but now I can't stop. I hardly recognize myself: Dark circles surround my eyes, my face is yellow and sickly, my collarbone pokes out from beneath the black tank, and I'm swimming in this pair of gray armor pants. And my nose—it's definitely crooked.

Felix is waiting for me. "Jo, there's no time for this. I need to search the building, see if anyone's left alive."

"*Alive*? What are you talking about?"

"If you'll come on, you can see for yourself."

He rushes from the showers, and I stumble after him. As I reach the doorway, I see a guard lying on the ground, dark blood pooled around his head. Past him, the hallway is littered with debris: furniture, pieces of jumpers, cell-made weapons, bullet holes, more blood.

The mess hall is even worse. More dead guards. Piles of women in orange jumpers. I spot a blond woman crumpled against the magnetic roll call wall, her face bashed in, a streak of blood on the wall above her. The thump in my chest tells me the woman is Goldie.

I call after Felix as we make our way though the corridors. "What happened?"

"The Plan went through. Alias hacked every FutureTech security system and turned it against us. They broke down the border, took control of the drones, got the sympathizers any military equipment they wanted."

"I thought they were *cyber* terrorists."

"They were. But they're bigger now, and once they realized they could breach our security systems, they decided to go full out. This is war, Jo."

"And they attacked the *prison*?"

"This prison is a FutureTech system. Once the security went down, the Alias members inside orchestrated the breakout."

"What about everybody else? Why are there still so many women in here?"

He looks over his shoulder. "I think you know."

My insides tumble. "Flake …"

"We call it Voxoclon. You're lucky it wasn't in your system long enough for it to have the full effect on you. It's designed to pacify a victim to the point that they forget how to survive."

"I was ready to die in the bin."

He stops abruptly and grabs my chin, lifting my face toward him. "Don't say that, Jo. You can't die yet. I won't let you." He stares at me, his hazel eyes fiercely focused, then jerks to look down the hallway. "Can you hear that?"

There's the faint sound of someone calling for help, deep inside the walls. Felix races down the corridor and finds an office door that's been blockaded from the outside with tables and squares of concrete. I take my time following, gliding my hand along the steel wall for support. He has the door open by the time I get there, and I hover in the hallway out of sight.

"Hathaway!" Felix says. "Why are you still here?"

"Oh thank god, Felix! I thought you forgot about me."

"How did you get trapped in here?"

"The women, they staged a riot. They jumped the girl. They blockaded me in during the breakout. I was certain I would starve to death—"

I creep around the doorway and Hathaway stops talking when she sees me. Her ears flatten against her head like a cat under threat, and her mouth droops open.

Felix hands her a canteen of water and a fruit bar, unaware of my presence. "C'mon, we need to get out of here."

But Hathaway keeps her eyes trained on me. "You need to put her back."

Felix sees me standing in the doorway. "There's no time for this, Hathaway. We need to leave."

"You need to put her back."

"I can't put her back. I came here to bring her home."

Hathaway jumps to her feet and towers over Felix. "You what? What is this? You were supposed to come rescue *me*. That was our deal."

"You were supposed to keep her safe, keep her away from the Voxoclon. I told you it was dangerous."

Hathaway heaves. "You told me about the new drugs after I was transferred out of Level Three, which—by the way—was *her* fault."

Felix goes on, ignoring Hathaway's argument. "And then you broke the deal when you locked her in the bin."

Hathaway pauses, inhales, then lets out a roar. "She murdered someone with her bare hands!"

The memories of my fist breaking LaRae's face floods my mind, and I know I'm about to react. *BAAM!* goes my fist into the wall.

"They schemed against me." My voice is hoarse and the words scratch my throat. "They wanted me to kill Klein."

Hathaway takes an uneasy step sideways. "What if it had been me in the yard? I swore to keep you safe because I owe it to Felix and good god what an idiot I've been. I knew there was something wrong with you from the moment I laid eyes on you. You are a monster."

The rage in her face is contagious, and I feel the blood pulsing through my veins, getting hotter with each pump. I snatch a broken block of concrete from the floor and hold it above my head. Felix yanks the block from my hands and tosses it aside, and Hathaway's eyes go wide as she watches the concrete dent a metal chair. I move toward her and Felix steps in front of me.

"Stop this. Jo, listen to me."

I don't listen. I come at him, the rage surging, arms flailing, throwing punches into his chest. He doesn't fight back; he stands there and lets me hit him.

"Let it out, Jo!"

My fist connects with his jaw and he grunts. I pause, fist in the air, waiting for his reaction. I can sense he's about to flash his signature grin, so I take another swing. He dodges my punch and tackles me out into the hallway, pinning me face-first against the cold steel, one arm wrapped around my waist and his other elbow in the middle of my back.

"All right," he whispers into my ear. "Calm down. I'm here."

His voice is soothing. My heart races as the adrenaline pulses through it, but the strength and weight of his body on mine is a comforting embrace.

"You have to put her back." Hathaway emerges from the office and slides against the opposite wall. I twitch with the need to punch her in the mouth, despite that she's a head taller than me and could knock me out in one blow.

Felix whispers into my ear, "I'm gonna let go now. Okay?" It takes all my concentration to will my body to relax. He senses this, slowly releases me, then turns to Hathaway. "We need weapons. What do you have in your office?"

"Felix—"

"I'm not leaving her. I promised I'd get her out. I'm trying to help her."

"She's beyond help."

"She's not. I know that. And I made her a promise that I'd get her out of prison. That's why I'm here. Now listen, Hathaway, we can't defend ourselves without more weapons—"

Hathaway cuts him off. "You were supposed to come get *me*."

"I didn't think you'd still be here."

"You've got to be shitting me, Felix. You expect me to believe Lone Wolf came all the way out here to rescue this lunatic?"

"Lone Wolf isn't here. It's just me."

Hathaway looks like she's choking on her tongue. "I held up my end of the arrangement …"

Felix stands tall. "For christ's sake, Hathaway, where are your guns?"

They have a stare-off in the corridor, sizing each other up, trying to break the other down, all the while displaying some kind of unspoken understanding. However these two know each other, it's obvious even in my disturbed state that there is a deep-rooted relationship between them, one that I feel a little left out of.

Despite Hathaway's physical dominance over Felix, she crumbles under his persuasive glower. "There's a safe in my office," she says. "I keep extra sidearms in there."

I follow them down the corridor, and I can't tell what's real anymore. I keep flickering, here, then there, and back again. Like a computer glitch. A bad graphic. A bug in the system. My eyes fight light and shadows, but my mind can't focus on any one sense or space. And I really want to hit something.

BAAM!

"You have to stop doing that." Felix has me by the wrist. The scabs on my knuckles break open and start bleeding.

"I can't."

"You have to."

"I need drugs …"

"No drugs. They're tainted."

"I can't do this."

"There has to be something. What else keeps away the visions?"

"Visions?" Hathaway has returned, covered in weapons and armor.

"They're not visions anymore," I tell Felix. "It's real. It's all real."

He grabs my shoulders and peers into me. "There has to be something else that helps."

Hathaway sighs. "Of course. The library."

"What?" says Felix.

"She was okay when she was painting in the library."

They're having this conversation like I'm not even here.

"What are you saying?"

"I don't know. It seemed like a good idea at the time, but then she stabbed that girl with the paintbrush …"

Felix snaps his fingers. "Yes! Where's the library?"

"Right behind you."

He zips away and Hathaway scowls in my direction, her eyes flickering around my head. "For a time I actually believed you were worth protecting," she says. "I never expected you'd become this. Dr. Baydar told me about the visions, but if you'd come clean with me—"

"It's too late." Why'd I say that? I don't mean that—I don't *want* to mean that. But is it true? I don't know, but now Hathaway is backing away from me.

Felix returns. He grabs my arm and places something in my hand: a paintbrush.

"What's this for?"

"If you think you're having a vision, pretend you're painting."

"Pretend?"

"Wave it around like a wand and imagine you're painting something."

"I'm not a wizard."

"Jo. *Pretend.*"

I jostle the paintbrush between my fingers, and Hathaway clutches her rifle tighter. Her sleeves are rolled up, and for the first time I see a tattoo of a white wolf on her forearm, the same wolf as the one on Felix's neck. She twitches when she realizes I'm studying her.

"We need to go," she says.

"The helo is outside the gate," says Felix.

He leads the way from the building, and Hathaway keeps close pace with him. I'm stuck fumbling behind on my weak knees, dragging my oversized boots across the dusty concrete floor.

"Alias is making their way up the state," says Felix. "Lone Wolf is in Los Angeles bracing for attack, but there's not enough man power to protect the city."

"I thought the military was prepared," Hathaway says. "They were supposed to be waiting in San Diego."

"San Diego is destroyed. Alias has neutron bombs."

"*Neutron* bombs?" Hathaway is so stunned she nearly trips over a dead guard.

The yard is a mess. There are bodies everywhere, guards and inmates. Dozens of women in orange jumpers lie in the dirt, curled up as though asleep. But they're not asleep. Every single one of these people is dead. The great outer wall is a crumpled mess of concrete and steel, as though a rocket burst through. Alias had it easy.

I follow Felix and Hathaway through the blasted wall, and I'm out of prison. Just like that. I'm free, yet the fresh air is suffocating. I have never felt more vulnerable.

Felix goes on. "No one expected them to have n-bombs. Not even us. They took the *X* in *Alias-X* very seriously. We're not sure where the weapons came from. The drones are taking out everything else. They're headed straight for LA and there's no one to stop them."

"But low-radiation neutron bombs suggest they want to reinhabit the city," Hathaway says. "Why would Alias do that?"

"Hard to say," Felix says, keeping his eyes straight ahead. "The bomb completely destroyed San Diego. There's nothing left to inhabit, low-radiation or not."

"Jesus ... Where the hell is Washington?"

"Using their pricks to write a peace treaty, is my guess. I'm flying us to LA to support Lone Wolf. At the moment, being with them is our best option for survival."

Felix is the first to reach the helicopter, but Hathaway stops short.

"Wait. Felix, what are you not telling me?"

Felix pauses, his hand on the aircraft door, his eyes focused west, on the flat expanse between us and LA. "A lot has changed, Hathaway. The rules have changed. Everything has changed." He glances at me, then pulls himself into the pilot's seat.

Hathaway heaves then takes the co-pilot's seat. She looks out to see me standing in the dirt. "Get in," she says.

I don't have much of a choice. I'll never survive alone out here, so I fasten myself in and we take off toward LA. Felix and Hathaway chatter through their headsets, and I stare out the window, watching the landscape drift past. I can't stop twitching. My hand clenches and jabs the air and I start hitting the window.

"Paintbrush!" Felix calls out.

It's on the seat. The moment I feel the smooth surface of the handle, my hand stops shaking. I graze the bristles against the window, outlining the hills. He's right, it does help. My brush follows the flow of the land, the clouds, the sky. I turn to see the distant skyline of downtown LA in the front window. I outline the buildings, some tall, some short, some with sharp spires. The mountains over here, the valley over there, the long line of AEVs stuck on the eastbound auto-way.

There is a light so bright it is instantly blinding, filling my pupils with white. It comes out of nowhere, a brilliant flash, right in the middle of the skyline. Then the sound, a thunderous roar that pierces my eardrums. An instant later the shockwave pounds through the helicopter, and we're tossed in the air like a leaf.

26 trigger happy

The helicopter flips over and over. I see the ground, then the fireball, then the sky, then the ground again. Felix is shouting. Hathaway is screaming. I hit my head on the window, and my sight fills with spots. The mountains level out. A huge mushroom cloud looms in the sky, blocking the sun.

"Oh my god!" Hathaway hollers. "They've bombed Los Angeles!"

Felix shouts into his headset. "Lone Wolf, are you there? Lone Wolf, do you read me? We're over Pasadena. Give me your position."

"Watch out!"

The words leave Hathaway's mouth just as a large silver unmanned aircraft swoops down and, without warning, drops explosives onto the suburbs below. Flames reach like dancing fingers into the sky.

"It's Alias! They have the drones!"

Felix steers the helicopter away from the mountains. "I told you, they have control of everything!"

A cluster of military helicopters comes at us from the other side, spraying us with bullets. Our turbulent movement in the sky pummels my body with g-forces, and I'm really feeling like I'm gonna puke.

"There," says Hathaway. "Land us in that parking lot."

She points to an open lot in front of an old-fashioned building with a red brick tile roof and a scorched hole blasted in the towering dome, making it look like a busted egg. People scurry around the building like cockroaches as the drones and aircraft fire down on the city.

"I can't land there! We need to get out of here and find—*Oh shit*!"

The helicopter shudders as bullets find the engine and we're sent tumbling down.

"Hang on!" Felix warns, but it's no use because I'd neglected to strap myself in tightly enough, and now I'm slammed against the window with my stomach in my throat. The helicopter spins around and around until the asphalt comes up through the floor and I'm sent flying into the ceiling.

"Is everyone okay?" Felix says after a moment. But we're not okay. We're a crumpled heap of bodies.

The engine bursts into flames, and Felix unbuckles my straps and pulls from me the helicopter. I struggle to find my feet beneath me and tumble over the body of a young woman sticking out from under our helicopter—a victim not of the exploding bombs, but of our haphazard landing in the parking lot. My head throbs and I desperately try to get away from the scene of the crash, only to stumble over more bombing victims, and my stomach can't take it anymore.

Hathaway calls out. "Felix! Get me a med kit."

"The helo's in flames!"

"We need to help these people!"

"We need to *get out of here*!"

I'm on my knees, vomiting all over the ground, as people stumble past me, swarming Hathaway as she tries to bandage the bleeding head of a man with his own shirt. The rumble of bombs and the screeching of alarms are overtaken by the screams. A little boy sits on a sidewalk, arms wrapped around his knees, howling up to the heavens. A mother wanders in circles, calling out for her lost children. A man pulls himself along the ground, dragging his legless torso toward the building steps. The cries envelop me, catching me in a hellish vortex—an echoing, endless loop of heart-wrenching agony and terror.

Felix pulls me to my feet. "Come on. Time to move."

Hathaway calls after us. "We need to help these people."

"We can't help them," Felix says. "There's too many."

"We can at least help one!"

"We *are* helping one," he says as he glances at me.

Hathaway is quick on her feet, and she hops over the bodies and skids in front of us. "Have you lost your mind? These people are dying, and you're concerned about *her*?"

"I made a promise to protect her."

"Yeah, and you made *me* promise to do the same. But I gave that up when she beat a woman to death."

My fingers ache because I'm clutching the paintbrush so tightly I can feel the wood flex and splinter.

"Alias has control of the drones," says Felix. "The ground force is probably here. We need to find Lone Wolf or else we'll be picked off with the rest of them. If you want to stay here, be my guest, but I'm taking Jo to find Lone Wolf."

Hathaway stands trembling in the middle of the parking lot. "I don't believe this. I just don't believe this."

Felix turns to me, his shoulders pulled forward and stiff. "Jo, have you ever fired a gun?"

In real life? Never. In my visions? At least once a week since I was a kid. "I'll figure it out."

He crumples his face like he's about to retract his suggestion.

Hathaway shakes her head. "No, Felix, you can't do that. Don't give her a gun!"

He completely ignores her and hands me a pistol. "Gun in one hand, paintbrush in the other. Got it?"

I nod and take the pistol from Felix, which has a scope attached to the top of the barrel. It's heavier than I expect. Solid. Cold. Hathaway's eyes bulge as she clutches her own gun tighter, and I'm actually relieved to have some sort of self-protection. I just have the weapon nestled in my palm when an explosion roars behind us; our helicopter has blown itself to bits and caught the surrounding civilians in its blast.

"Go that way!" Felix leads us down the street as the flames consume even more victims.

Pasadena is a scene of apocalypse. Block after block of boutiques and shops are reduced to piles of brick, concrete, and glass. Windows are busted out, cars scorched, buildings littered with bullet holes. The ground shakes periodically, the roar of explosions ring in the distance. Bodies litter the street. People run in circles or huddle against buildings in anticipation of another attack. And over the hill looms the gray mushroom cloud, casting a dull haze over the valley as it stretches miles into the sky. Felix leads us west, toward the cloud, and we reach a part of the boulevard that dips further into the valley. We pause in the street, looking down at the fire and smoke and chaos.

Fear of being blown to smithereens by the drones is not what turns in my mind. What alarms me most is the stimulation. All five of my senses are on high-alert—the stench of burning flesh and wood, the sight of bloody gore, the sound of screams and ricocheting bullets, the taste of ash and sulfur, the heat of tickling flames. Every part of my body is attuned to the sensation of pandemonium, every part except my sense of emotion. It's not empathic turmoil that squeezes my lungs and churns my stomach as it forces its way up through my throat, it's purely a gut reaction.

Stuck in this spot in the street looking down on what used to be Old Town, I'm suddenly pissed that Felix rescued me from prison. Maybe Hathaway was right, maybe I would have been better off if Felix had put me back. At least in the bin it was only my own cries echoing in my ears.

But Felix didn't think about that. He has some other motivation, regardless if it threatens our safety. He waves us to keep moving and we trot down the street.

Out of nowhere, three masked men in black uniforms with large red AX emblems jump from a parked armored Humvee and run for us.

"Stand down!" Felix shouts, his gun aimed and ready.

Hathaway fires a warning shot at their feet, yet it does nothing to slow their attack.

"Get out of our way!" one man says. "This is Alias territory now!"

Another Alias fighter breaks off in my direction. I can see the fury in his eyes through the gap in his mask. I don't know if he's going to kill me, but I have a pistol in my hand and the natural thing for me to do is aim and fire. The trigger senses what I'm about to do and a red laser beams out from the scope, and the light finds the gunman's chest, making my objective that much easier to fulfill. One shot, right through the heart, like I've done a hundred times in my visions. But it's even better. I feel the jerking recoil of the gun, smell the gunpowder, hear the shell casing clatter on the asphalt.

My ears adjust after the booming sound. It's quiet, too quiet. The weight of the gun pulls me back to reality—*but I was in reality.*

The other two men shout at me, shout at each other, shout at Felix and Hathaway. I aim my gun at the next closest Alias guy, my fingers clutching tightly around the grip of the weapon. Then the men turn hard on their heels and run down the street, shouting all the way.

Hathaway races toward me, her gun aimed at my head. "What is wrong with you? You can't just go around killing people!"

Felix chases after her. "Hathaway, stop this!"

They both come at me, Hathaway screaming at me and Felix screaming at her. "You're gonna get us killed!" she says. "You're gonna get *me* killed!"

A drone circles overhead and people hobble past us. Felix sees it, and pulls me toward a building, but Hathaway grabs my other arm and I'm stuck between them in a human tug-of-war.

"You can't be serious, Felix. She's a monster."

"I have to protect her."

"You're going to get us killed."

"Then leave us, goddammit! I don't need you here anyway."

The look of betrayal in Hathaway's face is unmistakable; her hardened battle-ready expression drops instantly, and for a moment I think she might cry. Felix has to look away. We're standing there in the middle of the street, Felix with one of my arms and Hathaway with the other, people screaming and running around in every direction, the drone casting its shadow on us, and these two former Army comrades are caught in a stalemate. One soldier wants to save me, the other wants to destroy me. I'm a Thanksgiving turkey wishbone and the winner of this debate will be decided by who rips off the most of my body.

A bomb erupts and we're showered in glass and plaster. Hathaway's hand loosens first and I tear my arm away. My former prison guard stares at me, wide-eyed and alarmed. It's such an intense and focused glare that it occurs to me this is the first time Hathaway has ever looked me in the eyes.

The foundation of the building next to us crumbles into the street, and Hathaway's gaze is broken.

"Take cover!" Felix shouts.

He drags me to find shelter, and I look back as Hathaway stands still, fixed in this rigid position as a mob of people swarm around her. Another set of Humvees converge in the street, mowing the innocents down with machine guns.

"Jo! Come on!"

Felix pulls me into a building, and Hathaway is lost from my sight. My foot catches and twists on a pile of rubble and a sharp pain shoots up through my shinbone. I yelp in pain but Felix won't let go. He drags me—hobbling leg and all—through the building and into a stairwell. The door shuts and suddenly it's so quiet I can hear my heartbeat. An emergency light strobes overhead, making our movements appear jerky and robotic.

Felix plops down on the step and fidgets with his visor, whispering into the headset like someone will find us in this dungeon of a stairwell. "Lone Wolf, are you there? Come in, Lone Wolf. For the love of god, please, someone answer me."

My consciousness tucks inside my mind, enveloping me in a haze. I can't nail down the most prominent thought in my head because there are so many, all of them equally disturbing.

A bomb exploded over Los Angeles … and yet, I don't feel sad. I can't feel sad about the flattened city that was my hometown. There's no telling how many people I knew under that bomb—hopefully not my mom, and not Lyle and the dads, who are surely in Denver by now. But despite all those dead people, my entire life was in LA. My artwork, my past and my future. At least, I thought it was my future. Not anymore. My future was taken from me the moment I was charged with murder and sentenced to prison. My past has been turned into a soap opera melodrama and all the people and things that gave me fulfillment were torn away well before the bomb fell. I thought I'd had a chance to become the girl I so desperately wanted to be—an artist—but I wonder now if that was all an illusion. Who's to say I ever stood a chance even without all that's happened in the last year? That city gave me nothing but grief and torment, and barely was there ever a glimmer of hope that I'd find a place within it. LA is gone, and so is the previous incarnation of Josephine Bristol.

And then there are the visions. No, I no longer have visions, not since the day I killed LaRae in the yard. Just flickers. And that masked assailant—well, sure, he was likely going to kill me had I not shot him first. But still. I don't even feel bad about it. It was like I was in a vision, where there is no emotion. Only death.

I'm consumed by my fading adrenaline, the lack of food, the exhaustion of being in the bin for a week, my throbbing foot, the circling drones, the realization that my visions have become reality. So when Felix asks "Are you all right?" I want to scream. Of course I'm not all right. I just listed six contributing factors to prove how much I'm not *all right.* There's not much more that could happen to make me any less *all right.*

"I'm fine."

"You don't look fine." Felix's face is sunken in, his eyes hollow, lips pursed thin. He looks like shit, and he's worried about me?

"Well, I've added another to my kill roster. All that considered, I'm fine." Not only are my visions my real life, but my head-to-mouth filter has been completely obliterated.

He winces. "Where's your paintbrush?"

I go to show him but one hand has the pistol and the other is empty. "Guess I lost it."

"Jo—" he starts, but I'm not in the mood for a lecture.

"I didn't have a vision. I don't need the paintbrush."

"You shot someone."

"I did what I had to do."

Felix looks away. "Look, Jo, this obviously isn't the situation I'd meant to drag you into, I meant to keep you safe, but I couldn't leave you in prison. You would have died in the bin."

My anger has subsided. The blood pulsing through my veins has slowed. All I have left is an empty feeling in my gut, and not because I'm starving. "Maybe it would have been the better option."

"I'm trying to keep you safe. I'm trying to protect you."

"You still haven't told me why."

"Why what?"

"Why you give a crap about me."

"I'm trying to protect you."

"But *why*? A war has started, and you're more concerned about me. It doesn't make sense."

Felix flexes his left hand. "I have my reasons."

"What about Hathaway?"

My answer comes in the form of Felix's wristlet ringing. He answers it. Hathaway bellows into the holo display, her face beaten and bloody, and when she speaks, her voice is muffled. "Felix …"

"Stay here, Jo!"

He's on his feet in a flash and bursts through the stairwell door. The sinking feeling in my gut tells me to stay put, but then I hear gunshots—a calling, a beckoning signal—and my instant reaction is to head to the sound of the gunfire.

The street is ablaze and the smell of burnt rubber is suffocating. Melting asphalt sticks to my boots. A wall of smoke separates me from the opposite sidewalk, but I can hear the voices.

A man speaks with a ragged flutter of anxiousness. "Tell us where to find Lone Wolf and we won't kill her."

"I'm not telling you anything," says Felix.

"All right then. This isn't gonna end well," the man says, and there's a *thump* and a whimper.

"We don't have any information!" Felix says.

The ragged voice laughs. "You expect me to believe you're not informed? Your ignorance is your death sentence. You're as good as dead."

A gust of wind clears a hole in the smoke, and then I see Hathaway on her knees, her face bloody, surrounded by five masked men, two of them the ones I'd nearly shot earlier. One man has a rifle pointed at the back of Hathaway's head. The others point their guns at Felix as he stands frozen in the street. And then the guns are on me.

"No!" Felix shouts, his voice rattling with fear. "Stay back, Jo!"

The Alias guys hesitate just long enough for me to become fixed on the dark depths of the gun barrels. The sight taunts me, it sucks me into the void like a hypnotic mirage. No vision comes, but I react as though I were in one. My legs move on their own volition, despite the pain shooting through my ankle.

Felix shouts out to me. "Jo! Not again!"

The terrorists are stunned, frozen in place, as I'm walking across the street with the pistol in my raised arm, red scope laser aimed at the man with the rifle. The pain in my ankle ignites a chain reaction of cramps in my leg, yet I keep walking. Hathaway watches me, hands behind her head, shivering. I walk all the way up to the rifleman until my pistol jabs into his chest. No one moves. No one speaks. The rifleman twitches, his eyes on my gun. My finger pulls the trigger and sends a bullet through his chest. The man hollers and falls to the ground.

The shouting starts. Felix screams. Gunshots ring. I catch sight of movement in my peripheral and move my arm and fire again. Movement on the other side, another bullet fired. Then two more shots, two more men down.

"Please … please … don't kill me." The rifleman gasps, spurting blood from his mouth. "I'm just … following orders."

He huddles at my feet, clutching his bleeding chest. Hathaway is crouched next to him, hands still on the back of her head. She heard him, and she looks to the rifleman and back at me. My pistol is aimed at his head, and I swear I didn't move it. Hathaway inhales, looks away, bends over, and buries her face into the asphalt.

I don't want to hear this man's crying. It doesn't matter who he is or where he came from or why he's even with these Alias assholes who are murdering innocent people in the street. It doesn't matter if this is not the proper retribution for his crimes. This isn't retribution. This is nothing more than instinct because I am the Psycho Schoolgirl Slicer.

One more shot. Right through the forehead.

27 soldier's mark

The bullet shell casing flies back and hits me on the forearm. The hot metal sears my skin, but I don't care. The man I'd just shot through the head had begged me to let him live, but I don't care. Hathaway kneels on the melting asphalt, and her broken face has turned blank and pale, but I don't care. Felix stares at me through heavy eyes, but I don't care.

My hand buzzes from the vibrations of rapid fire of the pistol. The metal is warm, the grip slippery with sweat. My mind has gone completely numb, but it's not the same as my drugged-out days in prison where the world swirled around me in a soupy haze and all of my senses were muddled. Now, I am keenly aware of every physical response. My senses are heightened, my perception focused and alert, yet my mind is devoid of all emotion. Like a soulless robot. I am a bothead.

The streets have gone silent. The drones have moved on. The mushroom cloud has expanded across the sky, turning the evening sun a murky brown. The wandering people have collapsed in the street, their faces expressionless, neither pained nor relieved. Simply empty.

Hathaway gets to her feet and wipes the blood from her lip, then gathers weapons from the dead assailants. "More will show up. We've gotta move." She tosses the weapons into the Alias Humvee and turns to the civilians. "You need to get to safety. Come on, get out of the streets." No one looks up at her; they stare into the smoldering rubble around them. "You need to find shelter."

Felix stands watching. "Leave them alone," he says, his voice flat and listless.

Hathaway tries to pull one man to his feet, but he's dead weight against her. "Felix, help me."

"They don't want our help. Leave them alone."

Hathaway straightens abruptly. "For christ's sake, Felix! What are you trying to prove?"

Felix is immobile, his arms hanging limply at his side. "My objective is to find Lone Wolf."

"Lone Wolf is gone! Can't you understand that? After all this…" she waves her hand at the bomb cloud "…you really think you're gonna find them?"

"I'm not going to divert from my objective." His eyes flicker to me.

"We need to get to safety. We're going to Denver. Get in the truck." Hathaway brushes past him and throws herself into the driver's seat.

Without hesitation, I slide into the backseat, despite Hathaway's glare. Felix stands in the street, flexing his left hand. Then he looks through my window in the truck as I stare back at him. He lets out a long sigh and climbs into the passenger side.

Hathaway drives us through the mess and toward the eastbound auto-way. The suburb is destroyed, buildings and houses crumpled to a heaps. AEVs and gassers and bodies and trees create an obstacle course that slows our retreat considerably, and it takes us all night to make it out of the valley.

None of us have the words to speak. Hathaway turns on the console screen and plays a video broadcast of a presidential address, as though to help make sense of the chaos, or possibly to break the tortuous silence.

"There is no doubting this is a tragic incident as we have lost many civilians in San Diego, Los Angeles, and Las Vegas," says the President. "I understand that while many US civilians sympathize with the Alias agenda, I encourage all of you to realize that by joining this war you are fighting against the people of the United States."

The President rambles on, clearly not emotionally prepared to be making such a significant speech. "The Secretary of Defense is making every attempt to open a line of dialogue with Alias so that we might come to some kind of peace agreement. However, since we are without the means to fight the terrorists on the ground, I encourage all citizens in the path between Las Vegas and Washington D.C. to find safety.

"In the meantime, I have faith in the Anti-Cyber Terrorism Agency militias to protect the citizens from violence. God speed to ACTA and many thanks of gratitude to FutureTech and for funding these armies. March 11 will be remembered as a day of great sadness in United States history."

"Huh," I say without thinking. "What do you know, it's my birthday today. I'm eighteen." Felix and Hathaway exchange a glance, and I continue babbling. "It's weird, when you think about it. I killed Rick on my seventeenth birthday. And now …"

Felix turns to look at me, but I avoid his eyes and look out the window. The sunrise crests in the front windshield. To the north, the cracking dry mountain range is hidden behind a heavy brown cloud, and to the south the landscape is littered with destruction. Smoke hovers over the entire valley. Streets that once contained tall buildings have been flattened to nothing. AEVs are stalled on the auto-way. The suburbs are eerily still; the people in these neighborhoods have already fled—or are dead. And along the auto-way stand screen after screen of FutureTech propaganda, the only survivors of the bombings. "*Keep your family safe with FutureTech's latest security systems*," one sign reads. As we pass by, I notice the fine print: "*Your survival is important to us.*"

My hand feels clammy and sore. The pistol is still clutched tightly in my palm. It feels good, and it feels powerful. It feels natural. Felix is watching me. I really wish he'd leave me alone. I'm tired of explaining myself. I don't know *how* to explain it. It just happened.

"It just happened, okay?"

Hathaway makes a gurgling sound.

Felix twitches. "How did it just *happen*?"

"I donno. I can't explain it."

"Was it a vision?"

"No, I don't have visions anymore."

"Jo—"

"I did what I had to do. I saved Hathaway's life, didn't I?" Felix reaches for my arm as I'm waving the gun around in the air, but I pull back. "I got it."

He squints at me. "You're gonna hurt somebody."

"Right, because I shot some guys who were shooting at us, now I'm a loose cannon who's gonna kill everybody." I catch Hathaway's eyes in the rearview.

"You were worried things would get out of your control," Felix says.

He's twisting my words around, and I really want him to shut his judgment-flapping mouth. "That's what I thought, too. But the visions are gone, okay? It's done."

"What's done?"

"I don't know! It doesn't matter. You don't need to protect me anymore. You're safe to release me into the wild."

I can't for the life of me understand the expression in Felix's face. He looks disappointed—in me, I suppose—but there's also this twinge of regret. And his eyes have been traveling over every inch of my body since we started this conversation. Maybe he's looking for a cancerous mole that he can slice off and heal me of this infectious ailment.

"I'm not done with you yet."

His voice is low and kind of creepy, but also kind of sexy because there is this heart-fluttering rumble when he whispers. Dammit. I'm so angry with him for judging me and acting like I'm a hell-fueled lunatic, and yet he's gazing at my collarbone and it's giving me goose bumps. It makes me so angry I want to jam the butt of my pistol across his face. I can't come up with a response for him, so I return my gaze through the window.

We drive through a gap in the mountains and descend into the desert. There are AEVs and gassers everywhere—on the road, lined up along the shoulders, and some that have careened into the dirt.

"Where are all the people?" Hathaway says.

"I have no idea," says Felix. "We should keep going."

We continue along as we pass through town after town of abandoned cars and houses. Charging stations and grocery stores have been blown to bits. The cookie-cutter towns of the outskirt cities are still burning.

"They're not just after Washington," Hathaway says. "They're taking out the whole country."

"Stay off the main roads, in case the drones are still here."

Hathaway turns us off the highway and down a dusty road into the middle of the desert, toward the early morning sunlight as it rises above the horizon.

Felix mumbles into his wristlet. "Lone Wolf, are you there? Lone Wolf, come in."

Hathaway peers at him through the side of her eyes. "Felix, you'll never get a response."

Hathaway is the one busted and bleeding with a manic killer in the backseat and she's composed and temperate. Felix—who is supposed to be the self-assured one—squirms and mumbles into his wristlet the entire ride.

"Lone Wolf, this is Oscar Romeo. We are on our way to Denver, now past Victorville. Give me your position. Come in Lone Wolf."

"They're gone, Felix."

We keep driving. And driving, until finally we see a plume of smoke emanating from a trailer park. Two dozen abandoned trailer homes sit rusting in the sun, all odd shapes and sizes, some sleek airstreams with buffed metallic siding and others angular trapezoids with tiny round windows. Trash and colorful graffiti fill and empty concrete pool. A handful of rusting gassers are parked along the road. It could be a child's playground, if children liked to play in creepy clown dreams.

Hathaway parks on a paved road that circles the park. "I'm going to look for survivors." She gets out and heads straight to the closest trailer.

"Stay here," Felix says to me.

"I need some air."

"It's safer for you in here."

"Safer for me, or safer for *you*?"

"Jo, don't do this."

I burst through the door and slide onto the road. The heat of the desert sucks the air from my lungs, and there is no place for me to hide from the heat, so I pace back and forth along the asphalt.

Felix follows after. "Jo, stop. I'm trying to help you."

"Why are you helping me? You don't owe me anything. I've made everything worse since you rescued me from prison."

Felix points to the Humvee bumper. "Jo, sit down."

I'm still pacing and my sprained foot is really starting to hurt. "I don't want to sit down."

"Sit down!"

"Stop telling me what to do! I'm not your pet!"

He lets out a sigh and takes his time settling himself on the bumper. I'm hoping he'll leave me alone, but no. Instead, I get an old *Hollywood Life Story*.

"It's about time I tell you about myself. I also went to East Hollywood Trade School. I'm twenty-five, so that would have been what—how long ago?"

Is he seriously waiting for me to do the math? "Get to the point."

"You have somewhere to be?" he says and waves his arm across the desert. I groan. "I didn't have the same opportunities as you. I never got close to the PEAD program. Hell, I don't even know what it means."

"Programmed Education and Development."

He rolls his eyes. "Ha, now I'm really glad I wasn't in it. Sounds like a brainwashing cult."

"Quite an ineffective one for me, obviously."

"You're still ages smarter than I am."

"Is there a purpose to this story?"

"I was there for a whole year before I learned Principal Torres was my dad," Felix says. "He didn't know until then, either. Well, he had his suspicions, but my mom was a pathological liar and wouldn't tell him the truth."

"Sounds a lot like my mom."

"Your mom forgets things. My mom deceives people."

"Like you?"

"No, that's not my *tick*."

He's using my word, and I hate the way he says it. "Okay then, what *is* your tick?"

"That's irrelevant to this story. See, when I was a teenager I didn't know my dad and I had a lying psycho of a mom, and I was into drugs and I loved tattoos." He holds up his arm as though I'm needing confirmation of that part of his story. "My Junior year I found a bunch of wicky artwork from some kid in LA. One piece in particular stuck in my head."

"You steal artwork for tattoo ideas?"

He shifts on the bumper; I think I'm finally irritating him. "A month later I was caught with a pocketful of spinners and got sent to rehab. I was having trouble getting clean and the doctors wanted to sign me up for a brain adjustment. That scared the shit out of me, but thankfully my dad suggested I join the army instead. He told me everyone has their own shit to go through, and the ones who fight through the toughest shit come out the strongest."

"A real twenty-first-century philosopher, your dad is."

Now he's ignoring my remarks. "Once my dad said that, I kept thinking about that kid's drawing. I felt connected to it somehow, like I understood why the kid drew the image in the first place."

"So you got the tattoo."

"You're rushing the story."

"I'm helping to get it over with."

"I was really messed-up back then. I was lost. And this tattoo—this *drawing*—did something for me. Not to get all *sunshiny* on you, but this image was my inspiration to see my way through the dark and into the light."

"Did you find any rainbows and leprechauns along the way?"

"Don't make a joke of this, Jo. I'm being serious. I'm being *honest.* My point is, this tattoo gave me a reason to want to return the favor."

"To who?"

"To the kid who drew the image."

Felix pulls open his shirt and reveals his beautifully sculpted chest and those beautifully drawn tattoos, and then I see the image over his heart: A fire-red phoenix flying toward the sky, balancing scales in her beak. I know that drawing. I know it because—

"That's *my* drawing!"

A smile tugs on his lips. "Is this finally making sense to you?"

It's the same painting that Principal Torres showed me that day in his office. *That's* how he knew about this piece. *That's* why he gave a crap about getting me a scholarship. *That's* how Mr. Torres and Felix tied themselves into a net with the intent of capturing me like a wild animal … this goddamn painting.

"I've been keeping an eye on you ever since I got the tattoo. Yeah, I know that makes me sound like a creepy stalker. I followed your Connex port before you took your stuff down, but by then I already felt like I knew you. I felt connected to you. But you wouldn't believe how hard it is to explain all this to my girlfriends." Felix chuckles, like this whole conversation is just hilarious to him.

"I really don't need to hear about your girlfriends."

He waves me off. "Anyway, I heard you left the PEAD program, and I had my dad promise to help you. And then you were all over the news for killing Ricardo Salazar—"

"Thanks for that reminder."

"None of that matters to me. I see who you really are. It's in this tattoo. And I know—I just *know*—that the girl with the ability to reveal such beauty within pain is still inside you."

"No. You're wrong. That girl died the day I killed Rick. I'm not an artist anymore. I'm a killer."

"I know you're not."

"I am. I have to be."

"You have to be an artist."

"I can't be an artist and expect to survive. I can only survive if I don't give a shit anymore."

"You know that's not true."

"What do you know about it?"

Felix pushes off the bumper and stands, like he's about to give another counter-argument. Instead, he slumps his shoulders and sighs. "Everah. Forget it."

"Trust me, I plan to."

He looks at me sharply, and I can see the defeat in his eyes. I want this conversation to end. I don't want him telling me this. I *hate* him for telling me this. I hate him for suggesting that he knows who I am. He doesn't know a damn thing about me. I'm in the middle of a war, and I have no room for sentiments in my quest for survival. I don't deserve to get out of this alive, but that's all I have left. Survival of the Fittest, or in my case, "survival of she who shoots first and doesn't give a shit about asking questions." What would he have me do, wave a canvas in the air and plead for sympathy? That's not survival, that's suicide. I might as well slit my wrists right here and save him the trouble of trying to protect me.

"That's what all this is about? A goddamn tattoo?" Hathaway appears around the truck, her eyes flickering between us.

I take a step away, but Felix holds onto my arm. "It's more than just that," he says.

"You told me she was your cousin," says Hathaway. "But she's not, is she? She's not even related to you."

"You're missing the point."

"Felix, I don't give a shit what the *point* is anymore, but you made me risk my job to keep her safe in prison."

"It doesn't matter now." The words came out of *my* mouth—not Felix's—and even though they both know the statement is true, they stare at me in disbelief. "Everah. I'm thirsty. Is there water and food in the trailers?"

Felix lets go of my arm. "My pack is in the Humvee," he says quietly. "Fill it up with whatever you can, and we'll get going."

I don't hesitate to tear myself from the two soldiers. I take Felix's pack and leave them arguing in the scorching sun.

I burst into an airstream trailer, taking no caution if anyone might still be here. It's been ransacked, the whole living space turned upside down. The kitchen area is mostly intact, and I find a few bottles of warm water and bags of nuts and other snacks, but not much else.

Something catches my attention behind the couch. There is a pair of boots on the floor, belonging to a man lying on the ground. He's been shot in the head. I've seen more blood and gore this week than most people will see in their lifetimes, and yet the sight of this man's brains spilling out onto the carpet churns my stomach. I feel my hand twitch. It used to do that when I was in proximity of art and I ached for a paintbrush. Now, the trigger is blood, and my hand yearns for the feel of a pistol grip.

I'm snapped from my thoughts by the siren. I rush to the doorway of the trailer and see a drone in the air, flying straight for us, throwing dust in its wake. Hathaway shouts at Felix, then runs to our Humvee, leaving Felix hollering after.

"Hathaway! No!"

Hathaway doesn't listen. She jumps into the Humvee and starts off into the desert. She's finally had enough of my destruction; she's leaving me to die in the hands of the terrorists.

Felix yells at me. "Take cover!"

The drone is too fast. I'm still in the doorway of the trailer when the aircraft fires down on the Humvee, which explodes and flies into the air, with Hathaway inside. The shockwave sweeps

Felix off his feet, and he hurdles to the ground, engulfed in a dust cloud. The trailer rocks on its unstable foundation, and I'm tossed outside, glass flying all around me. The roar of the explosion thumps my eardrums and everything goes silent.

I lie on my stomach in the dirt. Felix shouts something at me, but I can't hear him. He points at the drone as it hovers above the burning Humvee, and then he points at the rusting gassers parked along the road. *Go,* he mouths. *Go!* There's blood spurting from his leg, mixing with desert sand. I feel the instant sting of fear in my chest. I haven't been afraid in a very long time—I'd nearly forgotten what it felt like. Felix is hurt and he's pushing me away. "*Go!*" he says, and this time I hear him.

I scramble on my hands and knees toward the gassers. Sharp sand cuts into my bare palms. The drone moves toward Felix and lasers scan the ground. Something shoots down from the drone as the dust cloud settles around the trailer park. I feel a rush of adrenaline pulse through my veins. *Fight or flight, Jo.* I can't fight the drone, so I run like hell.

I sprint over to a large truck. The sharp pain in my foot brings tears to my eyes, but I keep running. I can't look back, I can't bring myself to see if Felix is dead. I hop into the gasser, feel the leather of the seats as it sears my skin, punch the START button, and take off in a sideways skid into the desert.

Only one thought rattles through my head: This is not the best time to learn how to drive.

28 fuel for fire

I have absolutely no idea what I'm doing. The truck speeds across the desert, skidding along the sand. I despise gassers, and worse, I don't know how to drive one. I jab and pull and kick the controls looking for the brake and somehow get the truck to speed up. I press a red button and the car dies, coming to an abrupt stop and painfully jamming my stomach into the steering panel.

Through the rearview mirror I see the Alias drone hovering above the trailer park. And then I see the line of Humvees racing across the flats toward Felix. I don't know if he's still alive. I don't know what Alias will do to him. Torture him for intel, probably. And once they're done with him, they'll come looking for me.

I punch the START button and I'm off across the desert again. The console map shows I'm headed west. There's nothing west. Not even a road. I should turn back. Or go north—that's where the highway is. We'd driven so far into the desert that it'll take me hours to get to the highway. Alias is probably there. They'll see me coming and bullets will rain down on me from their drones.

Just keep driving. The sun is rising higher in the sky. Plumes of smoke loom in the west. I don't see a single person. I spot a few houses and buildings that were abandoned decades ago, and two cows and a jackrabbit, but no humans.

An alarm blares from the console. "What is that?" I say, as though the truck will understand me. The screen flashes two words: LOW FUEL. Of course. This is a gasser, an old one at that. If this were an AEV I'd at least have solar panels to charge the batteries. This is how I die. Not by terrorist guns or drone-dropped bombs, but from thirst, starvation, and exposure because I'm out of gas in the middle of the freaking desert.

The LOW FUEL warning keeps on flashing. Now it says DANGEROUSLY LOW FUEL. The truck starts whining, and then it slows to a stop. I jab my finger into the START button. "C'mon, stupid truck!"

NO FUEL, says the console screen. Thanks for that clarification.

Now what? I still have Felix's pack, which I thankfully filled with water and food. I sit and nibble for a moment, trying to wrap my brain around how I ended up in this ridiculous predicament. Mushroom clouds. Drones. Alias guerilla soldiers. Felix. Me, the Teenage Killing Machine. I should call up the media and demand they upgrade my name. Oh wait, I can't. They were all incinerated in the n-bomb.

When did I become such an insensitive jerk? It wasn't that long ago that I wrote essays for my PEAD classes about the importance of human compassion in modern society. And now I haven't an ounce of empathy for anything. I guess this is what psychologists consider emotional acclimating. There must be a scientific term for that. If not, they should add it in their files next to a photo of me. Hell, they could fill a whole damn book with my issues.

I can't eat anymore. I can't sit here and think of the million ways I'm screwed-up. There must be something out here in the desert to help me, there *must.* I can use the scope on Felix's gun to look around, so I grab the gun and get out of the truck.

Holy crap it's hot. I've only been to the desert once, when Perfect Family took me to Laughlin by the river. It wasn't too bad then, but today is not even bearable. The air is so dry the moisture is sucked right out of my skin, like I've stuffed myself into a pizza oven.

The scope catches some weird illusions as I peer into the horizon. The ground shimmers as a brown sea, glinting in the sunlight. I spot a building at the edge of a low line of hills. It's what, three, four miles away? Ah hell, I don't know. It's far. And it's hot. And my ankle hurts.

And I have to walk.

I rummage through the trunk and find a gallon-sized plastic can that I'm hoping I can fill with gas. Felix's pack also has a switchblade knife—which I place on my belt for easy access—and a military-grade visor. I stuff the pistol in my waistband, put on the visor, grab the gas can, and start walking.

I'm amazed at how ruthlessly bright it is. Everything is a shade of beige, like a sepia-filtered photo, except for the sky, which is so blue it looks like a manufactured color. It won't be blue long; the smoke clouds are filling the sky. I pass a few stubby trees that resemble cheerleaders holding pom-poms. There's nothing out here to cheer for, just a lot of beige rocks sitting on a lot of beige dirt.

The air is still and heavy, so quiet that I'm aware of every sound I make, hear every grain of sand crunch beneath my boots, every whirr of oxygen as it swirls inside my crackling lungs. Something circles overhead: a hawk, or maybe a vulture. Up higher, I spot an aircraft. A drone, perhaps, or a jet. Or Superman. God, I really hope it's Superman.

I walk faster. The sharp pain in my ankle brings tears to my eyes, which evaporate the moment they touch the dry air. There's no moisture left in my swelling tongue to quench my chapped lips. The exposed skin of my neck and shoulders feels like it's on fire. The heat of the earth seeps through the rubber of my boot soles. It is taking me forever to reach the hills.

Just as I'm about to collapse into the sand and allow myself to be turned into human jerky, I spot a sign. Letters rise from a squat building that spell GAS. Sounds promising, but there's not much more there than a run-down gas station with a store attached. One small shed behind it. A dirt road leading through. No sign of people. I decide it's worth a chance, and walk closer.

Clack!

The gas can flies from my hand and tumbles several feet behind me.

"Don't come any closer or I'll shoot!" The voice is high-pitched, childlike.

I freeze, trying to peer into the shadows through a broken window into the store.

"I said, don't come any closer!" Yep, it's a kid.

"I'm not moving!"

"I'll shoot!"

"You already *did* shoot!"

"What do you want?"

"I need gas. Although, now I can't because you shot a hole in my can."

"Go away. This is my store."

"Are you here alone?"

There's a pause, then an unconvincing "No …?"

"I need to get out of the sun, okay?" I take one step and a bullet grazes my boot. "Jesus!"

"I said, go away!"

"I'm not here to hurt you."

"Then why are you here?"

"I told you, I need gas. Weren't you listening?"

"Are you armed?"

It takes me a moment to decide how to answer the question, but considering this kid probably has the gun aimed at my head, I figure it's best to answer truthfully.

"Yes, I'm armed."

Another pause. "Show me."

"Are you serious?"

"Just do it!"

I groan and pull the pistol from my waistband. I don't know what this kid expects me to—Another *clack!* and the pistol flies from my hand.

"Holy crap, you're a good shot!"

"Is that it? Was that your only weapon?"

I still have the knife strapped to my belt, but I'm going to need some sort of protection against Billy the Kid if this escalates any further. "Yeah, that's all I've got."

"Okay," says the little voice, and a blond head pops up behind the broken window.

I expected to see a young kid, but I certainly did not expect to see a young *girl.* She's no more than ten or eleven years old, her long sun-bleached hair tied back in braids, her face darkened by years in the desert, dressed in a faded yellow T-shirt and cut-off jean shorts likely worn by two other people before her. She clutches a rifle tightly in her arms—it's almost as long as she is tall.

We pause, staring at each other through the window, her studying me just as much as I'm studying her. The hawk *cawh*s above.

"Hey, um," I say, "now that we've got that outta the way, can I come out of the sun? It's really freaking hot."

She squints at me. "You're too white to be in the desert."

I look down at my reddening skin. "Yeah, no shit."

She giggles. It's a perplexing sight to see this kid in braids and a smile holding a semi-automatic weapon. "Okay, you can come in. But don't touch anything."

I keep my eye on her gun, and she keeps her eye on me as I hobble into the store. It looks like this girl has been the only one in here for some time. Dusty bags and cans of food sit on shelves. Huge cartons of water rest in the back. A tent of packing blankets hangs in front of the counter.

She frowns at my shoes. "What happened to your foot?"

"It's a long story," I say. "Why are you out here by yourself?"

"It's a long story," she mirrors. "You gonna get your gas, or what?"

"I can't. You put a bullet through my can, remember?"

She tilts her head. "You're not from around here, are you?"

"Is it that obvious?"

She giggles again. "Yeah."

This kid is baffling. She's a master with that rifle; she has to be. I mean, what if I'd been a pedophile come to kidnap her and burn the place down? She's forced to look after herself. And now that she's met me—all skin and bones and blistering with a sunburn—perhaps she's not so threatened.

"I'm Jo," I say and hold out my hand.

She jumps at the movement, then shakes my hand. "Evie."

Jeez, even her name is cute. "Where'd you learn to shoot like that, Evie?"

She beams proudly. "Daddy taught me. We shoot snakes and lizards." Her smile drops. "*Used* to. Anyway, there's not many snakes left around here."

"Probably because you shot them all."

She chuckles and hugs her rifle. "Probably."

"Where's your dad now?"

"Don't know. He works in Barstow. The drones went over and then Daddy never came back. It's just me."

I look around and nod. "Well, looks like you've got a good place for yourself."

Evie studies me a moment, then places her rifle on the counter. "I have another gas can." She skips to the storage room and emerges with a bright red plastic carton.

"Oh wicky. I've never done gas before, though."

"You've never pumped gas?"

"*Pumped*? That's what it's called? No, I've never driven a car before today."

Evie rolls her eyes. "Ah jeez. All right, come on."

She leads me outside to a pump. I've only seen these kinds of things in old movies, and I've never actually witnessed anyone pump gas. Evie's a pro. It takes her all of ten seconds to get the nozzle in the carton and start filling it up. The smell of the fumes is sharp and burns my nose. Evie notices my expression and rolls her eyes again.

"Okay, there you go."

She hands me the full carton. It's heavy and I wonder how I'm going to carry it the four miles back to the truck.

"Thanks," I say. I look out into the scorching desert. "Well, it was nice to meet you, Evie."

I take a few steps and her voice squeaks. "Wait! You can stay here."

"What? No, I don't want to do that. I'm just gonna fill up the truck and head to the highway."

She shakes her head. "You won't get to the highway on one gallon of gas."

I gaze into the beige infinity. The hawk circles again. And I swear it's even hotter now. "Oh. Well, what *can* I get to?"

"Depends how good your mileage is."

"My *what*?"

Evie groans. "You can drive the truck back here for more gas."

"Yeah, okay. That's what I'll do."

"Tomorrow."

"I can't wait until tomorrow."

"You're a freaking tomato! Stay here tonight and you can go in the morning, before the sun gets up too high."

I can't help but feel like she's trying to keep me as company a little longer. Maybe it won't be so bad. Honestly, it's not like I have any better options for keeping out of sight from the Alias drones. It doesn't hurt that she's a great shot with that rifle.

Evie walks out to the driveway and picks up my pistol. "You're gonna want this," she says as she hands it back to me. There's a sharp dent in the barrel from where she'd shot it out of my hand. "C'mon, I'll show you around."

It isn't a lengthy tour. The store has a bathroom with running water—amazingly enough. The refrigerators don't work, but they're still cool, and I gulp down a two-liter of orange juice as Evie watches in amazement. Most of the food has gone stale, yet the bag of crunchy chocolate chip cookies calls my attention.

"Chew!" Evie says with a grimace.

"Ah koobeb hab coobie baug hub," I say through a mouthful of crumbly sugar.

She giggles. "What?"

I swallow more orange juice. "I couldn't have cookies back home. They don't sell sweets in LA. It's part of their health legislature bullcrap."

Evie raises her eyebrows. "You're from LA? What's it like?"

I shrug. "It's gone."

She shrinks six inches. "Sorry …"

"Hey, it wasn't your fault."

"I know my daddy's dead too."

"Why do you say that?"

"He'd have come back for me."

She flops under her makeshift tent, and I sit on the floor in front of the counter.

"How'd you end up out here, anyway?"

She takes a big breath. "My uncle. He owns this store. We were driving out to get my daddy and we heard about the bombs on the news. He dropped me off and told me to wait while he went to get him."

"And neither came back?"

"Nope. You're the first person I've seen in two days. Other than the drones."

"They're still around?"

"Yeah, they fly over every once in awhile, but they don't bother with this place. Too small, I guess."

I nod, but Evie doesn't want to talk anymore. She's lost in her thoughts as she lies on her side with her back to me—I think she might be crying. That's okay because I'm too exhausted for conversation, even though my brain won't shut up. Evie hands me a blanket. She's so sweet and innocent, yet here she is, alone in the middle of the desert with no one left to come rescue her. She's just a kid. What kid deserves to be left to fend for herself?

I sit in the doorway of the gas station and watch the sun set behind the heavy cloud of smoke on the western horizon. The beige expanse of drab landscape transforms into a sea of purples, pinks, and oranges. I've never seen a sunset so colorful, like it's painted onto the sky, like the gods had pity on their human minions and granted a moment of mercy. As darkness envelops the desert, out come the stars that could never be seen amid the illuminated lights of LA. Despite the looming dangers that lurk in the desert, this place is strikingly peaceful at night.

I maybe have my eyes closed for ten minutes before I hear the vehicle rumbling straight for the gas station.

29 three's a crowd

Guns fire at the building before they're close enough to hit anything. Evie has her rifle positioned at the window in a matter of seconds.

"They're coming right at us!" she says.

Headlights grow in the distance. Bullets pelt the building, sending shattered glass and plaster in all directions.

"Shoot 'em, Evie!"

She whips around, her eyes widened with fear. "*What?*"

"Shoot them!"

"I can't shoot them!"

"Why not?"

"I've never shot a person before!"

"You shot at me!"

"I wasn't trying to *kill* you!"

"*Gargh!*" I swing open the door and hide my body behind the doorframe. I can't see where I'm aiming in the dark, but I fire round after round at the incoming headlights. A window shatters, someone hollers, and the truck screeches to a halt, not fifty feet from the store.

The truck door opens and someone yells. A figure moves in front of the headlight and my scope laser catches the movement. I fire and he falls to the ground. Another man yells from the truck. One more shot, and then it's quiet.

I look over to see Evie wide-eyed, hunkered below the window. I'm given mere seconds to catch my breath, and then I'm shot at again, this time with a weapon more powerful than I've witnessed in real life. The store is being torn to shreds and there's no way I can fire back and protect myself at the same time.

I dive behind the wall and flatten myself on the floor as plaster rains down on me. "Evie! Shoot him! If you don't kill him, he will kill us!"

Evie looks at me for an absurd amount of time as the wall disintegrates above me. She squeezes her eyes shut, and I'm certain we're done for, but then her trembling hand reaches for the trigger and she blinks through the scope. Finally, I hear the *clack!* of the rifle and the gunfire stops.

There's a thud as a body hits the dirt. Evie is frozen. I peek my head through the door. No sounds, no movement. I walk outside, carefully, and find one man crumpled in front of the truck. Dead. The windshield is blown out. Another man is hunched over in the driver's seat. Dead.

Evie's voice whispers through the window. "I killed him …"

I walk to the last guy laying in the dirt, a machine gun on the ground next to him, his neck ripped open and blood gushing though his mouth. Definitely dead.

"You sure did. Right through the throat. Come look."

Evie takes her time walking out with her rifle cradled in her arms, and when she sees the hole in the guy's throat she lets out a choking snort. "I've never killed anyone."

"There's a first time for everything."

She looks up at me, her face ghostly in the bright headlights. "You've done that before, haven't you?"

"Done what?"

"Killed someone."

Her question catches my breath, and I can't find the words to answer her. Thankfully, I don't have to, because we both hear the voice.

Evie jumps. "Did you hear that?"

I jerk around and pull the knife from my belt. Evie sees the blade and frowns.

"Hey! You lied to me. You said you didn't have any more weapons."

"I forgot I had it."

I'm pretty sure she doesn't believe me, but I can't stand here arguing my necessity for self-defense. We hear the voice again. It's coming from the back of the truck, and if my mind isn't playing tricks on me, I could swear it's calling for help. I put my finger to my lips to signal silence. Evie raises her rifle. I clutch my knife, and yank open the back of the truck.

"*Whoa*!" says the voice.

Evie shines her rifle light into the face of a man: Felix.

My stomach lurches. "What are you doing here?"

"It's nice to see you too, Jo." Felix says, shielding his eyes from the light. He's on the floor of the truck, one arm bound to a rail, his pant leg soaked with blood.

"You know him?" says Evie.

"Is that a *kid*?" he says.

"I'm not a kid! I'm eleven!"

"Jo, why is an eleven-year-old pointing a rifle at me?"

"This eleven-year-old just saved both our asses, so why don't cha shut the hell up?"

"Yeah!" Evie echoes. "Shut the hell up!"

Felix stares at us, dumbfounded.

"How are you still alive?" If I cared, I might be concerned that I sound indifferent.

"The drone tracked the Humvee. That's how Alias found us. I told them I was with ACTA and they were gonna take me to a military bunker for ransom."

"Because you're so important to ACTA, right?"

"I'm the last surviving Lone Wolf soldier. That's kind of a big deal. Now are you gonna help me out of here?"

I'm not so sure I should. I'd nearly made my escape. I could have run off with Evie the Sharpshooter and lived a life where no one knew a damn thing about me, and now here's my past, come running to catch up.

Felix notices my hesitation. "Jo?"

I have no words for the guy. I don't even take much caution about hurting him as I slice my knife though the rope around his arm.

"Thank you," Felix says, rubbing his wrist.

I walk back into the store, crunch my boots over the glass and plaster, and head straight for the liquor shelf. Most of the bottles are shattered from the gunfire, and I reach for the first full bottle I find. Whiskey? I don't know. I pop the top and take a swig. It burns my throat and I spit it out, and then take another drink. This one stays down.

Felix leans against the bullet-riddled doorframe, carefully removing the weight from his injured leg. "Oh, so you're drinking now?"

I glare and take another drink. Damn this stuff is vile. I don't care because Felix is getting blurry, and I don't want to see that look of expectation and disappointment on his face.

"Hathaway is dead," I say, forcing my voice past the burning alcohol in my throat.

He looks at his feet. "That was an unfortunate turn of events. But a lucky one since you weren't in the Humvee with her."

"She was leaving me. She was going to leave me in that trailer—"

"Is that what you think? Jo, she wasn't *leaving* you. The drone would have bombed the trailer."

"So she got the hell out of there."

Felix's face hardens. "She drew the drone away from the trailer park. Created a diversion. She sacrificed herself…" now his voice cracks "…for both of us."

"Why would she sacrifice her life for me?"

"That's the kind of woman she is … *Was*."

The last thing I want to think about is how a good woman traded her life for that of a psychopath, and yet here we are. I take another drink of liquor to numb the swell of heat in my abdomen; it only amplifies the sensation.

"And," he continues, "maybe she saw in you what I do."

"Clearly you're both delusional."

Felix huffs. "Yeah, okay."

Evie enters the store and notices Felix's bleeding leg. "You're hurt!"

He smiles at her. Really? He's *smiling*. What an ass.

"I'm all right. Nothing to make a fuss over."

"You should sit down," Evie says.

"Nah, I'm fine. I like the pain."

"Sit down!" She's sure got a knack for bossing people around.

"All right, kiddo. Calm down."

"Don't call her *kiddo*," I say.

"What, are you her guardian now?"

He's infuriating. I should at least be happy he's alive. At *least*.

"Are you hungry?" Evie asks.

He smiles again. "Starved."

"Then *sit*."

Felix collapses onto the blankets, and Evie brings him some cookies and a bottle of water. She plops next to him and watches him eat like it's the most fascinating thing she's ever seen, and he keeps on grinning at her.

It makes my blood boil. My head is swimming in alcohol now. I kinda like it, but at the same time I'm even more furious that I have no control over the spatter coming out of my mouth. "What do you mean, *you like the pain*?"

"Heh. I never did tell you what my tick is, did I?"

"What's a *tick*?" says Evie.

"Just a weird thing that people do. For example, Jo here likes to kill people."

Evie's eyes go wide, and I know I haven't done a good job of disproving that statement due to our recent Alias shoot-out. And I can feel her eyes on my scabbed and scarred knuckles.

"Mine's a little different," he says, pulling Evie's attention from me. "I like pain."

"You *like* pain?" Evie says, her nose scrunched in disgust.

"Yeah. Not self-inflicted—that kinda takes the fun out of it. I like when people hurt me. I'm a little masochistic that way."

"That explains why you keep dragging *me* along," I grumble, and I hate that Felix smiles in response.

Evie leans in. "Are you her boyfriend?"

He lets out a snorting laugh. "Who, *me*? No, Jo can't stand me."

"What I can't stand is the chariot you rode in on."

That makes Felix laugh even more, and he elbows Evie. "Yeah, whatever *that* means, right?"

Evie nods but her face remains scrunched. "It's just … you act like you are."

Felix winks at me. "I think she's saying we argue like an old married couple."

Evie giggles. "I think you'd make a cute old married couple."

"Aw, shucks," Felix says. "But I doubt I'd have a shot because I'm sure Jo has a line of drooling boys waiting for her back home."

"There is no more *home*, jackass," I say.

"Okay. Then, speaking theoretically …"

I groan.

"Well, not a *line* of boys. How about that *one*?"

Another swig of whiskey.

"Not *one*?" He squints at me. "*Ever*?"

"Do you have a point to make here?"

"Holy crap you're a virgin!"

I feel the blood rush to my cheeks. "Yes, thank you. You've found me out. I'm not yet a woman."

"Don't say that. I think it's wicky."

"It's *wicky* that I'm a virgin?"

He shrugs. "Yeah."

"I'm a virgin, too!" Evie blurts with such a sweet inflection that I expect cherubs to float down around her.

Felix laughs. "Good for you!"

I'm blushing from the embarrassment of Felix's revelation, and I'm fuming with anger for him bringing it up in the first place, and my skin is painfully sunburnt and the alcohol has raised my body temperature to unreasonable levels ... Basically, my face is on fire.

I look away. "Why are we talking about this?"

"I donno, beats talking about killing people."

"Are you a virgin?" Evie asks him.

Felix scoffs with a nonchalant shrug. "Well, that's kind of a long story."

I have to put a stop to this. "What are you doing?"

"What?" he says, giving me his best puppy-dog eyes. "She asked me a question."

"What about you, Jo?" Evie says. "What's your story?"

"Oh god ..."

Felix's face lights up. "Yeah, Jo, what's your story?"

"Stop. I am not having a conversation about my sex life in front of an eleven-year-old."

Felix mumbles under his breath. "We can't talk about your sex life if you don't actually *have* a sex life."

Evie giggles.

"You can't talk about this kind of stuff with a kid!"

"Gimme a break, Jo. This *kid* just shot a guy through the throat."

"That was one time. Once we get out of here she can go back to being a little girl."

"You think she can afford to be a little girl? Out here? In the goddamn desert in the middle of a goddamn war?"

"Yes! I can't sit back and watch her turn into a killer!"

I expect Felix to shout something back, but all I hear is the sound of my own breath bellowing through my nose. Evie lifts the rifle out of her lap and places it on the floor beside her. And Felix stares at me—hard.

"Like *you*?" he says. "You don't want her to become a killer like you."

"Yes! Okay? Is that what you want me to say? I don't want Evie to turn into a monster like me."

"Jo, this monster you claim you've become is a load of bullshit."

"Tell that to those media assholes who plastered my life story on the news."

"You have to move on from that."

"I've tried to forget, I've tried to move on, but here you are, time and again, reminding me of my past, of all the horrible things I've done."

Evie's voice is so faint I barely hear it, but the quiver it sends through the air makes my hair stand on end. "You really do like to kill people?"

Felix won't look at the girl; he keeps his eyes on me. "Is that how you want to be remembered?"

I shake my head. The whiskey makes my brain slosh around in my skull. My heart trembles in my chest, and I wonder if it's about to give up, if it's nearing the end of the line, too exhausted and tormented to continue pumping life through me.

"No," I say. "I don't want to be remembered at all. I want to be anonymous. Forgotten."

"I can't forget you," Felix says, his voice lowered. "I won't ever forget you."

"Oh really," I say flatly, unwilling to give in to this so-called sensitive movement. "Why won't you forget me?"

He pulls his shirt open and reveals the tattoo of my phoenix and scales on his chest. I knew it was coming, but I was hoping he wouldn't go there.

"I know who you are, Jo. I knew who you were. I know who you can be."

"Oh come on, Felix! I can't afford to be an artist in the goddamn desert in the middle of a goddamn war."

"Don't twist my words around."

"What am I gonna do? Paint pretty pictures on drones and Humvees?" My whole body is trembling, and I can't get enough air in my lungs for a full breath. Felix lets out a long sigh and I'm afraid he's consuming all the oxygen.

"If you keep your eyes open you'll figure it out," he says.

"Like you? At the ripe old age of twenty-five you've got yourself all figured out?"

"Are you kidding? I barely know who I am. I became a soldier because I didn't have to think about it. I don't have any special talents. If they were to build a doomsday shelter where they only let in people with contributable skills, I'd never even get considered."

"They wouldn't consider a convicted murderer, either."

"But you're more than that, Jo. You actually have something to contribute. Besides, painting helps with the visions."

"I told you, the visions are gone. Painting doesn't matter. I have nothing left to offer the world other than a thousand ways to kill a man."

"You know better than that."

"My artist days are done. I'm not the least bit inspired to create anything. And even if I was, there's no telling how long it'll be before the depression consumes me and I wind up bleeding out like my dad."

Felix doesn't have a response for that. The color has drained from his face, and he leans back against the counter, studying me as though I were a science experiment gone wrong.

Evie catches my eye as she sits under the tent, pouting like a kid, but looking older at the same time, like she's aged a decade in an hour.

I can't stand the sight of either of them. The alcohol has completely muddied my mind. The hot air sucks what little breath I have left in my lungs, and I start dry-heaving.

Felix shifts and I know he's getting ready to start another lecture.

"Just stop. Please."

He holds out his hands. "I wasn't—"

"I'm too exhausted for this. In case you haven't been keeping track, I've killed eight people in the last two days."

Evie's eyes widen like she's pondering the suggestion that I find sport in the activity.

"We don't know for sure they're all dead," says Felix.

"Like that matters? I *tried* to kill eight people. *Eight*! That doesn't include Rick or LaRae. And you want to know the worst part? I don't even care. I feel nothing."

"You've also inhaled a quarter bottle of whiskey," he says. "I'm surprised you're still standing."

"I just want to go to sleep. Can I do that? Please?"

"If you'll allow …" I roll my eyes but Felix continues. "Remember what I said about the base near here? It's a real place."

"What base?" says Evie. "There's no base around here." Evie's not convinced, and therefore neither am I.

"ACTA built a bunch of them in anticipation of the war."

"No," I say, shaking my head. "I don't want to go to any base."

"That's the only place we'll be safe," Felix says. "We can't keep wandering around in the desert like this."

"Fine. You go to the base. I'll stick it out on my own. If anyone threatens me, I'll shoot them." I hold out my pistol and Evie reaches over for her rifle.

"And you're gonna let her risk her life too?" Felix says, and nods to the girl.

"Take her to the base with you."

Evie gets to her feet, rifle in arms. "Nu-uh. I'm staying with you, Jo."

"It'll be safer if you go with Felix—" I start, but Evie won't have it.

"You're not my daddy. You can't tell me what to do." Evie jerks her body toward me, her blond braids whipping over her shoulders. "I go where you go."

I can see a smile tugging at the corner of Felix's mouth. "She goes where you go," he says.

Evie nods, her shoulders puffed up like she's trying to seem taller. The girl is going to follow in my shadow. How far? All the way to Hell? Because that's where I seem to be heading.

All my energy evaporates from my body, and I slump on the shelves. "I'm just so freaking tired …"

"We can't stay here," Felix says. "I've never left you behind, Jo, I don't aim to start now. Get some sleep. At the first light, we're hopping in that truck. That base is out there and we are going to find it."

My knees start to give out. "Fine. Everah. I just want to close my eyes."

"Jo, you can sleep in the tent if you want," Evie says.

"Come on down next to Poppa," Felix says, patting the blankets next to him.

I lie down as far from him as possible. "Keep your sneaky hands away from me. I'd at least like to stay a virgin through the night."

Felix chokes on his laugh and I squeeze my eyes shut, the bottle of whiskey still clutched in my hand.

30 guys and dolls

The light. The noise. The pressure. The pain.

"Ah! First hangover! How's it feel, champ?"

A hard object pokes my ribs when I roll over. I pull it out from underneath me—the whiskey bottle. "I thought alcohol was supposed to make you feel *good.*"

"Says the girl who detoxed from drugs. Twice."

"You're not helping."

He kicks my boot. "Get up. It's time to move. We're finding that base."

The room spins. Why does he have to talk so freaking loud? I squint into the light and see Evie has packed several boxes of food and water. Felix leans on a makeshift cane made of a metal pole, his leg wrapped in a towel, which has done nothing to stop the bleeding.

"Your leg looks like shit," I say.

"You're not looking any better. Now c'mon, you need to get the boxes in the truck. I can't carry anything."

"I'll take the smaller box," Evie says. No lack of energy from this one.

We pile in the abandoned Alias truck, and of course I'm designated to drive since Felix has to lay out his leg in the back. The next few hours are an uncomfortable and nerve-racking experience. The busted-out windshield lets every grain of sand fly under my visor and scratch my dry eyeballs. My face, neck, shoulders and arms are so burnt and blistered that the tickling of my hair causes excruciating agony. Add to that my hazy hangover head and I'm surprised we're moving at all. This truck is even trickier to drive than the gasser; I have no gauges since the windshield display is gone and the center console is riddled with bullet holes, and the steering panel is motion-sensored and any slight movement sends us winding in the other direction.

"Did you ever learn how to drive straight?" Felix hollers from the bed of the truck as he ping-pongs back and forth.

"She never learned to drive!" Evie laughs even though she's been white-knuckling the seat this whole time.

"That's not very encoura-*ugh*!" Felix slams into the side again. "Do you even know where we're going?"

"I thought *you* knew where to go! We don't have any sensors!"

Felix leans in and pushes a few manual buttons and music blares through the speakers, some ear-splitting, guitar-heavy madness that makes my head pound.

"The radio still works!" He tosses his head around to the beat. Evie laughs and joins in.

"Felix!"

"Alright, alright." He turns the music down. "Use your visor to search for metallic signatures."

I tap the side of the visor. "Show metallic signatures."

"There are no metallic signatures in current view," it responds.

"I don't see anything," I say moments before I spot the tiny flashing speck in my visor, signaling something spotted against the foothills. "Felix!"

"I see it. Keep going."

I squint into the sun, and that's when I see the cloud of swirling dust. "It's coming right for us!"

Felix cuts the music and now we hear the alarm warning us about whatever it was we couldn't see through the broken sensor screens.

"Where'd that come from!" Felix hollers.

"What is it?"

"Drone! Behind us! Go north! Go north!"

I pull a hard left and Evie buckles herself in. Felix wedges himself between our seats.

A second vehicle shows in my visor. "They're surrounding us!"

"One Humvee," Felix says. "I can't tell what the other one is. What is that—a *bus*?"

The Humvee splits off, trapping us between the bus and the drone as we barrel toward the foothills. The bus makes an abrupt stop, and so does the Humvee, and I slam on the breaks barely a hundred yards away, unsure what to do. Two people jump out of the bus and position themselves against the vehicle with a rocket launcher, aimed right at us.

"Oh my god!" Evie cries.

The rocket launcher fires. The missile whistles as it flies over us and explodes in the air.

"They took out the drone!" Felix opens the back hatch to see the remains of the drone fall to the ground in a fireball.

There's a honk from the bus, and Felix honks back four times. The rocket launcher team lowers their weapon.

Our truck radio springs to life. *"What the hell are you guys doing out here?"*

Felix depresses a button on the console. "Who are you?"

"You're asking me?"

"Yes, jerk-off, I'm asking you!"

Evie tugs Felix's sleeve and speaks in a tiny voice. "Maybe you should be nicer to them since they have the rocket launcher."

"This is Alpha Dog, Ranger Hogs."

Felix groans. "Oscar Romeo, Lone Wolf."

The guy on the radio laughs so loud it distorts the speaker. *"Oh of course it is! Good lord, Lone Wolf. I thought you were all dead!"*

"They are. I'm the only one left."

There's silence on the radio, then a sigh. *"What about the dolls driving your truck? Civilians?"*

Felix locks eyes with me. "Something like that."

"Well all right then. Get on over here so we can have a proper look at cha."

Felix shuts off the radio. "Time to make friends. Don't say anything stupid."

He slides out of the truck before I can scowl at him. Evie and I follow as a big, dark, burly guy with a big black beard and a toothy smile jumps from the bus wearing the same charcoal gray body armor as Felix, covered in beige dirt.

"What do have we here?" the man says, eyeing me with a grin.

Felix moves in between us, standing as tall as he can on his wounded leg. "I know there's a Foxhole around here. We need to find it."

"Huh. Well ain't that fascinating."

"Don't be an ass, Dog," says one of the other soldiers—a woman, tall and slender and wearing fitted jeans and a black tank-top with a scarf wrapped around her head.

Dog mumbles something behind his beard.

"What now?" The woman walks over and unwraps her scarf, revealing silky brown hair and flawless olive skin. "I'm Dakota," she says to Felix with a Miss America smile. She's absolutely gorgeous. And Felix can't take his eyes off her.

"Oscar Romeo," he says. "Actually, Felix. My name is Felix."

"Pleasure," she says. "Sorry about the scare back there. It took us a minute to realize you two weren't together."

"Heh," Felix chuckles. "Nah, we're just friends."

Dakota grins. "No, I mean, the drone. We thought you were Alias."

"Oh! We thought *you* were."

"Well, I'm glad we realized in time," says Dakota. She notices Evie with her giant sniper rifle and me swaying next to her. "You two look a little young to be ACTA agents."

Felix waves his hand. "They're not … this is … we …"

"I'm Evie," the girl says and reaches out her hand. "I'm eleven. And this is Jo. She's … well, not eleven."

Dakota laughs and shakes her hand. "Is that *your* rifle, Evie?"

"Yup!" she says. "It was my daddy's. I have a smaller one at home. But daddy's dead so I guess she's mine now."

Dog's beard twitches as he peers at Felix, who still hasn't taken his eyes off Dakota. "What are you, some kinda rolling orphanage?"

"I'm not an orphan." I don't even know if that's true, but I needed to say something. Anything to break Felix away from that woman.

"Okay," says Dog. "Then what are you?"

I open my mouth to announce that I'm a heartless desert assassin when Felix grabs hold of my arm.

"We really need to get to that foxhole," he says. "We can't keep wandering around in the desert like this."

"No, you can't," Dakota says. "Alias is snatching up the locals. It's not safe. You should ride with us."

"We'll follow you," Felix says.

"No, you're getting in the bus with me." She points to the bright red towel around his leg. "I need to get a look at that injury."

"I'll drive the truck," I say. "Evie and I."

"Yeah," nods Evie. "We got it."

Dog steps in close, his boulder of a chest heaving in my face. "I don't recommend you do that."

"Why not?" I say.

"Because it'll be dark well before we get to Foxhole," Dog says. "Alias moves at night and you can bet someone will be waiting for us beyond the foothills."

"Jo, let them drive the truck," says Felix.

"No, we got it," I say. "Evie's a killer shot. If we get in trouble we'll just shoot them."

Evie holds her rifle tighter, and Dakota raises an eyebrow.

A man wanders over from the Humvee with short buzzed hair and such a smooth face he looks like he's had the hair lasered off, and I see he's wearing the same gray body armor as Felix and Dog. "You two, get back in the bus. We need to move."

"They're coming with us," Dakota says. "It's not safe out here."

Dog tilts his head down at her. "If you wanna take up babysitting, that's your choice, sweetheart."

"I'm not babysitting anyone, and don't call me sweetheart."

Dog pauses, then grins. "*Eeaah*, you're killin' me, doll."

The clean-shaven guy looks between Dog and Dakota and taps his foot impatiently. "Let's *go*."

"Don't get your panties in a bunch, Solano," says Dog. "We're gathering the perishables."

The man sighs then heads back to the Humvee.

Dakota looks us over again. "Are you sure you'll be all right?"

"We'll be fine!" Evie says. "We can take care of ourselves. We've done it before. Jo's a good killer."

Dakota raises her other eyebrow, and I stand there awkwardly because I'm annoyed with Felix and Dog and this heat and my hangover, and on top of all that I can't figure out how this woman is out here in this filthy desert and still looks that good.

"All right. Just be careful." Dakota holds her arm out to Felix. "You're coming with me."

Felix moves to follow her, then glances over his shoulder to me. "Stay close."

Of course I'll stay close—I don't care how angry I am with Felix and how nice Dakota is. I wouldn't dare let him run off with Miss America.

Evie and I climb back into our scorching, windowless truck and follow the bus toward the foothills. Bomb clouds cover the valley, casting a gray shadow over everything. It's at least slightly cooler—my visor reads a breezy 108 degrees and 3% humidity—and there's an oddly metallic taste in the air, like an aluminum can.

It's pitch-black by the time we reach the foothills. Dog's voice comes over the radio. "*Turn off your floods, doll.*"

I flip on the mic. "I can't turn off my floods, I won't be able to see where I'm going."

"*If you wanna make it through these hills alive, you'll do as I say.*"

Everyone else's lights are off and I'm forced to do the same. My visor provides at least some sense of direction, displaying the metallic and heat signatures coming from the bus. I can't see anything beyond that; nothing more than black and more black. Not even moonlight.

"*Sniper! Eleven o'clock!*"

Dog barely finishes his statement when a machine gun flickers at the top of the hill. Bullets pelt the ground around us, and through the visor I can see that whoever is shooting is doing so atop a large truck.

"*Keep moving! Do not stop! I repeat, do not stop!*"

"They're gonna hit us!" Evie says, just as three bullets ricochet off our truck.

I'm starting to panic, I'm losing all proper motor skills. I move to engage the accelerator and our truck skids on loose gravel.

"You gotta keep us straight!" Evie has her rifle positioned in her arms, resting on the dashboard, aimed through the broken windshield at the sniper on the hill.

"Evie, what are you doing?"

"Keep it straight!" She takes a couple shots, yet the sniper still rains bullets down on us.

"What the hell are you doing back there?"

"Gah!" Evie says. "I can't see unless he's firing at us!"

I hand her my visor. "Use this."

"Ah-*ha*!" she says, and takes aim again.

Now I'm completely blind. I'm driving in the dark with dust blowing in my eyes, and all I see is the flash of the machine gun on the hill. Bullets *ping* off the bus and off our truck, and the closer we get to the hill the better chance the sniper has at taking us all down.

Evie is taking her time. "Steady … breathe … ready …"

Her rifle fires and a half second later the sniper's truck explodes into a giant fireball that lights up the entire hillside.

"Will you look at that!"

"Nice shot!"

"Got 'em." Evie sits back and cradles her rifle, grinning.

"Dog, you know that guy had company."

"Yeah, I know, Solano. Keep your eyes open."

"They're slowing down," Evie says.

She gives me back the visor, allowing me a visual of the other vehicles as we climb into the rocky hills.

"What the hell …"

"Quiet!"

We roll to a stop with the other truck to my right, the bus beyond that. At first I don't know why we've stopped, and then my visor picks up the heat signatures. People, at least two dozen of them, including children, all in a row in front of us. No one moves, not even the kids. They just stand there, like a front line of soldiers. A blockade.

Two voices come through the radio at once: "*Nobody move!*" "*Go around them!*"

Evie flips off the receiver and I realize these people could probably hear everything through our busted-out windshield.

"Are they bad guys?" Evie whispers.

Through the visor, I see one person off to the side with something metallic next to his head. Another person stands behind the first with a gun. And I realize, whoever these people are, they're prisoners.

I see movement in the truck next to me. I can't hear Solano, but judging by the way he's flailing his arms, he's probably arguing with the radio.

This is no time for arguing; something is wrong here, and Evie knows it too. I grab my pistol and Evie clutches her rifle.

"On three," I whisper. "Lights on, get out, aim." Evie nods. "One … two … three."

I flip on the floodlights, fling open the door, and take cover behind it. The people stand frozen, stunned, shielding their eyes from the light. They are varying levels of dreary and sun burnt, their clothes covered in dirt. I move around the truck door, and that's when I see the lights. Tiny flickers of blue flash behind every right ear. These people have been hijacked. I don't know what signals they're receiving, or who's in control of the transmitter, but Alias must be nearby.

No one moves. Not Solano in the truck, not Dog or anyone in the bus, not a single one of the civilians. I walk forward along the edge of the headlights, crouching with my pistol aimed and ready. I go to the man I suspect is being held hostage. He doesn't have a flashing device behind his ear, and neither does the masked man in black behind him. The hostage twitches his hand and I recognize he's sending me a signal, counting down on his fingers: *four, three, two, one*—The hostage drops to the ground and the masked man is startled and moves his pistol. I shoot first, right into his chest. The masked man tumbles into the dirt.

The hijacked civilians don't even flinch. Further down the line, a couple of adults turn their heads to look at me. Bullets whiz past, whistling in my ear. A second masked man hops out of the shadows and into the beam of the headlights, firing his gun furiously. I raise my pistol over a young boy's head, and fire at the same time as the gunman. My pistol makes a clanking sound and the barrel shifts backwards, indicating I'm now out of ammo. It doesn't matter, because blood spurts from the gunman's forehead; my last bullet killed him instantly.

The young boy yelps and falls to the ground. He rolls in the dirt, moaning. I'd unknowingly used him as a shield. And now he's been shot.

A hijacked man looks down at the boy bleeding in the dirt. "Man down," he says in a flat, monotone voice, watching as a pool of blood surrounds the boy.

There's rustling at the back of the group and another man in black races into the hills.

"Evie!"

"I got 'em!"

The *clack* of the rifle flutters over the hills. Last one down.

The injured boy moans in the dirt while the hijacked civilians stand silently still. I kneel down next to him and put my hand on his back, causing him to whimper, and I reel in my hand to find it covered in blood. The boy is bleeding to death, and no one is doing anything about it. Evie stands silhouetted in the headlights, her rifle crossed over her body. Solano sits in the truck, motionless through the windshield. There is no movement in the bus.

The hijacked man gives me a blank stare. "This civilian will require medical treatment," he says.

"Do something!" I say, and the man looks back to the boy and does nothing else.

Then, the flashing light behind the man's ear changes from blue to orange. He blinks. Looks around. Shakes his head. He looks at me, and at first his eyes narrow. When he notices the boy, he blinks again and his eyes fly open in wild excitement. "Jacob! Oh my boy, you're hurt!" He drops to the ground and sweeps up the boy in one arm. With the other hand he grabs my shirt, and screams in my face. "What do I do? Tell me what to do! I can't help him. You have to save him!"

A handful of the other civilians swarm around us, clutching their chests or faces. All of their lights flash orange.

"Someone has to help," says another man, his eyes wide with fear. "I don't know what to do."

"Oh, it hurts too much," a pregnant woman cries.

I jump to my feet and address the woman. "What are you talking about? What is going on?"

She avoids making eye contact with me; instead, she tosses her head back and forth with agony, clutching her protruding belly.

Dog jumps from the bus door. "I told you to stand down!"

"The boy needs help!" I say.

Dakota bursts through the crowd and kneels next to the injured boy, assessing the wound. "We need to get him on the bus. Someone help me."

Dog stands with his pistol in hand. The civilians wander in circles, crying to the heavens.

The pregnant woman grabs my arm. "It's too much. I can't handle it. There's no way I can survive through this."

Dakota waves her arms. "Someone help me!"

"Get away from them, Dakota." Solano rushes to her and pulls her to her feet. "We need to get out of here. Now."

"Solano, the boy's been hit!"

"These civilians are still hijacked."

Dog waves his pistol at the crying civilians. "Then how did the optrodes turn off?"

"They didn't turn off," I say. "They changed to orange."

Dakota looks around. "How could they change if the agents are all dead?"

"I did it. I switched the transmitter." A man walks up to us, holding a small black box with flashing buttons. It's the same hostage that counted down so I could shoot the masked man behind him. He stands at the edge of the headlights, the darkness allowing him some anonymity, but I can't help feeling there's something familiar about him.

The civilians holler and point at the man and back away, mumbling words that are incomprehensible amidst their bawling.

Dog aims his gun. "Put that down!"

The man holds up his hands, still holding the transmitter. He's just as disheveled as the rest of the group, with dirty clothes and an overgrown beard, yet no optrode. "Give me the chance to explain."

"Who are you?" Dog says, moving closer. "Are you with Alias?"

"No, I'm not with Alias. My name is Marius. I'm a civilian."

"Then what are you doing with the transmitter?"

"He had it," Marius says as he points to the dead Alias agent, the first one I'd shot.

Dakota looks him over. "You aren't implanted."

"They picked me up yesterday. Found me wandering the desert."

I'm being squashed as the pregnant woman pulls me into her body, her face nearly touching mine. She's terrified, her cheeks drenched in tears, jaw so clenched she can barely talk. "It was him, it wasn't our fault ..." she breathes into my ear. "It was him ..."

"It was who?" I ask.

The rest of the people chime in, sounding like a chorus of hissing snakes. "It wasn't our fault ... it was him ..."

"Get off of me!" I push at them and look around for help, but no one else seems to notice I'm drowning in a mob of hissing and crying botheads—no one except for the transmitter man.

"I swear I'm telling the truth," Marius says, twitching with every word.

Dog thrusts his gun in his face. "Make me believe you."

The chanting is getting louder now. "*It was him* ..." and finally it catches Dakota's attention.

"What are they saying?"

Before I can answer, the implants flash from orange to blue. The civilians freeze, roll back their shoulders, straighten their posture, wipe tears from their cheeks, and carefully back away.

"I will not be frightened," says the pregnant woman, talking to me as though she were hypnotized. "They will help us survive."

Dakota turns to Marius. "What did you do?"

"I'm not with Alias, I swear!" Marius holds the transmitter at the end of his fingers, away from his body as though its proximity threatened him. A *clack* rings over the hill and the transmitter flies from his hand. He looks to Evie, who holds her rifle in his direction, but the hostages are still hijacked, blue lights are still flashing.

A tall soldier emerges from the bus. "The communication lines are on the fritz. Alias is either here or on their way. We need to go before we lose connection to Foxhole."

"That's just a dandy idea, Oshiro," Dog says, "but what do you suggest we do with the botheads?"

"We need to take the boy with us," Dakota says.

"Leave the boy," Solano says and grabs Marius by the arm. "This is the only one we need. The rest of you, get in the bus. I'm not spending another minute in the open like this."

"There aren't any more Alias guys." Marius winces in Solano's grasp. "They shot all four."

Solano squints at Marius. "You're gonna tell me the goddamn truth or I'll execute you myself."

The pregnant woman waddles over to Solano. "You are addressing your fear at the wrong person. He is here to help you."

"Excuse me, miss," Solano growls, "but who the hell are you to talk to me about fear? You're the one being held hostage by terrorists."

"You will survive only if you know where to turn for help."

The civilians nod in silent agreement. The soldiers exchange glances of confusion. I'm pretty sure the injured boy is now officially dead.

"Time to get out of crazy town." Dog grabs me by the arm. He's got Evie in the other hand. "You two, in the bus. Now."

I'm pushed up the steps into the bus, which has been gutted to a metal shell and filled with piles of ammo and water tanks. Felix hobbles up from the back of the vehicle, his leg bound in a carbon-webbed sock. He looks me over as I crouch on the floor, hugging my knees.

"What did you do?"

I can't believe he's blaming me. "I didn't do anything. They're all hijacked."

Dog glares at us and heads to the radio console. He scans through channel after channel of static, mumbling to himself.

The tall man slides into the driver's seat. "I told you, communication is jammed."

"I got it, Oshiro. Just drive."

Solano appears in the doorway, holding Marius by the arm. Both men look straight at me.

Dog glares at them while blindly fussing with the radio. "I hope you're planning to tie that asshole up."

Dakota appears beside them, huffing. "Send another team out. We can't leave those people here. We already let one boy die."

"Sorry to be a jackass, sweetheart," says Dog, "but lots of people have died out here. I won't risk my team to save a bothead."

"Which is why you brought these girls on the bus," Solano says with a wave in my direction. Dog glares back and returns his attention to the radio.

"We'll send out another team to round up the civilians," says Oshiro. Dakota still looks concerned, but she nods back.

Marius stands in the middle of the bus, trembling. His floppy gray hair is dusted with beige dirt, and a beard mostly covers his face, but now I am absolutely certain that I recognize him. I know exactly who he is. This man was the neurologist called as a witness for my trial. For my botched defense. For my incarceration. Dr. Marius Frey of San Diego. The brain adjuster. This is the man who could have saved me from going to prison. But didn't.

Marius knows I recognize him. I don't know what my own face is doing, but his eyes go wide with alarm, and he bounces on the balls of his feet, poised to run.

I feel a pressure inside my gut, like my intestines are being tugged out through my belly button. This is not a vision; this is rage. I am overwhelmed with the need to hurt this man because I got sent to prison and this man did nothing to stop it. He saw my brain scans, he saw the oddities. Hell, he could have made something up. But this man sat on the stand, in front of the judge and the jury and the whole world, and he did nothing to prove that I didn't deserve to go to prison. In fact, he helped me get there.

And that makes me hate him.

Marius can sense my growing fury. I can tell by the way he pulls his arms in front of his body like a shield. I don't know if he's more afraid that I recognize him or because he knows how badly I want to punish him.

Solano shakes Marius, grabbing his attention. "You had better be straight with us, or this is gonna be bad news for you."

Marius looks between Solano and me. "I told you, I'm a civilian. I don't know anything about brain implants."

He's lying. I know he's lying. *He* knows I know he's lying, but if I open my mouth I'll sell myself out as the Schoolgirl Slicer and lose the opportunity to seek my revenge. I have to keep quiet, at least for now. I must do everything I can to rein in the raging bull inside my china shop body.

Voices carry through the windows as the civilians surround the bus, chanting, "*You will not survive alone. You will not survive alone.*"

The vehicle sways like a boat on open water as the civilians push into it from the outside. Evie grabs onto me, cautiously watching the rest of the soldiers. Felix moans in pain from the movement of the bus. Oshiro clutches the steering wheel as Dakota stares worriedly through the window. Solano stands guard next to Marius, who peers at me through the hair over his eyes.

Dog glares at every one of us and then lets out a roar. "I hate this goddamn desert!"

31 identity crisis

Foxhole 221. A concrete formation tucked inside the hills. A series of glass-walled watchtowers form a circle along the outer wall. It's not all that impressive from where I'm looking. A section of the wall slides open and the bus leads us into a clearing where one of two rock mounds open like a mouth, and we drive down a ramp into the garage filled with a dozen Humvees and trucks. Inside, armed soldiers in gray body armor form a line by a set of huge steel doors.

Marius curls himself against the wall of the bus. Felix flexes his left hand. Evie stares wide-eyed at the ACTA soldiers. My stomach tumbles inside me. We're all uncertain of where we're going, all for completely different reasons.

"Who are these people?" Evie whispers into my ear.

The bus door swings open from the outside and a female soldier with wild brown hair pokes her head in. "Good evening, everyone. Nice of you to finally show up."

Dakota gets to her feet. "Nadia, make sure Tuttle sends out another squad. There are people in the hills who need help."

Nadia raises her eyebrows. "More people?"

"You let me worry about the civilians," says Solano as he brushes past Nadia through the bus door. "Everyone move!"

"Tuttle ordered the newbies straight downstairs," Nadia says with a shrug. "I don't know anything about any civilians."

"ID scans are not more important than innocent people left in the desert," says Dakota.

Nadia plants her hands on her hips. "Those are the orders. There's no need for you to get in my face about it."

Dog groans. "If you ladies are gonna fight, can you let us off the bus first?"

Both women glare at Dog as he towers over them with his hands raised in an expectant shrug.

Oshiro squeezes through to the door. "I can't stand looking at the transmitter man's stupid face any longer," he says, then points to me. "And that girl is creeping me out."

Solano calls through the door. "I said, *move*!"

Dog pulls Marius off the bus by the arm. "You heard the man."

Once the men are gone, Nadia whispers to Dakota, "What the hell happened out there?"

Dakota didn't hear the question because she's too busy looking at Felix, who has his eyes trained on the line of ACTA soldiers. Nadia follows Dakota's gaze.

"You're Lone Wolf, aren't you?" Nadia motions to her neck. "The tattoo, I'd know it anywhere."

Felix doesn't answer. Instead, he grabs my elbow and leads me from the bus. We head through the large garage, and Felix carefully scans the space.

"Do you think we'll be safe here?" Evie's voice is so sudden I'd forgotten she was hovering in my shadow. She shifts the rifle in her arms, and it's clear she's getting tired of lugging it around.

I use Felix's body as a shield and keep my eyes on the back of Marius's head as Dog escorts him toward the base doors. Marius glances over his shoulder a few times, and once he finally spots me his eyes widen at the sight of my pistol, unaware it's empty of bullets. Dog pulls him to face forward again, and Felix notices.

"Be careful around him," Felix whispers to me. "That man is dangerous."

"I know who he is," I say.

Felix already knew that, because he slaps his hand over my mouth and looks over my shoulder. "Be careful what you say."

Dakota and Nadia pass by, eyeing us intensely. Felix removes his hand from my mouth and pretends nothing is going on between us. Nadia rolls her eyes, and she reaches the door first and pulls it open. "Welcome to Foxhole 221."

My chest tightens as we walk down the corridor. The place has an eerie resemblance to the women's prison—all white-washed cement and steel, cold and musty. Bright white lights illuminate every corner. Our steps echo off the walls.

"Where is everybody?" Felix asks.

"It's nearly eleven," Nadia says. "Curfew is at ten."

There's that twinge again. *Breakfast at seven, lunch at noon, dinner at seven, lights out at ten. Stand up, sit down, spread 'em and show 'em.*

I look over to see what Felix thinks of the place and notice the light reflecting the grease and dirt on his forehead. The illumination enhances the circles under his eyes. If he looks that bad, I can't image how horrible I must be.

We cram into an elevator that is way too small for nine passengers. Dog's huge body blocks the door terminal as Nadia taps our destination, so I have no clue where we're headed. The elevator descends and then opens to a dim hallway with six doors, three on each side.

Nadia leads the way to the first door on the left and holds her hand on the terminal. A green light flashes and the door opens. She starts to enter the room, then turns to Solano. "You don't all need to be here for this."

"Oh, but we do," Dog says. "Everyone wants to know the identity of the transmitter man."

"And I want to know why the last remaining Lone Wolf is wandering around with a couple of girls," Solano says as he pushes his way through the group and into the room.

Felix tenses again, and I'm hoping he'll come up with some excuse to get us out of this situation, whatever it may be. Instead, Dog pushes me through the door. Once inside, my eyes take a moment to adjust to the darkness. Sparse colored lights flash and flicker, reflecting off of the slick tile floor. Nadia taps the door terminal. The lights turn up slightly, and I'm able to get a clearer look.

The room is full of brain scanners. Dozens of them, all different kinds. Some old, some new. Some I recognize from the PEAD scans, one is similar to the scanner at the jail, and one looks to be in pieces, a patchwork of parts—all instruments of neurological intrusion.

My muscles tighten in preparation for instantaneous movement. Any aggressive action is certain to sell me out as a threat to these ACTA people, so when my legs flinch with the need to run, I jerk them back into place and nearly trip over my own boots. I bump into an equipment tower and my pistol connects with the metal with a *clink.*

Everyone turns to me. I tuck the pistol behind my back before anyone notices. Not that it matters, because Evie is standing next to me with her giant rifle in her arms.

"Holy shit," Nadia says, "are they still armed?"

Solano glares at Dog. "You let them walk in here with loaded weapons?"

I hold up the pistol. "Actually, it's empty. I used the last one on the Alias guy."

All eyebrows raise, Nadia's especially.

Felix steps in front of me. "Is it really necessary for us to be here?" he asks Dakota. "You told me the girls wouldn't have to go through the ID scans."

Nadia wedges herself between him and Dakota. "Everyone goes through the ID scan. Don't think you're special just because you're a Lone Wolf."

"It won't even work," he says. "Alias took out the data system."

"Not the *whole* system," Dog says with a smirk. "What does it matter, anyway? Lone Wolf can't come scolding us for twisting the rules if they're all dead."

Felix steps up to Dog's huge chest. "For christ's sake, stop saying that. Yes, they're all dead. They were my friends. I'd appreciate it if you'd shut your shithole mouth and leave it alone."

Dog puffs his chest into Felix's face.

"Let's calm down, all right?" Dakota lays a hand on Dog's huge arm. The big man looks down at the woman as she gives him a pleading gaze, trying to ease him from his attack. It works, and Dog takes a step back.

Felix flexes his left hand, looks Dakota over, and waves his other hand at the scanner. "Let's get this bullshit over with."

Oshiro grunts. "You got somewhere to be, Lone Wolf?"

Felix flinches and stuffs his hands in his pockets. Evie looks like we're about to be probed by aliens. I'd almost prefer that. The ID scan will show that I am a convicted murderer who has escaped from prison. No wonder Felix is hesitant. It doesn't matter that Marius is here. They'll find out who I am, regardless. And then it's all over for me. They'll lock me away in a dungeon. Or worse, send me back into the scorching desert to be picked apart by vultures or turned into a bothead by Alias terrorists.

Nadia waves her hand to a chair, and Felix eases himself into the seat. The scanner crane shines down on Felix, making him the most noticeable thing in the dim room. His body is stiff, his balling fist the only body part moving. I shift, and he gives me that *keep your mouth shut* glare.

Nadia smiles like she's enjoying watching Felix's discomfort. She takes her place behind a computer station complete with a hologram-projecting desktop. "All right, let's do this."

A blue laser light sweeps over his head, and a hologram image of his face floats above the desktop. His name flashes under the holo-head: *Diego Manuel Felix.*

"Lone Wolf sector of ACTA," Nadia reads from the display. "Like we needed confirmation of that."

"I still want to know why you're the only one left," Solano says. "What happened to the rest?"

Felix squints into the darkness behind the lights. “They were under the bomb.”

“And where were you?” says Solano.

“Rescuing a fellow Lone Wolf in Riverside,” says Felix.

“Where is he now?”

“*She* didn’t make it. Do you want to hear about Lone Wolf or do you want to finish the ID scan?”

”Anything else we should know?” Nadia asks.

Felix runs his palms down the front of his pants. “All you need to know about me is in my report.”

”There’s nothing else in your report,” she says.

“Then we’re done here.” Felix slides from the chair. His face is blank, but more relaxed. He nods his head once, just enough for me to notice.

Solano grumbles something to himself and Nadia studies the holo desktop, chewing on her fingernails.

“The transmitter man is next,” says Dog.

Marius sinks back into the dark corner, searching the room for an exit. “I told you, I’m not with Alias.”

“The brain scan will prove it,” says Solano.

He grabs Marius and nearly throws him into the chair. Light illuminates him from above, washing out the color in his face and reflecting the gray in his hair like silver wires.

Nadia positions the scanner. “Hold still.”

The blue laser sweeps Marius’s face, which is frozen in horror. My arm cramps because I have my pistol in a death grip. I have no doubt they’ll find out who he is, and once he loses his animosity, he’ll sell me out. He’s already ruined my life once before. I don’t doubt he’d do it again to save his own skin.

Marius's face appears in the holo and Nadia reads the display. "Marius Frey. San Diego. Not a known Alias Sympathizer."

Marius sighs with relief. Dog rolls his eyes. Solano's stern face never flinches. Felix's eyes flicker to me.

"Marius Frey … Frey … Why does that sound familiar?" Dakota looks over Nadia to the desktop. "Does it say anything else? What's his occupation?"

Lying Piece of Neuroshitter, is what it should say.

Nadia raises her eyebrows. "He's an accountant."

The blanket of tension is removed from my body. My arms feel like they're elastic, stretching down to my ankles. The pistol slips from my hand and hits the tile floor.

"You're shitting me," says Dog. "Millions of people have died but the *accountant* survived?"

Nadia shrugs. "That's what it says."

Solano waves over to me. "We'll investigate this later. The girls are next."

Evie is moved into the chair and the laser scans her face, her holo projection contorted in the baffled look she's had since we arrived here.

"Evie St. John," Nadia reads. "Resident of Daggett, California. She doesn't even have a report."

"Because she's a kid," Dakota says.

"I'm not a kid!" Evie shouts. "I'm eleven!"

Nadia rolls her eyes. "Moving on …"

It's my turn. Everyone else has been scanned into innocence, even the lying neurologist has a cover story. I didn't even want to come to this base in the first place. I had a chance to get out of this. I had a chance to live the rest of my life free and clear of my past.

Dog pulls me to the scanner chair and pushes me into the seat. The light above my head floods my eyes and makes it difficult to see into the shadows. All I see is Nadia behind the holo desktop, pressing the buttons that will lead to my demise. The blue scanner light sweeps over me and creates a representation of my dirty face, greasy hair, and crooked nose.

"Josephine Barker," Nadia reads.

My chest tightens at the sound of my name, but something isn't right. Did she say … *Barker*? Who is Josephine Barker? I don't know why I feel so compelled to correct Nadia for her mistake, but suddenly Felix's hand is on mine as it grips the chair arm. I can barely make out his face, but there is that glare again: *Keep your mouth shut.*

"Resident of Los Angeles. Nothing in her report either." Nadia looks up, her eyes narrowed and nostrils flared. "This can't possibly be right. You two are not who you say you are."

"Leave the girls alone," says Dakota. "They did good up on that hill. Can't you see they're exhausted?"

"What do you suggest we do with them?" Solano says, sarcastically. "Let them in the Desert Patrol Squad?"

"If that's your idea of a counter-offense tactic, I need to reconsider your recent promotion, Solano."

The voice came from the doorway, where a tall, sinewy man with overly tan skin and overly white hair stands with his hands on his hips. Everyone straightens to attention at the sight of the him, even Felix.

"Commander Tuttle," Solano says. "It isn't necessary for you to be here for the ID scans. This is standard procedure."

Tuttle looks him over. "I'd appreciate you not telling me what is necessary or not, Solano. I've been waiting hours for your report, and here I find you all having a gala in the scanner room. What is going on? And why does this kid have a rifle?"

Everyone turns to look at Evie as she wraps her arms around the weapon. "It's my daddy's," she says.

"She's not a threat, sir," Oshiro says.

"I'd certainly hope not. And what's this I hear about these two teeny-boppers taking out Alias members while the rest of you sat with your hands under your asses?"

"It's true," Dog says. "The kid's one hell of a shooter. Took out a truck a click away from a moving vehicle."

Tuttle stares at Dog. "This isn't a child's playground. I don't care if she took him down with a slingshot; I'm not letting teenage girls in my combat unit."

"I understand, sir," Dog says as he puffs out his chest, "but there aren't many civilians on base willing to take up arms. Clearly you're aware of that."

So that's why they brought us here? To enlist Evie and me to be soldiers? They see us as dispensable pawns. We'll be played in the first round as bait to lure out the enemy.

"Clearly I do know that," Tuttle says, "but what do these girls know about combat?"

Evie tugs on my arm. "She taught me how to kill."

Oh god, why'd she have to say that? Everyone turns to me expectantly, especially the overly-tan white-haired man.

"Evie's not a killer," I say.

"Ah, c'mon," Evie says. "They just said I—"

"You're not a killer!"

I'm suddenly so dizzy I think I might pass out. It would be nice, at least, if Felix would say something about all this. He's just standing there, staring at the hologram representation of my head as it hovers in the display. Right above my new fake name: Josephine Barker.

"Sir," Dakota says, "we need to send another team out. Two dozen civilians are still there, and they're hijacked."

Tuttle shakes his head. "I'm losing my patience with those goddamn botheads. We already have too many, and they're pissing me off. I'm about ready to send them all back into the desert. They're disruptive and a nuisance."

Dakota shakes her hands. "I know, but it's not right to let Alias do this to these people."

"No one is arguing against that, Dakota," says Nadia with a frown. "We're not as insensitive as you think we are."

"Once you figure out how to remove the implants, we'll talk," Tuttle says. "In the meantime, enough with the charades. I want my report, Solano."

"Yes, sir," Solano says.

"And honestly," Tuttle says, "apprehend the weapons. You know the rules."

"What about the girls?" Dog says.

Felix steps forward. "I'm in charge of them."

Tuttle looks him over with a stern face. "Lone Wolf. A Lone Wolf is in my base and I don't know about it?"

Solano starts, "Sir, I—"

"We need to talk, Solano. After you give me that goddamn report." Tuttle swivels on his heels and leaves the room.

Solano grabs Felix by the shirt. "You'd better watch yourself, Lone Wolf. I've got an eye on you."

The muscles in Felix's face twitch as the two men have a stare-off. Dog and Oshiro stand with their arms crossed, watching.

Dakota gets antsy and whispers into Solano's ear. "Calm down, Solano. He may be a Lone Wolf, but he's still on our side."

Nadia rolls her eyes. "Don't be so naive, Dakota."

Dakota ignores Nadia and rests her arm on Solano's. "We can't afford to make enemies with our allies."

Solano's body relaxes, and he looks at Dakota and nods. "Give him a room. All of them. Even the transmitter man."

Nadia throws her hands in the air as Oshiro leads Marius through the door. Marius turns to look back at me, his floppy hair covering one widened eye.

Solano reaches out for our weapons. "Hand 'em over."

Evie protests. "This is my daddy's rifle. I can't lose it!"

Dog gives her a toothy grin. "Don't fret, kitten. I'll make sure you get your gun back."

Evie ponders his promise, then hands the rifle to Solano, relaxing with the sudden relief of weight. I surrender my pistol, and I'm left feeling vulnerable and weak. Dog replaces the void with a clear plastic badge with a black stripe that he sticks to my shirt and pats down on my chest more times than should be necessary. Nadia shines a green flashlight at me, and the badge turns opaque with my horrible photo from the ID scan. And my new name. Felix and Evie are given badges with their real names, and I'm actually a little envious.

"This way," Dakota says and waves us into the hallway.

Felix pulls me aside. "I'm going to take a look around, see if I can learn anything helpful. Get some rest. You look like you need it."

I'd give some snarky retort, but I'm too tired to come up with anything witty. "Yeah, all right."

He cranes his neck down to look into my eyes. "You are safe here," he says, and I shrug in response.

Felix stays in the hallway as Dakota leads Evie and myself to the elevator, and for a moment I wonder if he means the same for himself. None of these ACTA guys seem to trust him, all for his Lone Wolf status and that target he now wears on his back.

We go up a few floors and down another corridor. Dakota taps on the door terminal and we're invited into a quaint living space of rough concrete, complete with two small beds, a bathroom, a dresser, and a desk.

"Let me know if you need anything, I'm right across the hall," Dakota says as she closes the door behind her.

Evie flops on a bed. "Eeh. It's lumpy."

Even though the room is better furnished than my prison cell, I'm still unable to find the will to consider this place comforting. Evie recognizes my hesitation and mirrors my frown.

"You don't like it here, do you?" she asks.

I don't have the words to answer her. I decide to busy myself with mundane activities. I open the drawers of the dresser and find it filled with clothes: black pants and tank tops for the women, and cargo pants and T-shirts for the men. I look down at my borrowed prison guard clothes and realize just how filthy I am. The last time I showered I was a half-step from death. In fact, showers seem to have a strange relation to death. A normal girl would be emotionally tense about the thought, but I am not a normal girl and I am too drained and dirty to care.

The water stings my sunburn, yet I stand under the cool shower for twenty minutes, letting the heat be sucked from my skin and flow down the drain. The console beeps, telling me I've surpassed my water quota for the day and it's about to shut off. I have just enough time to rinse out my hair before the blowers start.

I wrap myself in a robe and peek into the room. "Evie, you'll have to wait to shower. I used up the water."

She's fast asleep on one of the beds. My eyelids are heavy and I can barely stand any longer. I crawl into the other bed, close my eyes, and wonder if they'll ever open again. I nearly hope they won't.

32 down the foxhole

I wake to someone poking me in the ribs. My eyes fly open and there is Evie, wringing out her hair and splashing water on the floor. "It's breakfast time," she says with a smile.

My stomach grumbles in response, and Evie giggles. After pulling my limp body from the bed, I dress in black pants and a tank top from the dresser and slap the ID badge on my chest. When I open the door, I expect to find the hallway swarming with people, but instead it is completely empty.

I call back into the room and notice Evie is wearing the exact same outfit as me, although hers is two sizes too big. "Are you sure it's breakfast time?"

"You didn't check the time first?" The voice startles me, and I peer around the doorframe to see Felix leaning against the corridor wall, arms folded, a bent leg planted on the wall behind him.

"I assumed we'd be told when to eat," I say.

"Ha. You're a free civilian now. It's your responsibility to remember to feed yourself. You're back in the real world."

Felix looks so causal leaning there with a smirk on his face. He's cleaned up, even trimmed his goatee. But no matter how good he looks doing … well, *anything*, the shit that spurts out of his mouth puts me on edge.

"The real world has been bombed to bits," I say.

Felix frowns. "You need to lay off the pessimism."

"You need to stop telling me what I need to do."

He tilts his head. "Got up on the wrong side of the bed, huh?"

Evie appears in the doorway, clutching the waistband of her pants. "How is there a wrong side to get out of bed? I've gotten out on the right side and the left side, and they both worked just fine."

Leave it to Evie to break that one down. Felix smiles wide at her. The opposite door opens and Dakota appears in the threshold. Nadia rustles around in the room behind her, ranting about something. Felix pushes himself off the wall and straightens his posture as Dakota looks him over with surprise.

"Good morning, everyone," Dakota says, ignoring Nadia's discussion behind her. "Sleep well?"

Evie stretches. "The bed is lumpy."

Dakota chuckles. "With all the funding to build this place, you'd have thought they could afford decent mattresses."

"Mine was pretty soft," Felix says, and he flinches when he notices me glaring at him.

Nadia's voice carries from the room. "… I know you're determined, but I can't risk my rank because of some hunch you have." She appears behind Dakota as she stares at Felix. "Dakota!"

Dakota jerks from her stance and makes room in the doorway. "I have the right to make that call. I'm the only one on base with a medical degree."

"You don't know that," Nadia says, sliding into the corridor. "Any one of those civilians we picked up could be a doctor."

I notice Felix's jaw shift. He's thinking what I'm thinking. *Marius Frey.* "You'd know that based on the ID scans," he says.

"Yes," Nadia says, "but that doesn't mean the information hasn't been tampered with. Right, Lone Wolf?"

Felix's eyes twitch between the two women as they squint back at him. His wristlet rings and breaks up the ogling party. "I'm being summoned."

Dakota waves at him. "Don't delay on that. Tuttle is known to punish people for being late."

Felix studies Nadia for a moment, then turns to me. "Will you be all right?"

What does he think is going to happen if he leaves my side for five minutes? "Yeah," I say with a wave. "We'll eat breakfast."

Evie clutches her stomach. "I'm *starving*."

Felix adjusts my ID badge. "I'll see you later," he says and hurries down the corridor.

Nadia rolls her eyes—again—and turns to Dakota. "See what I mean?"

I ignore the commentary. "Where's the dining hall?"

"I'll take you there," Dakota says. "Give you a tour of Foxhole as well."

"There's no time for a tour," Nadia says. "Solano wants these two in the training sessions as soon as possible."

"Training for what?" I ask.

"War," she says. "Sure you can shoot, but you'll need to learn battle tactics and commands if you're gonna be out in the field."

I shake my head. "We're not soldiers."

Nadia groans and rolls her head back. "Take the compliment, will you? Besides, if you're not gonna be a soldier, then you need to find some other sector to work in."

"Evie shouldn't have to work," I say. "She's just a kid."

"I'm not a kid," Evie says with an exacerbated sigh.

Dakota keeps her eyes on me as she elbows Nadia in the arm. "Hey, we can discuss this later, yeah?" Nadia scrunches her face, but Dakota continues. "Okay, you two, let's go eat."

Dakota heads down the corridor with Evie at her side. I hesitate long enough for Nadia to zero in on me.

"You're not Josephine Barker, are you?"

I shudder, my body unable to decide if now is the time to run or stay put and argue.

Nadia folds her arms across her chest. "I was a criminal investigator before all this. Suspect profiling was my specialty. I read people, I figure them out. And I'll tell you, your profile doesn't add up."

My itch to run does not overpower my need to say something, regardless if my words will damn myself. "Does it matter?"

She tilts her head. "I don't know. Does it?"

"Well you know what they say, curiosity killed the cat."

Nadia dips her chin and peers at me from underneath her brow. I know I've said something I shouldn't have.

Evie's voice rings down the corridor. "Jo! You coming?"

"They're waiting for me," I say and shuffle down the corridor before Nadia can retort.

Dakota escorts Evie and myself through the base. She's familiar and comfortable with this place, all the while I'm becoming more unsettled by the moment. The similarities to the prison create terrifying flashbacks of my time spent there, yet there are notable differences. No tracker cuffs to magnetize me to the walls. No bright orange jumper. No guards at my side. I'm not even certain the cameras are on. We enter the elevator and Dakota presses the button for the third floor.

"This place is strange," Evie says, holding up her sagging pants.

"Makes you miss home, doesn't it," Dakota says. "I'm from LA too," she says, nodding to me. "You a PEAD kid?"

I'm not really in the mood to talk about the PEAD program, but Dakota keeps right on going.

"I missed the program, thankfully. Got my medical degree the old-fashioned way. Not that it makes any bit of difference now. M.D. or not, there's nothing I can do for these hijacked civilians."

Our elevator opens to a huge, three-story hall. A podium is erected on a platform on one side and huge florescent lights provide bright artificial sunlight. Two giant wall screens display reports of the devastation, and I'm caught on a slow-motion replay of the n-bomb detonating over Los Angeles. If I look closely enough I can see the tallest FutureTech building explode into a billion pieces. The sight of my hometown being flattened to rubble hypnotizes me, and for a moment I actually feel kind of sad, until my attention is broken.

A handful of blue-flashing hijacked civilians walk in my sight line, blocking the TV screens. The younger ones don't seem to notice the screens, and the two older adults glance at the destructive replay with vacant expressions, as though it were nothing more than a FutureTech infomercial. One man bumps into me from the side—not enough to hurt me, but certainly enough to incite some form of an apology, or at the very least, acknowledgement—but he doesn't seem to know I'm there.

Evie clutches a handful of my shirt and peers around my shoulder. "What's wrong with them?"

Dakota stops one young man and points to the screens. "Do you know what this is?"

The young man blinks at Dakota, then slowly turns his head to the screen. "They bombed Los Angeles," he says, his voice flat.

"Yes," Dakota says, nodding her head eagerly. "How does that make you feel?"

The young man blinks again, then continues his path around her and follows the others. Dakota watches them, wide-eyed and gaping, as the people pass her and disappear through the doorway.

"They were like that on the hill," I say. "When that boy was shot, the adults acted as though nothing was wrong."

Dakota hesitates to answer, her gaze caught on the TV screens. "Whatever those implants are designed to do, they're blocking all emotional reaction. I don't understand it. I don't understand the *point*."

"Maybe Alias doesn't want the civilians to be afraid of them," I say.

Dakota looks at me sharply. "Then why bomb us at all, if fear is not the purpose?"

I shrug because it doesn't make sense to me either, and quite frankly I'm not as eager to figure it out.

"I'm scared of them," Evie says in a faint voice.

Dakota shakes her head. "I can't turn off the optrodes. I can't even block the signal. The first transmitter we'd ever come across was the one Marius Frey had—"

"Which I shot," Evie says and hides behind me. "Sorry."

"Even those who are not implanted have been acting strange," Dakota says. "They're overwhelmed by their fears. Some civilians have begged me to implant them. They envy the botheads and their lack of emotional pain."

Dakota gazes off as Evie and I watch her. Even with her tall and strong body, she now looks frail and beaten. She's not as pretty when she's frowning.

"Can you implant people?" I ask.

She snaps out of her thoughts and peers at me. "No, I'm not a neurosurgeon. And even if I was, I'd never do it. These people need to face what's coming, not run from it."

"It's so sad," Evie says as she watches more people slog past us. This bunch is not comprised of botheads, but normal sobbing civilians, their eyes red and puffy.

Dakota's wristlet lights up. "I have to go. The dining hall is right over there. Get in line, you'll be fine." And with that, she races to the entrance of another corridor.

The dining hall is crammed with two hundred people: men and women, young and old, children and babies. They're sunburned, bruised, and exhausted. Many are crying, others sit with their arms tucked in, desperate to avoid physical contact. Evie and I make our way through the line and reach a serving counter where a woman ladles oatmeal into a bowl. Even the food reminds me of prison.

"Do you have anything else?" I ask, unreasonably hopeful.

The woman stares back at me, a hollow emptiness in her eyes.

We sit at a table with a young family. Twin boys sit staring at their food as the mother fusses with a crying infant. The father sloshes a spoon through his oatmeal. None of them are eating.

Evie inhales her bowl of oatmeal in a matter of moments and peeks over at one of the twin boys. "Hey, you gonna eat that?" The boy looks at Evie and instantly starts wailing. He swings off the bench and runs through the room, hollering at the top of his lungs. Evie flinches, then turns back to me, mouthing *"okay ..."*

I shrug and slide my bowl across the table. I've lost my appetite, but Evie, unaffected, shovels the oatmeal into her mouth like it's her last meal.

Something about these people doesn't add up. Bothead or not, they've lost the willingness to keep going. If that was the Alias plan, they sure as hell succeeded. My chest flutters as my heart pumps an extra beat, reacting to a thought that has been floating in the back of my head ever since I realized that the transmitter man was Marius Frey: It was he who implanted the optrodes. I just know it. And now he's been identified as a harmless accountant, free to wander the base while everyone else is none the wiser. As much as my anonymity is important to me, that man ruined my life and has ruined the lives of so many of these people. I have to know what he is up to.

"I'm gonna take a look around," I tell Evie. "I'll see you back in the barracks."

"I'm done eating." Evie pushes her bowl away and stands. "I'll go with you."

"No, Evie. I need to do this alone."

She rolls her eyes. "You don't have to protect me, Jo. I'm not a kid. I can take care of myself."

"I'm not trying to protect you."

Her voice raises to match her insistence. "Then let me go with you!"

"It's a really bad idea for you to follow me."

"Jeez, Jo, are you always this uptight?"

That comment stings a little. "You think I'm uptight?"

She gets to her feet. "You're not thinking clearly. I'm going as back-up. For your safety."

She plants her hands on her hips and eagerly waits for me to follow. A surge of pride seeps into my mind because this is exactly how I would react were someone passing me off as being too weak or small to join an adventure. That positive feeling is instantly replaced by a twinge of regret, because if she's this similar to me as a kid, what's in store for her in a few years?

Evie dances on her feet. "We going, or what?"

"Suit yourself, but don't blame me if you get hurt."

She groans. I slide off the bench and head through the dining hall with Evie on my heels. As hard as I try to shake her between the clumps of slow-moving civilians, she's a slippery little one. She's there at every turn, right behind me.

I make a wide circle around the third floor and pass by a man with a silver-striped badge and a gun holster.

"Excuse me," I say, "where are the brain scanners?"

He looks me over and frowns at Evie. "Why is everyone asking about the brain scanners? I told the other guy, no civilians are allowed on the eighth floor." He holds a green flashlight over my ID badge and I turn away before he can catch a glimpse of my fake name.

"Oh, my mistake," I say. "Thanks anyway."

The man watches us leave, and I slow my pace to pretend I'm not going where he told me I couldn't go. We round the corner and I prepare to run, but find my path blocked by a group of staggering botheads following a pair of ACTA soldiers, their implants flashing blue.

Evie slithers alongside me. "Jo, wait up."

We squeeze into the elevator after a couple of normal people with blue-striped badges. They eye us curiously, and I stand tall to pretend I belong. The people get off on the fifth floor and I jab the button for the eighth floor.

"Back to the brain scanners?" Evie asks. "I don't like that room."

"I told you to stay in the dining hall."

Evie opens her mouth to argue, but when the elevator door opens, a scream rips through the air. Evie squeaks. My body tenses as blood pulses through it, legs and arms reacting with impulse.

I sprint toward the sound, and slowly step through the open threshold as quietly as possible. The room is dark, speckled by flashing lights of color from at least a dozen scanners and computer screens. It takes me a moment to sort through all the stimulus, and then I spot Marius hovering in a corner, looking as pale-faced as ever. I knew I'd find him here, but now that I know I was right, I'm more uneasy than before.

"What did you do?" cries the screaming voice, a sound of pure terror that flutters my heart. Dakota is on the other side of the room, her hands clutched over her mouth, staring down at a woman in a scanner chair. "How could you do this?"

A man responds, a third person. "I don't want to feel like this. I want to be like her. I need to stop this madness in my head."

I motion for Evie to stay in the doorway and then creep through the scanners. My movement catches Marius's attention and he gasps, lurching back into the shadows. I'll deal with him later. As

I approach the scene I see a thirty-something man sprawled on the floor next to the chair. His hands and arms are covered in blood. The woman in the chair isn't moving, her stomach oddly distended. Blood trickles from the back of her head and pools on the shiny floor. Light from the scanner flashes on her face and I recognize her as the pregnant bothead from the hill.

"You *killed* her," Dakota says. "And her *baby*. Why would you do that?"

The man is dry-heaving so hard he can barely get his words out. "I begged you to implant me. You didn't do it. So I took hers." He holds up his hand and shows a small silver electronic device with light tubes dangling from it, covered in blood.

Soldiers burst into the room, bustling about and knocking things over. Solano rushes to Dakota. Nadia appears at my side, seemingly more interested in my presence than the dead woman.

"Is this him?" Dog says. "Is this the murdering son of a bitch?"

The man protects his face from Dog's verbal assault. "I need the implant. I need to stop feeling like this."

"The implant can only be removed by someone who knows how they were implanted in the first place."

Everyone turns to look at the person who muttered those words. Dakota is just as surprised as everyone else to see Marius crouched in the corner. Checkmate, Dr. Frey.

Solano jabs his finger in Marius's face. "What the hell are you doing here?"

"I got lost," he says.

Bullshit.

"How do you know how the implants work?" Solano asks.

Marius clutches the collar of his shirt with a trembling hand. "That's what I heard Alias say. It's some kind of fail-safe."

I open my mouth to call him a goddamn liar when a hand lands on my arm.

"Why is this room unlocked?" Felix says over my shoulder. "Civilians should not even be allowed on this floor."

Nadia's face hardens. "You've got quite the nerve to blame this on us, Lone Wolf."

"Who do you want to blame, then?" says Felix.

"Stop this!" Dakota says. "We can't let this go on. More civilians are going to die if we don't figure out who is behind the implants."

"Alias is behind the implants," Felix says as he straightens his posture.

I know Felix can sense me glaring at him, but he keeps his eyes averted. Meanwhile, Marius cowers in the corner, not doing a damn thing about the pregnant woman whose blood is as much on his hands as the man who pulled out the implant.

That's it, I've had enough of this. "I have something to say."

Felix's eyes go wide in anticipation, Marius sinks further into the shadows, and Nadia crosses her arms, expectantly.

"I know who—"

As soon as I begin my rant, a deafening siren drowns me out. A dozen ACTA soldiers in charcoal gray armor burst into the room, apprehend the murderer on the ground, and swoop the dead woman into a body bag. I'm trapped within the commotion, bumping back and forth between bodies and scanners. Somehow I end up in the elevator, squashed between Solano and Dog. Evie is behind me, while Felix stares at me from the other side.

We're escorted to our barrack, and Dog pushes Evie and me inside without a word. Felix gazes through the doorway as I stand in the middle of room, trembling.

"Why did we come here, Felix?"

He frowns. "I brought you here to keep you safe." He huffs and balls his left fist a few times. Then he backs into the hall and shuts the door.

Evie sits cross-legged on the bed and watches me pace the room. Even from the corner of my eye I see the deep furrow of her brow. I've been taking the same path for what feels like an hour, and if I keep dragging my feet like this I'm bound to dig a trench in the concrete.

"What's going to happen next?" Evie says.

I shake my head, not breaking my stride. "We should have never come here."

"Do you think they'll let us leave?"

I hadn't thought of that. I shake my head again. "They wouldn't risk it."

"Why not?"

"We could get captured by Alias and they could implant us. Or they'll hook us up to brain scanners and extract information."

"But I don't know anything!"

"You know about Foxhole. That's reason enough for Alias to probe you."

Evie screeches and cups her hands over her ears as if to keep any information from seeping out and sending signals to the enemy. "Jo … I'm scared."

She really is. I don't know why I'm saying these things. Am I really thinking I can scare her into staying hidden? She'll most certainly follow after me. Or worse—she'll get sucked into the bottomless pit of emotional desperation that has consumed the civilians of Foxhole 221.

My chest tightens and I can't get a full breath of air. There must not be any circulation of oxygen in this place, it's all being replaced by carbon dioxide and I'm going to suffocate—

I need to find Felix. He is the one with the answers to my questions.

"Stay here," I tell Evie.

"Where are you going?"

"I'll be right back."

"Stop trying to leave me!"

"I'm not leaving. I just need some air."

"Me too," she says as she hops off the bed.

"You're going to get hurt if you keep following me around! Find some kids to play with. Just be normal!"

Disappointment floods her face, and I feel a stab in my chest. She darts back to the bed, and I leave the room quickly because I can't bear to look at her pout any longer.

I aimlessly weave my way through the barracks level corridors. They all look the same. I don't even know which room Felix is staying in. I wonder why he never bothered to tell me.

I pass a handful of people in the hallway. They shake their heads and mutter to themselves like crazy hobos. Someone pokes me in the side and I turn to see a girl a few years older than me with a streak of green in her black hair. She's unkempt and sunburnt, and even though she's not old enough to have wrinkles, the bright lights bring out every dirt-penetrated crease in her face.

"Let me go back," she says, "let me go back to the way I was." Her cheeks are damp, her eyes red and splotchy. Her ID badge shimmers under the lights, and I catch her name: Suki Lin. She turns to look past me and reveals patch of blood-stained gauze behind her ear. "Let me go back …"

The girl is freaking me out. She reaches out for me, and I position myself to sprint away when someone latches onto me.

"Jo, wait." Felix yanks hard and pulls my back into him. He wraps his left arm around my waist, my right wrist in his right hand as he leads me through the crowd. "Hey, we must look like we're dancing."

I shout into his ear. "How do you always know where I am?"

He taps my ID badge. "Tracker chip."

Maybe this place isn't that different from prison after all. "Felix, tell me what is going on."

He *shushes* and leads me in a gliding tango down the corridor. I nearly trip over a man sitting against the wall, his body limp like he's lost all control over it. Felix and I pirouette around some hijacked botheads who don't notice we're there. The *normal* people watch the botheads with—if I'm not mistaken—longing.

I tilt my head back to look at him. "Who is Josephine Barker?"

"A girl from LA." He dances me into the dining hall where dozens of people sit in silence, staring blankly around the room. "I stole her identity and gave it to you. Do you know how to waltz? My sister was really into dancing."

We glide around and around, barely missing sideswiping civilians at the tables. *One*-two-three, *one*-two-three …

"Won't Josephine Barker need her own name?"

"No," he says. "She died in the bombing. I switched your identities in the system because I knew she wouldn't need it after the invasion."

The air is sucked from my lungs and my body ceases all function, but Felix won't let me stop dancing. He spins me again and pulls me into his body in a slow-dance pose, his cheek pressed into mine so I can't see his face.

"Things have gotten complicated," he whispers. "This war isn't a real war. The President is in hiding, the government has surrendered the counter-attack efforts to ACTA. FutureTech has assumed control over the country."

FutureTech? The corporation who controlled my life in LA, who sent me to prison, who built this bunker of isolation—now controls my future? Not just my future, *everyone's* future.

"What aren't you telling me?" I say, desperate to get a look at his eyes. "Felix, what does Lone Wolf have to do with this?"

His body stiffens and I crash into him because I have no warning to stop my momentum. He looks past me, across the dining room, the playful smile lost under his veil of thoughts.

"ACTA was never going to get you out of prison," he says.

"*What*? You told me—"

"I trusted them to get you out. I really did. And then they stopped answering my messages. Thankfully I realized this before it was too late. I knew the Alias attack was coming. So then I went to Plan B."

I put myself in his line of sight, and he blinks like he's startled to see me. "What is really going on?"

"I don't know. I'm trying to get back in the loop, but they're reluctant to let me in. But nothing is more important right now than you staying out of the way of Marius Frey. I don't trust him."

"That's why I was following him."

"Jo, he knows who you are. You need to stay *away* from him."

"He knows I'm a killer. If you want to prove that wrong, then why aren't you trying to keep these ACTA guys from turning me into a soldier?"

He grabs my shoulders. "I am trying. But for now, if you're in the squad, I'll be able to keep an eye on you. It's my job to protect you."

His voice was just loud enough for a handful of nearby botheads to hear him. Their eyes go wide, the skin of their faces pull taut. They move toward him as though in a state of hypnosis, Suki among them.

"You are here to protect us," Suki says. She touches the ACTA patch sewn onto his sleeve. "You will help us survive."

The others join in, and soon they're chanting. "*You are here to save us.*" They grab his arms, fist his shirt, pull him in all directions. I'm shoved out of the way, but Felix holds onto me with his left hand.

"It's not my job to save you," he tells the botheads, his voice cracking. "You have to help yourselves. You have to help us fight back."

But the botheads don't listen. They go on chanting, insisting Felix is their savior. One man still has the implant behind his ear, only it is turned off—no blue or orange light flickers—but the fear and panic in his face is unmistakable. He's not asking Felix for help; he's desperately begging for it.

Felix squeezes my hand in his, pulsing his clench, crunching my knuckles together. The pain shoots up my forearm and I pull back.

"Felix, let go."

He doesn't hear me. The botheads grope his arms and torso, and each time someone cries out, Felix winces, the muscles in his neck strain, his eyes squeeze shut. His grip on my hand tightens even further, and I'm afraid he'll break bones. I use my other hand to slide from his grasp. Just as I am free, Felix balls his left fist and stares at it, wide-eyed and panicked.

"Leave him alone, you crazy botheads!" My plea goes unnoticed, even from Felix. There's nothing I can do for him now, and I can't stand another moment in the dining hall with these people. I back away, weaving through the tables and chairs while keeping an eye on the swarm. As I reach the doorway Felix finally looks up. His faced drops, the tightened knit of his brow loosens, and his body wavers with the movement of the botheads.

33 a bad deal

I race through the corridors, desperate to find my way to the garage. There isn't any signage or directions to lead anyone anywhere. I spot a guard up ahead and shout out to him. "Excuse me!" The guard turns and I recognize him as the one who'd mistakenly directed me to the scanner rooms. His eyes widen when he sees me, and he speaks into his wristlet as he comes in my direction. Am I in trouble? Has there been some kind of issued lockdown that I'm unaware of? It's possible, for this guy seems intent on catching me. I turn to run back through the corridor when two more guards round the bend.

A door next to me opens, and a hoard of botheads flow into the hallway like a wave crashing through a tunnel. Dozens of them crowd the space, some crying and moaning, others walking blindly and bumping into me. The botheads create a buffer between the guards and me as they come at me from either end of the corridor. I can see them waving to each other, barking orders into their wristlets.

I latch onto the jacket of a tall man and hover behind his back, following along with the flow of bodies. They don't seem to have a specific destination, for when we reach a split in the walkway, half go in direction and the rest the opposite way. Still holding onto the man's jacket, I shuffle along, sandwiched inside the group, until we reach the doorway to the dining hall. I've made a full circle.

There's no way I'm getting out of here, is there?

I've lost the guards, but found my way back to the beginning of my escape plan. I don't even know where to find the exit. And then, what would I do, wander the desert aimlessly until I die of exposure or heat stroke?

The man with the jacket is gone, somehow detached himself from me. The botheads make their way to the food windows, because even in their hijacked state they still know it's lunchtime. I don't see Felix anywhere. It's just as well; I don't know how I'd explain why I left him drowning in a sea of people.

I walk through a different corridor—this time at a pace not meant for escape—and replay the events of the last few days over in my mind. Felix knows something he's not telling me. Felix knows a lot he's not telling *anyone.* He knows about the government handing control of the war over to FutureTech, but I sense there's something else. There's some reason in FutureTech assuming the responsibility of the fight; after all, it was their company that caused Alias to be created for retaliation in the first place. But there's another missing piece to this puzzle, and I can't seem to put my finger on it. Not without more answers.

In my mindless wandering, I've somehow arrived in the main hall of the third floor, and what I see is not only unexpected, but also strange and confusing. A dozen kids are on their hands and knees in the middle of the room, slithering around, heads tilted in thought, dragging colored sticks across the concrete.

Evie enters from another door with a small cardboard box in one hand. Her face lights up when she spots me. "Jo! You're still here!"

"Of course I am. There's nowhere to go."

Evie grins, then waves me to the group. "C'mon, I found some chalk in a storage room."

"Chalk?"

"Yeah! Haven't you ever drawn with street chalk?"

Evie reaches into the box and hands me a piece of green chalk the size of a hot dog. It's lighter than I expect, the texture brittle and dry. We didn't play with chalk in LA. All of my art classes were digital. I hated it. I much preferred real paint, despite how hard it was to come by. But chalk? I've never even seen the stuff.

The memories of home flood me with a stomach-churning ache, and the thought of drawing only makes it worse, so I sit against the wall and watch. The kid's illustrations are pretty silly. One boy has drawn a forest with a rainbow and a family of stick figures, and he's quite proud of his creation. He shows another kid, who immediately draws over it with white chalk in the shape of a mushroom cloud, making the first boy cry.

Evie steps in. "Hey, that's not nice. Why'd you do that?"

"His picture was stupid," says the mean kid.

"Why is it stupid?" Evie asks.

"Because there's no more trees or rainbows. Just bombs. All bombs!" The kid goes nuts, covering everyone's drawings with mushroom clouds while mimicking explosion sounds.

The crying boy hollers and the other kids follow suit, creating an echoing wail in the oversized room. Evie tackles the mean kid to the ground. I glance around for some angry parent to come rushing in, but Evie's already wrestled the chalk from his hand.

"Do you wanna draw or not?" she scolds. All the kids sit quietly. She snatches a brown piece of chalk from the box and drags it across the concrete. "Okay. Help me draw some birds."

"Why birds?" a girl asks.

"Because I like birds." Evie goes on drawing, but the kids aren't interested anymore. One by one, they get up and saunter away until Evie is the only one left.

She spots me watching her from my spot against the wall. "They didn't like my bird."

"I don't think it's the bird."

"What then?"

"They're sad and scared. Just like their parents."

"Then why not try to be happy?"

"I guess they don't have anything to be happy about."

"Do *you*?"

I take a moment to consider my answer and scoot across the floor to her. "I haven't been happy about anything in a long time."

"Why not? You're alive, aren't you?"

"Barely."

Evie shakes her head. "So they won?"

"Who won?"

"The people who bombed us." She looks over at the mean kid's mushroom clouds. Then she points to her bird drawing. "It's an eagle. My daddy's favorite. He was really good at drawing them, he had an eagle tattooed on his arm. I could never get the shape right."

I study her drawing. "He's a little fat."

"That's mean!" Evie laughs and it makes me smile.

"Maybe he got extra roadkill for dinner."

"What's your favorite bird?"

"I don't have a favorite bird."

Evie crunches her face. "Well, how about a crow?" I shake my head and she argues. "It matches your hair. Here, I'll draw it for you."

Evie grabs some purple chalk and doodles on the ground. Underneath the bird she scribbles *Jo the Crow.*

"My dad's favorite was a green parrot," I say.

"A parrot?"

"Yeah. He grew up in Burbank. The place was infested with thousands of these green parrots. He said they were so loud you could barely hear yourself talk when they flew over."

"Do you remember what they looked like?"

I do, actually. I spent years staring at my dad's parrot painting as it hung in the kitchen of my Los Feliz house. Until my mom burned it.

As if instinctually, my hand glides the chalk across the floor. Out comes a green parrot, with a dash of red on the head and orange in the neck, its beak open in a call. Evie watches carefully as I draw, her lips curled into an amused smile.

My head spins and I slump onto the floor. The drawing took every ounce of energy from me. Evie's not concerned. She leans over and writes *Jo's Dad* underneath the parrot.

"Do me next," she says. "I like ducks. You know those tall white ones that chase you and bite your ankles?"

"No, I can't."

"Ah, c'mon! We can do birds for everyone. Felix, Dakota, even Dog! I wonder what his favorite bird is."

"Probably a vulture," I say.

She snorts. "Yeah! Draw a vulture!"

"Evie, I can't."

"Sure you can. You're good. Maybe they'll put you in the art department. They could give you a rainbow badge …"

Evie's voice fades and I hear ringing. This isn't possible, I don't have visions anymore.

I'm standing in the middle of the empty hall in front of a bathtub. A streak of blood rolls over the side and drips onto the floor. I find a clone of myself curled inside, naked and bleeding from the wrists. My dad is next to me, he holds out his hand and looks down at mine. I squeeze my left fist and feel the sharp pain of a razorblade slicing my palm. My dad takes the blade, dabs a paintbrush it in the blood, and hands me the brush. He smiles and nods his head to the bathtub. My naked clone climbs out and I realize she's not covered in blood, it's red paint—

"Who's that one for?" Evie asks.

The vision clears and I look down to see I have a piece of white chalk in my hand and I've outlined a five-foot dove. I jerk my hand back. I had a vision. I had a vision where I did not murder someone. I had a vision about my dad. I had a vision about myself covered in my own blood. No, not blood … paint.

I speak without even thinking. "This one is for all the people who died."

Evie nods. "I like it." She writes *RIP* underneath the dove.

We sit on the ground for another hour as I fill out my giant dove, shading in the feathers and making it lush and beautiful.

I can't get the visual of my dad out of my head, of that paintbrush with my blood. I wish more than anything that my dad were here, right now, to help me figure out what it is he's trying to tell me.

The barrack is pitch-black when I wake up. I try to roll over but someone is lying on my arm. I panic, thinking Felix has somehow snuck in, but then I hear a faint, high-pitched sigh. Evie. She's left her own bed to join me in mine.

The display on the wall shows it's 5:08 a.m. I don't know why I'm awake. It could be because of the sparse but incessant beeping coming from the door terminal. I pull my arm from under Evie, careful not to wake her, and turn on the display. *Unread Message*, it says. I tap the screen. *Meet in room 803 at 5 a.m.*

What could be so important to be summoned at five in the morning? I remember what Nadia said about Tuttle's insistence of the rules, so I pull on my boots and leave Evie in bed.

The base is quiet, free of wandering botheads. I take the elevator to the eighth floor and find the hallway illuminated by one small light at the end. Every door is closed, even the scanner room is locked, probably to keep civilians from ripping out implants. I put my ear to the door and swear I hear a clinking of metal from inside.

Then I hear a roar from down the hall. "Ah, you sonofabitch!"

I know that roar. It's Dog's, coming from the last room on the left. I press my ear against door 803 and hear more voices. I knock and the voices go silent.

I hear Dog clearing his throat followed by snickers of laughter.

"Who is it?"

"It's Jo," I say.

The door flies open and Dog stands in the threshold, flashing a toothy. I smell liquor on his breath. "You're late."

"I was sleeping."

"This is no time for sleeping!"

"Give the girl a break, will ya?" Dakota's voice calls from behind him.

"Well, get in here!" Dog laughs and steps aside.

I'm invited into a storage room, most of the space taken up by metal chests and containers. A large table is in the center of the room, and huddled around it are Solano, Oshiro, Dakota, and Nadia. Two whiskey bottles are on the table, one nearly empty.

"Good morning." Felix appears on my side and gives a half smile, and then Dog slaps him on the shoulder.

"*This* guy, huh?" Dog says. "He may be a Lone Wolf, but he was smart enough to bring us some spirits to lift our spirits." He laughs at his own joke, and everyone else rolls their eyes. "This is for you," he says, and hands me a glass of whiskey.

Felix jerks. "Wait, she's not—"

"Oh relax, Lone Wolf," Dog says. "Just because you won't drink doesn't mean your lady can't enjoy herself."

Felix forces a smile. It seems like he's found his way back into the loop, with liquor. Dog shoves me into a seat, and Oshiro pushes a pile of coins across the table.

"Nadia!" Dog hollers. "Re-deal. We've got a seventh player."

Nadia frowns. "If we bring more people into this game, we're not gonna have enough cards."

"You gonna whine or you gonna deal?" Dakota tosses her handful of ragged playing cards across the table. The guys laugh and do the same.

Felix leans over. "Do you know how to play poker?"

"I've never touched real cards before," I say.

Nadia raises her eyebrows. "You've never played cards?"

I shake my head and everyone groans and rolls their eyes again.

"I'm not dealing to someone who doesn't know a damn thing about poker," Nadia says.

Dakota jumps to her feet and leans over the table, and everyone gets an eyeful of Miss America's cleavage pouring out of the top of her tank. "Woman, I've had enough grumpy attitude from those goddamn botheads, and I don't need it from you too. So if you won't deal, I will."

The men chuckle. Nadia blinks at her.

"You!" Dakota points at me. "Drink!"

She's intimidating like this, so I take the glass and toss the burning liquor down my throat. I wince and gag and Dakota slaps me a high five.

"Can we get back to the game, now?" says Oshiro. "Ya'll are screwing up my mojo."

"We wouldn't want to un-mojo you," says Solano. I think he's trying to crack a joke but no one reacts. At least the whiskey has loosened him up a bit.

Nadia deals. Dakota tries to explain the rules of poker, but she's too drunk to keep things straight. All I remember is something about Texas, a river and getting hit. It sounds like a ridiculous game. Even worse is that I'm distracted by Felix. All these guys are dressed in the same charcoal pants and black t-shirt, and I don't know if Felix got the wrong size or what, but his shirt is so tight I can see every muscle in his torso. Every breath moves his wondrous pecks, and the slight movement of tossing a coin across the table makes his tattooed arms ripple.

Dakota has stopped blabbering. I look over to pretend like I've understood her explanation of the rules, but she's leaning back, her legs crossed and an arm tossed over the back of her chair. She's grinning at me. Her eyes flicker to Felix and I follow her gaze just as Felix turns away from me with a jerk. I look back at Dakota, and she winks at me.

"I'll start at twenty," says Solano, and tosses a few coins into the center pile.

"Call," Oshiro says from behind his hand of cards. "So, Jo. What's your deal?"

Nadia's eyes narrow as she reads my reaction.

"What do you mean?" I say.

"Raise ten," says Dog. "He means, how do you know how to shoot like that?"

"I donno. It just … came naturally."

"You're a natural hitman?" Oshiro asks.

Dakota chucks a coin at him. "Hit-*woman*."

I shrug. "I guess I am."

Felix butts in. "She's a good shot, is all."

"No way. I don't believe that," Solano says. "I was in the Marines for four years and I puked my guts out anytime I shot somebody."

Nadia grimaces. "Jeez, Solano. Were you shooting babies?"

"No. They were terrorists. But that's not the point. It's not easy to kill someone. Especially if you're … exactly how old are you?"

"Eighteen." I probably should have lied, because even Dakota gapes at me.

"*Eighteen*?" she says.

"You knew she was young," Nadia says. "Don't act so surprised."

"Yeah, but ..." Dakota says, "I hadn't really thought about it like that."

"Your call, Felix," says Oshiro.

Felix looks up from his lap, suddenly remembering about the game. "Fold," he says, and drops his cards.

"Pansy," Dog scoffs. Then says, rather casually, "I've never killed anybody."

Solano squints. "You're joking."

Dog shrugs. "What? Just 'cause I talk big doesn't mean I like killing people. Not like Miss Teen Hitwoman over here. It's her turn, by the way."

Everyone's eyes narrow. They peer right at me, struck by something. A realization. A familiarity. I can see the wheels turning in Nadia's head. I follow Felix's lead and drop my cards.

Dakota wavers in her chair, then throws a handful of coins into the center pile. "I raise one hundred."

"Goddammit." Nadia flips her cards over.

"What's with the little one, then?" Oshiro says. "Is she also a natural-born killer?"

"No," I say. "She grew up hunting snakes and lizards. She's not a killer."

"Except she's killed two people," says Dog.

"Three," I say, and immediately wish I hadn't.

"*Three*?" Nadia asks. "How many have *you* killed?"

"Ten, before the night on the hill. I guess now it's twelve."

There's a horrible tension in my stomach. I see a flash of memory of that day out in the yard, the day I bludgeoned LaRae to death with my fists. And now I'm sitting here with a table of soldiers who assume those nicks in my kill belt are all Alias, but they're not. Not exactly, anyway.

A hand on my leg interrupts my thoughts, and I catch Felix's gaze. He flutters his eyebrows.

"Not like it matters," Dog says. "We're wasting our ammo rescuing those thankless jackasses."

"Are you kidding me?" Dakota says, bursting through her drunkenness.

"Look, Dakota, you know just as well as I do that most of these people act like we're dragging them to prison. Or worse."

"You can't blame them," Nadia says, holding her glass of whiskey to her nose. "This place is pretty much that."

Felix takes his hand off my leg and balls his fist a few times.

"They're innocent people who were left defenseless in the desert," says Dakota.

"Ah, c'mon, Dakota!" Dog roars. "Either they'll die out there or they'll drown in their self-pity in here."

"It's not their fault. They're affected by the implants. Can't you see that?"

"But for what?" Nadia asks.

"For mind control, obviously," Felix says in his smart-ass voice. At least I'm not the only one he uses that on. Nadia shoots him a mocking look.

"But, *why*?" Dakota says. "And how did Alias get all these optrodes in the first place?"

Felix shifts in his chair. All heads at the table go back and forth between Miss America and the Lone Wolf.

"Alias is international," Felix says, his eyes fixed on his fist. "They had their own scientists."

"The optrodes were made in the US," Dakota says.

"That doesn't mean anything."

Dakota glares at him. "Yes, it does."

"What about the transmitter man?" Dog asks.

"You already know the identity of Marius Frey," Felix says a little too quickly. I'm starting to wonder if there's some ulterior motive behind keeping the doctor's animosity hidden. "You're wasting your time with him."

Nadia leans across the table. "I'd appreciate you not insulting how our time is spent, Lone Wolf." She cocks her head. "Besides, I'm running a diagnostic on the ID database. It'll catch any discrepancies between old and new information—"

"If there are any," Felix says, cutting her off and effectively turning the woman red.

Oshiro tosses his cards on the table. "I donno. This all seems like a bigger scheme than Alias is capable of."

Dakota thumps her fist on the table. "If we had paid more attention, really looked into The Plan ..."

"I know you want the truth, Dakota," Dog says, "but no one in this base is willing to sacrifice themselves to uncover it."

Everyone is silent, except for Dakota. "I am."

Dog nods at her. "Well, you're a bigger man than the rest of us, sweetheart."

There's a long awkward silence, until Felix turns to Dakota. "Do you think this has anything to do with the Voxoclon?"

Dakota squints at him. "How do you know about Voxoclon?"

"I know they were circulating the drugs into the prisons, passing them off as flake to the non-Alias inmates. There might be some connection."

Everyone stares suspiciously at Felix. I'm really curious how he's going to explain his connection to the prison without selling me out.

Nadia leans in. "How you know they got Voxoclon into the prison?"

Felix swallows so hard I can see his Adam's apple rise and fall underneath his beard scruff. "A fellow Lone Wolf soldier was a guard in the SoCal Institute for Women."

Right. Hathaway. Good call, Felix.

"After the invasion I went to the prison to rescue her," he says. "You should have seen the place. You could tell who took the Voxoclon. The inmates didn't even fight when the Alias members busted out. They just … lay down and died."

"So the Alias members got out and the rest died?" Nadia says. "You didn't find any other survivors in the prison?"

He clears his throat. "No. No other survivors."

"It can't be Voxoclon that is affecting these botheads," Solano says. "We've yet to find anyone who survived past the initial hallucinogenic phase."

My body jolts at the memory of the drugs, causing my chair to squeak, and everyone looks at me.

"Are we sure they didn't develop a new version of it?" Felix says.

Oshiro rubs his chin. "We still don't know what the first batch was for."

"Fatal pacification," Solano says with a glare. "Didn't you read the report?"

Dakota waves her arms. "Look, a man murdered a woman to get her implant. He wasn't on Voxoclon. He wasn't hijacked. He and so many of these other people will do anything to hide from reality."

"I think we all understand the reality—" Dog starts, but Dakota wags a finger at him.

"The reality is that everyone is too busy trying to *forget* the reality instead of letting themselves feel emotion and mourn the dead."

Solano leans back. "So what do you want us to do about it? We're soldiers, not counselors."

"He's right," Dog says. "If you wanna help these people you go ahead. My job is to keep them alive. I can't do that if I'm holding their hands."

I get it now. These people—most especially Dakota—aren't here to lay the law down on everyone. They want to help. Hell, they all lost loved ones in the invasion too. They're determined to fight back. And I've been holding onto a secret ever since I arrived, a secret that not only could unravel the protective layer Felix has wrapped me in, but a secret that could help. I can't hold this burden any longer. I have to tell them about Dr. Marius Frey.

"There's something you need to know," I say, and all eyes land on me.

Right on cue, a siren blares into the room. Everyone jumps to their feet, forgetting I was talking. Felix looks at me and I expect him to frown, but his face is soft, his lips quivering.

Nadia pulls up a hologram on her wristlet of the desert landscape, displaying a dot moving through the sky. "It's a drone!"

The soldiers head straight for the elevators. Felix grabs me and follows everyone else to the top levels. Tuttle is in the corridor when we reach the third floor.

"One of the civilians had a tracker," he says. "The drone followed him here."

"The civilians from the hill?" Dakota asks.

"I knew we should have left them," Dog grumbles.

"Get to the towers," Tuttle says. "We need to take out the drone before it gets an aerial visual of Foxhole."

"Wake up the girl," Solano says.

My heart lurches. "Evie? No! Leave her out of this!"

But Dog has already retrieved her rifle from Tuttle's office.

"It's okay, Jo." Evie shuffles down the hallway, rubbing sleep from her eyes. "I can do it."

"No, no, no!" I can't stop shaking and I have the real need to punch something, but the closest one to me is little Evie. "No, you can't do this. Evie, you're not a killer!"

"You just told us she's killed three people," Nadia says.

Dog growls. "Look, we can argue this all day long, but in case you've forgotten *there's a drone coming*!" He shoves the rifle in Evie's arms and leads her down the hall. "We need to go. Now!"

Everyone follows Dog down the hall, except Felix, who stands in my path. "You should stay here."

"I need to help Evie!"

"Jo, the deeper you get into this, the harder it will be to get out."

"What the hell are you talking about? They're gonna turn Evie into a sniper and you're worried about *me*?"

"If you're not thinking clearly, you'll never be able to help Evie."

"I can't let her do this."

"You have to take care of yourself first."

"It's too late for me, Felix. You know that. But dammit it's not too late for Evie!" I barrel past him, leaving him alone in the corridor, standing there like a fool. I'm on my own now.

Running around the exterior hallway, I search for the way to the towers. I reach a dead end and find a door that houses a stairwell. Voices ring out above me. I race up the stairs and through another door and find myself in a lighthouse watchtower. Dog, Solano, Nadia, and Dakota are huddled around a hologram display table of radar information.

"Look," Solano says, pointing at a moving object in the holo. "It's circling."

"Maybe it'll pass by," Nadia says.

"No, he's right," says Dog. "Look at the flight path."

"The sun is coming up," Dakota says from the window. "It'll be able to see us soon."

Evie emerges from the corner, holding her rifle. She gives me an uneasy smile. "Ready, Jo?"

The others are surprised to see me, but I don't have time to bother with them. I go to Evie and grab her shoulders. "Evie, listen. You don't have to become a sniper, okay? You can do something else to help."

"Oh gimme a break," Dog groans.

"I don't have anything else, Jo. My daddy's dead and my mom is long gone. I'm a good shot. What else can I do?"

"We don't have time for this," Solano says.

I ignore the soldiers and force all my focus onto Evie. "You don't have to do this."

"What are you so worried about, Jo? You do it. These guys do it. Besides, it's just a drone … I'm not killing anybody."

Oshiro's voice comes over the speaker. *"What the hell are you waiting for?"*

Dakota waves over to the next tower. "We got it under control," she says, then looks at me. "Don't we?"

"We're running out of time. We need to take it out now!"

Before I can protest, Evie is led to the window where she sets up her rifle to the east. The drone is a dark speck in the pink sky of the early morning sunrise.

"See it?" Solano asks her.

"Yeah, I got it," Evie says.

"You gotta take it out with one shot," Solano says. "Two at the most. But don't dawdle in between."

"Hurry up!"

I collapse against the window as I watch this girl become Foxhole 221's lead sniper. Evie. My little Evie.

Dakota leans next to me. "It's good you're looking out for her, Jo, but there's nothing to worry about. A lot of women become soldiers, just like me and Nadia."

I glare at her. "She's not a woman. She's just a *kid*!"

"Well, we could say the same about you, and you've already killed twelve Alias terrorists."

I thought this woman was on my side, and now she's sitting back and watching Evie be turned into a weapons system. I'm so angry that I reach for the handle of the knife on my belt.

"I didn't just kill Alias terrorists."

Nadia jerks around. "What do you mean by that?"

The holo display starts beeping and the flying icon flashes.

"Oh shit, you guys! It's not a drone!"

Dog and Solano rush to the table.

"Is it a rocket?" Solano asks.

"No," Dog says.

Then Evie's voice calls from behind the rifle scope with a frightened twinge that sends a shiver down my spine.

"It's an airplane!"

34 birds in flight

The dark spot in the sky grows larger in the dawning light of the sun. The hologram display flashes and beeps. Voices scream through the receivers. This glass-framed watchtower is in unrelenting turmoil.

"It's a civilian aircraft!"

"*It's gotta be Alias!*"

"We don't know that!"

"Control, are you seeing this?"

"*We're getting four heat signatures from inside the aircraft.*"

"Any radio communication?"

"*They're not responding.*"

"That's it, they're here to take us out!"

"They could be survivors!"

"What do I do?" Everyone's forgotten little Evie peering through the scope of her rifle, aimed at the incoming plane.

"*Somebody's gotta take the shot!*"

"Shoot it down!" Dog hollers.

"*No!*" I fling myself at him. "Don't make her do it. Don't make her take the shot!"

"You've gone mad, girl!"

I claw at Dog's mountain of a chest. "There are people on that plane!"

"Listen, crazy. There are two hundred civilians down in that Foxhole. I don't give a *damn* about four unknown people flying at us."

Evie calls out. "It's getting closer!"

"Don't make her take the shot."

Dakota moves in. "This is war, Jo. We have to do what's necessary."

"Do what's necessary, I don't care. Just don't make Evie do it!"

There's a *clack* and moments later the aircraft explodes in the air in a brilliant yellow fireball. We all turn to look at Evie.

She shakes her head. "It wasn't me."

Dog looks around. "Who took the shot?"

"*I did,*" Oshiro says over the speaker. "*The kid's not the only one who can shoot.*"

Evie sinks back into the shadows, and I stand heaving in the middle of the watchtower. I can feel the muscles straining in my neck. My teeth clatter together. My body is so tense it hurts.

"Why did you want her to do it?"

Everyone is still, their arms held up and their eyes trained on my hand. I've grabbed my knife from my belt and I'm holding it out like a street fighter. "*Why?*" Still no one moves. "You didn't need her to take that shot. Why did you want her to do it?"

Nadia speaks flatly. "This is how things need to be. We all have a job to do."

"Evie's not a soldier. She's just a kid."

Dog is the next to speak. "Not anymore."

"Don't you dare say that!"

I lunge at him with the knife, and Dog pulls his pistol from his belt and aims it at my head. I skid to a halt inches from Dog's gun with my blade at his stomach.

A split-second later, Tuttle bursts through the door. "What the hell is going on here?" No one dares to attempt an explanation.

Dog gives me a sideways grin. "Huh. I thought you looked familiar. I couldn't place you at first—your face is a little different—but now I see it. It's that look in your eyes. It's familiar."

"Dog, what the hell are you talking about?" Tuttle asks.

Nadia squints at me. Solano and Dakota are perplexed. And Evie's eyes are suddenly wide, her voice is a quivering whisper.

"The Schoolgirl Slicer …"

My heart sinks. Out of all people, I did not want Evie to know the truth. I feared the day that her perception of me would be overshadowed by the realization that I am not only capable of shooting terrorists for survival, but that I have in fact committed cold-blooded murder. Twice. All I wanted was to prevent this sweet little girl from following my path into the darkness, into the depths of Hell that have consumed me.

"I knew it," Nadia says. "I knew you're not who you say you are. You're a murderer. You're supposed to be in prison."

"What the hell are you doing in my combat unit?" says Tuttle.

"Lone Wolf …" Dog says.

"Arrest the Lone Wolf!" Tuttle says.

"He's not the one you want." I step forward, closing the gap between my head and Dog's gun. I can't see beyond the muzzle of the pistol, and all I really want is to get Evie the hell out of this watchtower.

Dog never wavers. "Are you the Schoolgirl Slicer?"

Evie's voice squeaks from the shadows. "Jo …?"

Dog hollers, his voice rattling the windows. "Are you the Schoolgirl Slicer!"

"Stop calling me that!" I blink away the tears. I can't let them see me so vulnerable, not after all that's happened. Not with Evie here. "I'm a terrible person, and I know that. I don't deserve to be here. I don't deserve to be alive. But Evie … she's just a girl. I can't let her become a monster like me." I take one last step and the cold barrel of Dog's gun presses against my forehead. "Do it. Shoot me. Please."

"Jo! Stop!" Evie cries.

"Dog, you will stand down, that is an order!" Tuttle says.

"Get rid of me. I'm a disease. Don't you see that? I've ruined everything. It's my fault that Evie killed anyone in the first place."

Dog doesn't flinch. "You know I won't kill you, but I promise I'll lock you away."

I scream at him. "No! It's not enough! You have to get rid of me!"

Tuttle tries again. "Stand down, Dog!"

"Do it, you coward!"

Dog slams the pistol across my face and I hear the crunch of my cheekbone before I feel the pain. The tears that had been building up in my eyelids break through and stream down my cheeks.

"Leave her alone!"

"Evie!" Dakota screams. "What are you doing?"

I blink away the tears and see Evie pointing her rifle at the back of Dog's head. "Drop it!" she says. "I'll do it! Don't think I won't! I've already killed three people! I'll do it again!"

Dog lets go of the pistol and it clatters to the floor.

"Evie, stop! This is exactly what I didn't want to happen."

"It doesn't matter anymore, Jo. We're the same. You and me. We're killers. It's in our blood. It's who we are."

A harsh, prickling sensation flows over my body. My cheekbone throbs, but it's not any worse than the pain I feel inside me. I failed her, and the longer I'm on this earth, the more like me she will become. It has to end here. It has to end with me.

I drag the blade of my knife against the inside of my wrist, the warmth of my blood trickles down to my hand. The pain is excruciating, yet the wound relieves the some of the pressure built up inside my veins. Evie is crying. Dakota is crying. Dog, Tuttle, Solano, and Nadia all gape at me as I stand there trying to slice through my arm with the knife.

The door bursts open and there is Felix, sweating, his chest heaving, interrupting my attempt at relief.

"No, stay away!" I shout at him, waving my bloody knife in the air. "You're too late. You couldn't save me."

He barrels at me, taking no caution of the weapon in my hand or the fact that Evie's got Dog at gunpoint. He shoves me against the window, rips open his shirt, grabs the arm that holds my knife so I can't finish the job, and points the tip of the blade at his chest—right in the heart of the phoenix tattoo.

"Right here, Jo. You wanna end it? You think you've gotta wipe the earth clean of every sign of your existence? Then put your knife right here."

"It's *me* Felix! I'm the one who has to die."

"Don't be so goddamn selfish. If you're the heartless killer you say you are, then kill me. Josephine Bristol, if you are a killer then *kill me*!"

"It's me that has to go …"

I turn the knife around and inch it toward my neck. Felix knows what I'm doing—I can sense it in his grip—but he won't take his eyes away from mine.

"Just like your dad?"

His words crush me. "Don't talk about my dad!"

"Is that it, Jo? You think that Evie will be better off if you kill yourself? You think she'll be inspired to turn her life around if you bleed out in front of her? Your dad killed himself because he thought he'd spare you his pain, that you'd be better off without him. Are you better off? Did he spare you the pain?"

"Stop it! You know nothing about my dad."

"You're terrified of painting because you're convinced it will drive you to kill yourself. How's that working out for you now, huh?"

"You want to insult me while I'm holding a knife between our necks?"

"I'm trying to get you to shut the hell up and look around, Jo!"

"I can't change the world with a paintbrush!"

"And you think you'll make a difference with a *knife*?"

"I'm not the person you think I am!"

"Then show me who you are!"

"I'm a killer!"

Felix twists my wrist around and digs the knife into his chest and the tip breaks his skin. "Show me who you are!"

His eyes are wide with fury, his hot breath blowing over my face, his strong arms holding me in place. Just a moment ago I felt the adrenaline pulsing through my veins, my soul fighting back with the rage of a girl turned to the dark side, and now … Felix is crushing me from the inside out. I have nothing left to brace myself, no desire to keep the pain from penetrating through that soft spot of my heart. All my strength is gone, and I've given up.

How did I end up here? How did I become this monster? How did I completely forget everything that I ever wanted to be and traded it for the thing that everyone else says I am? Why did I ever try so hard to convince myself that I could be someone else?

Because there was a time when I believed I was a decent person. There was a time before all this, before the blood and the killing and the Schoolgirl Slicer that I believed I knew exactly who I was.

But not anymore.

Felix is waiting for me to say something. They all are. He's backed off, released his body from mine. I don't want to look at Evie, but her eyes draw me to her. She looks so broken, so alone, so lost, so haunted by everything that came before in her short life, and everything that lies beyond in the vast unknown of her future. I know that expression; I use to see it in the mirror every night. And I can't bear to look at it any longer.

I move before anyone has the chance to snatch me. I race across the tower and burst past Tuttle and through the door. I hear them shout and clamor as I race down the stairwell. They'll have to let me loose; like a bird trapped in a house, leave the windows open and wait for me to find my escape. And that's exactly what I have to do. I must leave this place and everyone behind. It's the only chance Evie or Felix will have to survive through this … without me.

I hear footsteps above me, heavy boots thumping against the metal rungs, vibrating every connecting piece of the stairs. I glance behind me to see a man coming down, taking the steps two at a time, leaping down to catch me. I can't let him catch me.

The entrance to the garage is on the opposite side of the base. Had I thought this through I would have chosen a better route from the watchtower to the garage, because the only way I can go now is straight through the main hall. But I can't pass through. A few dozen people crowd the room, standing in a ring in the center. I don't know why they're here, but I wish they would all go away. I'm so desperate to disappear that the last thing I want to do is see their pathetic faces.

I'm still running, still giving in to the pulsing influence of flight in my legs, that when a side door opens I barely have the sense to stop my momentum before I run over a handful of botheads creeping into the room, huddled together in a tight group. They are doe-eyed, like deer in headlights, faces ashen and damp. They whimper when they see me and compact together even tighter, hands and arms keeping their pack secured. One woman screeches when she spots the blood trickling down my arm. When the woman turns back to her group I see a patch of gauze behind her ear with a bright-red splotch. All of these botheads have the same patches; one even has blood trickling down his neck.

The botheads have gathered the attention of the normal civilians standing in the circle. I feel eyes on me, lots of eyes, examining me in my most vulnerable state, with the layers of my armor stripped away. I want nothing more than to cast a spell and become invisible to everyone, ever.

And then I see Marius, following behind the botheads. Right behind him comes Suki. She's no longer howling in agony; in fact, she looks rather natural. Suki tries to get Marius moving, but he's stiff, stuck in his position, his face twitching. I can't move either, even though the adrenaline has moved into my arms and down my fingertips and I'm itching with fury.

"Jo … stop …"

The words are said between rapid breaths of air, but the insistence, the fierceness, the determination … all of that is unmistakably Felix. He's behind me. I can feel his breath against my neck, smell his cowboy scent mixing with the sweet smell of sweat, his fingers grazing my arm.

Tuttle's voice rings across the hall. "I am putting you *both* under arrest!"

Boots tread into the room, along with clanking gear and huffed grunts. The soldiers have followed us down, Tuttle at the helm. Marius glances over my shoulder and his eyes go even wider as he coils his arms inward. The botheads start crying, and the civilians stand watching. This once expansive room feels cramped and stifling. And I have somehow lost the knowledge of how to move.

"I don't know what you're up to, Lone Wolf," Tuttle says, "but I oughtta lock both of you away for a long time."

Marius looks at me again and tilts his head. I do my best to keep from locking eyes with him, but I'm too livid to not glare at him, and I'm unwilling to turn and face the white-haired man's incriminating face.

Felix presses his back to mine, his lungs tremble when he speaks. "I can explain. This isn't what you think it is."

"She interfered with a defense operation," says Tuttle, "and you encouraged it. That's all there is to it."

The group of botheads creep closer, and the wailing woman reaches a hand out to me. I have nowhere to go but up against Felix's back.

"They're hurting us. They're going to kill us!" she says as tears stream down her face. "You have to help us!"

"Jesus," Tuttle says, gesturing to the botheads. "I can't deal with these idiots too. Get them out of here."

"All right," I hear Dakota say, "everyone calm down. We don't need to do this here."

"And where shall we take them," Dog says, "the dungeon?"

"Give me a chance to explain," Felix says.

The room is in audible chaos. Every soldier is shouting, including Felix. The botheads wail louder as though to drown out the argument. The ring of people in the middle of the room chatter with each other and point in my direction. Felix and I are back to back, the soldiers yelling at him, and the botheads hollering at me.

Then my attention is caught on a young boy standing amongst the circle of civilians, and I recognize him as the one who'd had his drawing blown to bits by the mean kid. One hand is wrapped tightly in the fist of a grown man, and the other holds a piece of orange chalk. He looks at the soldiers, then at the crazy botheads, up at the man he stands next to, then right at me. The kid puffs out his chest, raises the piece of chalk in the air, and screams, "This is a funeral!"

The last shouts and cries echo off the walls, and the room goes silent. Even the botheads stop wailing. Curious attention is drawn to the boy as he stands there with the chalk raised above his head.

Dakota is the first to speak. "What did you say?"

"I said," the boy takes a breath, "this is a *funeral*."

The boy gestures with his chalk as he turns around, and the circle of civilians move away, clearing a view to the center of their group. It takes me a moment to realize what these people had been doing when I first arrived in the hall. They weren't frantic or chaotic. They were hugging. Kissing on the cheek. Patting each other's backs. Holding hands. Crying, but smiling. They were mourning.

And that's when I see the birds.

The crowd has been standing in a ring around the center of the hall, around a cluster of chalk birds. Hundreds of them. Every color, every shape and size, varying from ornate to rudimentary. Names are sprawled underneath, noting birth dates, relationships, significance. These aren't just drawings of birds; they're headstones for the loved and recently lost.

And there in the middle is my giant white dove.

35 marked with blood

I stand frozen and shivering from some unknown source of chilled air, like an ice age has moved across the room. My senses fire at an achingly slow pace, and it takes forever for the signals to reach my brain. I wonder if time has stopped completely or if it is me who is gradually being turned into stone.

No one speaks as I stare down at the rainbow of birds. So many of them, so uniquely drawn with love and passion, so perfectly placed in a wreath around my white dove. One bird in particular catches my eye, a red cardinal with a phrase written underneath: *I miss you, Daddy.*

The air is sucked from my lungs and my legs give out. I collapse to my knees. The cold chill is replaced by an invisible blanket of warmth. Voices and sounds swirl around my ears, colors blur into nonsensical shapes in my sight.

It seems to take a moment for it to sink in for everyone else, except for Evie.

"The birds!" she cries. "There's more! Oh, it's so beautiful!"

The little boy wanders over to me, the only other movement in the room. "You're Jo, right? I found your crow. Don't be mad, but I erased it. These birds are for dead people. You're not dead. You're right here."

My heart implodes and I start sobbing. I can't stop myself. My lungs quiver uncontrollably as the entire room of people watches me bawl my eyes out.

Suki walks to the center of the room. "These birds are for our loved ones." She motions for the botheads to follow her. "You should see them. It'll help, I promise."

I watch from down on my knees as Suki leads the botheads to the birds. The wailing woman touches her behind the ear—next to her streak of green hair. Suki nods. She still has gauze patch, but the blood is dark brown, the edges of the tape have lifted and frayed. The civilians make room for Suki and the woman as they approach the birds.

Suki points down at a bluebird. "For my husband, Eric."

The woman drops to her knees and runs her fingers gently over the chalk. "My son's name was Eric," she says, her voice cracking. She takes a deep breath, wipes the tears from her cheeks, and looks up at the mourners. "I understand now. Thank you."

The other botheads join the rest of the group and mingle with the mourners, and suddenly it's as though there is no differentiating between bothead and civilian.

Strong hands lift me from the ground and there is Felix. His arms wrap around me in a tight embrace, and I sob into his bare chest. His voice travels into my ears as though he's the only source of sound in the universe.

"Still think you can't change the world with a paintbrush?"

I look through a waterfall of tears. "I didn't change the world."

"You've changed these people. And in here—down in this cave—this is their world. You made a difference in here."

"I didn't *mean* to."

He grabs my arms and the blood from my wrist dribbles to the floor. "You didn't have to. It came from your heart. You didn't just draw with chalk. You drew with your *blood.* You've shared pain, and sharing your suffering has lifted the weight from your shoulders."

"You can't know that."

"I can, Jo. I see it in your eyes. It's a beautiful sight."

My dad dabs the paintbrush in the blood, and hands me the brush. But it's not blood, it's red paint—

"Did you have a vision?"

I barely whisper. "Yes."

Worry floods his face. "Damn ..."

I shake my head. "It wasn't a vision of killing. It was a vision of my dad handing me a paintbrush, dipped in my own blood."

Felix's eyes fill with tears and for the first time since I've known him he looks frail. His own pain had been bubbling right at the surface of his soul for so long, and at this very moment it is unleashing itself. Right into me.

But we're not alone enough for such a display.

"Someone had better explain what the hell is going on here," Tuttle says.

"It looks like a rainbow vomited on the floor," Dog says, and a few soldiers chuckle.

"Jo drew the dove!" Evie says. She races over to me and wraps her arms around my waist. I grunt as she squeezes the air from my lungs.

"It is beautiful …" Dakota says as she walks over to get a closer look.

Everyone—even the soldiers—peer through the crowd to see the birds. They're confused but awestruck, mouths hanging open like the words are caught on their tongues. At this moment I wonder if for once I've truly done the right thing, and maybe it's enough to be forgiven for all the insanity in my past.

But I'm not out of the woods yet.

Nadia's wristlet beeps. As she reads through the display, she narrows her eyes and juts out her jaw, bringing the screen closer to her face. "You've gotta be joking." She's speaking to herself, but I still heard her. I'm the only one who did.

Nadia goes up to Dakota and jabs her in the side. Dakota can hardly tear herself from the birds, but when Nadia pokes her again she swivels around.

"What is it?" Dakota says sharply.

Nadia holds her wristlet so Dakota can read it. Her eyes go wide, and they both jerk their heads to look across the room. At first I don't know who they're looking for, but then I see him. Marius. Hovering against the wall.

"Commander?" Dakota says. "I think you need to see this."

"Tell me," Tuttle says.

"My program finished running the diagnostic on the ID database," Nadia says.

Felix lets out all the air from his lungs and the breadth of his body narrows like a shriveling balloon.

Dakota points to the man along the wall. "We've discovered the true identity of Marius Frey."

Felix and I look to Nadia at the same time. While all other heads follow the direction of Dakota's arm, Nadia has locked eyes with Felix. No words are said, just the slight dip of Nadia's chin and Felix's shift of stance.

"Then tell me who the hell he is!" says Tuttle.

Marius flattens himself against the wall and glances quickly between the soldiers and the door. The men are about to move in when Suki steps between them and Marius, placing one palm on the man's chest and the other held out to the room.

"Wait," she says. "He'll tell you who he is." She turns to him. "Won't you?"

Marius lowers his head and rakes his hand through his floppy gray hair. He looks to Suki, and she nods encouragingly.

"Yes, all right. I'll tell you who I am." Marius walks across the room and stops a few feet from Tuttle, in clear view of me, like he wants to see my reaction. "I'm not an accountant." He scratches his cheek. "I'm Dr. Marius Frey of San Diego, Experimental Neurologist."

The men shift, and I hear Dog cackle.

"He took out the implants." Suki says and pauses, waiting for the news to sink in, then points to the gauze behind her ear.

Dakota lowers her voice. "How do you know how to do that?"

Marius clears his throat. "Because I'm the one who put them in."

All guns are on Marius. The man tucks in his arms, recoiling like a frightened snake. Felix shields Evie and me behind his back. Solano rushes over to Marius and grabs him by the collar of his shirt.

Here we go. This is where the shit hits the fan.

"Did you hijack these people?" Solano says.

Marius winces, but keeps his position. "Yes, I did."

"Why? Why did you do it? Are you working with Alias?"

"They made me do it. They kidnapped my son. They killed my wife. They threatened to kill more people if I didn't do as they said." His eyes dance over to me. "I'm sorry I lied. I wanted to be sure I could remove the implants before I revealed myself."

Suki puts her hand on Solano's arm. "He's telling the truth. I was there. I remember everything now that he's removed the implant. I am no longer overwhelmed by the panic."

Solano releases Marius and the neurologist straightens his shirt.

Dakota sounds like she's choking on her words. "Is that what the implants are for? To induce panic?"

"Not exactly," Marius says, looking at the floor. "They're designed to trigger certain parts of the brain and shut off natural emotional responses. Once the implants are removed, however, all those bypassed emotions flood the brain, causing hysteria. I don't think this was their exact intention. There's a glitch in the programming."

Dakota blinks. "Who would create such a device? And *why*?"

"I don't know the purpose of it. They never told me, but I designed the implant. They came to me because I was working on a similar device."

Marius looks right at me. His eyes bore holes into my skin. Felix notices and jerks with the anticipation of attack.

"It was my job to help people," Marius says. "Patients came to me to heal themselves of their emotional abnormalities. Alias became interested in my work and forced me to create the implants. I swear, I didn't want to do any of it."

"You implanted people with mind-altering devices and then lied about it. What do you expect us to believe now?" Solano says.

"What if he's telling the truth?" I don't remember telling my mouth to move.

Felix grabs my arm, holding me in place. I can't feel the touch of his skin on mine, only the pressure of his fingernails digging into my tendons. Marius stares at me, the skin of his mouth and around his eyes pinched together in the middle of his face.

I keep talking. "Maybe there's something we can all get out of this if we work together. Maybe, instead of locking Dr. Frey away, he can keep removing the implants. Maybe he can even help me."

"What makes you think I'd agree to that?" Tuttle asks. "I should lock *all* of you up."

Dakota steps forward. "No, she's right. Marius is the only one who can remove the implants. And the birds have clearly helped with the emotional healing process. We can't have one without the other. We need them both."

Marius pulls back his shoulders and rubs his beard. The civilians group together, nodding and pointing down at the birds.

"We have to help the rest of them," says Suki.

"Commander," Dakota says, "you ordered me to find a way to help these people. Jo has done something that has sparked these people back to life. She can help. We need her."

Tuttle glares at everyone for what feels like an eternity, and we all stand awaiting the master's verdict. He throws an arm in the air and groans. "I let one goddamn Lone Wolf into my Foxhole and suddenly the whole base throws itself upside down."

Felix twitches again but stays quiet.

"Listen, you two…" Tuttle breaches the space between Marius and myself, waving an accusatory finger "…I won't have any more dicking around on my base. I have a command to run, and these are my orders. Get the little one out of the squad. Get the rest of those implants out of the civilians. And you…" his finger lands on me "…I don't know what your deal is, but these birds are … helping." He says the word like it tastes bad on his tongue. "If you're going to contribute something positive to Foxhole, then you'd better make it worth it."

Tuttle heaves a jagged breath then turns back to his soldiers. "Get moving. There's a war going on out there, and we need to be ahead of the game. Make it happen." He walks the length across the hall and through the door.

"You heard the man, let's move," says Solano.

Everyone shuffles at once, moving in every direction. Nadia stays behind. She seems to have relaxed some, but the curious expression in her face has twisted into something more troubled.

Dakota comes up to us, her beautiful eyes bright and sparkling. "You have quite the expectation on your shoulders, Jo. But I have faith in you. I'd like to help."

Felix nudges me with his shoulder, and Evie looks up from her entanglement around my waist, but I can't think of anything to say. I'm so overwhelmed by the events of the last few hours that I feel the energy being drained from my body and expelled through holes in my shoes.

Felix shrugs and turns to Dakota. "What do you have in mind?"

An amused smile breaks across her face. "Paint?"

My body jerks involuntarily and I nearly knock Evie's arms away from me. She holds on tighter. I must have a perplexing expression on my face, because when I look to Felix, he's flashing that signature grin.

"Paint." He says it like it's the most important word ever, like it holds the answer to life itself. The weight of those five letters simultaneously pushes down on my shoulders and creates lift under my feet, squishing me together like a rubber ball.

Dakota smiles. "I'll see what I can do. Come by the clinic first. We'll fix up that gash in your arm."

She pulls Nadia away, says something to Marius, and the three of them exit the hall, leaving Felix, Evie, and myself alone. Finally. Felix has his eyes on my bleeding wrist, and I'm now grateful he didn't let me finish. For so many reasons.

Evie jerks against me and I look down to see that she's laughing. "It was just a bird, Jo," she says, squeezing me in her arms.

"Yeah," I say, finding the strength to speak again. "It was just a bird."

36 vanishing point

A month after that fateful night in the watchtower, I find Evie in the dining hall surrounded by younger kids, rallying them like a camp counselor. It's Saturday, and the kids are excited for a morning free from their assigned duties, not that doing minor tasks like sweeping floors and taking photos of inhabitants are difficult jobs.

"Listen," Evie says. "We can't do the scene with the drone unless the props department actually finishes the props."

The kids groan.

"I need more glue," one says.

"All right, fine. We'll move on to the scene with the married people."

"Do I really have to kiss him?" one girl squeaks.

"It's more realistic," Evie says.

The kids give a collective "*eeew!*" and Evie rolls her eyes. She spots me sitting by myself at a table and rushes over.

"Hey, Jo!"

"Are you a director now?" I ask her.

"Trying to be. I mean, it's not like we have a playground or anything. So Dakota suggested we make a movie."

"Sounds complicated."

"Uh, you have no idea." She snags a scoop of my oatmeal and spies the paint under my fingernails. "How's the mural coming?"

No one has been allowed to see my mural thus far. I really don't care either way, but Felix insisted I keep it covered when I'm not working on it. I haven't even seen the whole thing myself.

"It's getting there," I say.

"I'm sure it's beautiful. There's gonna be a big ceremony, right?"

"Oh yeah, I forgot about that. It seems so silly."

"It's not silly!"

"What if everyone hates it?"

"Well," Evie says, "that'll be their problem, not yours."

"You're not very encouraging."

She giggles and lifts her arms into the air. "I am the voice of *reason*!"

"If that's true, we're really in trouble."

We both burst out laughing and everyone gives us strange looks.

Evie pats my arm. "I can't wait to see it, Jo."

"Thank you, Evie. Hey, you may wanna get back to your film crew. They're scattering."

She whips around to see the kids scampering away. "Hey! Where are you going? I didn't call wrap yet!"

On my way to the main hall, I pass a common room that has been converted into a communications hub where TV screens project news from around the country. Felix says the information coming in is convoluted, but I'm not terribly interested in knowing what's really going on out there; it's all been a bit overwhelming. When it's time to move, Felix will let me know.

Dog is in the hub, barking orders to a man fussing with a series of computers. He spots me and waves me over. "Jo, you said your mom was in Valley Mental Hospital, right? Lauren Bristol?"

"Yeah. Did you find her?"

He smiles. "Sure did. I searched for her *find me* bulletin over the public broadcast. Communication has been sketchy because Alias keeps breaking it down, but it hasn't stopped us."

"Do you know where she is?"

"The hospital was evacuated to Foxhole 167," Dog says. "Don't ask me why they thought it was crucial to save the crazies, but whatever. Here's her bulletin. From Lauren Bristol to Josephine Bristol."

He points to a tab. The message is addressed, "*My dearest daughter, Jo.*"

My heart jumps. I can't decide if I'm prepared to hear what she has to say, but she's my mom. And I miss her now more than ever.

I open the message.

Josephine,

I hope with every atom in my body that you are safe and well. The only thing I have to look forward to in life is hearing that you are alive. If you are reading this, then know I am safe too.

Before the bombings, the hospital was busy repairing my brain. I'm not fully healed, but I'm getting there. I'm remembering things, Jo. Your father, the abuse from Rick, the hacking … None of it was your fault.

I curse my damn brain for causing this illness and putting you in so much turmoil. I never wanted that. You're my daughter and a wonderful and beautiful girl and you deserved better than that. You will be successful in whatever you put your mind to, because if you are still the girl I knew, you are determined to survive.

I love you so much, I hope to see you soon.

Love, Mom

"Hey, you're getting the tab wet," Dog says, elbowing me in the arm.

Tears stream down my face and splatter on the screen. I wipe my eyes with my shirt. "Sorry."

He shakes his head. "Notta worry. How's the mural coming?"

"It'll be done soon."

"Well, hurry it up, will ya? I wanna see it."

I'm an emotional wreck from my mom's words, and I can't stop trembling as I make my way to the main hall. I pass by several people who nod their heads at me, a polite acknowledgement that I still have yet to get used to. Everyone knows me now. They know my story and they know I was the inspiration behind the chalk bird headstones, which have been sealed under a clear lacquer and protected from being washed away. Now that most of the hijacked civilians have had their brain implants removed, they don't look at me with fright or apprehension, but with relief and gratitude. That's what my mural has to live up to. Too mellow and it won't be impactful enough. Too drastic and it might alarm the fickle minds of the botheads. I can only hope my hand has been deft enough to create a piece of artwork worthy of what everyone expects of me.

I reach the main hall and find a group of kids peeking under the thick sheets of opaque plastic that cover the mural. They see me coming and scurry off, giggling. The idea of a grand reveal makes me nervous. For all I know everyone could hate it, and then they'll be upset because I've spent the last several weeks painting instead of making some other useful contribution to the community. But Felix is insistent, and I won't let Felix down. Not anymore.

I sprawl out my collection of paints and brushes and get to work. There isn't much left to do to the mural, I have but a few finer details to add. A flame over here. A shoeprint over there. A little more highlight, a little more shadow. Up and down the ladder I go, pulling back the sheets of plastic, only revealing the small space on which I'm working. It's quite a physical feat because the mural itself is twenty feet high. I protested this, but everyone insisted it needed to be something of grandeur, something that every person who passed through this room would be forced to look upon, for if this piece is to be anything like the chalk-bird headstones, this will be something people *should* be bombarded with.

So here I am.

I'm adding specks of yellow in the sky when my hand starts to tremble. It's nearly done. In fact, I'm just fussing now, adding irrelevant colors to a piece already full of detail. My hand shakes so much that I drop the brush and it clatters to the floor twenty feet beneath me.

It's finished.

My legs grow weaker the longer I stand on the ladder. I grab onto the plastic for support and it moves slightly, tearing itself from the nails. And I have a thought: I don't want some grand reveal—I want to see it now.

I climb down the ladder as fast as I can, push everything to the side, grab hold of the plastic, and pull. The whole thing swooshes down on me like a parachute, and I scurry out from underneath before it suffocates me.

I glance up. There's one spot. It catches my eye, in the center near the bottom. I grab my brush, dab it in red paint, and two strokes later, it's perfect. I turn away from the wall, clamber over the crumpled plastic, walk to the center of the room, and turn around and look.

It is, undoubtedly, a dedication to my dad. I have taken my favorite of his pieces and remade it, blown it up to an unavoidable size, and plastered it on the wall.

The girl with the paintbrush in the burning city.

I've made some variations. On the right side is the landscape of a destroyed city, specifically Los Angeles. A mushroom cloud looms overhead, the FutureTech building bursting into a billion pieces. But on the left side, the sun is shining. The Hollywood hills are green, the buildings a shimmering silver. In the foreground is a girl. Possibly me, but most likely Evie, for I gave the girl lighter hair. In her left hand she holds a gun, and in her right hand, a paintbrush.

I hear whispers around me. A few people gather in the doorways. Recently healed botheads hover against the walls, gently touching the gauze-covered spots behind their ears and wiping tears from their eyes. They stare at the wall, hesitant to move into the room.

"I thought you were supposed to wait," Evie says, rushing over. Her smile is remarkable. "I see it. There's what happened," she says, pointing to the mushroom cloud, "and there's what's to come." She points to the green hills. "Right?"

I shrug. "Something like that."

"The artist is not supposed to explain her work. You're meant to interpret it however you need to." Felix saunters over, his smile wide. "Couldn't wait for the reveal, huh?"

I shake my head. "It just seemed … pretentious."

Felix laughs. "Well, we wouldn't want you getting full of yourself, now would we?"

Dakota and Suki lead more people into the room. They talk in hushed voices, pointing at my mural. A tingling sensation travels up my spine, and I realize this is the first time this many people have looked at anything I've painted at one time. It's overwhelming.

Felix senses my anxiousness and grabs me by the waist. "Hey, it's okay."

Oh, how I adore that smile. "I still don't understand why you were so intent on saving me."

He pulls his shirt over his head, and I know he's enjoying the act just as much as I am. He takes my hand and lays it over his bare chest, on top of the phoenix tattoo. I run my fingertip over the scar left from where my knife punctured his skin.

"There's something I haven't told you yet," Felix says. "Something you need to know. Something I know you're ready to know."

He takes my hand and holds out his left wrist. There are scars in his skin. They're old scars, thick and jagged. I trace the length of the tracks with my fingers. Felix jerks and balls his fist.

I look up at him. "How close did you get?"

"Too close. I was convinced it was over for me. And then, I looked down. Saw the tattoo. Remembered what it represented."

I can't think of anything to say but, "Wow …"

Felix inhales, then smiles. "This phoenix has been a part of me for the last five years," he says. "It's seen my light and it's seen my dark. I would have never made it through without this symbol as a reminder to keep going, to keep trying, to keep getting better. I was able to do it, but not without your help. Not without your symbol. But it was you, Jo. You were the window into me. You've always been in my heart."

I chuckle. "Well, next to it."

"Close enough."

He gazes into my eyes and I'm completely locked in, forced into his mind, right into his soul. For the first time in a really long time, I feel like I mean something to someone.

"You knew, didn't you?" I ask him. "You always knew I could do this."

Felix smiles and his whole face lights up. "I've spent a long time wondering if I'd ever get to know the girl who created the drawing that changed my life. Today I finally met her."

"So did I," I say, and a tear rolls down my cheek but I don't care anymore about hiding any vulnerability. It's been done. I've spilled my insides onto the wall. I've bared my heart and soul. Sure, it's been beaten and battered and bled from many wounds. Sure, I've seen the darkest depths of my heart and mind. There are still so many questions that I have yet to answer about myself and my brain and my tick and what it means to everyone else, but all said and done …

I'm here. I made it.

The hall fills with more people. Many gather around the mural, taking in the details as much as the full sight. A few come by to congratulate me, but most stand awestruck and moved. Dog stays at the doorway, a hand under his chin, laughing. Solano seems confused, but intrigued, and he can't decide if he wants to look at the mural from up close or afar. Dakota walks around talking to people, passing out hugs and good graces.

Felix and I stand in each other's arms, watching. I can feel his heart beating faster through his ribcage. Mine seems to have stopped. After all we've been through—after so many times he pulled me from the darkness—being with Felix makes me feel invincible. Something has cracked open inside my body, releasing the emotions that I've kept locked away because I didn't want him to know how badly I need him. And oh, I do.

I tilt up on my toes, inching my face closer. His body tenses, and for a moment I think he'll push me away. But then he puts his lips to my forehead and kisses me. It's not a real kiss, but better than nothing. Not that it could go any further, anyway, not with Evie around.

She pokes me in the stomach, giggling. "Jeez, guys. People are watching."

"Oh, leave us alone," I say and tickle her in the side.

Evie laughs and skips away, singing over her shoulder. "Everah, you old married people!"

I laugh, but Felix stiffens, and the moment is lost. His eyes are behind me, not on my mural. I turn to follow his gaze and see Nadia walking up to us with a nervous expression. She glances around to make sure no one is listening, then leans in.

"I know you were responsible for altering Jo's identity in the database," Nadia says in a hushed voice. "And I know about the missing information in *your* file."

Felix jerks, scanning the room. "We're not having this conversation here."

Nadia pulls on his arm. "Look. My brother was a Lone Wolf. He made it really difficult to trust him, and I hated him for it, but I've gone through the files. I know the things he did. He's dead now, so I can't hate him anymore, but I now understand why he kept so many secrets." She holds out her hand at waist level, a nanodrive pinched between her fingers. "And I understand why you need to keep yours."

Felix pauses, then takes the nanodrive and nods.

Nadia's shoulders drop as she exhales. She glances behind her, then at me. "The mural is incredible. You've got talent. Whatever secrets you have are not in your file. Keep it that way."

With that, Nadia disappears into the crowd.

Felix turns to me, his mouth opened like he's about to speak. I shake my head.

"I don't need to know," I say. "When it's time, and you're ready to reveal the truth, I'll listen."

He wraps an arm around my shoulder and nuzzles his chin into my temple. His hair tickles my skin. "I appreciate your trust in me."

"Well, I don't know if it's trust or that I know harassing you about it isn't going to get me anywhere."

Felix tilts his head. I chuckle and he gives me a wary smile.

And there it is again, that incessantly pestering feeling in my chest, that nagging thought in my brain that I've tried to ignore for the last month while I've been busy painting, desperately trying to disregard my true desire.

"Besides," I say, "I'm more concerned with wanting to know someone else's secrets."

"And whose secrets are those?"

"Mine." I look up at him and take a deep breath. "I want Marius to scan my brain."

Felix's eyes go wide. His face twitches, unable to settle on any one emotion, like he wants to both agree with my idea and scold me at the same time. "Are you sure? You heard what Nadia said."

Of course I'm not sure. I have no idea if Marius would even agree to this, but I can't ignore it. The anticipation of the truth bubbles under my skin, a sensation that won't go away. "I need to find an answer."

"You don't know that you will."

"It's worth a shot."

"What if you don't *like* the answer?"

I look into his eyes and realize I have somehow lost the ability to put on a hard face for him. Honesty is all I can give him now. "That's a very big possibility. It's probably more likely than not. Either way, I need to know."

He purses his lips together then leans over and kisses my forehead again. When he pulls away, he presses his hand into my back.

"Go," he says. "Go get your answers."

My heart leaps in my chest. I'm so anxious and nervous and giddy I find it hard to look up at him again. But once I do I see he's smiling, so I smile back.

"You'll be here when it's over?" I ask.

"And then some," he says and winks.

My feet are as light as air. I run through the base as though angels carry me, whisking me through the corridors, down the elevator to the eighth floor. Once the elevator opens at my destination, I pause in the corridor, catching my breath. The scanner room door is closed. The hallway is empty, yet a strange breeze sets my hair on end, like something or someone has brushed past me. The single light at the other end of the hallway flickers and makes my eyes tense with each flash of light, causing a dull pulsing thump in my skull.

"I was wondering when you were going to show up."

I turn to see Marius standing in the doorway of the scanner room, hands stuffed in his pants pockets. The room behind him is eerily and unexpectedly dark. He looks like he hasn't slept in weeks. Like he's been waiting down here for me this whole time.

"I was finishing my mural."

"You were wasting time." There's an edge to his voice that I've never heard before, a harshness unfamiliar from the mouth of the twitchy brain doctor. The tone rattles me, and when I see his eyes shift I realize he's *trying* to rattle me.

I can't give him that advantage. This day is about me, and I intend to get what I came here for. "The mural seems to be helping those people. You know," I lean in, "the people you hijacked?"

He scratches his cheek. "Is that why you're here? To instill more guilt into me?"

I take a deep breath and prepare myself to do the scariest thing I've ever done. "No. I want you to give me answers."

Marius jerks like my response surprises him. He glances into the scanner room, searches the space, then quickly closes the door. "I can't. I need to get my son back."

"I was sent to prison and you did nothing to help me. You at least owe me this."

He shifts, lost in some painful memory. But there's something else, something I could sense when I first came down here. Like a tingle on the back of my neck when a presence is nearby. An otherworldly warning.

I look him straight on. "You know something else, don't you?"

Marius stiffens and clamps his lips shut.

I stand taller. "What do you know?"

He stares at the floor and takes a few slow steps, closing the space between us, inch by inch, his body silhouetted by the flickering light. He's nearly on top of me before he finally looks me in the eyes, and his voice quivers when he speaks.

"Have you not wondered why it was your drawings that helped those people? Aren't you the least bit curious about the connection? Don't you see there's more to this story than you realize?"

I hadn't even considered a connection. Why would I have? With everything that has happened in the last year, there hasn't been much of an opportunity for me to concern myself with anything other than my own survival. I came to Marius for answers about my tick, not to be bombarded with his own personal qualms.

"That's not the question I'm here to ask," I say.

"You want to know more about your brain. I'm not surprised."

"Then help me."

He shakes his head with short jerking movements. "I can't. It's already too late. They know you're still alive. You painted that mural and thus signed your own death wish. And now they're going to want you to finish what you started."

What the hell does he mean by that? How dare he undermine the importance of my mural, of my healing process, of my own revelation. *How dare he …*

"Who are *they*?"

Marius sighs, and his shoulders slump over as he exhales. He's softened the edge of his aggression, though his words are no less terrifying. "It doesn't matter," he says. "You don't want to know the truth."

"I do!"

"No. You don't. Once you know you'll be forever burdened by it. You'll learn just how far your influence has spread. And if you choose to tell anyone—especially those whom you love the most—you'll only put them in the worst danger imaginable. It's not only your truth at stake. We'll all be at the mercy of your reality."

I'm at a complete loss for words. Dumbstruck. Body and mind emptied like someone pulled a drain plug. The air suddenly goes cold. Dry. Stale. My eyes focus on the flickering light at the end of the hall, and I cannot for the life of me tear myself away. It draws me in, beckons me like a beam at the end of a tunnel, paralyzing my body in place.

And then I see her at the end of the hallway, blending into the shadows, transposed over my sight like a double exposure ...

A girl stands with her back to me, implants behind both her ears, one flashing blue, the other orange. In one hand she holds a gun. In the other—

ALLISON ROSE is a storyteller of all sorts. Having begun as an aspiring screenwriter and director, she strapped on an electric guitar and tried her hand as a songwriter before discovering her love of writing science fiction and fantasy. A local of the Los Angeles area, where she based much of the setting for TICK, she spends most of her free time daydreaming about the future.

For news updates and blog posts, visit The Girl and the Book:
www.thegirlandthebook.com

Follow on Twitter:
www.twitter.com/AllisonRoseBook
and Facebook:
www.facebook.com/AllisonRoseBooks

Please leave a review!
www.amazon.com/author/allisonrose
www.goodreads.com/AllisonRoseBook

Edited by Maxann Dobson
www.polished-pen.com

Thank you ...

Husband—as you will forever be identified for as long as the Internet and social media exists—otherwise known as the man who tirelessly encouraged me to finish this novel and finally have something to call my own, thank you for never giving up on my dream. It is, and always has been, your love and perseverance that helped get me where I am today.

Francesca, first one to ever read this book, most incessant "no-bullshit" critic on the planet. Your enthusiasm kept me going to the end, and your brilliant—while often certifiable—ideas helped make this a complete story.

Max, my wonderful editor: I'm so glad I found you, and "I am looking forward to working with you" again.

Mom, for supportively reading everything I write, even if it is a little disturbing. Dad, for being the inspiration for me as a writer from my early teenage years. Bridget, for being a bigger inspiration to these characters than you realize, and probably more than you'd like the general public to know.

Zoe and Rachel, my beta readers of wonder. Jen and Kevin, friends are great, nerdy ones are even better.

To all my family—blood and married—and friends from all corners of the planet, thank you for your support. This book exists because of you.